PRAISE

"Almost every character in the book is based on a historical figure, and Moran fleshes out their personalities beautifully, highlighting the teenage pharaoh's arrogance and paranoia, underscoring his queen's ambition and insecurity . . . Moran has created an engrossing tribute to one of the most powerful and alluring women in history."

—*Boston Globe*

"Mutnodjmet as narrator is a stroke of genius . . . Beautifully written and completely engrossing, this first novel should enjoy wide readership."

—*Library Journal*, Editor's Pick

"[Moran] gets the details just right . . . in an epic that brings an ancient world to life."

—*Publishers Weekly*

"Before there was Cleopatra there was the notorious Nefertiti, Queen of the Nile. Moran recreates her story with a vibrancy, drama, and compassion that would make the queen proud. As in *The Other Boleyn Girl*, the relationship between sisters sets this novel apart and makes Nefertiti's story powerful and memorable. It belongs alongside the finest fictional biographies."

—*Romantic Times Book Review*

"*Nefertiti* is a gem of a novel—the atmosphere positively seethes with intrigue, passion, betrayal, and, above all, the searing and oppressive heat of sibling rivalry."

—*Daily Telegraph*

"*Nefertiti* is a fascinating window into the past, a heroic story with a very human heart. Compulsively readable!"

—Diana Gabaldon, #1 *New York Times* bestselling author of *A Breath of Snow and Ashes*

"A stunning debut . . . what a thrilling read! I found the whole book rich and compelling, exciting and haunting. [The character of] Nefertiti is a fine creation, both appealing and frightening, and she's surrounded by a thoroughly satisfying cast of characters, too. The whole world of ancient Egypt comes to life."

—Rosalind Miles, *New York Times* bestselling author of *I, Elizabeth*

Nefertiti

a novel

MICHELLE MORAN

THREE RIVERS PRESS
NEW YORK

This is a work of fiction. Names, characters, places, and incidents either are the product of the author's imagination or are used fictitiously.

 Published in the United States by Three Rivers Press,
an imprint of the Crown Publishing Group,
a division of Random House, Inc., New York.
www.crownpublishing.com

Three Rivers Press and the Tugboat design are registered
trademarks of Random House, Inc.

Originally published in hardcover in slightly different form in the United States
by Crown Publishers, an imprint of the Crown Publishing Group,
a division of Random House, Inc., New York, in 2007.

Library of Congress Cataloging-in-Publication Data

Moran, Michelle.
Nefertiti : a novel / Michelle Moran.—1st ed.
1. Nefertiti, Queen of Egypt, 14th cent. B.C.—Fiction. 2. Akhenaten, King of Egypt—Fiction. 3. Egypt—History—Eighteenth dynasty, ca. 1570–1320 B.C.—Fiction. 4. Queens—Egypt—Fiction. 5. Egypt—Kings and rulers—Fiction. 1. Title.
PS3613.O682N45 2007
813'.6—dc22 2006039184

ISBN: 978-0-307-38174-3

Printed in the United States of America

Design by Jo Anne Metsch

Map by Sophie Kittredge

10 9 8 7

To my father, Robert Francis Moran, who gave me his love of language and books. You left too soon and never saw this published, but I think, somehow, you always knew. Thank you for knowing, and for your magnificent life, which inspired me in so many ways.

To speak the name of the dead is to make them live again.

—Egyptian Proverb

The Eighteenth Dynasty

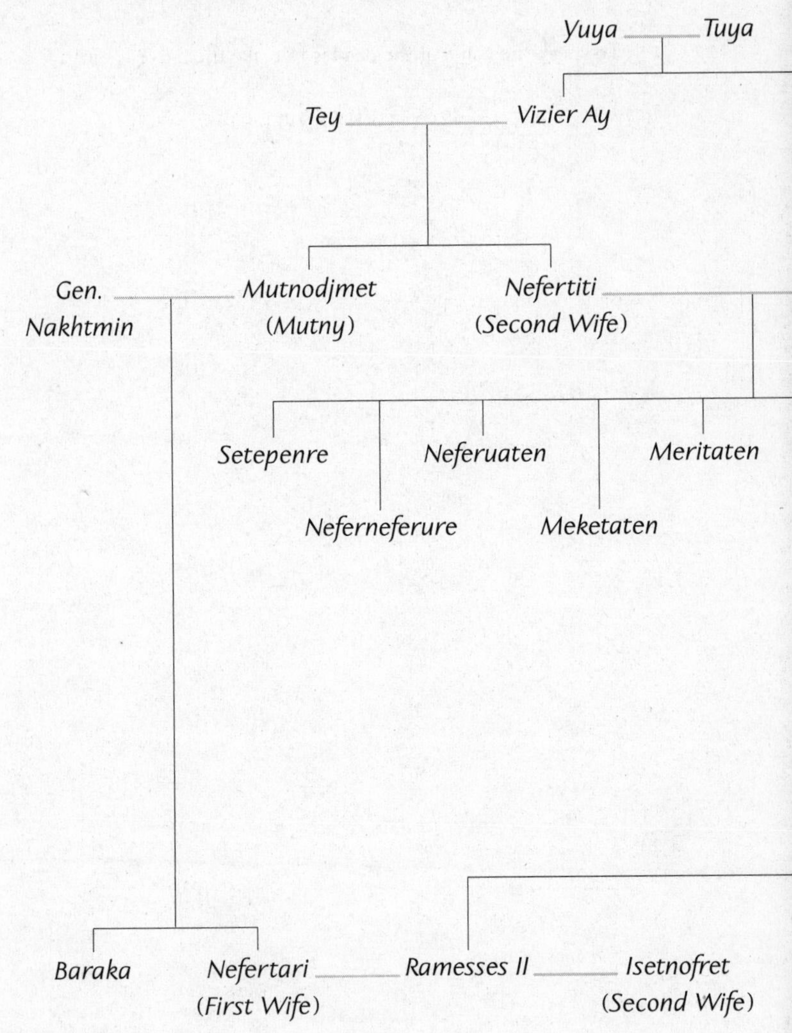

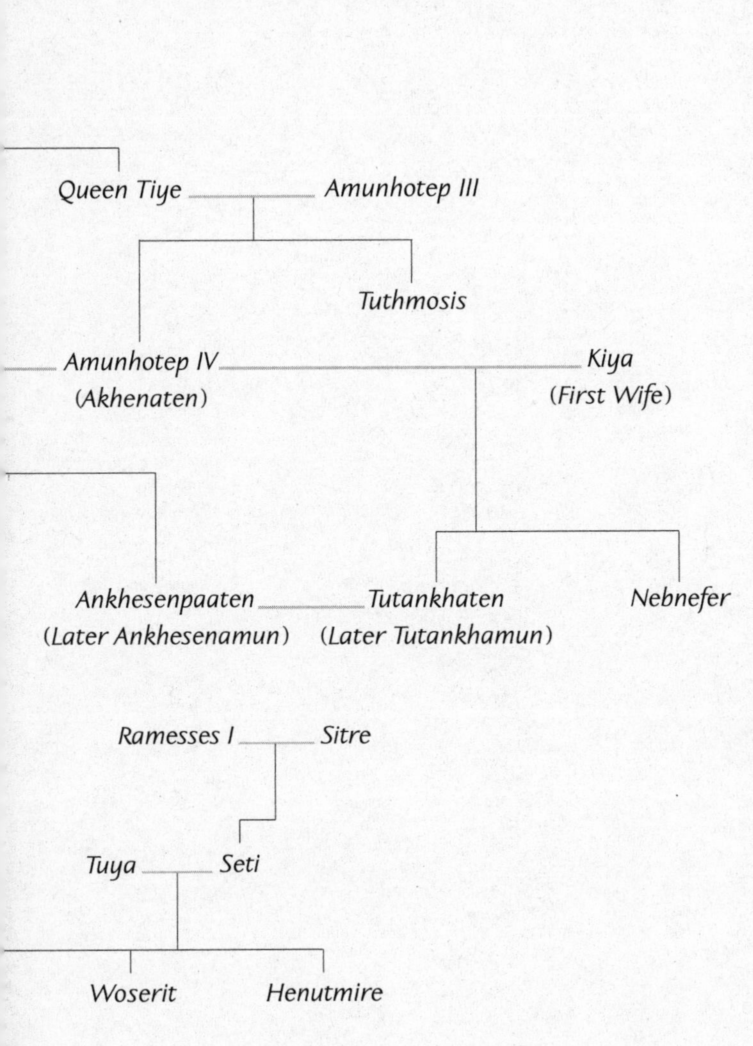
Queen Tiye
Amunhotep III
Tuthmosis
Amunhotep IV
(Akhenaten)
Kiya
(First Wife)
Ankhesenpaaten
(Later Ankhesenamun)
Tutankhaten
(Later Tutankhamun)
Nebnefer
Ramesses I
Sitre
Tuya
Seti
Woserit
Henutmire

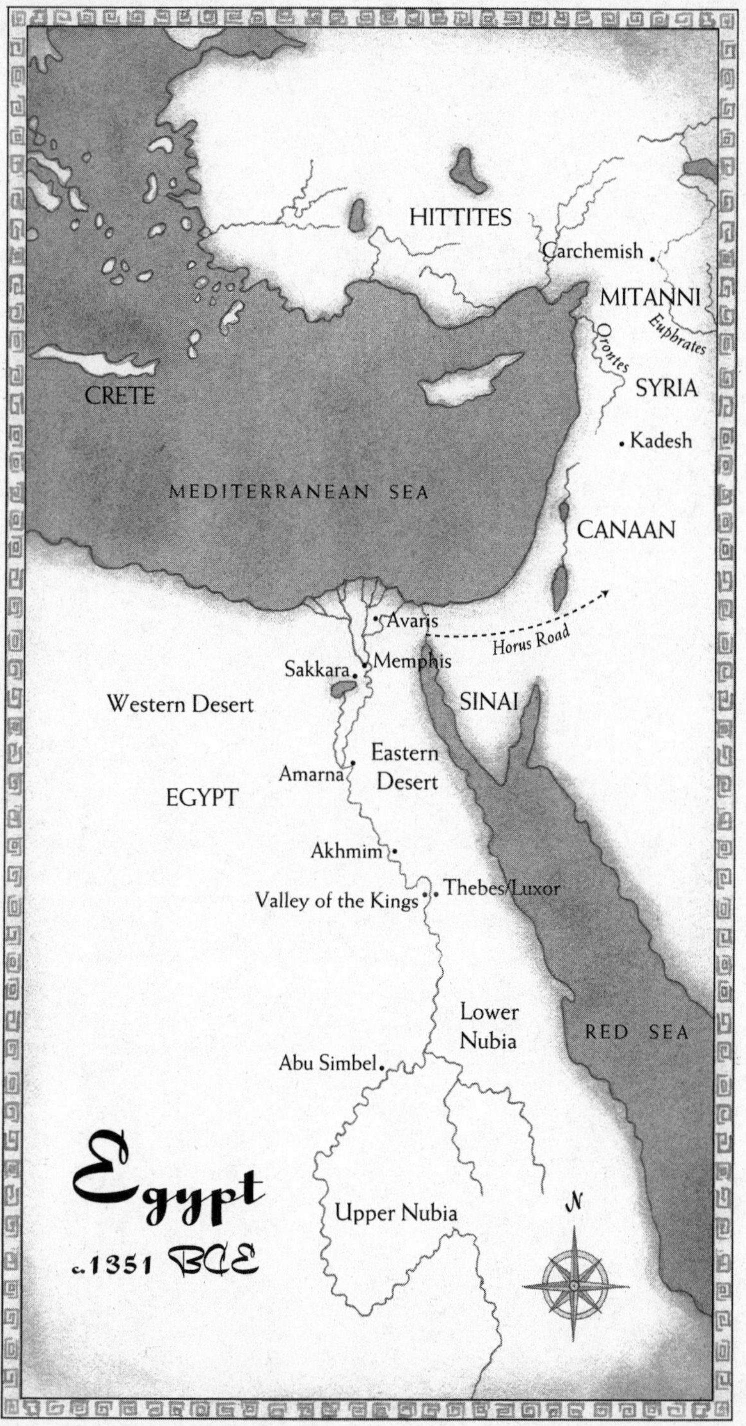
HITTITES
Carchemish
MITANNI
Euphrates
Orontes
SYRIA
Kadesh
CRETE
MEDITERRANEAN SEA
CANAAN
Avaris
Horus Road
Memphis
Sakkara
SINAI
Western Desert
Eastern Desert
Amarna
EGYPT
Akhmim
Thebes/Luxor
Valley of the Kings
Lower Nubia
RED SEA
Abu Simbel
Upper Nubia
N
Egypt
c.1351 BCE

Author's Note

IT HAS BEEN A long journey for me into Nefertiti's ancient world, a journey that began with a visit to the Altes Museum in Berlin, where her iconic bust is housed. The bust itself has a long and detailed history, beginning with its creation in the city of Amarna and continuing to its arrival in Germany, where it became an instant draw in its first exhibition in 1923.

Even three thousand years after her death, Nefertiti's allure still captivates tens of thousands of visitors each year. Encased in glass, it was her mysterious smile and powerful gaze that attracted me, making me wonder who she had been and how she'd become such a dominant figure in ancient Egypt.

Now the time is 1351 BCE. The great Pharaohs of Egypt have included Khufu, Ahmose, and the female Pharaoh Hatshepsut, while Ramses and Cleopatra are yet to come. Nefertiti is fifteen years old. Her sister is thirteen, and all of Egypt lies before them.

Prologue

IF YOU ARE to believe what the viziers say, then Amunhotep killed his brother for the crown of Egypt.

In the third month of Akhet, Crown Prince Tuthmosis lay in his room in Malkata Palace. A warm wind stirred the curtains of his chamber, carrying with it the desert scents of zaatar and myrrh. With each breeze the long linens danced, wrapping themselves around the columns of the palace, brushing the sun-dappled tiles on the floor. But while the twenty-year-old Prince of Egypt should have been riding to victory at the head of Pharaoh's charioteers, he was lying in his bedchamber, his right leg supported by cushions, swollen and crushed. The chariot that had failed him had immediately been burned, but the damage was done. His fever was high and his shoulders slumped. And while the jackal-headed god of death crept closer, Amunhotep sat across the room on a gilded chair, not even flinching when his older brother spat up the wine-colored phlegm that spelled possible death to the viziers.

When Amunhotep couldn't stand any more of his brother's sickness, he stalked from the chamber and stood on a balcony overlooking Thebes. He crossed his arms over his golden pectoral, watching the farmers with their emmer wheat, harvesting in the heavy heat of the day. Their silhouettes moved across the temples of Amun, his father's greatest contributions to the land. He stood above the city, thinking of the message that had summoned him from Memphis to his brother's side, and as the sun sank lower, he grew besieged by visions of what now might be. *Amunhotep the Great. Amunhotep the Builder. Amunhotep the Magnificent.* He could imagine it all, and it was only when a new moon had risen over the horizon that the sound of sandals slapping against tile made him turn.

"Your brother has called you back into his chamber."

"Now?"

"Yes." Queen Tiye turned her back on her son, and he followed her sharp footfalls into Tuthmosis's chamber. Inside, the viziers of Egypt had gathered.

Amunhotep swept the room with a glance. These were old men loyal to his father, men who had always loved his older brother more than him. "You may leave," he announced, and the viziers turned to the queen in shock.

"You may go," she repeated. But when the old men were gone, she warned her son sharply, "You will *not* treat the wise men of Egypt like slaves."

"They *are* slaves! Slaves to the priests of Amun who control more land and gold than we do. If Tuthmosis had lived to be crowned, he would have bowed to the priests like every Pharaoh that came—"

Queen Tiye's slap reverberated across the chamber. "You *will not* speak that way while your brother is still alive!"

Amunhotep inhaled sharply and watched his mother move to Tuthmosis's side.

The queen caressed the prince's cheek with her hand. Her favorite son, the one who was courageous in battle as well as life. They were so much alike, even sharing the same auburn hair and light eyes. "Amunhotep is here to see you," she whispered, the braids from her wig brushing his face. Tuthmosis struggled to sit and the queen moved to help him, but he waved her away.

"Leave us. We will talk alone."

Tiye hesitated.

"It's fine," Tuthmosis promised.

The two princes of Egypt watched their mother go, and only Anubis, who weighs the heart of the dead against the feather of truth, knows for certain what happened after the queen left that chamber. But there are many viziers who believe that when judgment comes, Amunhotep's heart will outweigh the feather. They think it has been made heavy with evil deeds, and that Ammit, the crocodile god, will devour it, condemning him to oblivion for eternity. Whatever the truth, that night the crown prince, Tuthmosis, died, and a new crown prince rose to take his place.

Chapter One

1351 BCE

Peret, Season of Growing

WHEN THE SUN set over Thebes, splaying its last rays over the limestone cliffs, we walked in a long procession across the sand. In a twisting line that threaded between the hills, the viziers of Upper and Lower Egypt came first, then the priests of Amun, followed by hundreds of mourners. The sand cooled rapidly in the shadows. I could feel the grains between the toes of my sandals, and when the wind blew under my thin linen robe, I shivered. I stepped out of line so I could see the sarcophagus, carried on a sledge by a team of oxen so the people of Egypt would know how wealthy and great our crown prince had been. Nefertiti would be jealous that she'd had to miss this.

I will tell her all about it when I get home, I thought. If *she is being nice to me.*

The bald-headed priests walked behind our family, for we were even more important than the representatives of the gods. The incense they swung from golden balls made me think of giant beetles, stinking up the air whichever way they went. When the funeral procession reached the mouth of the valley, the rattling of the sistrums stopped and the mourners went silent. On every cliff, families had gathered to see the prince, and now they looked down as the High Priest of Amun performed the Opening of the Mouth, to give Tuthmosis back his senses in the Afterlife. The priest was younger than the viziers of Egypt, but even so, men like my father stood back, deferring to his power when he touched a golden ankh to the mouth of the figure on the sarcophagus and announced, "The royal falcon has flown to heaven. Amunhotep the Younger is arisen in his place."

A wind echoed between the cliffs, and I thought I could hear the rush of the falcon's wings as the crown prince was freed from his body and ascended to the sky. There was a great amount of shuffling, children looking around the legs of their parents to see the new prince. I, too, craned my neck.

"Where is he?" I whispered. "Where is Amunhotep the Younger?"

"In the tomb," my father replied. His bald head shone dully in the setting sun, and in the deepening of the shadows his face appeared hawkish.

"But doesn't he want the people to see him?" I asked.

"No, *senit.*" His word for *little girl.* "Not until he's been given what his brother was promised."

I frowned. "And what is that?"

He clenched his jaw. "The coregency," he replied.

When the ceremony was finished, soldiers spread out to stop commoners from following us into the valley, and our small party was expected to walk on alone. Behind us, the team of oxen heaved, pulling their golden cargo across the sand. Around us, cliffs rose against the darkening sky.

"We will be climbing," my father warned, and my mother paled slightly. We were cats, she and I, frightened of places we couldn't understand, valleys whose sleeping Pharaohs watched from secret chambers. Nefertiti would have crossed this valley without pause, a falcon in her fearlessness, just like our father.

We walked to the eerie rattle of the sistrums, and I watched my golden sandals reflect the dying light. As we ascended the cliffs, I stopped to look down over the land.

"Don't stop," my father cautioned. "Keep going."

We trudged onward through the hills while the animals snorted their way up the rocks. The priests went before us now, carrying torches to light our way as we walked. Then the High Priest hesitated, and I wondered if he'd lost his bearing in the night.

"Untie the sarcophagus and free the oxen," he commanded, and I saw, carved into the face of the cliff, the entrance to the tomb. Children shifted in their beads and women's bangles clinked together as they passed each other looks. Then I saw the narrow staircase leading down into the earth and understood their fear.

"I don't like this," my mother whispered.

The priests relieved the oxen of their burden, heaving the gilded sarcophagus onto their shoulders. Then my father squeezed my hand to give me courage and we followed our dead prince into his chamber, out of the dying sun and into total darkness.

Carefully, so as not to slip on the rocks, we descended into the bowels of the earth, staying close to the priests and their reed torches. Inside the tomb, the light cast shadows across the painted scenes of Tuthmosis's twenty years in Egypt. There were women dancing, wealthy noblemen hunting, Queen Tiye serving her eldest son honeyed lotus and wine. I pressed my mother's hand for comfort, and when she said nothing, I knew she was offering up silent prayers to Amun.

Below us, the heavy air grew dank and the smell of the tomb became that of shifted earth. Images appeared and disappeared in the torchlight: yellow painted women and laughing men, children floating lotus blossoms along the River Nile. But fearsome was the blue-faced god of the underworld, holding the crook and flail of Egypt. "Osiris," I whispered, but no one heard.

We kept walking, into the most secretive chambers of the earth, then we entered a vaulted room and I gasped. This was where all the prince's earthly treasures were gathered: painted barges, golden chariots, sandals trimmed in leopard fur. We passed through this room to the innermost burial chamber, and my father leaned close to me and whispered, "Remember what I told you."

Inside the empty chamber, Pharaoh and his queen stood side by side. In the light of the torches, it was impossible to see anything but their shadowy figures and the long sarcophagus of the departed prince. I stretched out my arms in obeisance and my aunt nodded solemnly at me, remembering my face from her infrequent visits to our family in Akhmim. My father never took Nefertiti or me into Thebes. He kept us away from the palace, from the intrigues and ostentation of the court. Now, in the flickering light of the tomb, I saw that the queen hadn't changed in the six years since I had last seen her. She was still small and pale. Her light eyes appraised me as I held out my arms, and I wondered what she thought of my dark skin and unusual height. I straightened, and the High Priest of Amun opened the Book of the Dead, his voice intoning the words of dying mortals to the gods.

"Let my soul come to me from wherever it is. Come for my soul, O you Guardians of the heavens. May my soul see my corpse, may it rest on my mummified body which will never be destroyed or perish . . ."

I searched the chamber for Amunhotep the Younger. He was standing away from the sarcophagus and the canopic jars that would carry Tuthmosis's organs to the Afterlife. He was taller than I was, handsome despite his light curling hair, and I wondered if we could expect great things from him when it was his brother who had always been meant to reign. He shifted toward a statue of the goddess

Mut, and I remembered that Tuthmosis had been a cat lover in his life. With him would go his beloved Ta-Miw, wrapped inside her own miniature sarcophagus of gold. I touched my mother's arm gently and she turned.

"Did they kill her?" I whispered, and she followed my eyes to the little coffin beside the prince.

My mother shook her head, and as the priests took up the sistrums she replied, "They said she stopped eating once the crown prince was dead."

The High Priest began chanting the Song to the Soul, a lament to Osiris and the jackal god, Anubis. Then he snapped shut the Book of the Dead and announced, "The blessing of the organs."

Queen Tiye stepped forward. She knelt in the dirt, kissing each of the canopic jars in turn. Then Pharaoh did the same, and I saw him turn sharply, searching for his younger son in the darkness. "Come," he commanded.

His youngest son didn't move.

"Come!" he shouted, and his voice was magnified a hundred times in the chamber.

No one breathed. I looked at my father, and he shook his head sternly.

"Why should I bow to him in obeisance?" Amunhotep demanded. "He would have handed Egypt over to the Amun priests like every king that came before him!"

I covered my mouth, and for a moment I thought the Elder would move across the burial chamber to kill him. But Amunhotep was his only surviving son, the only legitimate heir to Egypt's throne, and like every seventeen-year-old crown prince in our history, the people would expect to see him enthroned as coregent. The Elder would be Pharaoh of Upper Egypt and Thebes, and Amunhotep would rule Lower Egypt from Memphis. If this son also died, the Elder's line would be finished. The queen walked swiftly to where her youngest son stood. "You will bless your brother's organs," she commanded.

"*Why?*"

"Because he is a Prince of Egypt!"

"And so am *I!*" Amunhotep said wildly.

Queen Tiye's eyes narrowed. "Your brother served this kingdom by joining Egypt's army. He was a High Priest of Amun, *dedicated* to the gods."

Amunhotep laughed. "So you loved him better because he could butcher what he blessed?"

Queen Tiye inhaled angrily. "Go to your father. Ask him to make a soldier of you. Then we will see what kind of Pharaoh you shall become."

Amunhotep turned, stooping rashly before Pharaoh in the midst of his brother's funeral. "I will become a warrior like my brother," he swore. The hem of his white cloak trailed in the dirt, and the viziers shook their heads. "Together, you and I can raise Aten above Amun," he promised. "We can rule the way your father once envisioned."

Pharaoh held on to his walking stick, as if it could support his ebbing life. "It was a mistake to raise you in Memphis," he pronounced. "You should have been raised with your brother. Here. In Thebes."

Amunhotep stood swiftly and his shoulders straightened. "You only have me, Father." He offered his hand to the old man who had conquered a dozen lands. "Take it. I may not be a warrior, but I will build a kingdom that will stand for eternity."

When it was clear that Pharaoh would not take Amunhotep's hand, my father moved forward to save the prince from embarrassment.

"Let your brother be buried," he suggested quietly.

The look Amunhotep gave his father would have turned Anubis cold.

It was only when we returned on barges across the Nile, with the rippling current to drown our voices, that anyone dared to speak.

"He is unstable," my father declared on our way back to Akhmim. "For three generations, our family has given women to the Pharaohs of Egypt. But I will not give one of my daughters to that man."

I wrapped my wool cloak around my shoulders. It wasn't me he was talking about. It was my sister, Nefertiti.

"If Amunhotep is to be made coregent with his father, he will need a Chief Wife," my mother said. "It will be Nefertiti or Kiya. And if it is Kiya . . ."

She left the words unspoken, but we all knew what she had meant to say. If it was Kiya, then Vizier Panahesi would have sway in Egypt. It would be easy and logical to make his daughter queen: Kiya was already married to Amunhotep and nearly three months pregnant with his child. But if she became Chief Wife, our family would bow to Panahesi's, and that would be an unthinkable thing.

My father shifted his weight on his cushion, brooding while the servants rowed north.

"Nefertiti has been told she will be a royal wife," my mother added. "You told her that."

"When Tuthmosis was alive! When there was stability and it looked as if Egypt would be ruled by . . ." My father closed his eyes.

I watched as the moon rose over the barge, and when enough time had passed, I thought it safe to ask, "Father, what is Aten?"

He opened his eyes. "The sun," he replied, staring at my mother. There were thoughts passing between them, but no words.

"But Amun-Ra is god of the sun."

"And Aten is the sun itself," he said.

I didn't understand. "But why would Amunhotep want to build temples to a sun god that no one has heard of?"

"Because if he builds temples to Aten, there will be no need for the priests of Amun."

I was shocked. "He wants to be rid of them?"

"Yes." My father nodded. "And go against all the laws of Ma'at."

I sucked in my breath. No one went against the goddess of truth. "But why?"

"Because the crown prince is weak," my father explained. "Because he is weak and shallow, and you should learn to recognize men who are afraid of others with power, Mutnodjmet."

My mother threw a sharp glance at him. It was treason, what my father just said, but there was no one to hear it above the splash of the oars.

Nefertiti was waiting for us. She was recovering from fever, but even so she was sitting in the garden, reclining by the lotus pool, the moonlight reflecting off her slender arms. She stood up as soon as she saw us, and I felt a sort of triumph that I had seen the prince's funeral and she'd been too sick to go. Guilt swept this feeling away, however, when I saw the longing in her face.

"Well, how was it?"

I'd planned on having the information drawn out of me, but I couldn't be cruel the way she could be. "Absolutely magnificent," I gushed. "And the sarcophagus—"

"What are you doing out of bed?" my mother scolded. She was not Nefertiti's mother. She was only mine. Nefertiti's mother had died when her daughter was two; she'd been a princess from Mitanni and my father's first wife. She was the one who gave Nefertiti her name, which meant *the Beautiful One Has Come.* And though we were related, there was no comparing us: Nefertiti was small and bronze, with black hair, dark eyes, and cheekbones you could cup in the palm of your hand, whereas I am dark, with a narrow face that would never be picked out of a crowd. At birth, my mother didn't name me for beauty. She called me Mutnodjmet, meaning *Sweet Child of Goddess Mut.*

"Nefertiti should be in bed," my father said. "She's not feeling well." And although it was my sister he should have been reprimanding, it was me to whom he spoke.

"I'll be fine," Nefertiti promised. "See, I'm better already." She smiled for him, and I turned to see my father's reaction. Like always, he had a soft look for her.

"Nevertheless," my mother cut in, "you were hot with fever and you will go back to bed."

We let ourselves be herded inside, and when we lay on our reed mats, Nefertiti rolled over, her profile sharp in the light of the moon. "So, what was it like?"

"Frightening," I admitted. "The tomb was huge. And dark."

"And the people? How many people were there?"

"Oh, hundreds. Maybe even thousands."

She sighed. She had missed a chance to be seen. "And the new crown prince?"

I hesitated. "He . . ."

She sat up on her pallet, nodding for me to go on.

"He is strange," I whispered.

In the moonlight, Nefertiti's dark eyes glittered. "How do you mean?"

"He is obsessed with Aten."

"With *what?*"

"With an image of the sun," I explained. "How can you honor an image of the sun and not Amun-Ra, who controls it?"

She was quiet. "That's it?"

"He's also tall."

"Well, he can't be that much taller than you."

I ignored her criticism. "He's much taller. Two heads over Father."

She wrapped her arms around her knees and replied, "This should be interesting, then."

I frowned. "What?"

She didn't explain.

"What should be interesting, then?" I repeated.

"Marriage," she said lightly, lying back down and pulling the linen cover over her chest. "With a coronation so close, Amunhotep will need to pick a Chief Wife, and why not me?"

Why not her? She was beautiful, educated, the daughter of a Mitanni princess. I felt a sharp stab of jealousy, but also fear. I had never known a time without Nefertiti.

"Of course, you'll come with me," she said, yawning. "Until you're old enough to be married, you'll be my Chief Lady."

"Mother wouldn't allow me to go to the palace alone."

"You wouldn't be alone. She'd come, too."

"To the palace!" I exclaimed.

"Mutny, when you're Chief Wife, your family comes with you. Our father is the greatest vizier in the land. Our aunt is the queen. Who would dare to say no?"

▣ ▣ ▣

In the middle of the night, a long shadow lingered outside our room, then a servant entered, holding an oil lamp above Nefertiti's head. I awoke at the brightness and saw my sister's face in the golden light, perfect even in her sleep.

"My lady?" our servant called, but Nefertiti didn't stir. "My lady?" she called louder. She looked at me, and I shook Nefertiti awake. "My lady, the Vizier Ay would like to speak with you."

I sat up quickly. "Is something wrong?"

But Nefertiti didn't say a word. She stepped into her robe, taking an oil lamp down from the wall and sheltering the sputtering flame with her hand. "What's happening?" I asked, but she didn't reply.

The door simply whispered shut in her wake. I waited up for my sister's return, and by the time she came back, the moon was a yellow disk high in the sky. "Where *were* you?" I scrambled up on my pallet.

"Father wanted to speak with me."

"Alone?" I challenged her. "And at night?"

"When else are all the nosy servants asleep?"

Then I knew at once. "He doesn't want you to marry Amunhotep," I said.

Nefertiti rolled her shoulders, playing coy. "I'm not afraid of Kiya."

"It's Vizier Panahesi he's concerned about."

"I want to be Chief Wife, Mutnodjmet. I want to be Queen of Egypt the way my grandmother was Queen of Mitanni."

She sat down on her pallet and we were silent, illuminated only by the flame of the lamp she'd brought in.

"And what did Father say?"

She shrugged again.

"Did he tell you what happened in the tombs?"

"So he refused to kiss the jars," she said dismissively. "What does that matter if in the end I'm sitting on the Horus throne? Amunhotep is going to be the Pharaoh of Egypt," she added, as if this settled the matter. "And Father has already said yes."

"He said *yes?*" I threw off my linen cover. "But he couldn't have said yes. He said the prince was unstable. He swore he would never give a daughter to that man!"

"And he changed his mind." In the flickering candlelight, I saw her lie down and draw up the covers. "Will you find me some juice in the kitchens?" she asked.

"It's night," I retorted, my voice tight with disapproval.

"But I'm sick," she reminded. "I have fever."

I hesitated.

"Please, Mutny. *Please.*"

I would go, but only because she had fever.

The next morning, the tutors ended our lessons early. There was no sign of illness on Nefertiti. "But we shouldn't tax her," my father said.

My mother disagreed. "These are all the lessons she will ever have if she's to be married soon. She should learn what she can."

My mother, who had not been raised among nobility like my father's first wife, knew the importance of an education, for she'd had to fight for hers when she was young and the daughter of a simple village priest. But my father turned his palm over.

"What else is there for her to learn? She excels at languages, and she's more proficient than the palace scribes at writing."

"She doesn't know the healing herbs like Mutny," my mother pointed out.

I raised my chin, but my father only replied, "That is Mutnodjmet's gift. Nefertiti has other skills."

We all looked at my sister, the center of attention in her short white sheath, her feet dangling in the lotus pools. Ranofer, the son of a local physician, had brought her flowers, a bunch of white lilies bound with twine. He was supposed to be my tutor, teaching me the secrets of medicine and herbs, but he spent more time watching my sister.

"Nefertiti charms people," my father said approvingly, "and the people she doesn't charm she can easily outwit. What does she need with herbs and medicine when she wants to be a leader of the people?"

My mother furrowed her brows. "*If* the queen approves."

"The queen is my sister," my father said simply. "She will approve of Nefertiti as Chief Wife." But I could see the concern in his eyes. A crown prince who defiled his brother's burial chamber, a man who couldn't control his own emotions? What kind of Pharaoh would he make? What kind of husband?

We stood and looked at Nefertiti until she saw the three of us watching her. She beckoned me over with her finger. I went to where they were laughing by the pools, my sister and my tutor.

"Good afternoon, Mutnodjmet." Ranofer smiled up at me, and for a moment I forgot what I had wanted to tell him.

"I tried the aloe today," I said at last. "It healed our servant's burns."

"Really?" Ranofer sat up. "What else?"

"I mixed it with lavender and there was less swelling."

He smiled wider at me. "You are surpassing even my teaching, my lady."

I grinned, proud of my ingenuity. "Next, I think I want to try—"

"Talking about something interesting?" Nefertiti sighed and leaned back in the sunshine. "Tell me, what was Father saying just now?"

"Right now?" I am a terrible liar.

"Yes. While you were standing there spying on me."

I flushed. "He spoke of your future."

She sat up, the ends of her black hair brushing her chin. "And?"

I paused, wondering if I should tell her the rest. She waited. "And that the queen might be coming," I said at last.

Immediately, Ranofer's smile vanished. "But if she comes"—his voice rose—"you will leave Akhmim."

Nefertiti frowned over Ranofer's head at me. "Don't worry," she promised lightly. "Nothing will come of it."

There was a moment between them, then Ranofer took her hand and they both stood up.

"Where are you going?" I cried, but Nefertiti didn't answer, so I called after my tutor. "What about our lesson?"

"Later." He grinned, but it was only my sister he really had eyes for.

* * *

Word arrived that the queen would pay a visit to our villa in Akhmim. In our family shrine, this was what Nefertiti had been secretly praying for, laying down bowls of our best honeyed wine at the feet of Amun and promising all sorts of wild things if he would only send the queen to our city. Now that Amun seemed to have granted her request, Nefertiti was unbearable in her excitement. While my sister preened, my mother rushed around the house, snapping at slaves and servants alike.

"Mutny, make sure the towels are clean. Nefertiti, the bowls please. Make sure the servants have washed them. *All* of them."

Our servants dusted the fringed wall hangings while my mother arranged our best inlaid chairs around the Audience Chamber, which would be the first room the queen would enter. Queen Tiye was my father's sister; she was a hard woman and would not approve of sloppy housekeeping. The tiles in the kitchen were scrubbed to gleaming, even though the queen would go nowhere near them, and the lotus pool was stocked with orange fish. Even Nefertiti did some work, actually inspecting the bowls instead of pretending she had. In six days, Amunhotep the Younger would be crowned at Karnak and made coregent with his father. Even I knew what this visit meant. The queen had not come all the way to Akhmim for over six years. The only reason to visit now would be for a marriage.

"Mutny, go help your sister get dressed," my mother said.

In our room, Nefertiti stood in front of the mirror. She pushed her dark hair from her face, imagining herself with the crown of Egypt. "This is it," she whispered. "I will be the greatest queen Egypt has ever known."

I scoffed. "No queen will ever be greater than our aunt."

She whirled around. "There was Hatshepsut. And our aunt doesn't wear the pschent crown."

"Only a Pharaoh can wear it."

"So while she commands the army and meets with foreign leaders, what does she get? *Nothing.* It is her husband who reaps the glory. When I am queen, it will be my name that lives in eternity."

I knew better than to argue with Nefertiti when she was like this. I mixed the kohl and handed it to her in a jar, then watched her apply it. She rimmed her eyes and darkened her brows, and the paint made her look older than her fifteen years.

"Do you really think you will become Chief Wife?" I asked.

"Who would our aunt rather see give birth to an heir? A commoner"—she wrinkled her nose—"or her niece?"

I was a commoner, but it wasn't me she was slighting. It was Panahesi's daughter, Kiya, who was the child of a noblewoman, whereas Nefertiti was the granddaughter of a queen.

"Can you find my linen dress and gold belt?" she said.

I narrowed my eyes. "Just because you're about to make a marriage doesn't make me your slave."

She smiled widely. "*Please,* Mutny. You know I can't do this without you." She watched in the mirror while I rummaged through her chests, looking for the gown she wore only to festivals. I pulled out her golden belt and she protested, "The one with onyx, not turquoise."

"Don't you have servants for this?" I demanded.

She ignored me and held out her hand for the belt. Personally, I liked the turquoise better. There was a knock on the door, and then my mother's servant appeared, her face bright with excitement.

"Your mother says to be quick!" the girl cried. "The caravan has been spotted."

Nefertiti looked at me. "Think of it, Mutny. You will be sister to the Queen of Egypt!"

"*If* she likes you," I said flatly.

"Of course she will." She glanced in the mirror at her own reflection, her small honeyed shoulders and rich black hair. "I'll be charming and sweet, and when we've moved into the palace, just think of all the things we can do!"

"We do plenty of things here," I protested. "What's wrong with Akhmim?"

She took the brush and finished her hair. "Don't you want to see Karnak and Memphis and be a part of the palace?"

"Father's part of the palace. He says it makes him tired, so much talk of politics."

"Well, that's Father. He gets to go to the palace every day. What do we ever get to do here?" she complained. "Nothing but wait for a prince to die so that we can go out and see the world."

I sucked in my breath. *"Nefertiti!"*

She laughed merrily. Then my mother appeared in the doorway, breathless. She had put on her good jewels and heavy new bangles I'd never seen before. "Are you ready?"

Nefertiti stood up. Her dress was sheer, and I felt a wave of pure envy at the way the material tightened across her thighs and emphasized the slenderness of her waist.

"Wait." My mother put her hand in the air. "We must have a necklace. Mutny, go and fetch the gold collar."

I gasped. *"Your* collar?"

"Of course. Now hurry! The guard will let you into the treasury."

I was shocked that my mother would let Nefertiti wear the collar my father had given her on their wedding day. I had underestimated how important my aunt's visit was to her, then. To us all. I hurried to the treasury in the back of the house, and the sentry looked up at me with a smile. I was taller than him by a head. I blushed.

"My mother wants the collar for my sister."

"The gold collar?"

"What other collar is there?"

He snapped his head back. *"Well.* Must be for something very important. I hear the queen is arriving today."

I placed my hands on my hips so that he knew that I was waiting.

"All right, all right." He descended into the underground chamber and reappeared with my mother's treasure, which would be mine someday. "So your sister must be getting married," he said.

I held out my hand. "The collar."

"She would make a fine queen."

"So everybody says."

He smiled like he knew my thoughts on the matter, the prying old donkey, then he held out the collar and I snatched it. I ran back to my room and held up the heavy jewel like a prize. Nefertiti looked to my mother.

"Are you sure?" She looked at the gold, and her eyes reflected its light.

My mother nodded. She fastened it around my sister's neck, then we both stood back. The gold began at my sister's throat in a lotus pattern, dipping between her breasts in droplets of various lengths. I was glad she was two years older than me. If I had been the one to marry first, no man would have chosen me over her. "Now we are ready," my mother said. She led the way to the Audience Chamber, where the queen was waiting. We could hear her speaking with my father, her voice low and grating and full of command.

"Come when you are called," my mother said quickly. "There are gifts on the table from our treasury. Bring them when you enter. The larger one is for Nefertiti to carry."

Then she disappeared inside, and we stood in the tiled hall to wait for our summons.

Nefertiti paced. "Why *wouldn't* she choose me to marry her son? I'm her brother's child, and our father has the highest position in the land."

"Of course she'll choose you."

"But for Chief Wife? I won't be anything less, Mutny. I won't be some lesser wife thrown into a palace that Pharaoh comes to visit only every two seasons. I'd rather marry a vizier's son."

"She'll want you."

"Of course, it's really up to Amunhotep." She stopped pacing, and I realized that she was talking to herself. "In the end, he'll be the one who chooses. He's the one who has to get a son on me, not her."

I winced at her crassness.

"But I'll never get to see him without charming his mother."

"You'll do well."

She looked at me, as if noticing that I was there for the first time. "Really?"

"Yes." I sat down in my father's ebony chair and called one of the household cats to me. "But how do you know that you will love him?" I asked.

Nefertiti looked at me sharply. "Because he's about to become the Pharaoh of Egypt," she said. "And I am tired of Akhmim."

I thought of Ranofer with his handsome smile and wondered if she was tired of him, too. Then my mother's servant came through the doors of the Audience Chamber and the cat slipped away.

"Are we to come?" Nefertiti asked anxiously.

"Yes, my lady."

Nefertiti looked at me. Her cheeks were flushed. "Walk behind me, Mutny. She has to see me first and fall in love."

We entered into the Audience Chamber with the gifts from our treasury, and the room seemed bigger than I remembered. The painted marshes on the wall and blue river tiles on the ground looked brighter. The servants had done well, even washing out the stain on the hanging above my mother's head. The queen looked the same as she had at the tombs. An austere face surrounded by a large Nubian wig. If Nefertiti ever became queen, she would wear such a wig. We approached the dais, where the queen sat in a large, feather-stuffed cushion on the chair with the widest arms in our house. A black cat rested on her lap. Her hand was on its back, and its collar was lapis and gold.

The queen's herald stepped forward and flung out his arm in a sweeping gesture. "Your Majesty, your niece, the Lady Nefertiti."

My sister held out her gift and a servant took the gilt bowl. My aunt touched an empty seat to her left, indicating that Nefertiti should sit next to her. As my sister ascended the dais, my aunt's eyes never moved from her face. Nefertiti was beautiful in a way that made even queens stare.

"Your Majesty, your niece, the Lady Mutnodjmet."

I stepped forward and my aunt blinked in surprise. She looked at the turquoise box I held out for her and smiled, a concession that in Nefertiti's presence she'd forgotten about me. "You've grown tall," she commented.

"Yes, but not as graceful as Nefertiti, Your Majesty."

My mother nodded approvingly. I had turned the conversation to the reason the queen had come to Akhmim, and we all looked to my sister, who tried not to glow.

"She *is* beautiful, Ay. More of her mother, I think, than you."

My father laughed. "And gifted. She can sing. And dance."

"But is she clever?"

"Of course. And she has strength." His voice lowered meaningfully. "She will be able to guide his passions and control him."

My aunt looked at Nefertiti again, wondering if this was true.

"But she must be Chief Wife if she is to marry him," he added. "Then she will direct his interests away from Aten, back to Amun and to politics that are less dangerous."

The queen turned directly to my sister. "What do you say to all this?" she asked.

"I will do what is commanded of me, Your Majesty. I will entertain the prince and give him children. And I will be an obedient servant of Amun." Her eyes met mine, and I lowered my head to keep from smiling.

"Of Amun," the queen repeated thoughtfully. "If only my son had so much sense."

"She is the strongest willed of my two children," my father said. "If anyone can sway him, it would be her."

"And Kiya is weak," the queen conceded. "She cannot do the job. He wanted to make her Chief Wife, but I wouldn't allow it."

My father promised, "Once he sees Nefertiti, he will forget about Kiya."

"Kiya's father is a vizier," my aunt said warningly. "He will be displeased that I chose your daughter over his."

My father shrugged. "It's to be expected. We are family."

There was a moment's hesitation, then the queen stood up. "So the matter is settled."

I heard Nefertiti's delighted intake of breath. It was over as quickly as it had begun. The queen walked down the dais, a small but indomitable figure, and the cat followed her on the end of a golden leash. "I hope she lives up to your promise, Ay. It is the future of Egypt that is at stake," she warned darkly.

For three days servants rushed from room to room, packing linens and clothes and small jewelry into baskets. There were half-empty chests lying open everywhere, with vessels of alabaster, glass, and pottery waiting to be wrapped and put inside. My father supervised the move with visible pleasure. Nefertiti's marriage meant we would all move to live in Malkata Palace in Thebes with him, and he would get to see more of us now.

"Mutny, stop standing around," my mother admonished. "Find something to do."

"Nefertiti's standing around," I tattled. My sister was at the other end of the room, trying on clothes and holding up pieces of glass jewelry.

"Nefertiti," my mother snapped, "there will be enough time to stand in front of the mirror at Malkata."

Nefertiti heaved dramatically, then took an armful of gowns and tumbled them into a basket. My mother shook her head, and my sister went out to supervise the loading of her seventeen chests. We could hear her in the courtyard, telling a slave to be careful, that her baskets were worth more than we'd paid for him. I looked over at my mother, who sighed. It hadn't become real that my sister would be queen.

It would change everything.

We would leave Akhmim behind. We'd keep the villa, but who knew if we'd ever see it again. "Do you think we'll ever come back?" I asked.

My mother straightened. I saw her look at the pools that my sister and I had played in as children, then out at our family's shrine to Amun. "I hope so," she answered. "We've been a family here. It's our home."

"But now Thebes will be our home."

She drew a heavy breath. "Yes. It's what your father wants. And your sister."

"Is it what you want?" I asked quietly.

Her eyes turned to the room she shared with my father. She missed him terribly when he was gone. Now she would be near him. "I want to be with my husband," she admitted, "and I want opportunities for my children." We both looked at Nefertiti, commanding the servants in the courtyard. "She will be monarch of Egypt," my mother said, a little in awe. "Our Nefertiti, only fifteen years old."

"And me?"

My mother smiled, the lines on her face coming together. "And you will be Sister of the King's Chief Wife. That's no small thing."

"But who will I marry?"

"You're only thirteen!" she exclaimed, and a shadow crossed her face. I was the only child the goddess Tawaret had given her. Once I was married, she'd have no one. Immediately, I felt sorry I'd said anything.

"Perhaps I won't marry," I said quickly. "Perhaps I will be a priestess."

She nodded, but I could see that she was thinking of a time when she would be all alone.

Chapter Two

THEBES

nineteenth of Pharmuthi

OUR BARGE WAS ready to set sail for Thebes four days after my aunt's visit to Akhmim. As the sun rose in the east above the temples of our city, I stood in front of my small herb garden and plucked a leaf of myrrh, holding it up to my nose and closing my eyes. I would miss Akhmim so much.

"Stop looking so sad." I heard my sister's voice behind me. "There'll be plenty of gardens for you at Malkata."

"How would you know?" I looked out over my tenderly cultivated plants. Cornflowers, mandrakes, poppies, a tiny pomegranate tree that Ranofer and I had planted together.

"Well, you'll be Sister of the King's Chief Wife. If there aren't, I'll have some built!" I laughed, and so did she. She took my arm in hers. "And who knows? Maybe we'll build an entire temple to you, make you goddess of the garden."

"*Nefertiti,* don't say such things."

"In two days I'll be married to a god, and that will make me a goddess, and you the sister of one. You will be divine by relation," she joked shockingly.

Our family was too close to the Pharaohs of Egypt to believe in their divinity the way the common people did, the way they were told to believe so they wouldn't challenge their authority. My father explained it one night, and I was afraid that next he would tell us that Amun-Re was not real, either, but he never did that. There were things you believed in for convenience's sake, and things too sacred to speak against.

Despite Nefertiti's promises, I was sad to leave my little garden. I took as many herbs with me as I could, placing them in small pots, and I told the servants to take care of the rest for me. They promised they would, but I doubted if they would really pay attention to the jujube or give the mandrakes as much water as they needed.

The trip to Thebes from the city of Akhmim was not a long one. Our barge pushed through the reeds and cattails, and then splashed through the muddy waters of the Nile south toward the City of Pharaohs. My father smiled at my sister from the prow, and she smiled back at him from her chair beneath an awning. Then he beckoned me over with his finger. "You have cat eyes in the sun," he said. "Green as emeralds."

"Just like Mother's," I replied.

"Yes," he agreed. But he hadn't called me over to speak about my eyes. "Mutnodjmet, your sister will need you in the days to come. These are dangerous times. Whenever a new Pharaoh sits on the throne there is uncertainty, and never more than now. You will become your sister's Chief Lady, but you must be very careful what you do and say. I know you are honest." He smiled. "Honest sometimes to a fault. But the court is no place for honesty. You must take heed around Amunhotep." He looked out over the waters. Fishermen's nets hung limp in the sun. At this time of day, all work was abandoned. "Also, you must rein in Nefertiti."

I glanced at him in surprise. "How?"

"By giving her advice. You have patience and you are good with people."

I flushed. He had never said that about me before.

"Nefertiti is hot-tempered. And I am afraid . . ." He shook his head, but he didn't say what he was afraid of.

"You told Aunt Tiye Nefertiti could control the prince. Why does a prince need to be controlled?"

"Because he is hot-tempered, too. And ambitious."

"Isn't ambition good?"

"Not like this." He covered my hand with his. "You will see. Just keep your eyes open, little cat, and your senses alert. If there is trouble, come to me before anyone else." My father saw which way my thoughts were tending and smiled. "Don't look so worried. It won't be so bad. After all, it's a small trade for the crown of Egypt." He indicated the shore with his eyes. "We're almost there."

I looked out over the prow. There were more ships now that we were nearing the palace, long vessels with triangular sails like ours. Women ran to the sides of their ships to catch a glimpse of our barge and to see who was in it. The gold banners flying from the mast identified my father as Senior Vizier to the Elder, and everyone would know that it was carrying the future queen of Egypt. Nefertiti had disappeared into the cabin, and now she reappeared in fresh linen. Rare jewels that our aunt had left for her hung across her throat and caught the sun. She came up and stood beside me on the prow, letting the spray cool her skin.

"Great Osiris!" I pointed. "Look!" There were fifty soldiers on the shore, and at least two hundred servants, all waiting for our arrival.

My father was the first to disembark, followed by my mother, then Nefertiti and myself. This was the order of importance in our family. I wondered how that hierarchy would change after my sister's coronation.

"Look at the litters," I exclaimed. They were gold and lapis with ebony carrying poles.

"They must be the Elder's," Nefertiti said, impressed.

We were borne up, each in our own curtained box, and I parted the drapes to see Thebes for the second time, sparkling under the afternoon sun. I wondered how Nefertiti could bear to sit back in her litter when she had never seen Thebes before. But I could see her shadow, proud and erect in the middle of her litter, restraining herself as we swept through the city our father had never taken us to. A dozen flutists played as we went, passing the sandstone houses with their hundreds of onlookers. I wished I could be in the same litter as my mother, sharing her joy as the acrobats and musicians entertained the gathering crowds. We passed the temple of Amunhotep the Magnificent and the colossal pair of statues depicting him as a god. Then, in the midst of the desert, a lake glittered on the horizon. I nearly toppled out of the litter, my urge to see it was so strong. It was a man-made pool dug in a half-moon shape, and it surrounded the palace. Boats with small sails slipped across the waters in a place where sand and palms should have been, and I remembered my father saying that Amunhotep the Magnificent had built a lake as a symbol of his love for Queen Tiye, and that it was unlike any other in Egypt. It shone like liquid lapis and silver in the sun, and the crowds moved away as we approached the palace gates.

I quickly sat back on the pillows and let the curtains fall into place. I didn't want to seem like a farm girl who'd never been outside of Akhmim. Even with the curtains closed, though, I knew when we had passed onto the grounds of the palace. The road became shaded with trees, and I could make out the outline of small sanctuaries, villas of public officials, a royal workshop, and small, squat quarters for servants. The litter bearers ascended a flight of stairs and we were set down at the top. When we parted the curtains, all of Thebes was spread before us: the half-moon lake, the mud-brick houses, the markets and farms, and, beyond them, the Nile.

My father dusted off his kilt and announced his intentions to the servants. "We will be taken to our quarters and unpacked. When we are bathed and changed, we shall meet the Elder."

The servants bowed deeply in a show of esteem, and I knew my mother was impressed at how much power her husband commanded in Thebes. In Akhmim he was simply our father, a man who liked to read by the lotus pools and visit the Temple of Amun to watch the sun set over the fields. But in the palace he was the Vizier Ay, one of the most respected men in the kingdom.

A male servant appeared sporting the side lock of youth. He was slight, with a kilt trimmed in gold. Only Pharaoh's servants wore gold on their cloth. "I will be the one to take you to your rooms." He began walking. "The estimable Vizier Ay and his wife shall be lodged in the courtyard to the left of Pharaoh. To his right is the prince, next to whom the ladies Nefertiti and Mutnodjmet shall be placed." Behind us servants scrambled to gather our dozens of chests. The palace was built in the shape of an ankh, the center of which was Pharaoh. Scattered around him in various courtyards were his viziers, and as we passed these open squares women and children stopped to watch our procession. *This is what our life will be like now,* I thought. A world of watching.

Our guide walked across several brightly tiled courtyards with paintings of papyrus fields, then into a chamber where everyone stopped. "The Vizier Ay's rooms," he announced ceremoniously. He threw open the doors and granite statues peered out from every niche in the chamber. It was a room full of luxury and light, with reed baskets and wooden tables with carved ivory feet.

"Take my daughters to their rooms," my father instructed, "then escort them to the Great Hall in time for dinner."

"Mutny, be dressed properly tonight," my mother warned, embarrassing me in front of the servants. "Nefertiti, the prince will be there."

"With Kiya?" she asked.

"Yes," my father replied. "We have arranged for jewelry and clothes to be placed in your chamber. You have until sunset. Mutny will help you with whatever you need." My father looked at me and I nodded. "I have also arranged for body servants to be sent. These are the most highly trained women in the palace."

"At what?" I asked ignorantly. We had never had body servants in Akhmim. Nefertiti flushed a mortified red.

My father replied, "At cosmetics and beauty."

There was a real bed in our chamber. Not a reed mat or stuffed pallet as we had in our villa back home, but a large, carved ebony platform overhung with linens that Nefertiti and I would share. A brazier was sunk into the tiled floor for colder nights when we would sip warm beer and wrap ourselves in heavy blankets by the fire. And in a separate room used just for changing there was a limestone toilet. I pulled up its lid, and Nefertiti glanced over her shoulder in horror. Our guide watched me with amusement. There was a ceramic bowl filled with rosemary water beneath. We would never have to use a toilet stool and bowl again. It was a room fit for a princess of Egypt, and our guide interrupted us to explain that I would be Nefertiti's bedmate until she was married, at which time she could choose to have her own bed.

Everywhere were the representations of growth and endless life. The wooden columns had been carved into flowers, then painted in blues and greens, dark yellows and reds. Egrets and ibis took flight along the walls, drawn by an artist skilled at his work. Even the tiled floor splashed with life, the mosaic of a lotus pond so realistic that like the gods, we, too, could walk on water. Our guide disappeared, and Nefertiti called, "Come look at this!" She touched the face of a mirror, larger than both of us together, and we stared at our reflection. Small, light Nefertiti and me. Nefertiti smiled at herself in the polished bronze. "This is how we shall look in eternity," she whispered. "Young and beautiful."

Well, young, anyway, I thought.

"Tonight I must be magnificent," Nefertiti said, turning quickly. "I have to outshine Kiya in every way. Chief Wife is only a title, Mutnodjmet. Amunhotep could send me to the back of some harem if I fail to charm him."

"Our father would never let that happen," I protested. "You will always have a room in the palace."

"Palace or harem," she dismissed, turning back to the mirror, "what does it matter? If I don't impress him, I will be a figurehead and nothing more. I will pass my days in my chamber and never know what it's like to rule a kingdom."

It frightened me to hear Nefertiti speak like this. I preferred her wild confidence to the reality of what would happen if she failed to become the favorite. Then I saw something move behind us in the mirror and froze. A pair of women had entered our chamber. Nefertiti turned sharply and one of the women stepped forward. She was dressed in the court's latest fashion, with beaded sandals and small golden earrings. When she smiled, two dimples appeared on her cheeks.

"We have been instructed to take you to the baths," she announced, handing us linen towels and soft bathing robes. She was older than Nefertiti, but not by many years. "I am Ipu." Her black eyes searched us appraisingly, taking in my disheveled hair and Nefertiti's slenderness. She indicated the woman next to her and smiled. "This is Merit."

Merit's lips curved upward slightly, and I thought her face was haughtier looking than Ipu's. Yet her bow was deep, and when she came up she flicked her bangled wrist toward the door, indicating the courtyard. "The baths are this way."

I thought of the cold copper tubs in Akhmim and my enthusiasm waned. Ipu, however, chattered brightly as we went.

"We are to become your body servants," she informed us. "Before you dress or leave your chamber, we will make certain everything is in place. Princess Kiya has her own ladies. Body servants as well as acolytes. The women of the court all follow her lead. However she paints her eyes, they paint their eyes. However she wears her hair, the women of Thebes follow. For now," she added with a smile.

A pair of guards ceremoniously pushed open the double doors to the bathhouse, and when the steam cleared from my vision I gasped. Vessels poured water into a long tiled pool that was surrounded by stone benches and sun-warmed stones. Thick plants, their tendrils escaping from vases to wind up the colonnades, grew toward the light.

Nefertiti surveyed the columned chamber with approval. "Can you believe that Father knew all about this and chose to raise us in Akhmim?" She tossed aside her linen towel.

We took seats on stone benches, and our new body servants instructed us to lie down.

"Your shoulders are very tense, my lady." Ipu pressed down to ease the tension in my back. "Old women have softer shoulders than you!" She laughed, and I was surprised at her familiarity. But as she massaged, I felt the tenseness in my shoulders come undone.

The beads from Ipu's wig clinked softly together, and I could smell the perfume from her linen sheath, the scent of lotus blossom. I closed my eyes, and when I opened them again there was another woman in the pool. Then almost at once Merit was moving, wrapping my sister in her robe.

I sat up. "Where—"

"Shh." Ipu pressed down on my back.

I watched them leave, stunned. "Where are they going?"

"Back to your chamber."

"But why?"

"Because Kiya is here," Ipu said.

I looked across the pool at a woman tossing her beaded hair in the water. Her face was small and narrow, her nose slightly crooked, but there was something arresting about her face.

Ipu clicked her tongue. "I have run out of lavender. Stay here, say *nothing*. I'll be back."

As Ipu walked away, Kiya moved toward me. She wrapped linen around her waist. Immediately, I sat up and did the same.

"So you're the one they're calling Cat Eyes," she said. She sat across from me and stared. "I suppose this is your first time in the baths?" She looked beneath my bench and I followed her gaze, seeing what I'd done. I had folded my bathing robe on the ground and now water had come and soaked its edges. "In the palace we have *closets* for these things." She grinned, and I looked over to where her robe was hanging and flushed.

"I didn't know."

She raised her brows. "I would have thought your body servant would have told you. Ipu is famous in Thebes. All the women at court want her for her skill with paint, and the queen gave her to you." She paused, waiting for my response. When she saw she would get nothing else out of me, she leaned forward. "So tell me, was that your sister?"

I nodded.

"She's very beautiful. She must have been the flower of every garden in Akhmim." She looked at me from under her long lashes. "I bet she had many admirers. It must have been difficult to leave him behind," she said intimately, "especially if she was in love."

"Nefertiti doesn't fall in love," I replied. "Men fall in love with her."

"*Men?* So there's more than one?"

"No, just our tutor," I replied quickly.

"The *tutor?*" She sat back.

"Well, not her tutor. He was mine."

Ipu's steps echoed in the courtyard and at once Kiya was standing, smiling brilliantly. "I'm sure we'll speak again, little sister."

Ipu saw us and alarm spread over her face. Then Kiya slipped out the doors, wearing only her wet linen. "What happened?" Ipu demanded, crossing the baths. "What did Princess Kiya say to you just now?"

I hesitated. "Only that Nefertiti was beautiful."

Ipu narrowed her eyes. "Nothing else?"

I shook my head earnestly. "No."

When I returned to our chamber, Nefertiti was already inside, dressed in a gown that cut below her breasts. Mine was identical, but when I put it on, no two sisters could have been more different. On me, the linen was long and loose, but on Nefertiti the gown hugged her little waist, coming up below her breasts to push them higher. "Wait!" Nefertiti exclaimed as Merit poised the brush above her head. "Where's the safflower oil?"

Merit frowned. "My lady?"

"Safflower oil," Nefertiti explained, glancing at me. "My sister says to use it. To prevent losing your hair."

"We don't use safflower oil here, my lady. Shall I find some?"

"Yes." Nefertiti sat back and watched Merit go. She nodded approvingly at my gown. "You see? You can look nice when you try."

"Thanks," I said flatly.

It took fully until sunset to prepare us; Ipu and Merit were as capable as my father had promised, and with steady hands they meticulously rouged our lips and applied kohl to our eyes, hennaed our breasts, and at last placed Nubian wigs on our heads.

"Over my hair?" I complained. Nefertiti glared at me, but the wig looked hot and heavy, full of braids and tiny beads. "Does everyone do this?"

Ipu stifled a laugh. "Yes, Lady Mutnodjmet. Even the queen."

"But how will it stay?"

"With beeswax and resin."

She tied my long hair into a knot and placed the wig on my head with expert care. The effect was surprisingly becoming. The braids framed my face and green beads brought out the color of my eyes; Ipu must have chosen the color for me, for I saw that Nefertiti's beads were silver. I sat still while my body servant applied a cream across my breasts, then delicately removed the lid from a jar. She poured a handful of glittering fragments into the palm of her hand and then blew softly, and I was covered in gold dust. I caught a glimpse of myself in the mirror and gasped. I was pretty.

Then Nefertiti stood.

There was no sign of the boat journey we had taken from Akhmim. She was wide awake with nervousness for this night, and she shimmered with the brilliance of the sun. Her wig came below her shoulders and behind her ears, emphasizing her cheekbones and slender neck. Every strand of hair played music when the beads came together, and I thought there wasn't a man in any kingdom who could refuse her. Her entire body glittered with gold, even her toes.

The two body servants stepped back. "She's magnificent."

They switched places to inspect each other's work, and Merit hummed approval as she looked into my face. "Green eyes," she said. "I have never seen eyes this green before."

"I rimmed them in malachite," Ipu replied, proud of her work.

"It's beautiful."

I sat straighter and my sister cleared her throat, interrupting my moment.

"My sandals," she announced.

Merit fetched sandals encrusted with gold, then Nefertiti turned to me.

"Tonight I meet the Prince of Egypt," she said. She held out her arms and her bangles tinkled at her wrists. "How do I look?"

"Like Isis," I said honestly.

We were led to the Great Hall at sunset and could hear the festivities from several courtyards away. As each guest arrived, they were announced, and as we waited in line, Nefertiti squeezed my arm. "Is Father in there yet?" she asked, thinking that because I was tall I could see over the heads of a dozen people.

"I can't tell."

"Stand on your toes," she instructed.

I still couldn't see. "Don't worry. Everyone will see your entrance," I promised.

We moved up several places in line, and now I could see that the Elder and Queen Tiye were both within. The prince, too, was there. Men kept turning in line to look at my sister, and I realized that my father had chosen correctly when instructing us to arrive after everyone else.

The line kept moving, and soon the entire hall was spread before us. Of all the rooms I had yet seen in Malkata, it was easily the widest and most beautiful. The herald cleared his throat and stretched out his arm. "The Lady Nefertiti," he announced grandly, "daughter of Ay, Vizier of Egypt and Overseer of the King's Great Works."

Nefertiti took a step forward and I heard conversation in the Great Hall falter.

"The Lady Mutnodjmet, sister of Nefertiti, daughter of Ay, Vizier of Egypt and Overseer of the King's Great Works," the herald continued.

Now I stepped forward, and I watched as the guests turned to see Ay's two daughters, fresh from the tiny city of Akhmim.

Women stared as we walked to the dais. Our father stood to greet us from behind a long table, and we were brought before the three Horus thrones of Egypt, bowing with our arms outstretched. The Elder sat forward on his chair, and I could see that his sandals were carved of wood and that the bottoms were painted with images of his enemies. He stared at Nefertiti's round hennaed breasts, though there were enough pairs in the Great Hall to keep him occupied for the entire night.

"Rise," the queen commanded.

As we did so, Prince Amunhotep's gaze met my sister's. Nefertiti smiled back, and I noticed that next to him Kiya was watching us closely. Then, because Nefertiti was not yet queen, we were taken to a table directly beneath the dais where the viziers ate and where my father was sitting.

Nefertiti hissed through her perfect smile, "It's an insult, to have to sit beneath her."

My father stroked my sister's golden arm. "In a few days, she will be sitting here, and you will be Queen of Egypt."

The men at our table talked over each other to ask Nefertiti about her journey to Thebes, if the weather had been good, whether the ship had stopped at any cities along the way. I watched Amunhotep, and his eyes never left my sister's face. She must have known this, because she laughed and flirted, tossing her long neck back when a handsome son of another vizier approached her and asked about her time in Akhmim. I saw Kiya try to speak with the prince, to tear her husband's gaze away from my sister, but Amunhotep would not be distracted. I wondered what he thought of his future wife, and I studied the way Nefertiti held men in her power. She spoke softly, so they had to bend closer to hear, and she gave her smiles sparingly, so that when she laughed a man felt like he had been bathed in her light.

When the food was served and we began to eat, I didn't know

where to look first. The dais, where the Elder leered at naked women whose limber bodies bent backward in dance, or the prince, who looked sharp and controlled, a different man from the one I remembered in the tombs. I looked at Panahesi across the table. The vizier wore the signet ring of the king, and he was tall like my father. But in all other ways they were opposites. Where my father had blue eyes, Panahesi's were black. Where my father had the high cheekbones Nefertiti had inherited, Panahesi's face was longer and fuller. Gold rings shone on each of his fingers, whereas my father rarely wore his jewels. I studied our family's rival until the musicians struck up a tune and everyone left the tables to dance, women in one circle, men in another. My father took my mother's hand to lead her across the hall, and Kiya watched with critical eyes as Nefertiti got up to join the women.

"Aren't you coming?" Nefertiti asked.

"Of course not!" I stared at the throngs of pretty courtiers' daughters, all of whom had been raised in Thebes, all of whom would know the court dances. "I don't know any of the moves. How will you do it?"

She shrugged. "I'll watch and learn."

Perhaps Merit had given her instructions in private, for I was amazed to see my sister leap and spin in time with the others, a vision of lapis lazuli and gold. There were only a few women sitting, and I noticed with unease that I wasn't alone at our table. Panahesi remained as well. I glanced at him, the way his long fingers were templed under his clipped black beard, the only vizier at court who let his hair grow long. Then he caught me looking at him and said, "This must be very exciting for you. A young girl from Akhmim, coming to the palace with all its feasting and gold. So why aren't you dancing?"

I shifted in my seat. "I don't know the dances," I admitted.

He raised his brows. "Yet your sister seems so natural," he pointed out, and we be both looked at Nefertiti, who danced as if we'd been attending court functions all our lives. Panahesi looked from her to me and smiled. "You must be half sisters."

I hoped Ipu's rouge hid my mortification, and bit my tongue so I wouldn't reply with something sharp.

"So tell me," Panahesi went on. "With a sister in the king's harem, who will you marry?"

My ire rose. "I am only thirteen."

"Of course, a little girl still." His eyes traveled to my chest, and suddenly Nefertiti was beside me. The music had ended.

"Yes, but better a blossoming woman than a wilted old man." Her eyes traveled meaningfully to Panahesi's kilt. Then our father reappeared, taking his seat at the table.

Panahesi pushed out his chair. "Your children are very charming," he snapped. "I am sure the prince will come to love them dearly." He swept away, his white cloak trailing at his heels, and my father demanded, "What happened?"

"The vizier—" I began, but Nefertiti cut me off.

"Nothing."

My father looked long at Nefertiti.

"Nothing," she repeated.

"I warned you to be careful. The Vizier Panahesi has Amunhotep's ear."

Nefertiti set her jaw, and I could see that she wanted to reply, *Not when I become queen,* but remained silent. Then she searched the room and became agitated. "Where is the prince?"

"While you were charming the vizier, he left the hall."

Nefertiti faltered. "I won't meet him tonight?"

"Not unless he returns," my father said, and I had never heard his voice so deep or stern. This wasn't Akhmim. This was the court of Egypt, where mistakes couldn't be tolerated.

"Maybe he'll come back," I suggested hopefully, and both Nefertiti and my father ignored me. The musky scent of wine filled the hall. Kiya remained surrounded by her women, court ladies who were dressed, as Ipu had told us, in the fashion she dictated: long hair, sleeveless sheaths, and hennaed feet. They hovered around her like moths, her little belly evidence that she, and not my sister, was the future of Egypt.

"It's too hot in here," Nefertiti said, taking my arm. "Come with me."

Our father warned sharply, "Do not go far."

I followed Nefertiti's angry footfalls through the hall. "Where are we going?"

"Anywhere but here." She stalked through the palace. "He left, Mutnodjmet. He actually left without meeting me. His future queen. The future of Egypt!"

We went outside and found ourselves at the fountain. We put our hands beneath its flow, letting the water drip from our fingers to our breasts. The rippling water carried the scents of honeysuckle and jasmine. As Nefertiti took off her wig, a familiar voice pierced the darkness.

"So you are my mother's choice of wife."

Nefertiti looked up and the prince was standing there, clad in his golden pectoral. She wiped any trace of surprise from her face, and at once she was Nefertiti, flirtatious and charming. "Why? Are you shocked?" she asked him.

"Yes." But there was nothing airy in Amunhotep's response. He sat and studied Nefertiti in the moonlight.

"Is Egypt's prince tired of the dancing then?" She did it perfectly, hiding her nervousness by sounding coquettish.

"I am tired of seeing my mother bow to the High Priest of Amun." When Nefertiti smiled, Amunhotep looked at her sharply. "Is that funny?"

"Yes. I had thought you had come out here to court your new wife. But if you want to talk politics, I will listen."

Amunhotep narrowed his eyes. "Listen the way my father listens?

Or the way you listened to your tutor when he professed love in Akhmim?"

Even in the darkness I could see my sister blanch, and I realized immediately what Kiya had done. I thought I would be ill, but Nefertiti was quick.

"They say you are a great believer of Aten," she recovered. "That you plan to build temples when you are made Pharaoh."

Amunhotep sat back. "Your father keeps you well informed," he remarked.

"I keep myself well informed," she replied.

She was smart and she was charming, and even he couldn't resist the earnestness of her stare in the light of the oil lamps. He moved closer to her. "I want to be known as the People's Pharaoh," he admitted. "I want to build the greatest monuments in Egypt to show the people what a leader with vision can do. The Amun priests should never have been allowed to achieve such power. That power was meant for the Pharaohs of Egypt."

There was the crunch of gravel and the three of us turned.

"Amunhotep." Kiya stepped into the light. "Everyone is wondering where the Prince of Egypt has been." She smiled lovingly at him, as if his disappearing was both quaint and wonderful. She held out her arm. "Shall we return?"

Nefertiti nodded. "Until tomorrow then," she promised, and her voice was low and sultry, as if there was a great secret between them.

Kiya's arm tightened around Amunhotep's. "I felt our child move tonight. A son," she swore, loud enough for Nefertiti to hear as she steered him away. "I can already feel him."

We watched them walk into the darkness, and I noticed how tightly Kiya was holding on to Amunhotep, as if he might disappear at any moment.

▣ ▣ ▣

Nefertiti seethed, her sandals slapping across the tiles to our chamber. "What will he do in two days when we are united before Amun? Will he bring Kiya along and ignore me then, too?"

My father stood and closed the door. "You must lower your voice. There are spies throughout the palace."

Nefertiti sank onto a leather cushion and put her head against my mother's shoulder. "I was humiliated, *mawat.* He sees me as just another wife."

My mother caressed my sister's dark hair. "He will come around."

"When?" Nefertiti sat up. "*When?*"

"Tomorrow," my father said with certainty. "And if not tomorrow, then we will make him see that you are more than just his mother's choice of wife."

Chapter Three

twentieth of Pharmuthi

THE CORONATION OF Egypt's new Pharaoh and his queen was to take place on the twenty-first of Pharmuthi, and my father did everything in his power to put Nefertiti before Amunhotep's eye.

In the morning we entered the wide, bronze gates into the towering Arena that Amunhotep III had built for Amun. Nefertiti squeezed my hand, for neither of us had ever seen anything so high or magnificent. A forest of columns encircled a sandy pit and the painted walls stretched to the sky. On the lowest tier of seats, the nobility assembled while their servants held drinks and honeyed cakes. This was where Amunhotep liked to ride in the morning, so we were there, watching the prince sweep around the tracks in his golden chariot. But Kiya was there as well, and the Vizier Panahesi, so that when the prince was finished playing warrior an hour later it was Kiya he kissed, and Kiya he laughed with, while Nefertiti had to smile and look pleased before her rival.

At noon, we were in the Great Hall again, sitting below the dais, eating and chatting as happily as if everything was going our family's way. Nefertiti laughed and flirted, and I noticed that the more Amunhotep saw of his future wife, the less he could stop watching her. Kiya had none of Nefertiti's sleek charm. She couldn't turn a room the way Nefertiti did. But when the afternoon meal was finished, no further words had passed between the prince and Nefertiti, and when we returned to our chamber, my sister was silent. Ipu and Merit rushed around us, and I watched Nefertiti with a growing unease. Amunhotep still saw her as his mother's choice of wife, and I couldn't see how my father planned to change that.

"What will you do?" I finally asked.

"Repeat to me what he said in the tombs."

Merit stiffened, poised to apply gold across Nefertiti's chest. It was bad luck to speak of what happened below the earth.

I hesitated. "He said he would never bow to his brother. Never bow to Amun."

"And by the fountain he said he wanted to be loved by the people," Nefertiti stressed. "That he wanted to be the People's Pharaoh."

I nodded slowly.

"Mutnodjmet, go and find Father," she said.

"Now?" Ipu was applying kohl to my brows. "Can't it wait until after?"

"After *what*?" she asked tersely. "Kiya has birthed him a son?"

"Well, what are you going to tell him?" I demanded. I wasn't going to leave until I'd determined that it was worth disturbing our father.

"I am going to tell him how we can turn the prince."

I sighed, so she would know I wasn't happy about it, then I went into the hall, but I couldn't find my father. He wasn't in his room or in the Audience Chamber. I searched the gardens, made my way into the labyrinthine kitchens, then rushed into the courtyard at the front of the palace, where a servant stopped me and asked what I needed.

"I'm searching for the Vizier Ay."

The old man smiled. "He's in the same place he always is, my lady."

"And where is that?"

"In the Per Medjat."

"The *what?*"

"The Hall of Books." He could see that I did not know where this was and so he asked, "Shall I show you the way, my lady?"

"Yes." I hurried after him into the palace, past the Great Hall toward the Audience Chamber. For an elderly man, he was spry. He stopped short at a pair of wooden doors, and it was clear he could not go inside.

"In there?"

"Yes, my lady. The Per Medjat."

He waited to see whether I would knock or go in. I pushed open the doors and stood gazing up at the most magnificent room in all of Malkata. I had never before seen a hall of books. Two twisting flights of stairs in polished wood wound toward the ceiling, and everywhere there were scrolls bound in leather, held together by twine—they must have contained all the wisdom of the Pharaohs. My father sat at a cedar table. The queen was there, too, as well as my mother, and all of their voices were quick and tense. When I stepped inside, all three of them stopping speaking. Then two pairs of sharp blue eyes focused on me; I had not seen the strong resemblance between my father and his sister until then.

I cleared my throat and directed my announcement to my father. "Nefertiti would like to speak with you," I told him.

Ay turned to his sister. "We'll speak on this later. Perhaps today will change things." He glanced at me. "What does she want?"

"To tell you something about the prince," I said as we left the Per Medjat and entered the hall. "She thinks she has found a way to turn him."

Inside our chamber, Ipu and Merit had finished dressing Nefertiti. Matching cartouches jangled at her wrists, and there were earrings in her ears. I paused, then gasped and rushed over to see what our body servants had done. They had pierced her lobes not once, but *twice.* "Who pierces them twice?"

"I do," she said, lifting her chin.

I turned to my father, who only looked approvingly at her. "You have news about the prince?" he asked.

Nefertiti indicated our body servants with her eyes.

"From now on your body servants are your closest friends. Kiya has her women, and these are yours. Merit as well as Ipu were both chosen with caution. They are loyal."

I glanced across the room at Merit. She rarely smiled, and I was thankful my father had chosen Ipu, the merrier one, for me.

"Ipu," my father instructed quietly, "stand by the door and talk softly with Merit." He pulled Nefertiti to the side, and I could hear only pieces of what they said together. At one point, my father looked immensely pleased. He patted Nefertiti's shoulder and replied, "Very good. I thought the same." Then they went to the door and he addressed Merit. "Come. I have a job." And the three of them left the chamber.

I stared at Ipu. "What's happening? Where did they go?"

"To turn the prince away from Kiya," she said. She indicated the leather stool where she could finish my kohl, and I sat. "I only hope they succeed," she confided.

I was curious. "Why?"

She took out her brush and uncapped a glass vial. "Before she wed the prince, Kiya and Merit were good friends." I raised my eyebrows and Ipu nodded. "They were raised together, both the daughters of scribes. But Panahesi became a High Vizier and moved Kiya into the palace. It's how she met the prince. Then Merit's father was to become a lesser vizier at the palace as well. The Elder wanted to promote him. But Panahesi told the Elder he wasn't trustworthy."

I sucked in my breath. "How devious."

"Kiya was afraid that with Merit in the palace, the prince would lose interest in her. But Merit always had another man in mind. She was to marry Vizier Kemosiri's son, Heru, as soon as her father received his promotion. When it didn't happen, Heru told his father he was still in love with Merit, daughter of a scribe or no. They kept writing, hoping the Elder would discover that he'd been wrong. Then one day, the letters stopped coming."

I sat forward in my chair. "What happened?"

"Merit didn't know. Later, she discovered that Kiya had turned Heru."

I didn't understand. "Turned?"

"Turned his eye. Even though Kiya knew she was going to marry the prince."

"How cruel." But I could imagine Kiya smiling sweetly, the same way she had smiled at me in the baths. *All the girls must be in love with you,* she'd probably told him.

Ipu clicked her tongue softly, holding up the pomegranate paste. "Of course, once Kiya was married, what did it matter if Merit came to the palace?"

"And her father?"

"Oh." Ipu's dimples disappeared. "He's still a scribe." Her voice grew low and hard. "It's why Merit still hates Kiya."

"But how can Nefertiti take Kiya's place?"

Ipu smiled. "Gossip."

Chapter Four

twenty-first of Pharmuthi

ON THE MORNING of Nefertiti's marriage and coronation, rumors began spreading in the palace that a beauty never before seen in Egypt had descended on Thebes and would become the queen. Ipu suspected those rumors began with my father and involved the transfer of deben, which were rings of metal value, because by sunrise there was nowhere Nefertiti could go without servants peering through the windows at her. Ladies newly arrived at court for the coronation suddenly began appearing at our room on false errands, calling to see if Nefertiti needed perfume, or linen, or spiced wine. Eventually, my mother barricaded us in her chamber and drew the curtains on all four sides.

Nefertiti was irritable; she hadn't slept all night. She'd rolled around, stealing my covers and whispering my name every so often to see if I was awake. "Stand still or I can't fasten your necklace," I said.

"And be gracious," my mother advised. "These people are whispering in the prince's ear even as we speak, telling him about you."

Nefertiti nodded, while Merit applied cream to her face. "Mutnodjmet, find my sandals, the ones with amber. And you should wear the same. It doesn't matter that they're uncomfortable," she said, anticipating my reaction. "You can throw them away afterward."

"But no one will even see my sandals," I protested.

"Of course they will," Nefertiti replied. "They'll see your sandals, your linen, and your crooked wig." She frowned, interrupting Merit to lean forward and fix my hair. "Gods, Mutny! What would you do without me?"

I handed her the amber-studded sandals. "Tend my garden and have a quiet life."

She laughed and I smiled, even though she was being unbearable. "I hope it goes well," I said earnestly.

My sister's face grew serious. "It has to, or our family will have traveled to Thebes and exchanged our lives for nothing."

There was a knock on the chamber door and my mother rose to get it. My father stood at the threshold with six guards. The men stared into the room and I smoothed my hair quickly, trying to look like a Sister of the King's Chief Wife. Nefertiti, however, ignored them all, closing her eyes while Merit applied the last sweeps of kohl.

"Are we ready?" My father strode into the chamber while the guards remained at the door, studying Nefertiti's reflection in the mirror. They hadn't even noticed I was there.

"Yes, we're almost ready," I announced. The guards looked in my direction for the first time and my mother frowned at me.

"Well, don't just stand there." My father gestured. "Help your sister."

I flushed. "With what?"

"With anything. The scribes are waiting, and soon the barges will be sailing for Karnak and we'll all have a new Pharaoh." I turned to look at him because there was such irony in his voice, but he gestured for me to keep moving. "Hurry."

Then Nefertiti was ready. She stood, her beaded faience dress spilling to the floor as the sun caught her necklace and gilded bangles. She looked at the guards, and I studied their reaction. Their shoulders straightened and their chests expanded. Nefertiti moved forward, hooking our father's arm in hers, and she told him winningly, "I'm glad we came to Malkata."

"Don't get too comfortable," he warned. "Amunhotep will stay at Malkata only until Tiye has decided that he is ready to leave. Then we will go to the capital of Lower Egypt to rule."

"Memphis?" I cried. "We're going to Memphis? Forever?"

"Forever is a big word, Mutny," my father said. We walked out into the tiled hall and passed through the columns. "Perhaps not forever."

"How long then? And when will we return?"

My father looked at my mother, and it was understood between them that she should explain. "Mutny, your sister will be Queen of Egypt," she said in a voice used with small children, not thirteen-year-old girls. "When the Elder embraces the Afterlife, Amunhotep will move back to Thebes to rule Upper Egypt as well. But we will not return here until the Elder dies."

"And when will that be? The Pharaoh could live for twenty more years!"

No one said anything, and I saw from my father's look that the guards had probably overheard me.

"Now that the court is to be split, dangerous games are going to be played," my father said in a lower voice. "Who will stay with the old king, and who will place their bets on the new? Panahesi will go with Kiya to Memphis, since she is carrying Amunhotep's child. We, of course, will go as well. Your job will be to warn Nefertiti when there is trouble."

We entered the open courtyard outside the palace where the procession was waiting, and my mother took Nefertiti to Queen Tiye's side. I pressed my father's hand before he, too, could leave. "But what if she doesn't want to listen to me?" I asked.

"She will because she always has." He squeezed my shoulder gently. "And because you are the one who will be honest with her."

The procession was to begin at noon. The Elder and Queen Tiye were to ride in chariots. Behind them, the rest of the court would be carried in open litters shaded by thin canopies of linen. Only Amunhotep and Nefertiti would be on foot, as tradition decreed, walking through the city to Pharaoh's barge, which would be waiting on the waters of the Theban quay. From there, the barge would sail to Karnak, where the royal couple would proceed to the temple gates to be crowned Pharaoh and Queen of Lower Egypt.

As the courtyard filled with nobility, the guards grew tense. They shifted nervously from foot to foot, knowing if anything happened during the procession, their lives would be forfeit. I noticed one soldier in particular, a general with long hair and a pleated kilt. Ipu saw the direction of my gaze and said, "General Nakhtmin. Only twenty-one. I can make an introduction—"

"Don't you dare!" I gasped.

She laughed. "An eight-year difference is not so big!"

Nefertiti heard us laughing together and frowned. "Where is Amunhotep?" she demanded.

"I wouldn't be concerned," my father said wryly. "He won't miss his own coronation."

When the prince appeared, he was escorted by Kiya on one arm and her father, Panahesi, on the other. Both were whispering into the prince's ear, speaking quickly, and when they came to our place in line Panahesi greeted my father coldly. Then he caught sight of Nefertiti in a queen's diadem, and it looked as though he had bitten into something sour. But Kiya only smiled, touching Amunhotep softly on the hand as she prepared to take her leave of him. "Blessings to Your Highness on this auspicious day," she said with a sweetness that was sickening. "May Aten be with you."

Nefertiti met my father's eye. Kiya had just blessed Amunhotep in the name of *Aten.* So this was how she held him.

My father's eyes glinted. "Stay close," he warned me. "Once we reach Karnak, we will be walking to the temple, and there will be more commoners in the streets than you have ever seen."

"Because of the coronation?" I asked, but he didn't hear me. My voice was lost in the melee of horses and chariots and guards.

"Yes, and because rumors have been spreading through the city that the reincarnation of Isis has appeared."

I turned. The young general was smiling up at me.

"A beauty who can heal with the touch of her hand, if you listen to palace servants." He held out his arm and helped me into my litter.

"And what servant would say that?"

"You mean, why would someone pay a servant to say that?" he asked. "Because if your sister can win the people's hearts," he explained, "your family's stakes will have risen higher in this kingdom."

The litters were borne up, and in the swell of people the general disappeared.

As the procession made its way into the city, people began chanting the prince's name, and as we passed through the markets, we were overwhelmed by the passion of the thousands crushed into the streets, shouting my sister's name, begging for the blessings of Isis and chanting, "Long live the queen! Long live Nefertiti!"

As the people crushed against our litters, I tried to imagine the large chain of supporters my father must have called upon, and I realized how truly powerful the Vizier Ay was. The guards repeatedly pushed the people back, and I turned in my litter to see Amunhotep looking with astonishment on the woman who was so beloved in his kingdom. I watched as Nefertiti raised Amunhotep's hand in hers, and the roar that went up in the streets was deafening. She turned to him triumphantly, and I could read her expression: *I am more than just your mother's choice of wife.*

As we reached the barge, the cries throughout the city became "AMUN-HOTEP. NEFER-TITI."

The prince's face was aglow with the people's love. Nefertiti raised Amunhotep's hand in hers for the second time and proclaimed loud enough for Osiris to hear, "THE PEOPLE'S PHARAOH!" Then the crowds swelling along the riverbank grew untamable. The guards brought us to the quay with difficulty; we descended quickly from our litters and boarded the barge, but commoners had already surrounded the ship. The guards were forced to pry them off the ropes and from the hull. When the barge surged forward, it left thousands on the riverbank. The crowd immediately followed the barge along the shore, chanting blessings and throwing lotus blossoms into the water. Amunhotep stared at Nefertiti with the look of a man who'd been caught unawares.

"Is this why the Vizier Ay chose to raise his daughters in Akhmim?"

Nefertiti was flushed with triumph and her voice turned coy. "That, and the vizier didn't want us believing as his sister does in the power of the Amun priests."

I pressed my lips together in fear. But I saw what she was doing. She had taken her cue from Kiya.

Amunhotep blinked in surprise. "Then you believe I'm right?"

Nefertiti touched his arm, and I thought I could feel the heat of her palm as she whispered forcefully, "Pharaohs determine what is right. And when this barge reaches Karnak, you will be Pharaoh and I will be your queen."

We reached Karnak quickly, for the Temple of Amun was only a short distance from Malkata Palace. We could have walked, but sailing the Nile was tradition, and our fleet of barges with their golden pennants made an impressive sight in the midday sun. When the plank was lowered, thousands of Egyptians swelled around the barge. Their chants boomed over the water, and they struggled against the guards to glimpse the new king and queen of Egypt. Amunhotep and Nefertiti weren't afraid. They brushed past the soldiers and into the crowd.

But I stood back.

"This way." The general appeared at my side. "Stay close to me."

I followed him, and we were swept into a quick-moving procession. Up ahead, I could see the four golden chariots of the royal family. My mother and father were allowed to ride with the Pharaoh and his queen. The rest of us would walk to the Temple of Amun. On all sides of us women and children shouted, reaching out to touch our robes and wigs so they, too, could live for eternity.

"Are you all right?" the general asked.

"Yes, I think so."

"Keep walking."

As if I had a choice. The temple loomed ahead, and I could see the beautiful and nearly completed limestone sanctuary of Senusret I, and the towering shrines of the Elder. Sun spilled across the courtyard, and as we passed through the enclosure, the cheering fell behind us and everything grew suddenly cool and silent. Geese waddled between the columns, and shaven-headed boys in loose robes appeared, holding incense and candles. I listened to the crowds outside the walls, still chanting Nefertiti's name. If not for them, the only sound would have been trickling water and sandals slapping on stone.

"What happens now?" I whispered.

The general stepped back, and I noticed that his eyes were the shifting colors of sand. "Your sister will be taken to the sacred lake and anointed as coregent by the High Priest of Amun. Then she and the prince will be given the crook and flail of Egypt, and together they will reign."

My father appeared. "Mutnodjmet, go and stand by your sister," he instructed.

I went to Nefertiti. In the dim light of the temple, her skin shone like amber, and the lamps illuminated the gold around her neck. She glanced at me, and we both understood that the most important moment in our lives had come: After this ceremony, she would be Queen of Lower Egypt, and our family would ascend to immortality with her. Our names would be written in cartouches and public buildings from Luxor to Kush. We would be remembered in stone and assured a place with the gods for eternity.

Amunhotep ascended the dais holding Nefertiti's hand in his. He was taller than any Pharaoh that had come before him, and there was more gold on his arms than in my parents' entire treasury in Akhmim. The priests of Amun filed through the crowd, taking their places on the dais next to me, their bald heads like newly polished brass in the sun. I recognized the High Priest by his leopard robe, and when he came to stand before the new king, my sister passed Amunhotep a look full of meaning.

"Behold, Amun has called us together to exalt Amunhotep the Younger before the land," the High Priest announced. "Amun has appointed Amunhotep to be Chief of Lower Egypt, and to administer the laws of her people for all his days."

I could see the general from where I stood. He was watching my sister, and for some reason I felt disappointed.

"From Upper to Lower Egypt they have come. The Pharaoh of Egypt has declared that his son shall be made Pharaoh with him. The people have united to celebrate the new Pharaoh and his protector, Amun. From east to west there will be rejoicing. From north to south there will be celebration. Come." The High Priest held up a golden vessel filled with oil. "Amun pours his blessing on you, Pharaoh of Egypt." He poured the oil over Amunhotep's head. "Amun pours his blessing on you, Queen of Egypt."

The oil poured down Nefertiti's new wig and dripped onto her best linen gown. But my sister didn't flinch. She was queen. There would be many more gowns.

"Amun takes you by the hand and leads you to the sacred waters that shall wash you clean and make you new." He led them into the sacred pool, where he laid them back and the oil was washed away. The nobles who had been allowed inside the temple grew still and silent. Even the children knew that this was a moment they might never witness again.

"King Amunhotep and Queen Nefertiti," the High Priest proclaimed. "May Amun grant them long life and prosperity."

⁂

The sun was still high in the sky when we assembled in barges to return to Malkata from the Temple of Amun. On the boat ride from Karnak, Amunhotep studied my sister with open fascination: the way she talked, the way she smiled, the way she threw her head back and laughed. "Mutny, come," my sister called gaily. "Amunhotep, this is my sister, Mutnodjmet."

"You do have cat eyes," he remarked. "Your sister told me, but I didn't believe her."

I bowed, wondering what else my sister had time to tell him about. "I am pleased to meet you, Your Majesty."

"My husband has been talking about the temples he will build," Nefertiti said.

I looked to our new king to see if this was true, and Amunhotep straightened.

"Someday, Mutnodjmet, when I am Pharaoh of both Lower and Upper Egypt, I will raise Aten above all other gods. I will build him temples that overshadow anything built for Amun, and rid Egypt of the priests who take her gold to glorify themselves."

I glanced at Nefertiti, but she let him continue.

"Today a Pharaoh of Egypt can't make a decision without the priests of Amun. A Pharaoh can't go to war, build a temple, or construct a palace without the High Priest's consent."

"You mean the High Priest's money," Nefertiti offered.

"Yes. But that will change." He stood up and looked out over the prow. "My mother believes my worship of Aten will pass. But she is wrong; even my father will see in time that Aten is the god who has guided Egypt to glory."

I moved away to stand closer to my aunt, who was watching her new daughter-in-law with a critical eye. She beckoned me over with a finger to where she sat, a formidable woman, and smiled at me.

"You are a brave girl to have spoken to General Nakhtmin in front of my son," she said, then patted an armed chair next to her and I sat.

"Are they enemies?" I asked.

"My son dislikes the army, and the general has lived and breathed it since he was a boy." I wanted to ask more about General Nakhtmin, but she was searching for something else, something that had to do with Nefertiti. "So tell me, Mutnodjmet," she asked casually, "what is my son discussing with your sister?"

I knew to choose my words carefully. "They are speaking of the future, Your Majesty, and of all the plans Amunhotep wants to make."

"I wonder, do those plans include temples to Aten?"

I lowered my head and Tiye said, "I thought so." She turned to the nearest servant. "Find Vizier Ay and bring him to me."

I remained seated, and when my father came, another chair with leather arms was brought. All three of us watched Nefertiti on the prow, talking in earnest with her husband. It was impossible to think that just this morning they had hardly known each other at all.

"He is speaking of Aten," my aunt declared heatedly. "On his way from the Temple of Amun he is still rambling about something his grandfather once carved into his bedposts and onto his shields!" I had never seen my aunt so enraged. "He will be the unmaking of the country, Ay. My husband will not live forever! Your daughter must control him before he becomes Pharaoh of Upper Egypt as well."

My father looked across at me. "What has Nefertiti been saying?"

"She is listening to him," I said.

"That's it?"

I bit my tongue and nodded so I wouldn't have to lie.

"Give her time." Ay turned to his sister. "It's only been a day."

"In a day, Ptah created the world," she answered, and we all knew what she meant. That in a day, her son could undo it.

In Malkata Palace, Nefertiti and I were both undressed and given new gowns for the feasts celebrating the coronation. Ipu and Merit scurried like cats, finding sandals that would complement our sheaths and painting our eyes in black and green. Merit held Nefertiti's crown with awe, and placed it on her head while we all watched, holding our breaths. I tried to imagine being Queen of Egypt and wearing the cobra around my brow. "What does it feel like?" I asked.

Nefertiti closed her eyes. "Like being a goddess."

"Will you go to him before the feast?"

"Of course. I will walk in on his arm. You don't think I'd risk having him go with Kiya? It's bad enough he will go back to her bed."

"It's the custom, Nefertiti. Father said he'll be with her every fortnight. There's nothing you can do."

"There's *plenty* I can do!" Her eyes darted wildly across the chamber. "For one, we're not staying in these rooms."

"What?" I had arranged all my potted herbs along the windowsill. I had unpacked my chests. "But we're only in Thebes until Tiye announces when we'll move on to Memphis. I'll have to repack."

"Ipu will do it for you. Why should the Pharaoh and queen sleep apart? Our parents sleep in one room," she pointed out.

"But they aren't—"

"Power." She raised her finger while our body servants pretended not to listen. "That's why. They don't want the queen to have too much power."

"That's foolish. Queen Tiye is Pharaoh in all but name."

"Yes." Nefertiti began brushing her hair vigorously, dismissing Merit and Ipu with a wave. "In all but name. What more in life do we have but our name? What will be remembered in eternity? The gown I wore or the name I carried?"

"Your deeds. They will be remembered."

"Will Tiye's deeds be remembered, or will they be recorded as her husband's?"

"Nefertiti." I shook my head. She was aiming too high.

"What?" She tossed the brush aside, knowing that Merit would pick it up later. "Hatshepsut was king. She had herself crowned."

"You are meant to discourage him," I said. "You were talking about *Aten* on the barge!"

"Father said to control him." She grinned smugly. "He didn't say how. Come."

"Come where?"

"To the king's chamber."

She moved down the hall and I followed on her heels. In front of Pharaoh's room, a pair of guards moved aside. We swept into Amunhotep's anteroom and stood before the entrances to two separate chambers. One was clearly Amunhotep's bedroom. Nefertiti looked at the second room and nodded. "That will be yours after the feasts."

I stared at her. "And where will you stay?"

"In here."

She pushed opened the doors to the king's private chamber and I heard Amunhotep's gasp of surprise. I caught a glimpse of tiled walls and alabaster lamps, then the doors swung shut and I was alone in the king's private antechamber. There was silence for a moment, then laughter echoed through the walls. I waited in the antechamber for Nefertiti to come out, thinking the laughter would eventually cease, but the sun sank lower and lower in the sky and there was no indication of when they would emerge.

I seated myself and looked around. On a low table, hastily scrawled poems to Aten had been written on papyrus. I glanced at the king's door, which was firmly shut, then read them while I waited. They were psalms to the sun. *"Giver of breath to animals . . . Thy rays are in the midst of the great green sea."* There was sheaf after sheaf of poetry, each one different, each one praising Aten. For several hours, I read while inside Nefertiti spoke. The sound of Amunhotep's voice penetrated through the walls, and I didn't dare to imagine what they were speaking of so passionately. Eventually, evening fell, and I began to wonder if we would ever go to the feast. When someone knocked on the door, I hesitated, but Nefertiti's voice rang out brightly, "Mutny can answer it."

She knew I'd still be waiting.

On the other side of the door was General Nakhtmin.

He stepped back, shocked to see me in the king's antechamber, and I could tell by the way his eyes shifted to the king's door that he was wondering if Amunhotep had taken both sisters as lovers. "My lady." His gaze focused on the closed inner chamber. "I see that the Pharaoh is otherwise . . . occupied."

I flushed a brilliant scarlet. "Yes, he is busy now."

"Then perhaps you can give him the message that his father and mother are awaiting his presence in the Great Hall. The feast in his honor has been going on for some hours."

"Perhaps you can give him the message?" I said. "I . . . would hate to disturb them."

He raised his brows. "All right."

He knocked on the king's door, and I heard my sister's voice call sweetly, "Enter." The general disappeared and reappeared a moment later. "They have said that they will come when they are ready."

I did my best to hide my disappointment, and the general held out his arm to me.

"That doesn't mean you should miss the feasts."

I looked at the closed door and hesitated. If I left, Nefertiti would be angry. She would accuse me of abandoning her. But I had studied the same mosaics in the antechamber for hours and the sun had already set . . .

Rashly, I held out my arm, and the general smiled.

On a dais in the Great Hall were now four golden thrones. Beneath them a long table had been arranged where my mother and father were sitting; I could see them talking and eating with the viziers of the Elder's court. The general brought me over to them, and I was aware of my aunt's sharp eyes following us.

"Vizier Ay." The general bowed politely. "The Lady Mutnodjmet has arrived."

I felt a small thrill that he knew my name. My father stood, frowning over my shoulder to ask harshly, "This is well, but where is my *other* daughter?"

The general and I looked at each other.

"They said they would come when they were ready," I replied. I could feel the burn in my cheeks, and someone at the table inhaled. It was Kiya.

"Thank you," my father said, and the general disappeared.

I sat down and bowls of food appeared before me: roasted goose in garlic, barley beer, and honeyed lamb. Music was being played, and over the clatter of bowls it was difficult to hear what my parents were speaking of. But Kiya leaned across the table, and her voice was clear.

"She's a fool if she thinks he's going to forget me. Amunhotep adores me. He writes me poetry." I thought of the psalms in Amunhotep's chamber and wondered if they were his. "Pregnant in the first year, and I already know it's going to be a son," she gloated. "Amunhotep's even picked out a name."

I bit my tongue to keep from asking what it was, but I needn't have done so.

"Tutankhamun," she said. "Or maybe Nebnefer. Nebnefer, Prince of Egypt," she imagined.

"And if it's a girl?"

Kiya's black eyes went wide. Rimmed in kohl, they looked three times their size. "A *girl*? Why would it be—" Her response was cut off by the sound of trumpets announcing my sister's entrance. We all turned to see Nefertiti enter on Amunhotep's arm. At once Kiya's ladies began whispering, tossing glances in my direction, then in my sister's.

From the dais, Queen Tiye asked her son sharply, "Shall we dance, now that the night is nearly over?"

Amunhotep looked to Nefertiti.

"Yes, let's dance," my sister said, and my aunt did not let her son's deference go unnoticed.

***

Many of the guests would stay in their drunken stupor throughout the night and into the next, to be carried off in their litters when the sun rose. In the tiled hall leading to the royal chambers, I stood with my parents and shivered in the cold.

"You are shaking." My mother frowned.

"Just tired," I admitted. "We never had such late nights in Akhmim."

My mother smiled wistfully. "Yes, many things will be different now." Her eyes searched my face. "What happened then?"

"Amunhotep was with Nefertiti before the feasts. She went to him, and Nefertiti said he asked her to spend the night."

My mother cupped my chin in her palm, seeing my unhappiness.

"There's nothing to be afraid of, Mutnodjmet. Your sister will only be a courtyard away."

"I know. It's just that I've never spent a night without her before." My lip quivered, and I tried to steady it with my teeth.

"You can sleep in our chamber," my mother offered.

I shook my head. I was thirteen years old. Not a child anymore. "No, I shall have to get used to it."

"So Kiya will be displaced," my mother remarked. "Panahesi will be angry."

"Then he may be angry for many nights to come," I said as Nefertiti and my father joined us.

"Take Nefertiti to your rooms," my father instructed. "Merit is waiting." He squeezed my sister's shoulder to give her courage. "You understand what to do?"

Nefertiti reddened. "Of course."

My mother embraced her warmly, whispering words of wisdom in her ear that I couldn't hear. Then we left our parents and walked through the painted corridors of the palace. The servants were dancing at the feast and our footfalls echoed in the empty halls of Malkata. Tonight, our childhood would pass.

"So you are going to Amunhotep's bed," I said.

"And I plan to stay until morning," she confided, striding ahead.

"But no one spends the entire night with a king," I exclaimed and quickened my pace. "He sleeps by himself."

"And tonight I shall change that."

In our room, the oil lamps had been lit. The paintings of papyrus fields swayed in the flickering light. Merit was there, as my father had promised, and she and Nefertiti whispered together. Ipu was in our chamber as well. "We will both bathe your sister and get her ready," she said to me. "I will not be able to assist you tonight."

I swallowed. "Of course."

Merit and Ipu led Nefertiti to the baths. When they returned, they changed her into a simple sheath. It took both of their hands to powder her legs and perfume her hair, making sure every scent Amunhotep encountered was sweet.

"Should I wear a wig?" It was me that Nefertiti was asking when it should have been Merit, who would know about these things.

"Go without it," I offered. "Let him see you as yourself tonight."

Next to me, Ipu nodded, and together we watched as Merit applied cream to Nefertiti's face and sprinkled lavender water over her hair. Then my sister stood and our servants stepped back. All three turned to see my reaction.

"Beautiful." I smiled.

My sister hugged me, and I inhaled deeply so I would be the first to smell her like this, not Amunhotep. We stood together in the dim light of the room. "I will miss you tonight," I said, swallowing my fear. "I hope you brushed with mint and myrrh," I added, offering her the only advice that I could.

Nefertiti rolled her eyes. "Of course."

I pulled back to look at her. "But aren't you afraid?"

She shrugged. "Not really."

"And Ranofer?" I asked quietly.

"We never did anything."

I gave her a long look.

"Only touching. I never—"

I nodded quickly.

"Not that it would matter. It only matters that I remain faithful to him now." She tossed her head and her dark hair fell across her shoulders. She caught her reflection in the polished bronze. "I'm ready for this. I'm ready to be the queen my mother swore I would be. She married our father hoping someday it would lead to the throne, and this is it."

"How do you know that?" I had never thought of my father's first marriage in that way. I had never thought that a princess of Mitanni might marry a queen's brother for a chance to place her child on the throne.

Nefertiti met my eyes in the mirror. "Father told me."

"That she didn't love him?"

"Certainly, she did. But first and foremost was the future of her child." She turned to Merit and her look was firm. "I'm ready."

Chapter Five

twenty-second of Pharmuthi

NEFERTITI CAME TO my bed the next morning. She shook me from a deep, exhausted sleep and I sat up quickly, afraid that something had gone wrong. "What? What happened?"

"I made love to the king."

I rubbed the sleep out of my eyes. I looked at her side of the bed. It was unmade. "And you spent the night!" I threw off my covers. "So what was it like?"

She sat down and shrugged one of her brown shoulders at me. "Painful. But then you get used to it."

I gasped. "How many times could you have done it?" I cried.

She smiled wickedly. "Several." Then she looked around our chamber. "We should move rooms at once. The Queen of Egypt doesn't sleep in a bed with her sister. I will sleep with Amunhotep from now on."

I scrambled from my bed. "But we've only been in Thebes for four days. And tomorrow Tiye will announce in chambers when we're leaving; it could be within the month."

Nefertiti ignored my plea. "Have your servants pack up your herbs. They'll grow just as well in sunlight a few chambers away."

Nefertiti told no one about the move, and I wasn't going to be the one to let our father know. He'd said to come to him with any sign of trouble, and so far as I could see there was no trouble in moving a courtyard away. Besides, the entire palace would know soon enough.

"Kiya will be beside herself." Nefertiti grinned, practically dancing through our new rooms and pointing to tapestries she wanted moved.

"Be careful with Kiya," I replied. "Her father can make trouble for us. And if Kiya has a son, then Panahesi will be the grandfather to the heir of Egypt."

"By the end of Shemu I'm sure I'll be pregnant." We both looked at her belly. She was small and slender. But by Pachons she could be carrying Egypt's heir. "And my sons will always be first in line for the throne. If I can get five sons from Amunhotep, our family will have five chances." And only if all of her sons were to die would any of Kiya's sons stand in line for the crown.

I watched her pick up a brush and start on her hair, the deep, silky blackness of it framing her face. Then the door opened to the antechamber and Amunhotep strolled in.

"Queen of Egypt and queen of my—" He stopped short when he saw me in his room. His mood darkened quickly. "And what are you two sisters gossiping about?"

"You, of course." Nefertiti opened her arms, making light of his suspicions, and wrapped him in her embrace. "So tell me," she said intimately, "what is the news?"

His face lightened. "Tomorrow my mother will announce when we are to move to Memphis, where we will build such temples as the world has never seen."

"We should begin at once," my sister agreed. "Then in time you will be known as Amunhotep the Builder."

"Amunhotep the Builder." A dreamy look passed over Amunhotep's eyes. "They'll forget about Tuthmosis when they see what I do. When we leave for Memphis," Amunhotep said decisively, "my father's architect must come with us." He stepped away from my sister's embrace. "I will write to Maya to make sure he understands the choice that lies before him. To follow the future," he said as he walked swiftly to his chamber, "or be buried in the past."

The door swung shut behind him, and I looked at Nefertiti. She wouldn't meet my gaze. When there was a knock at the outer door, she rose quickly to get it.

"Vizier Panahesi!" she said delightedly. "Won't you come in?"

Panahesi stepped back, shocked to see her in the king's private antechamber. He stepped in gingerly, as if he thought he might wake from a dream. My sister's voice was not sweet when she asked him, "What do you want?"

"I have come to see Pharaoh."

"Pharaoh is busy."

"Don't play with me, child. I will see him. I am the Vizier of Egypt and you are just one of many wives. You would do well to remember that. He may be passionate for you now, but by the end of Shemu his ardor will cool."

I held my breath to see what Nefertiti would do. Then she spun on her heel and went to find Amunhotep, leaving me alone. The vizier nodded at the second room. "Is that your chamber now?"

"Yes."

"Interesting."

Amunhotep reappeared with my sister, and at once Panahesi swept him a bow. "You did well yesterday, Your Majesty." He moved quickly to the king's side and added, "All that's left is to sail to Memphis and ascend your throne."

"And wait for the Elder to die," Amunhotep said with brutal frankness. "He doesn't see the greed of the Amun priests."

Panahesi glanced at Nefertiti, then at me. "Do you think, perhaps, we should talk about this elsewhere?"

Nefertiti was quick. "My husband trusts me, Vizier. Whatever you have to say can be said in the presence of everyone here." She smiled sweetly at Amunhotep, but her eyes were full of warning. *I can stop loving you and the people's adoration will disappear.* She touched his shoulder briefly. "Isn't that true?"

He nodded. "Of course. I trust my wife as I trust Aten."

Panahesi grew furious. "Then perhaps Your Majesty might not want privileged information to be heard by younger, more impressionable women."

"My sister is neither young nor impressionable," Nefertiti said sweetly. "Perhaps you are thinking of your own daughter at her age?"

Amunhotep laughed. "Go on, Vizier. What is it you have to say?"

But by now Panahesi had lost his way. "I simply came to congratulate Your Majesty." He turned to leave, and then, as if on second thought, he added, "Though many may have wished for your brother yesterday, I know you shall rule with greater wisdom and strength."

"*Who* wished for my brother? Who wished for Tuthmosis to be on the throne?"

Panahesi had found a way past Nefertiti. "There are factions, my lord, who wish for Tuthmosis. Surely you see them. Of course, once we go to Memphis, it will be telling who chooses to come with us and who chooses to stay behind."

"Will the architect Maya come with us?" he demanded.

"It's possible." Panahesi spread his hands. "If we get to him."

"And the army?"

"It will be divided in two."

Amunhotep was silent, then he said with venom, "You will make sure this court knows that when I go to Memphis, either they are with me or against me. And they had best remember which Pharaoh will live longer!"

Panahesi bowed out of the chamber. "I will do as I am told, Your Majesty."

Nefertiti shut the door behind him and Amunhotep dropped into a gold and leather chair. "Why doesn't your father come to congratulate me on my coronation?"

"My father doesn't offer congratulations where none are needed. Everyone knows you were chosen by the gods to rule as Pharaoh."

Amunhotep glanced up from under his thick lashes. He was a boy. A sulking, insecure child. "Then why did Panahesi say—"

"He is lying!" Nefertiti exclaimed. "Who would be so foolish as to wish for your brother's rule when they could serve a Pharaoh like you?"

But a light flickered in Amunhotep's eyes and he turned. "If my brother had not died, you would be his wife."

"I would never have been Tuthmosis's wife," Nefertiti said quickly.

It was dangerous, the way the king's thoughts were tending. Amunhotep turned on me. "They say the sister of Nefertiti never lies. Did your father ever mention Tuthmosis in his house?"

Nefertiti turned white and I nodded slowly.

"And did he plan to marry your sister to him?"

I was wise enough to know that if I didn't lie now, Kiya would become the favorite in Memphis and my sister just another of the king's many wives. Amunhotep leaned forward and his face looked dark. It would take only one lie to change eternity, to ensure that our names lived forever on the glorious monuments of Thebes. I glanced at Nefertiti, who was waiting to see what I would do. Then I stared into Amunhotep's eyes and replied the way my father would have wanted me to, the way Nefertiti was hoping I would. "Vizier Ay always believed it would be you who would take the throne of Egypt. It was you whom my sister was intended for, even when you were a child."

Amunhotep stared at me. "Destiny," he whispered, sitting back in his chair. "It was destiny! Your father *knew* I would take the throne of Egypt!"

"Yes," she whispered, looking at me.

I swallowed the lump in my throat. I had lied for her. I had gone against my conscience to preserve our family.

The seventeen-year-old Pharaoh of Egypt stood up. "Ay will serve as Chief Vizier above all the land!" he proclaimed. "He shall be Overseer of Foreign Affairs in Memphis, and I will raise him above all other viziers!" Amunhotep looked at me again. "You may go," he said carelessly. "The queen and I have plans to make."

Nefertiti reached out her hand to stop me, but I shook my head sternly, slipping past her out the door. Tears welled in my eyes and I wiped them away with the back of my hand. I had lied to a king of Egypt, the highest representative of Amun in the land. *Ma'at will be ashamed,* I whispered aloud, but there was no one in the columned halls to hear me.

I thought of going to see my mother, but she would say that what I had done had been the right thing to do. I found my way into the gardens and sat down on the farthest stone bench. I would be punished by the gods for what I'd done. Ma'at would want vengeance.

"It's not often a queen's sister comes to the gardens alone."

It was General Nakhtmin.

I blinked away my tears. "If Pharaoh sees you with me, he will not be pleased," I said sternly, gathering myself.

"No matter. Soon the new Pharaoh will be in Memphis."

I looked up sharply. "You will not be coming?"

"Only those who choose to leave will be moving. Much of the army will remain in Thebes." The general took a seat next to me without asking my permission. "So why are you here, among the willows and all alone?"

My eyes welled up again. I had shamed the gods.

"What? Has a boy broken your heart?" he demanded. "Shall I banish him for you?"

I laughed, despite myself. "No boy is interested in me," I said.

We were quiet for a moment.

"So why all this weeping?"

"I told a lie," I whispered.

The general studied me and a smile began at the edges of his lips. "That's it?"

"It may be a small thing for you, but it is a great deal to me. I have *never* lied."

"*Never*? Not even about a broken dish, or somebody's lost necklace that you found?"

"No. Not since I became old enough to understand the laws of Ma'at."

The general said nothing, and I realized I must look like such a child to him, a man who'd seen war and bloodshed. "It doesn't matter," I mumbled.

"It does matter," he said seriously. "You value truth. Only now you've lied."

I said nothing.

"It's fine, your secret's safe with me."

I stood up, furious. "I should never have told you!"

"You think you will lose my respect over a lie?" He laughed kindly. "The court of Egypt is built on them. You will see that in Memphis."

"Then I will close my eyes," I replied childishly.

"At your own peril. Best to keep them open, my lady. Your father depends on it."

"How do you know what my father depends on?"

"Well, if you don't keep a sensible head, who will? Your beautiful sister? Pharaoh Amunhotep the Younger? They'll be too busy building tombs and temples," he replied. "Maybe even," he added treasonously, "dismantling the priesthood in order to control the gold it brings in." I must have looked scandalized, because the general asked, "Do you think your family is the only one that sees this? The new Pharaoh has everyone running. If the priests of Amun fall, so will many other wealthy men," he predicted.

"My sister has nothing to do with that," I said firmly and began walking back to the palace. I didn't like the way he implicated my family in Amunhotep's plans. But he followed after me, matching my stride.

"Have I offended you, my lady?"

"Yes, you have."

"I'm sorry. I shall be more careful in the future. After all, you will be one of the most dangerous women at court."

I stopped walking.

"Privy to the secrets that viziers and priests are paying spies very handsomely to procure."

"I don't know what you're talking about."

"Information, Lady Mutnodjmet," he said, and he kept walking toward the stables.

"And what do you think information can do?" I called after him.

"In the wrong hands," he replied over his shoulder, "it can do anything."

⊡ ⊡ ⊡

That night I prepared for bed in the room next to the king's private chamber, knowing my sister was next door but that I was unable to call to her. I looked over at my windowsill at the potted herbs that had endured the journey from Akhmim, and then a shuffling from one room to the next. Tomorrow, the queen would announce the date for our move to Memphis, and the plants would have to survive yet another uprooting.

When Ipu appeared to undress me, she saw my long face and clicked her tongue. "What is it, my lady?"

I shrugged, as if the matter was of little consequence.

"You miss your home," she guessed, and I nodded.

She slipped the sheath over my head and I put on a fresh one. I sat obediently on the bed so that she could braid my hair. "Don't you ever miss your home?" I asked quietly.

"Only when I think of my brothers." She smiled. "I was raised with seven brothers. It's why I get along so well with men."

I laughed. "You get along with everyone. I saw you at the feasts. There's not a person in Thebes you haven't met."

She lifted her shoulder casually, but didn't deny it. "This is how we are in the city of Fayyum. Always friendly."

"So you were born near Lake Moeris?"

She nodded. "A little farming village between the lake and River Nile." She described vast stretches of loamy soil rolling away into earthy green hills. And the vineyards dotting the blue-green Nile. "There is no place in Egypt better for gardening, for tending to crops or harvesting papyrus."

"And what did your family do?" I asked.

"My father was Pharaoh's personal vintner."

"And you left his gardens to work in the palace?"

"Only when he died. I was twelve, the youngest of five daughters and seven sons. My mother didn't need me, and I'd inherited her skill with paints." I studied her heavily made-up eyes in the mirror above our heads, the sweeps of malachite that never smudged in the sun. "The Elder found me a place as one of the queen's women. Eventually, I grew to become the queen's favorite."

And the queen had let her go to be with me. I thought of my aunt and imagined all the selfless acts that she performed that went unnoticed. And squandering her kindness away was her son, selfish and self-absorbed.

"Palace life is better than life on the vineyards," she continued. "To be in a city where women can buy whatever they need . . ." She exhaled thankfully. "Kohl, perfume, *real* wigs, exotic food. The boats come along the Nile and stop at Thebes. But no boats ever stopped in the Fayyum."

I sighed as she brought me my robe and linen socks. No boats. No people. No politics. Just gardens. I put on my slippers and sat near the brazier. Ipu remained standing, and I pointed to a stool. "Tell me, Ipu." I dropped my voice low, even though Nefertiti could never have heard me. "What is the gossip around the palace?"

Ipu gleamed. She was in her element now. "About you, my lady?"

I flushed. "About my sister and the king."

She raised her eyebrows and said with caution, "Ah . . . I hear the new Pharaoh is willful."

I sat forward. "And?"

She glanced briefly at the door that led to the antechamber and, outside of it, the king's private rooms. "And the new queen is beautiful. The other servants call her Neferet." *The Beautiful Woman.*

"And Memphis?" I asked. "Have the servants been told when to prepare for a journey?"

"Oh." Her dimples flashed. "That's what you want." She leaned close to me, her dark hair tumbling over her shoulders. She was a beautiful woman, full of curves and faience beads with glittery malachite eyelids. "Queen Tiye ordered three new litters today, and the Master of the Horse said that six new horses have already been purchased."

I sat back. "When will they be ready?"

"In six days."

⧉ ⧉ ⧉

The next day, I was summoned to the Audience Chamber early, before it grew crowded with the courtiers who would come to hear of Amunhotep's departure for Memphis. As I entered the double doors, my eyes were drawn first to the forest of closed papyrus-bud columns that culminated at a raised and painted dais. As I approached the golden thrones, the closed buds atop the columns slowly opened until the last two were carved into fully painted blooms—symbolic, I supposed, of Pharaoh opening his arms to embrace all of Egypt.

Beneath the dais, where my aunt and father were sitting, were images of bound captives, Hittites and Nubians, so that whenever Pharaoh ascended to his throne he would trod his enemies underfoot. The Audience Chamber was empty except for the three of us, and my father sat with his sister on an ebony bench with papyrus scrolls spread out before them.

"Your Majesty." I bowed. "Father."

Queen Tiye didn't wait for me to sit. "Your sister has moved into my son's private chambers." Her face was inscrutable, and I was careful with my reply.

"Yes. She has entranced the new king, Your Majesty."

"She has entranced the entire palace," Queen Tiye corrected. "She's all the servants will talk about."

I thought of Ipu calling my sister *Neferet,* and of what General Nakhtmin had said. "She is bold, Your Highness, but she is very loyal."

Queen Tiye studied me. "Loyal, but to who?"

My father cleared his throat. "We want to know what was said at breakfast this morning."

I realized what was happening and saw that I was being used as a spy. I shifted uncomfortably and replied, "They never ate breakfast. The servants arranged trays of food in the anteroom, and after I ate, the food was sent away."

"What did they do, then?" the queen demanded.

I hesitated, and my father said sternly, "It is important for us to know these things, Mutnodjmet. Either we find out or someone else will."

Someone like Panahesi. "They made plans for building temples to Aten," I told them.

Ay asked quickly, "*Drawings?*"

I nodded.

He turned to his sister and said hurriedly, "Amunhotep can do nothing until the Elder dies. He has neither the gold nor the resources for temple building. It's just talk—"

"*Dangerous* talk!" she flared up. "Talk that will continue until he becomes Pharaoh of Upper Egypt."

"By then he will understand that it is not so easy to rule without the support of the priests. He won't even be able raise an army without their gold. No Pharaoh can rule on his own."

"My son thinks he can. He thinks he will defy the gods and raise Aten above all of them, even Osiris. Even Ra. *Your* daughter was supposed to change this—"

"She will—"

"She is too wild and ambitious!" the queen shouted. She walked out onto the balcony and wrapped her fingers around the railing. "Perhaps I chose the wrong daughter as Chief Wife," she said.

My father looked over his shoulder to where I sat, but I couldn't read his expression. "Send him to Memphis," my father encouraged. "There he will see that it is not so easy to interfere with Ma'at."

In the Audience Chamber that noon, the queen announced our departure to Memphis. We were to leave on the twenty-eighth of Pharmuthi. We had five days to prepare.

Chapter Six

twenty-fourth of Pharmuthi

THIS TIME, WHEN we went to watch Amunhotep ride in the Arena, he gathered us in the stables and asked Nefertiti which horse she liked best. Kiya would have batted her lashes and answered that she liked the horse with the most beautiful mane. But Nefertiti observed their width and breadth, the strength of their muscles beneath their coat and the fire in their eyes, then replied in a firm voice, "The dark one. The chestnut champing at the gates."

Amunhotep nodded. "Bring out the chestnut!"

Kiya turned to the three ladies who were always with her, tall women who towered over my sister, and one of them said loudly so my family would overhear, "Next thing he'll be letting her pick out his kilts." They all snickered, but Nefertiti walked purposefully to where Amunhotep was standing near Panahesi and my father, and watched him fasten his leather gauntlets. "Have you always ridden?" Nefertiti asked.

Panahesi snapped, "Since the Pharaoh was a boy in Memphis."

Nefertiti looked to where a group of men were waiting, the sons of other viziers who practiced with the king. Amunhotep saw the direction of her gaze and added firmly, "Those men don't lose to me every morning because they have to. I can outride any soldier in my father's army."

Nefertiti stepped closer. "And you say you have done this since you were a child?"

Amunhotep strapped on his helmet and replied, "I rode the chariot as soon as I learned to walk."

"And what if I wanted to learn?" she asked him.

Across the stables Kiya retorted sharply, "Women don't ride in the Arena."

"I rode in Akhmim," Nefertiti announced. I glanced at my father, whose face was reserved. He said nothing, and Nefertiti took a helmet from the nearby shelf and placed it brazenly on her head. "I want you to teach me."

Amunhotep paused to measure the seriousness of her statement.

She added brilliantly, "I want to feel the exhilaration of riding with Egypt's finest steeds. I want to learn from the greatest rider in Egypt."

Amunhotep laughed. "Bring out the Master of the Horse!" he cried, and Panahesi and Kiya flew into action.

"She'll be killed!" Panahesi cried. Of course, his real objection was that his daughter hadn't been smart enough or quick enough to suggest it for herself. Now the Arena would be full of Nefertiti. Not even our father had thought of this, but it was perfect, really. An exquisite move. If she could sink her claws in Amunhotep's chamber, his politics, and now his pastime, where wouldn't they be united?

"But Your Highness—" Panahesi said.

Amunhotep turned and his look was dark. "*Nothing* more, Vizier. My queen wants to ride, and I will teach her."

In the wooden tiers beneath a linen shade, we watched them ride, and Kiya hissed to me, "What does she think she's doing?"

I looked down at my sister, laughing and radiant, tossing her long hair back in the sun. Amunhotep laughed with her, and I replied, "She's entertaining the king. What else now that her tutor is gone?"

"That was well done," my father complimented.

Nefertiti sat smugly in her chair, waiting for Merit to finish beading her wig. A pair of red riding gloves had arrived in her chamber, a gift from Amunhotep. She said, "It was fun."

"This once," my father warned.

"Why? I enjoyed it. Why shouldn't I learn to ride?"

"Because it's dangerous!" I exclaimed. "Aren't you afraid?"

"What's to be afraid of?"

"The horses. Or toppling over the chariot. Look what happened to Crown Prince Tuthmosis."

My father and Nefertiti exchanged glances. Ipu and Merit both looked away.

"Tuthmosis died at war," Nefertiti said dismissively. "And this isn't war." Merit strung the last beads over Nefertiti's wig, and when my sister stood up the glass made hollow music.

My father stood with her. "I will be in the Per Medjat drafting letters to foreign nations. They must know where to find your husband and address their petitions." He glanced across the room, where nothing had changed since yesterday's news. "We are leaving in five days," he reminded us quietly, "and both of you should be overseeing your packing."

When our father left, Nefertiti held out her arm to me, unconcerned with foreign nations. "Come."

I scowled. "You heard Father. He said we should pack."

"Not now." She took my arm and pulled me along.

"Stop. Where are we going?" I protested.

"To your favorite place."

"Why the gardens?"

"Because there's someone there we're going to meet."

"Amunhotep?" I guessed.

"And someone else."

We walked through the halls and entered the palace gardens with their tree-lined avenues and sprawling lakes. Someone with a very good eye for design had placed a fountain of Horus in the lotus pond, surrounding it with cattails and indigo irises. Stone benches were shaded by the heavy boughs of sycamores, and a path bordered by jasmine led to the bathhouses. Beyond that was the harem, where the lesser ranked of the Elder's women lived. I watched the dragonflies dart in and out of the grass, the sunlight catching on their blue-gold wings where we walked.

"The first thing we shall do when we get to Memphis is erect the largest temple ever built in Egypt. Once the people see Aten's glory"—my sister strode ahead—"there will be no need for the priests of Amun."

"Father says there are balances. The power of Pharaoh is balanced by the power of priests. Even our tutors taught us that."

"Did they also teach us that the priests control the purse strings of Pharaohs? Is *that* balanced?" Nefertiti's eyes darkened beneath the shade of a sycamore. "Mutny, the Pharaohs of Egypt are puppets. And Amunhotep is going to change that. He will take the focus away from Amun and raise Aten in his place. The Pharaoh and queen will be heads of the temples. *We* will control the calendar, declare the feast days, and be in charge—"

"Of all the gold that once flowed freely into the temples of Amun." I thought of the general and closed my eyes against the truth of his words. When I opened them, my sister's gaze was resolute.

"Yes."

"Nefertiti, you frighten me. You weren't this way in Akhmim."

"I wasn't Queen of Egypt in Akhmim."

At the end of the path, I stopped walking to ask her, "Aren't you afraid you will offend the gods?"

Nefertiti bridled. "This is Amunhotep's dream," she said defensively. "The more I do for Amunhotep, the closer he will be to me and no one else." She stared across the lotus pond and her voice became a whisper. "He is going to Kiya's bed tomorrow night."

I saw the worry in her face and said hopefully, "Perhaps he won't—"

"Oh, he will. It's tradition. You said so yourself. But it will be *my* children who inherit this land."

"Father thinks you've become too ambitious," I warned her.

Nefertiti glanced at me sharply. "You had a family meeting without me?"

I didn't answer.

"What did you talk about?" she demanded.

"You, of course."

"And what did Father say?"

"Nothing much. It's our aunt who does most of the talking."

"She doesn't like me. She doubts her choice. I know she must. Seeing another beautiful woman rise in the palace—"

"And humble as well."

She gave me a look and we continued to walk. "Don't tell me she isn't resentful."

"*Regretful,* maybe. You were brought here to bring balance, not tip the scales!"

"And how does anyone expect me to do that?" she asked heatedly. "I can't tell him what he believes is wrong; he would run to Kiya and I would be finished."

At the farthest end of the gardens, we came upon a bower. I heard Amunhotep's voice, low and intense on the other side of the tangled vines. I made to back away, but Nefertiti glanced sideways at me, then took my arm and pushed past the trees and into the clearing. At once, Amunhotep straightened. He was standing with a general, and both of them turned.

"Nefertiti," Amunhotep said with delight. Then he saw me and his smile thinned. "The inseparable sisters."

The general bowed. He was young, like Nakhtmin, but there was a seriousness in him that Nakhtmin didn't possess; a hardness in his eyes. "Queen Nefertiti," he said, as if the words didn't give him much joy. "Lady Mutnodjmet."

"General Horemheb will be coming with us to Memphis," Amunhotep announced. "He wishes to push the Hittites back and to reclaim territory that Egypt has lost since my father retired from the army. I have promised him a campaign in the north as soon as we reach Lower Egypt. And I have told him that all the booty the soldiers can collect may be kept by him and my army, so long as he can reclaim our land."

"That is very generous," Nefertiti replied, watching Amunhotep carefully; I saw that the general was watching Amunhotep with the same guarded look.

"Other soldiers can remain with my father to waste their careers, but Horemheb will follow me to glory!"

I glanced at General Horemheb, who wasn't moved by speeches.

"And has Your Highness considered where the money will come from for these campaigns?" he asked frankly. "To regain lost territory will be expensive."

"Then I will tax the temples of Amun," Amunhotep replied.

Nefertiti exchanged a quick glance with me, but the general didn't blink. "The temples of Amun have never been taxed. What makes you think they will give up their gold now?"

"Because you will be there to enforce my will," Amunhotep countered, and then I understood what was happening. He was striking a deal.

General Horemheb clenched his jaw. "And how do I know that

once the army has collected the taxes from the temples that the gold will be used to fund a campaign in the north?"

"You don't. But either you will trust me or you will spend your days in the service of a Pharaoh who is too old to fight. Only remember"—Amunhotep's voice took on a warning tone—"in the end, I will be Pharaoh of Upper Egypt as well."

Horemheb looked at Nefertiti, then at me. "Then I must trust your word."

Amunhotep held out his hand to the general. "I will not forget your loyalty," he promised.

Horemheb took Pharaoh's hand, but the look in his eyes was one of distrust. "Then I ask to take my leave, Your Highness." He bowed, and I felt a chill go down my spine as I wondered what would happen if Amunhotep wasn't as good as his word. I would not want a man like Horemheb for an enemy.

Amunhotep watched him go and turned to Nefertiti. "I will never bow to the priests of Amun again."

"You'll be the greatest Pharaoh of Egypt," Nefertiti swore.

"With the most magnificent queen of Egypt," he added, "producing Pharaohs that will sit on the throne of Egypt to eternity." He put his hands across her small taut stomach. "Even now, a little queen may be growing inside."

"We should know soon. I'm sure by the time we reach Memphis I will be showing." But she looked at me when she said this, as if I could influence the gods because I was the one who prayed every night and made obeisance at the shrine of Amun every morning.

Chapter Seven

twenty-fifth of Pharmuthi

"WHAT IF I'M not with child and Kiya gives birth to a boy in six months?" Nefertiti was pacing the floor of the antechamber. The sun had set, but Amunhotep was not with Nefertiti. He had gone to visit Kiya. "And who knows how long he'll stay in her room tonight? What if he's there until morning?" she panicked.

"Don't be foolish," I tried to comfort her. "Pharaohs don't sleep in bed with their wives."

"He sleeps in mine!" she shrieked and stopped pacing. "But he is not getting into bed with me tonight. He thinks he can go from one wife to the next? I'm no different from any of his other chattel?" Her voice rose. "Is that what he thinks?" She sat down before her mirror. "Kiya is not more beautiful than I am." It was a question.

"Of course not."

"Is she more cunning?"

I couldn't say.

Nefertiti spun around, and there was the light of a new idea in her eyes. "You must go and see what they are doing," she decided.

"*What?* You want me to spy on your husband?" I shook my head vehemently. "If I'm caught spying, the guards would bring me to Pharaoh."

"I *have* to know what they do together, Mutnodjmet."

"Why? What does it matter?"

"Because I have to be better than she is!" She raised her chin. "We all have to be. It's not just for me, it's for our family. Our future." She came and held my shoulders. "Please, just find out what he says to her."

"It's too dangerous!" I protested.

"I can tell you how to reach their window."

"*What? Outside?* You want me to crawl in the dirt? What if I'm caught?"

"Guards aren't posted beneath Second Wives' windows," she sneered. "Please, just put on a cloak," she encouraged.

With a deep foreboding, I put on a heavy linen and sat at the mirror to tie back my hair. Nefertiti watched my progress from behind me. "It's a good thing you're dark," she remarked. "No one will notice you."

I glared at her, but she was no longer watching me. All of her thoughts now were on Kiya, and she stared down the hall as if she could see what her husband was doing already. When I was done, I went and stood at the door. My father would have wanted me to do this. It was for the good of the family. And spying wasn't against the laws of Ma'at. I wasn't stealing, just listening.

"I need to know everything that he tells her," she said. She wrapped a long cape over her sheath and shivered. "I'll wait here. And Mutny—"

I frowned.

"Be careful."

I felt my heart in my throat as I slipped into the courtyard. The air was warm and reed mats slapped softly against the palace windows, moving in the breeze. No one was out. The moon was a sliver in the sky, and unless someone were looking for me, there would be no reason to walk beyond the palace doors in the middle of the night. I passed through a succession of courtyards, counting them as I went. I kept close to the walls, near the shrubs and ivy. When I arrived in Kiya's courtyard, I stopped to listen, but there was no sound. I crept along until I reached the third window. I glanced across the courtyard and saw no one, then crouched to listen. Now there were voices; I pressed myself flat against the wall, trying to hear what Pharaoh was saying.

When you set in western lightland, earth is in darkness as if in death. Every lion comes from its den. All the serpents bite. Darkness hovers, earth is silent, as their maker rests in lightland.

He was reciting poetry.

Earth brightens when you dawn in lightland. When you shine as Aten of daytime, as you cast your rays, the Two Lands are in festivity. Awake they stand on their feet. You have roused them!

"Let me read the rest." It was Kiya's voice. I heard the rustle of papyrus, and then she began to read.

Roads come open when you rise. The fish in the river dart before you. Your rays are in the midst of the sea. You are the One who makes seed grow, who creates life, who feeds the son in his mother's womb, who soothes him to still his tears. Oh, Nurse in the womb, oh, Giver of breath. You nourish all that you make.

So this was the spell that Kiya, with her long willowy legs, cast on him . . . the magic of quiet sanctuary. Away from Nefertiti's constant plans and politics, Amunhotep and Kiya read poetry together.

From beneath the window, I could smell burning incense. I waited to see what else they would talk about, and he began telling her stories of what life would be like in Memphis, where he'd grown up as a boy.

"My rooms will be in the center of the palace," he said, "and to my right I will place you and give you the best of everything."

I heard her giggle like a child. Nefertiti never giggled; she laughed, deep and breathy like a woman.

"Come!" He must have grabbed her, because I heard them fall heavily on the bed, and I covered my mouth in horror. How could he take a woman in pregnancy? He would hurt the child!

"Wait," she whispered, and her voice grew stern. "What about my father?"

"Vizier Panahesi? Of course he will come with us to Memphis," he pronounced, as if there was never any other option. "And I will give him the highest position at court."

"Such as?"

"Such as whatever he wants," he promised. "You never have to worry. Your father is loyal to me and my cause. There is no vizier in Egypt I trust above Panahesi."

I looked across the courtyard and there, in the silvery light, was the vizier listening to everything that I'd just heard. He was standing motionless, and I believe at that moment my heart stopped in my chest. When he saw that I'd recognized him, he smiled.

Then I was running, all the way back to Nefertiti's chamber. I forgot about Amunhotep's poetry and Kiya's questions. Nefertiti rushed to meet me at the door. "What happened?" she exclaimed, seeing my face, but I couldn't answer. "Mutny, what happened? Were you caught?"

My breath came in quick gasps. My thoughts raced, and I wondered if I should tell her about Panahesi. We had both been conspirators caught in the night. I hadn't said anything and neither had he.

She shook my shoulders. "Were you caught?"

"No." I breathed. "They were reading poetry."

"Then why were you running? What happened?"

"He said he trusted Panahesi above any other vizier in Egypt. He told Kiya he'd give her father the highest position at court!"

Immediately, Nefertiti was at the door, commanding one of the guards to fetch Vizier Ay. Our father came at once, and the three of us sat in a circle around the king's private brazier. If he returned, he would catch us conspiring about him.

My sister straightened. "I'm going to tell Amunhotep that Panahesi can't be trusted," she resolved.

"And risk his anger?" My father shook his head. "No. Panahesi can be avoided," he replied. "The bigger threat is growing in Kiya's belly."

"Then perhaps we should kill it," my sister said.

"*Nefertiti!*" She and my father both looked at me.

"The right mix of herbs in her wine . . . ," my father wondered. I didn't want to hear this. I didn't want to be part of it. "But she would only get pregnant again," he concluded.

"And the vizier would be suspicious," Nefertiti replied. "He would tell Amunhotep and that would be the end of us. I will simply have to outwit her."

"Keep doing whatever you're doing," my father agreed. "He's infatuated with you."

She raised an eyebrow. "You mean keep praising Aten?"

My father looked stern.

"It's the only way to keep him," Nefertiti said quickly.

"And it's what Kiya does," I pointed out.

"Kiya does *nothing*," Nefertiti replied hotly.

"She listens to his poetry. And he doesn't read it to you!"

"When we go to Memphis, he must be careful with the priests of Amun," my father interrupted. "He cannot interfere with them. Nefertiti, you must make sure of this."

I waited for my sister to speak of the deal Amunhotep had struck with Horemheb in the gardens, but she said nothing.

"If he grabs for too much power, it could topple us all. The Elder has other sons that could replace him if he should suddenly die."

My breath caught in my throat. "The priests of Amun would murder a king?"

My sister and father stared at me again, and then ignored my outburst.

Nefertiti asked, "But what if he *could* take power from the priests?"

"Don't think it."

"Why not?" she demanded.

"Because then Pharaoh would have total control of Memphis, and your husband is not wise enough to wield that kind of power."

"Then you could have it. You could be the power behind the throne," she tempted him. "You would be untouchable."

Now this was something new. A king's vizier could wield more influence if he only had to answer to Pharaoh, not to the priests and noblemen. I saw my father thinking, and my sister continued. "It's what he wants. He will be busy building his temples to Aten. And who would rule better, you or the High Priest of Thebes?"

I could see that my father was thinking she was right. If there was going to be a shift in the balance, why not come out on the better end? He had a better knowledge of foreign and domestic entanglements than a priest walled up in a temple to Amun. "Tiye will not be pleased," my father warned. "It's a gamble," he said. "It could all turn out wrong."

"How else am I to remain the favorite?" Nefertiti rose dramatically. "Tell him he will fail? He will go through with this whether I support him or not."

"Can't you take his mind away from Aten?"

"It's all he can think about."

My father stood and went to the door. "We will play this slowly," he decided. "There are men in this court neither you nor your husband would like to make enemies of."

We listened as his footsteps slapped across the tiles back to his own chamber.

Nefertiti collapsed into a chair. "So while Amunhotep is reciting poetry to that *whore,* the Queen of Egypt is spending the night with her sister."

"Don't be angry or he will resent you," I said.

She shot me a look, but didn't mock my suggestion.

"I will sleep with you tonight," she decided, and I didn't complain. I wouldn't have wanted my husband crawling into bed next to me after a night with another woman, either.

The next morning, I awoke at sunrise, then dressed myself quickly to pay obeisance at the shrine of Amun. I moved as silently as possible, but even so Nefertiti rolled over to grumble at me.

"You're not going to the shrine?" she asked with disbelief. "You don't have to pay obeisance *every* day," she said.

"I enjoy speaking with Amun," I replied defensively, and she made a disbelieving noise in her throat. "When is the last time you went?" I demanded, and she closed her eyes, pretending to be asleep. "Do you even know where Amun's shrine is?" I challenged.

"Of course. In the garden."

"Well, it wouldn't hurt you to come. You're Queen of Egypt."

"And you visit every day. You make my offerings for me. I'm too tired."

"To thank Amun?"

"He knows that I'm thankful. Now leave me alone."

So I went into the gardens by myself, as I had every morning since our arrival in Thebes, and picked a crop of flowers to place at Amun's feet. I took only the choicest flowers: irises as purple as deep summer's night, and hibiscus with petals like bloodred stars. When I was finished at the shrine, it was still quite early, and only servants were out in the gardens, watering the tamarinds with their heavy earthen bowls. Nefertiti was certain to still be asleep, so I walked to my parents' courtyard. My mother would be awake, placing offerings at Hathor's feet.

As I moved through the palace, I enjoyed the silence. Cats crept through the halls, sleek black with bronze eyes, but they took no notice of me. They were hunting for the remains of last night's dinner, a half-eaten honeyed fig dropped by a servant or a delicious morsel of roasted gazelle. I reached my mother's courtyard and found her sitting in the garden, reading a scroll with a familiar wax seal.

"News from Akhmim!" she announced brightly when she saw me. The morning sun gilded the new lapis collar that she was wearing.

I walked eagerly to her bench and took a seat. "And what does the overseer say?" I asked.

"Your garden is doing well."

I thought of my jujube with its ginger-colored fruit and the beautiful hibiscus I had planted last spring. I would not be there to see any of it ripen. "And what else?"

"The grapes are growing fast. The overseer says that in Shemu this vintage could produce sixty barrels."

"Sixty! Will they send them on to Memphis?"

"Certainly. And I asked for my linen shifts to be sent as well. I forgot them in the rush to pack."

We smiled at each other in the pale light of the courtyard, both thinking about Akhmim. Only her smile was wider and more innocent, because my father kept from her the things he couldn't keep from me, and she didn't see that we'd traded security for worry.

"So tell me about Nefertiti," she said. "Is she happy?" She rolled up the scroll, tucking it into her sleeve.

"As happy as she can be. He did go to Kiya last night." I settled against the cool stone bench and sighed. "So, we are leaving for Memphis."

My mother nodded. "Amunhotep will only grow restless here, waiting for the Elder to die. Perhaps not even waiting," she added ominously.

I glanced at her sharply. "You don't think he would hasten the Elder's death?"

My mother looked across the courtyard, but we were alone. "There is talk he sent Tuthmosis to an early burial. But that is just talk," she added quickly. "Servants' gossip."

"Except that servants are usually right," I whispered.

She lost some of her coloring. "Yes."

That night we took our meal in the Great Hall, but much of the court was absent, attending a funeral for the emissary to Rhodes. Both Queen Tiye and my father had gone, while the Elder remained at the palace with his wine and women. That night the Elder was in a particularly vulgar mood, singing and belching with abandon. I saw him grab one of the servant's breasts while she reached to replenish his wine, and when Nefertiti sat down to her husband's left he suggested she might want to sit near him instead. She declined without a word, and I flushed on her behalf, so Pharaoh turned to me. "Then perhaps I might have the company tonight of the green-eyed sister."

"Enough!" Amunhotep banged his fist on the table. The courtiers turned to us to see what was happening. "The Sister of the King's Chief Wife is perfectly fine where she is."

The Elder lowered his wine threateningly and stood, sending his chair clattering to the floor. "No weak-stomached son of mine will ever command me!" he shouted, reaching for his sword, but as he stepped forward his feet gave out beneath him. He crashed to the tiles, hazy with wine, and a dozen servants rushed to his aid. "No son of mine will teach me manners!" he raged.

Amunhotep jumped to his feet, commanding the servants, "Take him out of here! He is sick with wine." The servants looked between the Elder and his son. "Take him *now!*" Amunhotep shouted.

The servants rushed to do as they were bid. They carried Pharaoh toward the door. But the Elder broke free and rushed the dais violently.

Amunhotep reached for his short sword and my heart raced in my chest. "Nefertiti!" I cried.

Guards rushed to restrain the king, and the Elder shouted, "No prince who writes poems instead of fighting on the battlefield will control my kingdom! Do you hear? Tuthmosis was the *chosen* Prince of Egypt!" The guards hustled him toward the doors and he shouted violently, "The *chosen* prince!" The doors swung shut and suddenly there was silence. The diners in the Great Hall looked to Amunhotep, who sheathed his sword and flung his cup against the tiles. When it shattered into pieces, he held out his hand for Nefertiti. "Come."

Dinner in the Great Hall was over.

Inside the antechamber to our rooms, Amunhotep's mood was dark. "He's like a pig, stuffing himself with food and women. I will *never* be like him!" he shouted. "He was more interested in the serving girl than he was in me. If Tuthmosis was alive, he would have begged him to tell his stories. What did you shoot today?" he mimicked. "A boar? No! You wrestled a crocodile?" Amunhotep's pacing grew more fervent. Between the two of them, they would wear the polish off these tiles. "Why is Tuthmosis the *chosen* one?" he thundered. "Because I don't go off and shoot things like he did?"

"No one cares whether or not you hunt," Nefertiti said. She caressed his cheek, moving her hand through his tumble of curls. "Leave it," she suggested. "Tomorrow we begin preparing for our departure, and you will be a true Pharaoh and beholden to no one."

Chapter Eight

twenty-seventh of Pharmuthi

THE FOLLOWING DAY brought frenzied preparations to the palace. My parents were arranging litters and donkeys, and Nefertiti hollered into my chamber only when she wanted something from me. Should she bring her wigs or get new ones made? What should she wear on her progression to Memphis, and would Ipu and Merit be coming with us? No one was standing still in the palace. Even the army was in disarray, with the Elder choosing which men would stay with him and which ones would go. The generals were to decide for themselves.

I went out to the palace gardens, where there wasn't any commotion, and walked down the avenue of sycamore trees, their bright foliage shading the cobbled road. I wandered off the path, stopping to admire the flowering myrtles that clustered near the olive groves, their thick white blossoms used to treat coughs, bad breath, and colds. All around the palace grew plants with properties to cure or hurt. I wondered if the Royal Gardener knew that jasmine was good for exhaustion, and whether he'd planted the vines near the yellow and white chamomile flowers by accident, or if he'd known that chamomile was also used by the court physicians to ease tension.

I could sit in the gardens all day and no one would notice until Nefertiti wanted something. I picked up a pebble and tossed it into the water, and as the splash resounded I heard a high-pitched mewl. First one, then another kitten darted out of the brush, startled by the noise the pebble had made. One of the palace felines had just produced a litter and the kittens bounded after their sleek black mother, nipping at each other's tails and tumbling in the grass. I called one of them over to me, a green-eyed bundle who looked like her sire, and she curled up in my lap, mewling for food.

"I'll bet you like it here in these gardens," I said wistfully, chucking the kitten beneath the chin. "No one to bother you or ask you what kilt they should wear." The kitten ignored me and climbed up my shirt, nestling its tiny head in my neck. I laughed and pried it away. "Come here." It held out its tiny arms and claws, searching for something stable. "There." I tucked the kitten into the crook of my arm and she sat there, watching the dragonflies, fascinated by them.

"Mutny?" Nefertiti called from across the garden. As always, her voice was filled with urgency. "Mutny, where are you?" She appeared through the trees, walking the perimeter of the lotus pond to get to me. Her eyes brimmed with tears, but she wasn't crying. She never cried.

"What happened?" I sprung up, abandoning the kitten. "What's wrong?"

She hooked my arm in hers and steered me to a stone bench. "I bled," she confided.

I observed her quizzically. "But you've only been his wife for—"

Her nails dug into my arm. "Kiya is nearly four months pregnant!" she cried. "Four! You must know something you can give me, Mutny. You studied herbs with Ranofer."

I shook my head. "Nefertiti—"

"*Please.* Think of what he told you. You always listened to what he had to say."

While it was Nefertiti that Ranofer had been in love with, I was the one who had listened patiently as he rattled off the names of medicinal herbs. I would have smiled, but there was fear in her eyes, and I realized how serious it would be if Kiya had a son and Nefertiti was not even pregnant with a child. I tried to think. "There is mandrake," I said.

"Good." She sat straighter, the color coming back to her cheeks. "What else?"

"Honey and oil."

She nodded quickly. "I could get those things. Mandrake, of course, is more difficult."

"Try the honey," I prompted, and I knew it was useless to point out that it had taken Kiya nearly a year to conceive.

⊡ ⊡ ⊡

On the twenty-eighth of Pharmuthi, every courtyard in the palace was cluttered with litters. Heavily laden donkeys brayed loudly while bustling slaves bumped into each other and muttered sharp curses. Because this was nearly Shemu and the waters were low, our journey to Memphis would take many days. I asked Ipu to scour the markets for treatises on herbs that I could read while we sailed.

"On the ship? You want to read on the ship?" She stood in the doorway of my room and lowered the empty basket in her hands. By afternoon, it would be filled with my requests. This would be the last we'd see of Thebes, and who knew what kind of markets existed in Memphis? Everyone was in a panic, rushing into the city to find lotus oil, kohl, and coconut balm. "But how could you bear to read on the water? Won't you get sick?"

"I'll take ginger." I stood up from my bed and pressed several deben of copper into her hand. We walked outside together, so that I could join my sister. "Leather-bound tomes or good scrolls on anything to do with herbs."

The Elder had come into our courtyard to oversee the packing of Amunhotep's belongings, and he watched the loading of the articles with suspicion. Twice, when he saw something he wanted, he demanded that servants unload it.

"The gold vessel with turquoise was a tribute from the Nubians. It will remain in Malkata."

So the servants struggled with the standing vessel and returned it to its place in the rooms that Amunhotep had occupied. When the Elder saw a female slave he was particularly fond of, a nubile girl with long hair and small breasts, he demanded that she be brought back to the palace as well. The queen looked on with contempt.

"I shall never tolerate a lecherous husband," Nefertiti seethed. We stood together beneath an awning, watching the spectacle.

"She allows it because it keeps him occupied," I told her, realizing the truth of my words as I said them. "If he is in the bedchamber, then he cannot be in the Audience Chamber as well."

My mother joined us, and together we found seats and watched the chaotic proceedings. Fan bearers cooled us in the stifling heat, which Nefertiti didn't seem to mind. She left our shaded spot to supervise the loading of all the things that would soon be hers in Memphis, barking orders while the servants stared. They hadn't become used to her rare beauty, her almond-shaped eyes and long, sweeping lashes. And they mistook her beauty for complacence, not recognizing yet that she had limitless energy and a need for movement.

Queen Nefertiti, I thought, *ruler of Lower Egypt and someday Upper Egypt as well. Queen Mutnodjmet,* I imagined, then shivered. I would never want that. A low voice shook me out of my reverie, and I realized that Amunhotep was standing near our awning. He was wearing a long kilt with a golden belt and silver bangles. The kohl around his eyes was fresh. General Horemheb was standing across from him at arm's length, but a gulf separated the two, and with little surprise I realized, *The general doesn't respect this new king.*

"Seventy men are to follow on my heels with fifty in front. I won't risk assassination. If any peasant slips onto the boats undetected, he is to pay the penalty of immediate death." Runaway slaves would sometimes join a king's caravan so they could escape to the palace, where they could serve in luxury.

The general said nothing.

"And we shall travel from morning until dusk. Until it's too dark to see the currents," he commanded. "We will proceed straight to Memphis without stopping at any ports."

The first flicker of emotion crossed Horemheb's face. "Your Majesty," Horemheb interrupted firmly, "the men will need rest."

"Then they may take turns at the oars."

"In the heat of the day, the men could die. The cost would be great—"

"Then whatever the cost, it shall be done!" Amunhotep shouted. The bustle in the courtyard fell silent. Amunhotep was aware of an audience and the blood rushed to his face. He stepped toward Horemheb, who didn't flinch. "Are you questioning Pharaoh?" he asked dangerously.

Horemheb returned his stare. "Never, Your Majesty."

Amunhotep narrowed his eyes.

"Is that all?"

For a moment, I thought Amunhotep wouldn't answer. Then he replied. "That is all."

The general strode purposefully toward his men and Amunhotep moved in the opposite direction. Nefertiti looked at my mother and then at me. "What's happened?"

"Amunhotep was angry with the general," I said. "We are to proceed straight to Memphis without stopping. The general says the men could die in the heat."

"Then they can take turns at the oars," she replied, and my mother and I exchanged glances.

There was to be no Feast of Farewell before we left for Memphis. The sun rose higher in the sky and the time of our departure grew near. Panahesi appeared in the courtyard, and my sister and I saw him whisper something into Amunhotep's ear. They stood together on the verge of the commotion, away from the braying of the donkeys and the din of the servants. Nefertiti moved across the courtyard, pulling me with her, and Panahesi gave a bow and made a hasty retreat. "What did he want?" Nefertiti demanded.

Amunhotep shifted uncomfortably. "A litter."

My sister was quick. "For Kiya?"

"She's pregnant. She will need six bearers."

Nefertiti held tighter to my arm. "Has she grown so fat she must be carried by six men?"

I flushed. She was raising her voice to the King of Egypt.

"I must accommodate Panahesi—"

"Is Panahesi riding in it or is she? Only *queens* are carried by six servants! Is she queen now? Have I been replaced?"

I could sense the commotion in the courtyard stopping again, and on the border of my vision I saw General Nakhtmin.

"I . . . I will tell Panahesi she must only use five," Amunhotep faltered.

I gasped, but Nefertiti nodded and watched Amunhotep disappear to tell Panahesi that his pregnant daughter must use fewer bearers. As Pharaoh left, General Nakhtmin waded through the busy courtyard.

"I have come to wish the Queen of Egypt farewell," he said, "and to bid the Sister of the King's Chief Wife a safe journey. May you find as much joy in the gardens of Memphis as you have in Thebes, Lady Mutnodjmet."

Nefertiti raised her eyebrows. I could tell she was intrigued by the general. She liked his pale eyes against his dark skin. He looked at Nefertiti and I felt a sudden surge of jealousy. "You seem to be familiar with my sister, General." Nefertiti smiled and the general grinned back.

"We have met several times. Once in the garden, in fact, where I predicted her future."

Nefertiti smiled wider. "Then you are a fortune-teller as well as a general?"

I inhaled sharply. Only the priests of Amun knew the wishes of the gods.

"I wouldn't presume to go so far, Your Highness. I am simply an astute observer."

She moved closer to him, so that if she wanted to she could have brushed his cheek with her lips. They were playing a game I didn't like. His eyes swept over her small, powerful body and rested on the inky hair that fringed her cheek. She would not have allowed just anyone to look at her that way. The general stepped back, dizzy from her perfume. Then Amunhotep appeared and their dangerous game was over. She straightened. "Will you be coming to Memphis then, General?"

"Sadly, no," he answered, and he looked at me when he said it. "I shall be waiting here instead for your return. But I shall accompany Your Highness's caravan to the quay."

Nefertiti shrugged playfully. "Then we shall see you shortly." She moved to interrogate Amunhotep about the bearers, and the general held me with his eyes.

"Good-bye, General," I said coolly, then turned to join my mother beneath the awning.

The caravan was ready. The animals shifted uncomfortably in the warm courtyard, and there was nervousness in the air. The horses whinnied impatiently and servants stroked their muzzles to calm them. I had packed my plants into a carefully prepared chest, placing linen between the pots to stop them from rocking together on the short trip from the palace to the quay. On the ship, I could unpack them and place them where they could find sun. But there were only a dozen. The rest I left in the palace, taking clippings from their leaves and storing them in an inlaid ivory box. There were dozens of these, and in small, tightly bound linen bags I'd stockpiled some of the most useful plants. General Horemheb inspected the army, then Amunhotep knelt before his father, receiving the Elder's blessing.

"I will make you proud," Amunhotep swore. "The gods are rejoicing on this day."

I saw the Elder turn to Tiye, and I imagined they were both thinking of Tuthmosis, who should have been kneeling there instead of Amunhotep. Amunhotep saw this, too, and stood.

"You may wish for Tuthmosis," he hissed sharply, "but I am the son who rules Lower Egypt. *I* am the one the gods chose, *not* him."

Queen Tiye straightened her shoulders. "May the gods protect you," she said coldly. Pharaoh nodded, but there was no love in his eyes.

Amunhotep straightened his tunic self-consciously, and when he saw that the soldiers and servants were watching he cried out violently, "Move!"

My body servant appeared and shouted, "Into your litter!"

I scrambled inside. The caravan surged forward. I was behind Nefertiti and Amunhotep, who rode together. I parted the curtains and waved to my aunt. She waved back. The Elder, I noticed, looked solemn. We departed in a cloud of dust, riding the short distance to the bay that surrounded the palace. The glare off the moving water could be seen through the strips of linen protecting me from the sun, and then the caravan stopped where a fleet of impressive Egyptian ships had been moored. We were lowered in our litters and the royal family was taken onto the barges. Because we were part of the royal family now, my mother, father, and I would be traveling on Pharaoh's barge with golden pennants flying from the mast. Panahesi and his family had their own private ship. I was glad for the separation; no vessel could have held both Nefertiti and Kiya.

The barges could fit fifty-two soldiers rowing at the oars and another twenty passengers above or below decks. In the midst of the ships were wooden cabins with two chambers inside. The cabins were built of wood and covered in linen. "To protect against the heat," my father said.

"And where will the soldiers sleep?" I asked him.

"On the deck. It's warm enough now."

The ships looked handsome in the water. The ebony oars, inlaid with silver, caught the light, and the calls of an ibis searching for its mate echoed across the bay. I watched from the steps as treasures from the Elder's palace were packed: copper bowls, cedar wig chests, alabaster statues, and an altar of granite that was inlaid with pearl. The slaves strained under the weight of the many heavy baskets, loading Egypt's finest jewels onto the vessels last so that the guards could watch over them.

When the ships set sail, I went to find my parents in our cabin. My mother was playing Senet with the wife of Egypt's most honored architect. *So Amunhotep convinced him to leave Thebes after all,* I thought. "Where's Father?" I asked her.

My mother used her chin to indicate the stern of the ship, but she didn't take her eyes from the game. Like Nefertiti, she was good at Senet. I wandered out to the stern and heard my father's voice before I saw him.

"Why didn't you tell me this before?" he demanded.

"Because I knew you would be angry. But Horemheb is on our side. He understands what we are doing."

I peered beyond the door of the cabin and saw my father shake his head. "You are making enemies for this family faster than we can make allies. The sands of Memphis will swallow us whole, and if the people rise against you . . ."

"But they will love us!" Nefertiti promised. "We will build them greater temples than they have ever seen. We will hold more feast days, and we'll *give* to the people. This is Amunhotep's *dream.*"

"And yours?"

She hesitated. "Don't you want to be remembered?"

"For what? For taxing the temples?"

A short silence hung between them.

"You will be the most powerful man in the kingdom," she pledged. "I shall see to it. While he builds temples, you will rule this kingdom. He has no interest in politics. Everything will be left to you, and Panahesi will be like bronze to your gold."

Chapter Nine

Shemu, Season of Harvest

BY THE SECOND of Pachons, I began to recognize the sailors on board our ship. They nodded as I passed, but they were wearied and beaten, driven all day in the sun with only water and soup to sustain them. They always had time for Ipu, however. When she walked the decks with her heavy gold earrings and swaying hips, the men talked to her the way a brother might talk with his sister, and quietly, when no one was looking, they laughed. But they never spoke to me except to mumble politely, "My lady."

By the third day of the voyage, I had grown bored. I tried to read, learning about trees that grew in the Kingdom of Mitanni far to our north where the Khabur and the Euphrates overflowed their banks. I read all seven treatises that Ipu had collected in the markets of Thebes by the time we had spent seven days without disembarking. Then, on the eighth night, even Amunhotep grew weary of constant travel, and we were taken to shore to build fires and stretch our legs.

The servants gathered wood to roast the wild geese they had

caught on the river, and we all ate in the Elder's best faience bowls. It was a glad change from the hard bread and figs we had been eating, and Ipu joined me at the fire, holding a cup of Pharaoh's best wine. Across from us, at a dozen different fires, soldiers were getting drunk and courtiers were playing Senet. Ipu stared into her cup and smiled.

"As good as anything I've ever tasted," she said.

I raised my brows. "Even the wine from your father's vineyard?"

She nodded and leaned close. "I think they have opened the oldest barrels."

I sucked in my breath. "For *tonight*? And Pharaoh doesn't care?"

She glanced at Amunhotep, and I followed her gaze. While the courtiers laughed and Nefertiti spoke in low tones with our father, Amunhotep was staring into the fire. His lips were drawn into a thin line and the bones in his face appeared hollow in the flickering light. "He only cares about getting there," Ipu replied. "The faster he arrives in Memphis, the sooner he can take up the crook and flail of Egypt."

Panahesi was making his way toward our circle with an obviously pregnant Kiya. As they drew near the fire, Nefertiti turned and pinched my arm roughly. "What is she doing here?" she demanded.

I rubbed my arm. "She's coming with us to Memphis, remember?"

But Nefertiti didn't hear my sarcasm. "She's pregnant. She should be back on the ship." *And away from Amunhotep,* she wanted to add.

One of Kiya's ladies spread a feathered cushion on the sand and Kiya sat across from Amunhotep, resting her hand on her large hennaed belly. She was soft and fresh, natural in her pregnancy, while across the fire Nefertiti glittered with malachite and gold.

"We are halfway to Memphis," Panahesi announced. "Soon, we will arrive and Pharaoh will be enthroned in his palace." The small group around the fire nodded, murmuring among themselves, and my father watched him carefully. "Are the plans going well for the building, Your Highness?"

Amunhotep straightened, awakening from his stupor. "The plans are coming magnificently. My queen has a great mind for design. We have already sketched a temple with a courtyard and three altars."

Panahesi smiled indulgently. "If His Highness should need any help . . ." He spread his palms and Amunhotep nodded at his loyalty.

"I have already made plans for you," he said. At nearby fires, the courtiers stopped playing Senet. "When we reach Memphis," Amunhotep announced, "I want you to see to it that General Horemheb succeeds in collecting taxes from the priests of Amun."

The fire snapped and hissed, and Panahesi hid his shock, looking quickly to Nefertiti to see if she'd known, gauging how far the Pharaoh trusted her now. Then all of the viziers began talking at once.

"But Your Majesty," one of them interjected. "Is that prudent?"

Panahesi cleared his throat. "Of course, it is prudent. The temples of Amun have never been taxed. They hoard Egypt's wealth and spend it as their own."

"Exactly!" Amunhotep exclaimed. He struck his fist into his palm and many of the soldiers turned to hear what Pharaoh was saying. I looked at my father, whose face was a blank courtier's mask, but I knew what he was thinking: *This king is only seventeen years old. What will happen ten years from now, when power rests on his shoulders like a comfortably fitting cloak? What precedents will he topple then?*

Panahesi leaned over and said to the king, "My daughter has missed you these eight nights at sail."

Amunhotep glanced quickly at Nefertiti. "I have not forgotten my first wife," he said. "I will come to her again . . . when we are in Memphis." He looked across the fire at Kiya, who was feigning ignorance about what her father had just said. She smiled lovingly at him. *Little minx,* I thought. *She knows exactly what her father's doing.*

"Shall we walk along the beach?" Nefertiti said at once, grabbing my arm and whisking me up.

I held my breath as we walked away; I thought my sister would be enraged. But as we pressed our feet along the wet banks of the Nile, trailed by two guards, her spirits were high. She looked up at the wide expanse of stars and breathed in the fresh air. "The reign of Kiya in Amunhotep's heart is over. He's not going to visit her again until we reach Memphis."

"That's not so long," I pointed out.

"But *I'm* the one designing his temple with him. *I'm* the one who'll reign at his side. Not her. And soon I'll be with his child."

I glanced at her sideways. "You're pregnant?"

Her face fell. "No, not yet."

"Have you taken the honey?"

"Even better." She laughed as if she were intoxicated. "My servants found mandrake."

"And they made the juice?" It was a difficult process. I'd only seen Ranofer do it once.

"Yes. I took it last night. And now it could happen at any time."

At any time. My sister, pregnant with the heir to Egypt's throne. I stared at her in the silver light and frowned. "But aren't you ever afraid of his plans?"

"Of course not. Why should I be afraid?"

"Because the priests could rise against you! They are powerful, Nefertiti. What if they should try assassination?"

"Without the army, how could they? The army is on our side. We have Horemheb."

"But what if the people never forgive you? It's their gold. It's their silver."

"And we'll be freeing it from the stranglehold of the Amun priests. We will give back to the people what the priests have taken."

My voice sounded cynical even in my own ears. *"How?"*

Nefertiti looked out over the waters. "Through Aten."

"A god only you understand."

"A god *all* of Egypt will come to know."

"Because that god is really Amunhotep?"

She shot me a look, but she didn't reply.

▣ ▣ ▣

The next morning, the sailors were slow to start. They had taken too much wine, so by orders of Amunhotep no one was to be allowed onshore again. My mother and father said nothing, exercising their cramped legs on the deck, but three nights later word spread between the ships that six of Horemheb's men had died. The servants whispered that their deaths had been caused by tainted water and food.

"What does Pharaoh expect?" a vizier hissed at my father. "If we're not allowed onshore to find fresh water regularly, then men are going to die." Dysentery, someone called it, an ailment that could have been cured by any local physician had the men simply been allowed to go onshore.

Two nights later, news came that eleven more men had died. Then the general disobeyed Amunhotep's orders. In the evening, he stalked to the royal barge at the front of the fleet and came on board our ship, demanding an audience with the king at once.

We looked up from our Senet games and my father stood swiftly. "I do not know if he will see you, General."

Horemheb would not be turned away. "More men are dying and the dysentery is spreading."

My father hesitated. "I will see what I can do." He disappeared into the cabin. When he returned, he shook his head grimly. "The Pharaoh will see no one."

"These are *men*," Horemheb said between clenched teeth. "These are men who need *help*. A physician is all that they need. Will he sacrifice men to arrive sooner in Memphis?"

"Yes." The door to the innermost cabin opened and Amunhotep appeared in his kilt and *nemes* crown. "Pharaoh does not change his mind." He strode forward. "You have heard my decision!" he shouted.

Real danger flashed from Horemheb's eyes. I thought he might slit Amunhotep's throat with one slip of his dagger. Then Horemheb remembered his place and moved toward the door.

"Wait!" I cried, surprising myself. The general stopped. "I have mint and basil. It may cure your men, and we wouldn't have to go ashore for a physician."

Amunhotep tensed, but Nefertiti appeared in the cabin door behind him. "Let her go," she urged.

"I could use a cloak," I said quickly. "No one would even know I was gone." I looked to Amunhotep. "Then the people would think your orders have been obeyed and the lives of your soldiers would be spared."

"She studied herbs in Akhmim," Nefertiti explained. "She might be able to cure them. And what if the dysentery should spread?"

General Horemheb looked to Pharaoh for his decision.

Pharaoh raised his chin, feigning an air of munificence. "The Sister of the King's Chief Wife may go."

My mother's face was disapproving, my father's eyes unreadable. But these were men's lives. To let them die when we could save them would go against all the laws of Ma'at. What would the gods think if on our way to Memphis, to the start of a new reign, we let innocent men die? I ran to my pallet and collected my herb box. Then I threw on a cloak and in the shadow of darkness followed Horemheb onto the deck. Outside, the wind of the Nile rustled my cloak. I was nervous. I wished I could bend in quick obeisance to Bast, the god of travel, for safe journey. But I followed the general in front of me, who said nothing. We boarded the vessel, where the men were suffering and the stench of sickness was overwhelming. I put my cloak to my nose.

"A squeamish healer?" the general asked, and I dropped the cloak in defiance. He led me into his own cabin. "What do you need?"

"Hot water and bowls. We can soak the mint and basil and make it into tea."

He disappeared to collect what I needed and I studied his chamber. The cabin was smaller than the one that Pharaoh and Nefertiti were sharing and nothing hung on the walls, even though we had been on the river for almost twenty days. His pallet was neat and folded, and four armless chairs were arranged around a Senet board. I looked at the pieces. Whoever had been black had won the last game. I guessed it was Horemheb or he wouldn't have let the pieces remain.

"The water is heating," he said when he returned. He didn't offer me a seat. I remained standing.

"You play Senet," I remarked.

He nodded.

"You were black."

He studied me with an interested expression. "They said you were the wise one." He didn't add whether he believed them now, but he indicated a seat with his hand. He took one himself, crossing his arms over his chest while we waited for the water to boil. "How old are you?"

"Fourteen," I replied.

"When I was fourteen, I was fighting for the Elder against the Nubians. That was eight years ago," he said thoughtfully.

So he was twenty-two now. General Nakhtmin's age.

"Fourteen is an important age," he added. "It is a time when destinies are decided." He stared at me in a way that was unnerving. "You will be your sister's closest adviser in Memphis."

"I advise her in nothing," I said quickly. "She takes her own advice."

He raised his eyebrows and suddenly I wished that I hadn't said anything. Then a soldier came into the cabin bearing a steaming pot of water. A second followed with dozens of bowls.

I was surprised. "How many of the men are sick?"

"Twenty-four. And there will be more by tomorrow."

"Twenty-four?" What had Amunhotep allowed to happen? It was half of the ship. I worked quickly, tearing leaves of mint and placing them in each of the cups. The general watched, appraising my work, and when I was finished he said nothing to me. He took away the steaming bowls and led me out the way I had come. I thought that nothing else would pass between us, but as we reached the king's barge he bowed deeply. "Thank you, Lady Mutnodjmet." Then he turned and disappeared into the night.

Our fleet of ships was docked close enough together that a sailor could stand at the stern of one and speak with a sailor on the prow of another. This is how talk of what I had done for Horemheb's men spread from ship to ship, and whenever the barges docked for the night, word began reaching me of women looking to ease their monthly pain, or stop seasickness, or prevent the unwanted results of a casual encounter with a sailor.

"Who knew," Nefertiti said, lounging in my doorway, "that Ranofer's endless talk of herbs would be useful?"

I sorted through my box, handing Ipu ginger for seasickness and raspberry leaf for monthly pain. Preventing unwanted births would be more difficult. I had studied the combination of acacia and honey with Ranofer, but making it would prove more complicated. Ipu wrapped the herbs carefully in small strips of linen and wrote the women's names with a reed pen and ink. She would pass them along to the women who'd asked for them.

Nefertiti continued to watch us. "You should charge for this. The herbs are not grown free."

Ipu looked up and nodded. "I suggested that as well, my lady."

I sighed. "Perhaps if I had a garden of my own . . ."

"And what happens when these run out?" Nefertiti wanted to know.

I looked into my box. The mint was nearly gone, and in a day there would be no more raspberry leaves. "Then I will replace them in Memphis."

▣ ▣ ▣

When we finally arrived in the capital of Lower Egypt, the women ran onto the decks and the men crowded next to them, catching their first glimpse of Memphis. She was beautiful. A city of busy markets glittering in the early morning sun. The Nile's waters lapped against the steps of the Temple to Amun, and we could hear the calls of merchants unloading ships at the quay. The temples of Apis and Ptah rose over even the tallest buildings, their golden roofs shining in the sun. Nefertiti's eyes were wide. "It's magnificent!"

Amunhotep flinched. "I was raised here," he said, "with my grandfather's discarded treasure and unwanted wives."

The servants unloaded the ships, and chariots were brought so that Pharaoh and his court could ride the short distance to the palace. Thousands were waiting, pressed together in the streets, throwing petals, waving branches, and chanting the royals' names until the sound grew so loud it deafened the noise of horses and chariots.

Amunhotep swelled with the people's new love.

"They adore you," Nefertiti said in his ear.

"Bring me two chests of gold!" Amunhotep shouted, but the viziers couldn't hear him above the horses and cheering crowds. He motioned to Panahesi, who halted the chariots. Then he shouted a second time, "Two chests of gold!"

Panahesi dismounted from his chariot and ran back to the barge. He returned with seven guards and two chests, and when the people realized what was about to happen they grew wild in the streets.

"For the glory of Egypt!" Amunhotep took handfuls of deben and tossed them. There was a momentary silence, then the crowd closed around him, their chanting growing animallike. Nefertiti tossed back her head and laughed, taking handfuls of rings herself, tossing them to the people.

Crowds began running after the king's chariot, and Horemheb's soldiers blocked their passage with their spears. When we passed through the gates of the palace, the mob had grown uncontrollable. There were thousands now, but the chests were empty. "They want more!" Nefertiti shouted, seeing women hurl themselves at the gate.

"Then give it to them!" Amunhotep cried. A third chest was brought, but my father raised his arm.

"Is this wise, Your Highness?" He looked directly at Nefertiti. "The people will *kill* each other in the streets."

Panahesi stepped forward. "I say bring a fourth chest, Your Majesty. They will love you."

Amunhotep laughed jubilantly. "A fourth!" he cried.

A fourth chest was brought to join the third and debens of gold were scattered over the gates. Horemheb shouted orders to his men, telling them to arrest any citizen or slave who attempted to scale the walls.

"They're fighting!" I gripped my mother's sheath in horror.

"Yes." Amunhotep smiled. "But they will know that I love them." He strode from the gardens into the halls of the palace, servants trailing on his heels.

My father said angrily, "You cannot buy the people's love. They will come to disdain you."

Amunhotep stopped walking and Nefertiti reached out in a conciliatory gesture, putting a hand on his arm. "My father's right. There is such a thing as too much."

Panahesi sidled up to him. "But the people will be talking about the Great Pharaoh Amunhotep for months."

Amunhotep ignored my father's concern. "Take us to our rooms!" he commanded, and we were shown to our new chambers.

As always, Pharaoh's chamber was in the center of the palace. Nefertiti's clothes were brought into his rooms, and although the Memphis servants stared wide-eyed, the Malkata servants knew better. Vizier Panahesi and my parents were placed in a courtyard to the left of the king, and I was to Nefertiti's right in a separate chamber, divided only by a short hall. The standing army of nearly three thousand men would arrive in ten days and be housed in their own quarters, rooms just outside the palace but behind its walls. Of the soldiers who'd journeyed with us, nearly two hundred of them had died on the ships.

In my new room in the king's courtyard, I stared at my gilded bed with its carved images of Bes, the dwarf god of protection, who would keep away demons. The room was large, with plump feathered cushions in every corner and brightly glazed pottery on low cedar chests. The ceiling was held up by columns in the shape of lotus blossoms, and in a corner Ipu was already rearranging my belongings. She had seen how I'd placed my herb box in a cool corner of my room in Malkata and had done the same, even going through the trouble of hanging up the amber-colored leaves of myrrh the way I had, to sweeten the chamber. She hummed as she worked, and Nefertiti appeared in my doorway, smiling.

"Come see this," she said. She hooked my arm in hers and led me into the royal chamber. She stood back, grinning, and I gasped.

I would never see another room like it. It was exquisitely tiled and painted, furnished with gold statues honoring the most powerful Egyptian gods. From a wide, arching window, it was possible to see the manicured palace gardens and a tree-lined avenue sloping down to the Nile. There was a room for wigs that was scented with lotus, and an entire chamber where Merit could work. I went into this second room, where everything was laid out in preparation: pellets of incense for under the arms, hair curlers, tweezers, jars of perfume, and pots of kohl already mixed with date palm oil. A hand mirror had been cleverly carved into the shape of an ankh and makeup chests filled every available space. Every lamp was inlaid with ivory and obsidian.

Amunhotep sat in the corner, watching my expression. "Does the Sister of the King's Chief Wife approve?" he asked, standing and taking Nefertiti's arm so that she had to let go of mine. "You're the first person your sister ran to get."

I bowed. "It is beautiful, Your Highness."

He sat down and pulled Nefertiti onto his lap. She laughed, and indicated that I should sit across from them. She said merrily, "Tomorrow the builder, Maya, is going to begin the temple."

I sat. "To Aten?"

"Of course to Aten," Amunhotep snapped. "On the twenty-sixth of Pachons, the army will begin collecting taxes from the priests. On the first of Payni, we build. Once the temple is finished, we won't need the high priests. *We* will become the high priests." He turned to my sister in triumph. "You and I . . . and the gods will speak through us."

I recoiled. This was blasphemy.

But Nefertiti said nothing and avoided my gaze.

Dinner in the Great Hall was chaotic. Though the chamber was the same as it had been in Thebes, confusion turned the towering hall into a commotion of rushing people that I'd only ever seen the likes of in the marketplace. Servants were bowing to scribes and snubbing courtiers because they hadn't learned the faces of the Theban nobility. Only a few of Egypt's viziers were in attendance, and even Panahesi was absent, probably still seeing to his robes and his rooms. Women came up to thank me for my herbs, women I had never seen before, and they all wanted to know if I would continue to carry acacia, adding that they would be willing to pay me for it, and the raspberry leaves if I would continue to provide them.

"You should do it," Ipu encouraged me. "I could fetch any herbs for you at the quay. You might not have a garden, but if you told me what you needed . . ."

I thought a moment. It wouldn't just be acacia and raspberry. The women had asked for other herbs, too. Safflower oil for muscle pain and healthy hair, fig and willow for toothache, myrrh for healing. I could harvest some of those from my potted plants, but Ipu would have to find me the rest. "All right," I said hesitantly.

"And will you charge for them?"

"Ipu!" I gasped.

But she continued to stare at me. "The women in Pharaoh's harem charge for the linen that they weave. And your father does not work for free simply because he works for the royal family."

I shifted uncomfortably. "I might charge."

She smiled, pulling out my chair. "I will be back with your food, my lady."

My parents were in attendance at the royal table. Nefertiti would eat with Amunhotep at the top of the dais from now on, overseeing the entire hall. And tonight, because there was no arranged seating, the architect, Maya, sat with us beneath the Horus thrones. He and his wife looked cut from the same cloth, both tall Egyptians with watchful eyes.

"Pharaoh wishes to begin building a temple to Aten," Maya said warningly, and my father exhaled.

"He has said as much to you?"

The architect looked nervously over his shoulder. Nefertiti and Amunhotep regarded the proceedings with apathy, more interested in their talk of temples and taxes, and Maya lowered his voice. "Yes. And in two days' time, the army begins collecting taxes from the temples of Amun."

"The priests will not gladly hand over what has been theirs for centuries," my father said vehemently.

"Then Pharaoh will kill them," Maya replied.

"He has ordered this?"

The greatest architect in Egypt nodded solemnly.

My father stood up, pushing his chair from the table. "The Elder must be warned." He swept from the Audience Chamber with my mother on his heels, and for the first time the royal couple on the dais noticed something outside of themselves. Nefertiti beckoned me toward the thrones with her finger.

"Where has Father gone?" she demanded.

"He has heard that you intend on building soon," I said carefully. "He has gone to make preparations to clear the way."

Amunhotep settled back into his throne. "I have chosen correctly in your father," he said to Nefertiti. "Once every seven days," he decided, "we will hold court in the Audience Chamber. The rest of the time we shall let Ay deal with foreign emissaries and petitioners."

My sister glanced approvingly at me.

Chapter Ten

MEMPHIS

twenty-fifth of Pachons

ON MY FIRST morning in Memphis, my father and Nefertiti slipped into my room and shut the door. Ipu, who slept across the hall as both my servant and my guard, remained sleeping soundly.

I scrambled from beneath my covers. "What's happening?"

"From now on, this is where we meet," my father said. Nefertiti took a seat on my bed and I rubbed the sleep from my eyes.

"Why here?"

"Because Panahesi is in the same courtyard as Father, and if I make a habit of visiting, he will make a habit of sending spies."

I looked around the room. "Where's Mother?"

My father sat himself down. "At the baths."

Apparently, she wasn't to be included in our meetings. Just as well. She would only spend nights sitting up worrying.

"Tomorrow, Amunhotep begins collecting taxes from the temples," my father said, "and we will need a plan if it all goes wrong."

I sat forward. "If what goes wrong?"

"If Horemheb turns on Pharaoh and the priests revolt," my sister said shortly.

I felt fear rising in my throat. "But why would that happen?"

Nefertiti ignored me.

"If it goes wrong tomorrow," my father decided, "everyone in this family will meet behind the Temple of Amun. Take chariots from the north of the palace, where the gates are unguarded, and ride them to the docks. If the army turns, they will storm the palace from the south. At the water steps, a ship will be ready to set sail. If Pharaoh has been killed, we will return to Thebes."

Nefertiti's gaze flew to the door, to be sure no one was listening. "And if he hasn't?" she asked, her voice dropping.

"Then we all go by ship."

"And what if he won't come?"

"Then you must leave without him." My father's voice was stern. "Because he will be marked and will not live to see the night."

I shivered, and even Nefertiti seemed disturbed. "*If* it goes wrong," she repeated. "There is no indication that it will."

"We still prepare. Let Amunhotep make his rash decisions, but he will not take this family with him." My father stood, but Nefertiti didn't move. "You both understand what to do?" He looked at us and we nodded. "I'll be in the Per Medjat." He opened the door and disappeared into the Hall of Books.

Nefertiti looked at me in the glow of the rising sun. "Amunhotep's reign will be decided tomorrow," she said. "He has promised Horemheb all manner of things. War with the Hittites. New chariots, greater shields."

"Will he give them to him?"

Nefertiti shrugged. "Once he has collected the taxes, what does it matter?"

"I would not want to make an enemy of Horemheb."

"Yes." Nefertiti nodded slowly. "And I'm not foolish enough to think we are invincible. But Tuthmosis would never have had the courage to challenge the priests. Had I married Tuthmosis, we would still be in Thebes, waiting for the Elder to die. Amunhotep sees a new Egypt, a greater Egypt."

"What is wrong with the Egypt of now?"

"Look around! If the Hittites threatened our kingdom, who would have the money to send us to war?"

"The priests. But if a Pharaoh has all the power," I countered, "who will tell him which wars should be waged? What if he wants to fight a useless war? There will be no priests to stop him."

"What war has ever been useless?" my sister asked. "All were for the greatness of Egypt."

▣ ▣ ▣

We met in the Audience Chamber the following day at noon. Kiya was there, her round belly showing beneath her sheath. A servant helped her into a chair opposite mine on the first step below the throne, and I could see she had less than five months to wait before the child's birth. Her wig was new and she had hennaed her hands and heavy breasts. I noticed Amunhotep staring at them and narrowed my eyes, thinking he should only be looking at my sister.

Panahesi and my father seated themselves on the second tier, while minor officials sat in a small circle around the Audience Chamber. Maya, the architect, was at the center of court. I hadn't spoken with him, but I'd heard that he was clever. There was nothing he couldn't do, my father once said. When the Elder had wanted a lake in the middle of the desert, he'd done it. When he'd wanted statues of himself larger than any that had been carved, Maya had found a way. Now he would build a Temple to Aten, a god no one had heard of, a protector of Egypt only Amunhotep understood.

"Are you ready?" Amunhotep demanded from his throne.

Maya shifted the papyrus and reed pen in his hand. "Yes, Your Highness."

"You will take down everything," Amunhotep said, and the architect nodded. "I want the entrance to the temple flanked by a row of ram-headed sphinxes."

The architect nodded and wrote it down.

"There should be an open-air court flanked by lotus columns."

"And ponds stocked with fish," Nefertiti added. My father scowled, but Nefertiti ignored him. "And a garden. With a lake. Like the one you made for Queen Tiye."

"Only greater," Amunhotep pressed, and the builder hesitated.

"If this temple is going to be near the current Temple of Amun," Maya paused, "there may be no room for a lake."

"Then we will tear down the Temple of Amun to create space!" Amunhotep vowed.

The court burst into a frenzy of whispering. I looked at my mother, whose face was ashen, and she stole a glance at Nefertiti, who avoided her gaze. How could he tear down the Temple of Amun? Where would the god rest? Where would the people worship?

Maya cleared his throat. "To tear down the temple could take years," he warned.

"Then the lake can come last. But there will be towering stone pylons and heavy columns. And murals at every entrance."

"Depicting our lives in Memphis," Nefertiti envisioned. "The fan bearers and bodyguards, the viziers and scribes, the sandal bearers, the parasol bearers, the servants who walk the halls, and us."

"On every column, the Pharaoh and Queen of Egypt." Amunhotep reached out for Nefertiti's hand, forgetting his pregnant wife beneath him, and the two of them were carried away by a vision that only they could see.

Maya put down the reed pen and looked up at the dais. "Is that all, Your Highness?"

"For now." Amunhotep struck his scepter of reign on the floor. "Bring in the general."

The doors swept open and General Horemheb was shown into the Audience Chamber. As the architect left and the general entered, I detected a stiffening of backs among Egypt's viziers. *What do they fear from him?* I wondered.

"Has everything been prepared?" Amunhotep demanded.

"The soldiers are ready," Horemheb replied. "They wait on your orders." *And expect to be repaid in kind.* I could see this addendum on Horemheb's face, that the soldiers expected war with the Hittites to stop them from encroaching on our foreign territories.

"Then give them my orders and go." Horemheb moved toward the doors, but Amunhotep sat forward on his throne, stopping him before he reached the entrance. "You will *not* disappoint me, General."

The entire court craned their necks and Horemheb turned.

"I never disappoint, Your Highness. I am a man of my word. As I know you shall be."

When the heavy metal doors swung shut, Amunhotep stormed from his throne, startling the viziers. "This meeting is over!" The officials in the Audience Chamber hesitated. "Out!" he shouted, and the men scrambled to their feet. "Ay and Panahesi will stay behind."

I stood up to go, too, but Nefertiti held her hand in the air for me to stay. The Audience Chamber cleared and I resumed my seat. Kiya, too, remained where she was. Below us, Amunhotep paced.

"This general cannot be trusted," he determined. "He isn't loyal to me."

"You haven't tested him yet," my father said swiftly.

"He is loyal only to his men in the army!"

Panahesi nodded. "I agree, Your Highness," and with this concurrence Amunhotep made up his mind.

"I will not send him to war. I will not send him north to fight the

Hittites so he can come back with chariots full of weapons and gold that he can use to start a rebellion!"

"A wise decision," Panahesi said at once.

"Panahesi, I am sending you to supervise the temples," Amunhotep said. "You will go with Horemheb to see that *nothing* is stolen. *Everything* the army collects comes back to me. For the glory of Aten." He turned to my father. "Ay, you shall deal with the foreign ambassadors. Whatever matters come before the throne of Horus will be handled by you. I trust you above all other men." His black eyes held my father in their grip, and my father bowed respectfully.

"Of course, Your Highness."

On our third night in Memphis, the dinner in the Great Hall was muted. Pharaoh was ill-tempered and suspicious of everyone. No one dared mention General Horemheb's name, and the viziers whispered quietly among themselves.

"Have you seen the gardens yet?" my mother asked, reaching down and feeding a morsel of duck to one of the palace cats, making the servants envious. She was the only one who was merry at our table. She had been exploring the markets while Amunhotep was vowing to turn his back on the general as soon as Horemheb had raided the temples of Amun.

I shook my head. "No. I've been unpacking." I sighed.

"Then we shall go after dinner," she said cheerfully.

When the Great Hall cleared, we passed through the crowded courtyards and wandered into the quiet of the evening. From the topmost steps of the palace leading down into the gardens, I could see the windblown dunes of Memphis. The sand shifted in the waning light and dust billowed up in a shimmering haze. The sun was setting, but it was still warm, and that night the sky above was clear. I reached up and plucked a leaf from a tree. "Myrrh." I tore the leaf apart and rubbed its juices on my fingers, then held them up for my mother to smell. She craned her neck back.

"Awful."

"Not when you're in pain."

She looked at me in the fading light. "Perhaps you and I should have stayed in Akhmim," she said suddenly. "You miss your gardens. You were always so talented with herbs."

I glanced at her, wondering what would make her say such a thing now. "Ranofer was a good teacher," I replied.

"Ranofer has married," my mother said.

I looked up sharply. "*Who?*"

"A local girl. I'm sure she's not as beautiful as Nefertiti, but she will be loyal and love him."

"Do you think Nefertiti loved him?" I asked.

We watched as the sky deepened to violet. My mother sighed. "There are many different kinds of love, Mutnodjmet. The kind you have for your parents, the kind you have for children, the kind that's really lust."

"You think Nefertiti was in lust?"

My mother laughed. "No, she has too much self-control for lust. It's men who are in lust with her. But I think she loved Ranofer in her own way. He was there, he was attractive, and he followed her."

"Like Amunhotep."

She gave a little smile. "Yes. But Ranofer always knew Nefertiti was meant for Pharaoh. She is the daughter of a princess."

"And now he's married."

"Yes. I guess his heart has mended."

We both smiled. I was happy for Ranofer. He had married a local girl. A good wife, probably, who would water his herbs and bring him dinner when he came home from visiting his patients in the village. I wondered if my future husband would know about herbs or care about tending a garden. We walked back to the palace under the stars. My mother came into my chamber, startling Ipu, who executed a hasty bow as she lit the lamps. "Lovely." My mother ran her fingers over the paintings of Isis and Osiris. An image of my patron goddess was on the wall. "Mut," she said, staring at the feline head in the candlelight. She looked at my green eyes, then back at the goddess. "I wonder if our names determine our destiny, or if destiny leads us to choose certain names."

I had wondered that myself. Had my mother known I would have feline eyes before she'd chosen Mutnodjmet as my name? And could my father's first wife have known just how beautiful Nefertiti would become when she called her the Beautiful One?

My mother dropped her hand to her side. "Tomorrow will be a busy day," she said meaningfully. "The future of Memphis will be decided."

By a man that Pharaoh intends to betray. I wondered if she had heard the news from my father. I didn't say anything, and my mother smiled softly.

"You should sleep."

Like a child, I obeyed and climbed into bed. Then she kissed my forehead, the way she used to in Akhmim.

回 回 回

In the morning, I was woken by the sun, which filtered into my room through the lowered reed mats. The world around me was strangely silent. I got up and checked the door, but Ipu was gone. I looked into the courtyard, and none of the servants were around. I dressed quickly, thinking that something must have gone wrong. Had Horemheb betrayed us? Had the barges fled? I rushed down the hall. Had they left without me? How could I have slept so late? I quickened my pace, and when I saw a servant in the hall I demanded, "Where is everyone?"

The servant walked away from me, buried beneath an armful of scrolls. "The Great Hall, my lady."

"Why the Great Hall?"

"Because it wouldn't all fit in the Audience Chamber!"

At the Great Hall, two guards parted to let me through, and as I entered into the chamber I gasped. The windows had been thrown open to let in the morning light, but it wasn't the bright tiles or gilded tables that I noticed. It was chest upon open chest of treasure: silver scepters and wrought gold that Egypt's Pharaohs must not have seen for centuries. They were piled haphazardly around the room: ancient statues of Ptah and Osiris, gilded chairs, and chests filled with bronze and gold. Nefertiti and Amunhotep stood on the dais while the army carried more treasure into the room. My family was standing around surveying the scene.

"This must be all the gold in Egypt!" I exclaimed, and General Horemheb, who was passing me by, threw a sharp look in my direction. My father separated himself from the crowd of officials and took my arm.

"It's gone well."

"Is that why you woke me up?" I asked, offended that no one had thought to include me on such a momentous occasion.

"Your mother gave strict instructions not to wake you unless something went wrong." He patted my back. "We only have your best interests at heart, little cat. Don't be angry." We both looked across the Great Hall and he added warningly, "If there's to be a fight, it will happen before nightfall. They have not yet gone to the High Priest of Amun."

"He doesn't know they're coming?"

"He has been forewarned."

I lowered my voice. "So do you think there will be violence?"

"If the High Priest is foolish enough not to see the turning of the tide."

I glanced at him in shock. "Then you agree with this?"

My father closed his eyes briefly. "You can't change the desert.

You can only take the fastest course through it. Wishing it's an oasis won't make it so, Mutnodjmet."

Suddenly, the room grew hushed, and I noticed that Horemheb's men were gone. Nefertiti descended the dais to stand beside my father and me. "The soldiers have left for Amun's temple," she said excitedly. We looked over the treasure, gleaming in the sun. There was so much of it that I wondered whether the army hadn't simply taxed the temples but had stripped whatever they'd found in their treasuries.

"This can't only be taxes," I said aloud. "Look at it all. There's too much of it."

"Oh, there are dozens of temples in Memphis," Nefertiti said gaily. My father looked hard at her and she added defensively, "The men's orders were to take a fourth of the gold in their treasuries."

"And they are following those orders?" he demanded.

"Of course," Amunhotep replied. None of us had heard his approach. He stepped between my sister and me and placed his arm around her slender waist. "Panahesi is there to make certain it's done." He looked down into Nefertiti's dark eyes. She leaned her head into his shoulder. "How is it that since your arrival in my life all of my projects have come to fruition?"

Nefertiti shrugged provocatively, as if she knew the answer but wouldn't say.

The High Priest of Amun has still to part with his wealth, I thought darkly.

We waited in the Great Hall. For hours there was no word from the Great Temple of Amun and the court began to grow anxious. Amunhotep paced the floor while Nefertiti played a game of Senet with my mother. When at last the door swung open and Horemheb burst in, the Great Hall held its breath. The general strode toward the dais dressed in leather and armed, but empty-handed.

"Where is it?" Amunhotep cried. "Where is Amun's gold?"

"The High Priest will not agree to taxation of the temple," he said simply.

The anger built in Amunhotep's voice. "Then why are you here? You know the bargain. If he will not bow to Pharaoh, then he will pay the price!" There was an outburst of chatter as Amunhotep's viziers talked heatedly among themselves. "Silence!" he shouted. An immediate hush fell over the Great Hall.

"You must make an example of the High Priest," Panahesi advised.

My father stood. "His death could lead to rebellion. The people see him as the mouth of the gods. It is more prudent to arrest him."

Amunhotep looked to Nefertiti, and it became clear to the court how much influence she had gained. She descended the dais.

"You must do what you think right. Perhaps it is wiser to arrest him," she acknowledged, "but if he will not go in peace . . ." She held up her palm. She had placated everyone and condemned the High Priest in one breath.

Amunhotep faced Horemheb. "Arrest him! If he will not go in peace, then you will take his life."

Horemheb did not move. "My men are not murderers, *Your Highness.*"

"He is a traitor to the crown!" Amunhotep seethed. "A blight on the mighty glory of Aten!"

"Then I will arrest him and bring him here. In peace."

I could see Amunhotep's desire to lash out, but he needed Horemheb; the job was not finished. Nefertiti stepped forward, placing her lips against Horemheb's ear, and I could read what she was saying. "Amun's reign is over," she whispered threateningly. "Aten watches over Egypt now." They looked at one another, and a dozen messages were concealed in that glance. Horemheb made a bow, then turned to leave.

Amunhotep looked to Panahesi. "Follow him," he commanded.

There was a meeting in my chamber that night.

"You let him kill the High Priest of Amun!" my father raged. He paced the bedroom and his cloak swirled violently around his heels.

Nefertiti sat on the edge of my bed. She was visibly shaken. "He refused taxation," she said. "Had he gone in peace—"

"Panahesi didn't give him the chance to *go in peace!* This is against Ma'at," my father warned, and Nefertiti lost some of her color.

"The goddess understands—"

"Does she?" he demanded. "Are you willing to risk your *ka* for it?"

We both looked at Nefertiti.

"Nothing can be done now," she replied. "He's dead, and . . . and Amunhotep expects me back in his chamber." Her voice disappeared into itself. "There will be a feast tonight." She stole a glance at my father. "He expects you," she said hastily. "And Panahesi will be there."

Our father didn't reply. Horemheb hadn't betrayed the king, but something far worse, far more lasting had occurred. This deed of Amunhotep's wouldn't echo just on earth, it would echo among the gods. My father stormed from the chamber, and Nefertiti looked at me sharply. Then she disappeared after my father, and I was alone in my room.

When Merit arrived with instructions to wear my finest jewels to the feast, I shook my head angrily. "But the queen has requested it," she replied.

"Then tell the queen she will simply have to be the only daughter of Ay who looks stunning tonight. If I'm not mistaken, the court should be in mourning, not celebrating."

Merit looked puzzled.

"The High Priest has been killed!"

She drew her head back in understanding. "Oh. Yes. May Osiris embrace his soul," she mumbled. "I will return with your answer to the queen, my lady. But you will be going?" she confirmed.

"Of course," I snapped. "But only because I have no other choice."

She looked at me curiously, but I didn't care. I didn't care who knew I didn't think we should be celebrating the death of Ma'at. But in the end, I knew even my father would attend Pharaoh's feast. No one was above Pharaoh.

I stood in the center of my room and closed my eyes. "Ipu," I called. She didn't answer. "Ipu?"

My body servant appeared. "My lady?"

"I am to attend a feast tonight."

I could read the shock on her face, although for once she kept her silence. The High Priest of Amun, Holiest of Holies, had been dead for seven hours and a feast was being held. I sat silently while my hair and nails were done, even allowing my feet and breasts to be hennaed. When the door to my chamber swung open, I knew who it was before she appeared.

Her wig was shorter than the one she usually wore. The hair curved around her ears, showing her double pierced earlobes and then cutting straight to her chin. She looked beautiful and fearsome. She sat down next to me, but I ignored her.

"You aren't sulking, are you? We did what had to be done," she swore.

"Murder?" I exclaimed. "The gods will punish this family," I forewarned.

"We set an *example.*"

"What *kind* of example? That Pharaoh should be feared?"

"Of course, he should be feared!" Nefertiti straightened. "He is Pharaoh of the mightiest kingdom in the world, and there are only two ways of ruling. With fear or with rebellion." She held out her arm. "The building of our temple will begin tomorrow. It is a night for celebration no matter what you think." She smiled, indicating with her chin that I should stand up and walk with her. "Did you know the Elder sent his general here to find out what was happening?"

My breath came faster. "General Nakhtmin?"

"Yes." We moved swiftly through the halls of the palace.

"But what does the Elder expect the general to do?"

"He can do nothing," she said merrily. "You heard, of course, that the Elder has married again. A little princess from Nubia. Twelve years old."

I winced.

"But what do I care? A new sun has risen, and it will scorch every other star out of the sky. Including the Elder."

I was shocked by her aggression. "And our aunt?"

"Tiye is strong. She can take care of herself."

We walked briskly through the painted halls to the sprawling room she shared with the king. Amunhotep emerged from the inner chamber, and the sight of him drew my breath away. His kilt was long and formfitting, and his golden pectoral was one I had never seen him wear before. Perhaps it was from the treasuries of Amun. They kissed, and I turned my head.

"I said you would succeed," Nefertiti said softly. "And this is only the beginning."

The Great Hall opened its doors to us and trumpets blared.

The feasting stopped so the people could watch Pharaoh's entrance. I followed my sister, and behind the three of us trailed Ipu and Merit with beads of lapis and gold in their hair. I scanned the faces, but didn't see the general among the crowd. My parents were at their table beneath the double thrones. The architect was there, with Kiya and Panahesi. I was disappointed to see that Horemheb was also among them.

I took my place at the table and Amunhotep led my sister to her throne. The people watched as they ascended the dais together, looking like gods who had just come to earth. There had never been such a striking couple in Egypt, with their gold and faience beads and jeweled scepters of reign. The court shook their heads and there was a murmur of awe. Then dinner resumed, and everyone chatted merrily, as if a murder had not just taken place. I looked at my empty plate and handed it to Ipu so she could prepare a dish for me. Only Horemheb and I remained taciturn at the table.

"You are silent tonight, General." Kiya was sitting next to him, her pretty breasts exposed and her stomach an attractive mound beneath them. "Aren't you enjoying the feast?"

Horemheb regarded her incredulously. "I am here because those were my orders. Otherwise, I would be preparing for battle with the Hittites, who are raiding our villages and encroaching on our land."

Kiya laughed. "Hittites? You would rather be fighting Hittites than eating with Pharaoh?"

The general looked at her without saying a word.

"Are the Hittites really stealing Egypt's land?" I asked him.

"Every day that we let them," Horemheb replied.

"Do you think there will be war?" I asked quietly.

"If Pharaoh lives up to his word. What does the Sister of the King's Chief Wife believe?"

Kiya made a dismissive noise in her throat. "What do *little girls* know about war?"

Horemheb fixed Kiya with his eyes. "Apparently, more than the wives of Pharaohs." He pushed himself from the table and walked away. Then I stood up without waiting for Ipu to bring my dinner and announced that I had an urge to see the gardens.

Outside, a full moon had risen above the Garden of Horus. The lights from the palace illuminated the night and a fountain tinkled musically in the distance. I could hear laughter and the sound of happy feasting inside.

"I thought you might be here."

I froze. A man emerged from the shadows and I thought of running. It had been foolish to come out to the gardens alone. But when he stepped into the light, I saw who it was. I remembered our last conversation and smiled coolly. "Good evening, General Nakhtmin."

"Not even surprised to see me?" he asked.

He was wearing a long kilt and a short cloak of heavy linen. I studied him in the pale moonlight. "No. Should I be?"

"I just arrived in Memphis. Not even Pharaoh knows that I am here."

"But Nefertiti said . . ."

He shrugged. "They were warned of my coming."

"Then you should be inside." I indicated the palace. "They will want to speak with you at once."

The general laughed. "Do you think that Pharaoh cares what his mother has to say on his politics?"

I thought a moment. "No."

"Then what does it matter if I'm in there pretending to be enjoying myself, or out here with a beautiful *miw-sher,* enjoying myself for real?"

I flushed deeply. *Miw-sher* was what my father called me. It was something you would call a kitten, not a woman. "Nefertiti is inside. You could still enjoy the company of a beautiful woman."

"So *this* is why you are angry with me. I wondered—"

"I'm not angry with you at all," I said defensively.

"Good. Then you won't object to a stroll around the gardens."

He offered his arm and I took it hesitantly. "You will get me into a great deal of trouble if my sister finds us out here," I warned, but I enjoyed the feel of his arm against mine and didn't pull away.

"She won't come out here."

I glanced up at him. "And how do you know?"

"Because right now she's more concerned with building a temple to Aten."

It was true. I doubted if anyone at the feast was missing me at all. "So how is it in Thebes?" I asked glumly.

"Like Memphis. Full of politics," he said. "Someday I will leave it all behind and retire in a peaceful village somewhere." He looked at me in the moonlight. "And you? What are the plans for the Sister of the King's Chief Wife?"

I was fourteen, old enough to marry and run a household of my own. I pressed my lips together. "Whatever my father decides for me."

The general said nothing. I think he might have been disappointed with my answer. "They say you are a healer," he observed, changing the subject.

I shook my head earnestly. "I simply learned the use of a few herbs in Akhmim."

He smiled. "What's this, then?" he asked, bending down and picking a leaf from a small green plant. I didn't want to answer, but he held it higher, waiting.

"Thyme. With honey it can cure coughs." I couldn't help myself, and Nakhtmin laughed. We were at the edge of the garden. In a few steps, we would be at the palace.

"You don't belong here," he said, looking at the open doors to the Great Hall. "You belong with nicer people."

My voice rose with indignation. "Are you saying—"

"I'm saying none of that, *miw-sher.* But these games are not for you." We stopped at the verge of the courtyard. "I leave tomorrow morning," he said. He paused, and then added quietly, "Be careful here, my lady. Let history forget your name. For if your deeds are to live in eternity, you will have to become exactly what your family wants you to be."

"And what is that?" I demanded.

"A slave to the throne."

I sat in Nefertiti's chamber because she had called me there, and I watched her undress, flinging her expensive sheath to the floor. She held out her arms for me to slip on her robe, and I wondered if I was a slave to the throne. I was certainly a slave to Nefertiti.

"Mutny? Mutny, are you listening to me?"

"Of course."

"Then why haven't you said anything? I just said that tomorrow we are going to see the temple and you . . ." She sucked in her breath. "You were thinking of the general," she accused. "I saw you come into the Great Hall with him last night!"

I turned away so she wouldn't see my blush.

"Well, put him out of your mind," she snapped. "He's not a favorite with Amunhotep and you won't be seen with him."

"I won't?" I stood up, suddenly angry. "I'm fourteen years old. What gives you the right to tell me who to see?"

We stared at each other and the lines grew tight around her mouth. "I am Queen of Egypt. This is not like in Akhmim when we were just girls. I am the ruler of the wealthiest kingdom in the world and you will not be responsible for bringing me down!"

I gathered my courage and shook my head fiercely. "Then leave me out of it." I moved toward the door, but she barred my exit.

"Where are you going?"

"Back to my courtyard."

"You can't!" she exclaimed.

I laughed. "So, what? You're going to stand here all night?"

"Yes."

We stared at each other, then the tears welled in her eyes. I reached out my hand, but she waved it away. She walked over to the bed and threw herself down on it. "You want me to be by myself? Is that it?"

I went and sat down next to her. "Nefertiti, you have Amunhotep. You have Father—"

"*Father.* Father loves me because I am the daughter with ambition and cunning. It's you he respects. It's you he talks to."

"He talks to me because I listen."

"And so do I!"

"No. You *don't* listen. You wait until someone says what you want to hear and then you pay attention. And you don't take Father's advice. You don't take anyone's advice."

"Why should I? Why should I be a sheep?"

I sat silently. "You have Amunhotep," I pointed out again.

"Amunhotep," she repeated. "Amunhotep is an ambitious dreamer. And tonight he'll be with Kiya, whose vision doesn't extend beyond the end of her crooked nose!"

I laughed because it was true, and she reached out her hand to touch my knee.

"Stay with me, Mutny."

"I'll stay for tonight."

"Don't do me any favors!"

"I'm not. I don't want you to be alone," I said earnestly.

She smiled smugly and poured two cups of wine. I ignored her self-satisfied expression and sat next to her at the brazier, drawing a blanket over both of our knees.

"Why doesn't Amunhotep like the general?" I asked her.

Nefertiti knew immediately which general I meant. "He chose to stay in Thebes rather than come to Memphis." The fire from the brazier cast golden shadows on her face. She was beautiful even without her jewels and crown.

I protested. "But not every general could come to Memphis with us."

"Well, Amunhotep distrusts him." She swirled the wine in her cup. "And for that reason you can't be seen with him. Those who were loyal came with him to Memphis."

"But what happens if the Elder dies? Won't the army join together again in Thebes?"

She shook her head. "I doubt we'll be going back to Thebes."

I nearly dropped my cup. "What do you mean? Someday the Elder will die," I exclaimed. "Perhaps not soon, but someday—"

"And when he does, Amunhotep will not return."

"Has he said this? Have you told Father?"

"No, he hasn't said this. But I've come to know him." She looked into the flames. "He will want his own city. One outside of Memphis that will stand as a testament to our reign." She couldn't stop herself from smiling.

"But don't you want to return to Thebes?" I asked her. "It's the center of Egypt. It's the center of everything."

Nefertiti's smile widened. "No, Mutny. *We're* the center of everything. Once the Elder dies, wherever we are the court will follow."

"But Thebes—"

"Is just a city. Imagine if Amunhotep could build an even bigger capital." Her eyes widened. "He would be the greatest builder in the history of Egypt. We could inscribe our names on every doorpost. Every temple, every shrine, every library, even the art would be testaments to our lives. Yours, too." Her black hair shone in the firelight. "You could have your own building, immortalize your name, and the gods would never forget you."

I heard Nakhtmin's voice in my mind, that to be forgotten was the greatest gift that history could give. But that couldn't be true. How would the gods know what you had done? We both sat in silence, thinking. The fire in the depths of Nefertiti's eyes faded and her expression became haunted.

"We're so different, you and I. It must be because I am more like my mother, and you are more like yours."

I shifted uncomfortably. I didn't like it when she spoke about our different pasts.

"I wonder what my mother was like. Imagine, Mutny, I have

nothing left of her. No image, no cloth, not even a scroll. Just a handful of rings."

"She was a Mitanni princess. In her homeland, she must be painted on her father's tomb."

"Even so, I have no image of her in Egypt." Her gaze grew determined. "I will never let that happen to me. I will carve my image in every corner of this land. I want my children to remember me until the sands disappear from Egypt and the pyramids crumble to the earth."

I stared at my sister in the firelight and felt a deep sorrow. I had never known this about her before.

◙ ◙ ◙

The bulk of Amun's treasures had been secured in heavily bound chests, then stacked carelessly against the walls of the Audience Chamber. There were still golden sandals, leopard pelts, and crowns with gems the size of my fist piled in corners and strewn across tables. Where would it all go? It couldn't be kept safely in this public chamber, not even with three dozen guards watching over it.

"We should fetch Maya," Nefertiti suggested, "to design a treasury."

Amunhotep warmed to the idea at once. "The queen is right. I want a treasury built to withstand the sieges of time. Panahesi, find Maya."

Panahesi rose quickly. "Of course, Your Highness. And if Pharaoh desires, I would be happy to oversee the construction."

My father shot Nefertiti a swift glance and my sister said lightly, "There will be plenty of time for that, Vizier." She looked at Amunhotep. "First, we will find a sculptor to place your image at every corner. Amunhotep the Builder, guarding the wealth and treasures of Egypt."

Panahesi glowered. "Your Highness—"

But Amunhotep was carried away with the vision. "He can sculpt you as well. We'll be Egypt's mightiest rulers overlooking its greatest treasury."

Panahesi turned white at the thought of Nefertiti's image in the treasury of Egypt.

"Shall we see that a sculptor is summoned?" my father asked.

"Yes," Amunhotep commanded. "Do so at once."

Chapter Eleven

1350 BCE

Akhet, Season of Overflow

THE TREASURY TOOK precedence even over the Temple of Aten.

By the beginning of Thoth, a majestic two-story pavilion reared up in granite splendor next to the palace. The dust had not settled across the courtyard before Maya pushed open the heavy metal doors and we all stood in awe of what the architect had accomplished in so little time. From all four corners of the treasury, Amunhotep and Nefertiti stared down at us, larger than life, larger than the Elder's most magnificent statues in Thebes.

"Who created these?" I gaped, and Maya grinned at me.

"A sculptor named Thutmose."

It was magnificent. The statues were so tall, so breathtaking, it was as if we were saplings in a forest of sycamores. The group of viziers and courtiers behind us went quiet. Even Panahesi had nothing to say. Nefertiti walked up to one of the statues; her head reached as high as its foot. Her likeness was uncanny: the thin nose, the small mouth, and the wide black eyes under highly arched brows. She ran her hand down the sandstone skirt and mouthed to me, "I wish Kiya was here."

Amunhotep announced grandly, "Now we shall begin construction on the Temple of Aten."

My father stared as if this wasn't to be believed, but Maya looked unsurprised.

"Certainly, Your Highness."

"And Vizier Panahesi will oversee the building."

***

There was another meeting in my chamber. With the treasury built, the risk could not be run of letting Panahesi be placed in charge of its gold. Construction on the Temple of Aten would begin in Thoth, but once Panahesi's job overseeing the work was done, he would make a bid to be treasurer again.

"You will have to do something to stop it," my father said simply.

"We can give him a different job. Something that takes him out of the palace again. What about ambassador? He could travel to Mitanni—"

My father shook his head dismissively. "He will never agree."

"Who *cares* what he will agree to?" Nefertiti hissed.

My father hesitated. "We could make him the High Priest of Aten," he thought aloud.

Nefertiti recoiled. "Of my temple?" she cried.

"Would you rather him be treasurer," my father countered, "in charge of Egypt's wealth with a possible prince waiting to be delivered? No, we will make him High Priest of Aten," he decided, standing swiftly. "Nefertiti, you've had a dream. You've had a dream in which you saw Panahesi as the High Priest of Aten."

Nefertiti saw at once what he was doing. "He was dressed in leopard's robes. There was a golden light surrounding him. It must have been a sign."

My father smiled and she laughed. They were a perfect pair of hyenas.

◙ ◙ ◙

That afternoon, Nefertiti waited until the Audience Chamber was filled to announce to the court that she'd had a dream. "A vivid dream," she called it, and Panahesi looked sharply up at the dais. My sister continued. "A dream so realistic that when I awoke, I thought it had truly happened."

Amunhotep sat forward on his throne, intrigued. "Shall we call for a priest? Was it to do with me?"

Below the dais, Kiya and her ladies gathered closer together, whispering.

Nefertiti played coy. "It was to do with all of Egypt," she explained.

"Send for a priest!" Amunhotep cried, and my father was at the door before Panahesi could even stand.

"Any particular priest, Your Majesty?"

Amunhotep's lip curled. Until the Temple of Aten could be built, he must find his priests in the Temple of Amun. "An Interpreter of Dreams."

When my father disappeared, Panahesi glowered, sensing something in the air. "Your Highness," he offered, "wouldn't it be wise to hear the dream first?"

Nefertiti laughed easily. "Why, Vizier? Are you afraid I might dream something that would embarrass the king?" She swept her long lashes in Amunhotep's direction and he smiled.

"I trust my wife in all things, Vizier. Even her dreams."

But Kiya, with her growing belly, would not be outdone by Nefertiti. "Perhaps His Highness would like music while he waits?" If Nefertiti could please Pharaoh with a dream, she would please him with music. She waved a bangled wrist in the direction of the musicians who followed the court wherever it went, and they struck up a song. There was no mention of the petitioners who lined up outside the palace or of the viziers who wanted to know what should be done with Horemheb or the Hittites who were encroaching on Egypt's territories. Nefertiti's dream had taken precedence. Nefertiti's dream and Kiya's music. *The only time nothing gets done,* I thought, *is when Pharaoh decides to reign within his Audience Chamber.*

Amunhotep sat on his throne as the harpists played, then the doors to the Audience Chamber swung open and my father returned. Behind him, a robed priest of Amun swept across the tiles. My father announced, "The Interpreter of Dreams."

The old man bowed. "I am the priest Menkheperre."

Nefertiti spoke. "I've had a dream, Seer, that we want you to interpret."

"Please repeat it, Your Majesty, along with any details that you can remember."

Nefertiti stood. "I dreamed of leopard's robes beneath the sun," she said. I looked nervously at Panahesi, who met my eyes and knew immediately from my glance that some pot was being stirred.

"You have dreamed of the High Priest of Aten," Menkheperre announced solemnly, and there were whisperings all around the chamber.

"I also dreamed that a vizier was picking up these robes, and that as he put them on the sun shone brighter. So bright that the rays were almost blinding."

Everyone in the court sat transfixed and Menkheperre cried triumphantly, "A sign! Definitely a sign!"

Amunhotep stood from his throne. "Is the man from your dream standing here now?"

We all followed Nefertiti's gaze as it fell on Panahesi, then we all looked back at the priest.

Menkheperre spread his hands, and I wondered how much of my

father's gold might be found beneath his robes as he pronounced, "The meaning is obvious, Your Highness. Aten has chosen."

"No!" Panahesi stumbled from his chair. "Your Majesty, this was only a dream. Nothing more than a dream!"

Amunhotep stepped down from the dais, placing his hands lovingly on Panahesi's shoulders. "Aten has chosen."

Panahesi looked at me and then at my father, whose face was a perfect mask.

"Congratulations, Your Holiness," my father replied with an irony that only Panahesi understood. "The god has chosen."

Once we were outside the Audience Chamber, Kiya gloated to me. "My father is High Priest of Aten," she said, not seeing my family's hand in it. "With a prince in the making, now there will be no seat of Egypt my family won't fill. And the High Priest of Aten collects the tithes," she added. "Your sister has just helped us up the dais toward the throne."

"No, she has just pushed you down," I replied. "Your father may collect the taxes," I said, "but it is my father who will count them."

Kiya stared at me blankly.

"Before this meeting, Vizier Ay was named treasurer."

Chapter Twelve

seventh of Thoth

WE STOOD ON the top of a barren hill overlooking the Nile as it coursed through Memphis. A warm wind tore at our sheaths, snapping our short cloaks in the air.

"The temple will be two stories high and two hills across." Maya pointed across the sunstruck dunes. Their crests vaulted one after another, cones of white sand shimmering in the heat.

"Where will the materials come from?" Nefertiti asked.

"The men will use the rocks from the Eastern Quarry."

Amunhotep was impatient. "How long will it take?"

The wind picked up, drowning out the builder's words. Panahesi and my father moved closer.

"Six seasons, if the men can work daily."

Amunhotep's face darkened. "In six seasons, I could be assassinated!" he shouted. Since he had executed the High Priest of Amun, this was his fear. Everywhere he went, hired guards from Nubia accompanied him. They stood outside his door while he slept and hovered like ravens behind his chair while he ate. They were here now, clustered at the bottom of the hill, their spears ready to dispense with any enemy of the king. In the halls of the palace, Nefertiti had whispered to me that Amunhotep was afraid that the people didn't love him. "Why?" I'd asked her, and her look plainly answered. It was because of what had happened to the High Priest of Amun. Now Amunhotep could feel the people's anger in the streets, and none of his viziers were courageous enough to tell him this was true. But our father had warned Nefertiti. "How can you know?" she'd railed in my chamber, and he had produced a drawing found in the marketplace; it had the body of a serpent and the head of the king swallowing up a statue of the great god Amun.

Now Amunhotep paced on the top of the hill and his voice brooked no argument. "Six seasons is not acceptable!" he raged.

"What would you have me do, Your Majesty? There are only so many workers skilled enough to build a temple—"

Amunhotep set his jaw. "Then we shall use the army."

Nefertiti stepped forward, and her voice grew excited. "If soldiers helped build the temple, how soon could it be done?"

Maya frowned. "How many soldiers do we speak of, Your Highness?"

"Three thousand," Amunhotep replied immediately, not thinking about the war he had promised Horemheb or the borders of Egypt that would have to be defended.

"Three thousand?" Maya tried to hide his surprise. "It might take . . ." He paused a moment to calculate. "With so many men, it might only take three seasons."

Amunhotep nodded decisively. "Then every soldier who has come to Memphis will be employed tonight."

"What of Egypt's borders?" my father asked firmly. "They will need to be defended. The palace will still need to be guarded. Take a thousand," he said, though I knew the suggestion pained him. He passed a warning glance to my sister, who nodded.

"Yes. One thousand. We don't want Egypt's borders to go defenseless."

Amunhotep submitted, then looked to Maya. "But you will inform the men tonight."

"And Horemheb?" my father warned. "He will not be pleased."

"Then let him not be pleased!" Amunhotep snapped.

My father shook his head. "He could turn the army against you."

Panahesi was immediately at Amunhotep's side. "Pay the army more than they could ever take in booty from the Hittites," he suggested. "Placate them. There is more than enough money from the taxation."

"Good. *Good*." Amunhotep grinned. "The men will not leave me after what I'll pay."

"And the general?" my father asked again.

Amunhotep narrowed his eyes. "What general?"

The next day, the Audience Chamber was crowded with petitioners waiting to see Pharaoh. The building of the greatest temple ever raised had already begun and messengers arrived bearing scrolls from the construction site. While Kiya waddled through the palace halls, heaving herself from chair to chair like a heifer—as Nefertiti described it—servants came and went with details and measurements from the builder Maya. Then the doors to the Audience Chamber burst open and Amunhotep tensed. The guards closed around him and Horemheb laughed.

"I fought against the Nubians when I was nothing more than a boy," he sneered. "You think fifteen guards can stop me?" He advanced on the throne. "You *swore* to me that there would be war. I gave you the temples of Amun!"

Amunhotep smiled. "And I am very grateful."

If I were king, I wouldn't taunt this general, I thought.

At the base of the dais, Horemheb stiffened. "How long do you plan on using the soldiers of Egypt as workers?"

"Three seasons," Nefertiti replied from her throne.

Horemheb's gaze slid from Amunhotep to my sister. I shuddered, but she didn't shrink from his glare.

"Egypt must have its borders fully defended. That means every soldier," Horemheb cautioned. "The Hittites—"

"I don't care about Hittites!" Amunhotep walked down the dais to stand in front of Horemheb, knowing that in a room full of guards he was safe.

Horemheb inhaled, the leather of his pectoral straining against his chest. "You have lied to me."

"I gave your soldiers better, less-dangerous jobs."

"To build a temple to Aten? You defile Amun!"

"No." Amunhotep smiled dangerously. "*You* defiled Amun."

Horemheb's rage brought out the veins in his arms and neck. "We will be attacked," he warned. "The Hittites will come for Egypt, and when your men are better builders than soldiers you will be sorry."

Amunhotep moved closer to Horemheb so that only I, sitting on the lowest tier of the dais, could hear what passed between them. "The men follow you the way they followed my brother. I don't know why. But you will follow Aten. You will serve him, you will serve Pharaoh, or you will be stripped of your position and find yourself without a friend in Egypt. Horemheb the Friendless, they will call you. And anyone caught associating with you will be killed." He straightened. "Do you understand?"

Horemheb said nothing.

"Do you understand?" Amunhotep shouted, and his voice rang in my ears.

Horemheb clenched his jaw. "I understand you well, *Your Majesty*."

"Then go."

We watched the general leave the chamber, and I thought, *It is a very foolish thing he's done today.*

Amunhotep surveyed the chaotic scene in the Audience Chamber and declared, "I'm finished!" He looked sharply at the group of viziers clustered at the bottom of the dais. "Where is Panahesi?" he demanded.

"At the site of the new temple," my father said, hiding his pleasure.

"Good." Amunhotep turned to my sister and smiled indulgently. "Come. Let's walk in the gardens. Your father can deal with all of this." He waved a bangled arm to indicate the long line of petitioners outside the chamber.

Nefertiti looked at me, and it went without saying that I would be going, too.

We walked through the courtyard to the wide sycamore trees whose figs were ready to be harvested. "Did you know that Mutny can pick out any herb in the garden and name it?" Nefertiti asked.

Amunhotep regarded me suspiciously. "Are you a healer?"

"I learned a bit in Akhmim, Your Majesty."

Nefertiti laughed. "More than a bit. She's a little physician. Remember the boat?" Amunhotep stiffened, and I wondered why Nefertiti was reminding him about such a thing. "When I have a child, she will be one of my healers," Nefertiti said, and there was something in her voice that made the Pharaoh and me both turn.

"Are you with child?" Amunhotep whispered.

Nefertiti's smile widened. "The first son of Egypt."

I gasped, covering my mouth, and Amunhotep let out a great shout and hugged Nefertiti to his chest. "A *family,* and no child shall ever be adored as much as ours," he swore. He put his hand gently on my sister's belly. I thought with incredulity that at seventeen, Nefertiti would be a mother to a Pharaoh of Egypt.

She beamed at me. "Well?"

I didn't know what to say. "The gods have blessed you," I gushed, but I also felt fear. She would have a family now, a husband and children to pay attention to. "Have you told Father?" I asked.

"No." She was still smiling. "But I want my child blessed in Aten's temple," she said eagerly, and I stared at her in shock.

Amunhotep's face grew serious. "Then the temple must be finished within nine months," he said. "They must finish by Pachons."

▣ ▣ ▣

Inside the palace, there had already been whispers among the servants. There had been no blood found on Nefertiti's sheets and no stains on her sheaths. Of course, I didn't know. I was a courtyard away from her now, but Ipu wasn't surprised.

"You knew and you didn't even tell me?" I cried. Ipu lifted my robe over my head and put on another one for the night's celebration.

"I didn't know you wanted me to pass on gossip, my lady."

"Of course I do!"

Ipu smiled so widely her dimples showed. "Then all my lady had to do was ask."

Preparation for a celebration in the Great Hall officially began after Nefertiti told Amunhotep that she was carrying his child, but the dozens of tables and flickering oil lamps looked to have been prearranged. An army of servants must have decorated all afternoon, and every cook in Memphis must have started preparing dishes the same hour the news arrived in the palace. The dais, with its three steps leading to the Horus thrones, was bestrewn with flowers. On each step, servants had placed two chairs, high backed and well cushioned, for the highest members of the royal court. I would be sitting in one of those chairs, as would my mother and father, High Priest Panahesi, and, if she came, Princess Kiya. The last chair would be reserved for a chosen person of honor.

Once it came to eating, we would all ascend to the royal table where, most nights, the royal couple ate alone at the top of the glittering dais. But this night we would join them. This night was a celebration of our family. The royal family of Egypt.

Trumpeters announced our entrance to the room and we swept through the hall, making sure all the viziers could see how many golden bangles we were wearing and how many rings my father had donned. Kiya gave the excuse of pregnancy, but Panahesi walked with us in procession to the dais, and from beneath the Horus thrones my mother couldn't stop beaming.

"Your sister is carrying the heir to the throne of Egypt," she said in a voice full of wonder. "He will be Pharaoh someday."

"If it's a boy," I replied.

My father smiled sharply. "It had better be. The midwives say Kiya is carrying a son and this family can't afford a pretender to the throne."

The Great Hall was filled with talking, laughing people. Every noble in Memphis had come. Nefertiti descended the dais and held out her arm for me to walk the room with her. She glowed in her triumph.

"You can't walk alone?" I asked her.

"Of course, I *can*. But I need you."

She didn't need me, not really, but I hid my pleasure and gave her my arm. Heads turned as Ay's daughters made their way across the chamber, and for the first time I felt it: the giddiness of being both beautiful and powerful. The men stared at Nefertiti, but their eyes lingered on me as well.

"Such a beautiful little girl." Nefertiti chucked a woman's fat child under the chin. I stared at my sister. She couldn't possibly think the child was beautiful. But the mother smiled proudly and bowed more deeply than any of the other women at court.

"Thank you, my queen. *Thank you.*"

"Nefertiti," I protested.

She pinched my arm. "Just keep smiling," she instructed.

Then I saw that Amunhotep was watching us from his throne. Nefertiti and the sister of Nefertiti, charming and lovely and desirable and wanted. He descended the dais. He'd had enough of watching her bestow her graces on everyone but him.

"The most beautiful woman in Egypt," he avowed, pulling her away from me. He escorted her back to her ebony throne and she glowed.

▣ ▣ ▣

The child was all we heard about.

In the baths, at the Arena, inside the Great Hall, Nefertiti reminded everyone that she was carrying the heir to Egypt's throne. By the middle of Thoth, I believe even Mother was tired of hearing it. "It's all she ever talks about," I confided, sitting forward on the stone bench in the garden, watching the cats hunt mice in the tall grass.

"It's what she came here to do," my mother said. "To give Egypt a son."

"And to control the prince," I said pointedly. We stared into the lake, watching the lotus blossoms dance across the surface, their cupping flowers mirrored in the water.

"Let's just hope that it's a son," was all my mother said. "The people will forgive anything if there's a prince waiting for the throne and they know there won't be bloodshed for the crown. They may even forget that while the royal family is building temples in Memphis the Hittites are marching on Egyptian land in Kadesh."

I glanced across at her, surprised, but she said nothing more on it.

▣ ▣ ▣

"Get dressed, Mutny. We're going to the temple."

I started from my sheets. "The Temple of Amun?"

Nefertiti gave a dismissive sniff. "The Temple of *Aten*. They have finished the courtyard and I want to see it."

"They finished in fifteen days?"

"Of course. There are thousands of men working. Hurry!"

I rushed to find my kilt and sandals and a belt. "What about Father?"

"He will stay in the Audience Chamber enforcing Egypt's laws." My sister added proudly, "The perfect trio. Pharaoh, his queen, and the competent vizier."

"And Mother?" I slipped on my kilt.

"She's coming."

"But what will Tiye think?"

My sister hesitated. I thought there was real regret in her voice when she admitted, "Tiye is angry with me." Shame colored her cheeks. After all, Queen Tiye had been the one to place the Horus crown on her head. But now Nefertiti owed Amunhotep her loyalty, not Tiye. I knew she saw it this way, but she never discussed with me what the choice had cost her or the sleepless nights she had, her head on her palm, looking out at the moon and wondering how eternity would echo her decisions. She sat on my bed now and watched me dress. She used to make fun of how long my legs were and how dark my skin was. But she didn't have time for children's insults now. "She even sent messengers to threaten him. But what can she do? He was crowned. He will be Pharaoh of Upper and Lower Egypt as soon as the Elder dies."

"Which could be years," I warned, hoping the gods didn't hear the way her voice rose with hope when she spoke about Pharaoh's death. I followed her through the hall, and when we entered the courtyard I turned to Nefertiti in surprise. "Who are all these armed men?"

Amunhotep strode through the carved sandstone gates and answered me. "I must have protection, and your sister as well. I don't trust my father's army."

"But these men are part of the army," I pointed out. "If the army can't be trusted—"

"The *generals* can't be trusted," Amunhotep snapped. "The soldiers—*these* soldiers—will do as they're told." He stepped up into his gilded chariot, holding out his hand to help my sister. Then he cracked the whip in the air and the horses took off.

"Nefertiti!" I cried and turned to my mother. "Is it safe for her to be riding so fast?" I could hear Nefertiti's laughter above the horses' hooves and watched her disappear into the distance.

My mother shook her head. "Of course not. But who is going to stop her?"

The armed guards ushered us quickly into our own chariot, and it was a short ride to the site of the new Temple of Aten. When it reared into view, it was as though we had stepped into the midst of a city that had come under siege. Sandstone blocks lay scattered and soldiers picked their way through half-built debris, grunting and heaving and shouting orders. Panahesi, his long cloak billowing, stood with his arms folded over his chest, barking commands to the men. As my sister had promised, the courtyard had already been erected, and pillars, carved in Nefertiti and Amunhotep's likeness, were being pulled into place. The royal couple descended from their chariot and Panahesi rushed over, bowing.

"Your Highness." He saw my sister and tried to hide his disappointment. "Your Majesty. How kind of you to have come all the way here."

"We plan to supervise the building until it is done," Nefertiti said firmly, surveying the site. Although it appeared to be chaos, at a second glance, the land seemed to be divided into four distinct sections: the painters, the carvers, the movers, and the builders.

Amunhotep flipped his cloak from his shoulders and looked around. "Have the men noticed our arrival?"

Panahesi hesitated. "Your Highness?"

"Have the men noticed our arrival?" he shouted. "No one is bowing!"

The workers around us stopped and Panahesi cleared his throat. "I thought Your Highness wanted the temple to the glorious Aten finished as quickly as possible?"

"*Nothing* is more important than Pharaoh!" His voice echoed across the busy courtyards. I saw General Horemheb in the background, his face filled with quiet menace. Then the hammers stopped and the soldiers immediately fell to one knee. Only one man remained standing. An anger bright as fire flashed across Amunhotep's face. He moved forward and the crowds stumbled back to make way for him. Nefertiti inhaled and I stepped closer to her. "What will he do?"

"I don't know."

Amunhotep closed the distance between himself and Horemheb. They stood at the same height, but only one had the love of the army. "Why don't you kneel before the representative of Aten?"

"You put these men in jeopardy, *Your Highness.* The most elite of your fighting force is here. Men who ride chariots into battle are carving your likeness into stone when they should be defending our borders from the Hittites. This is not a wise use of trained men."

"*I* will determine what is wise! You are nothing more than a soldier and I am Pharaoh of Egypt." Amunhotep stiffened. "You will bow before me."

Horemheb remained standing and Amunhotep's hand flew to the dagger at his side. He stepped forward threateningly. "Tell me," he said, drawing the knife from its sheath, "do you think your men would rise against me if I were to kill you here?" He glanced around him nervously. "I think they would continue to kneel, even as your blood soaked into the sand."

Horemheb inhaled. "Then try it, Your Highness."

Amunhotep hesitated. He looked around at the thousands of

soldiers whose powerful bodies were clad in kilts, but were weaponless. Then he sheathed his dagger and stepped away. "Why don't you obey me?" he demanded.

"We struck a deal," Horemheb replied. "I obeyed His Highness and His Highness betrayed Egypt."

"I betrayed no one," Amunhotep said viciously. "*You* betray me. You and this army. You think I don't know that you were friends with Tuthmosis? That you were loyal to him?"

Horemheb said nothing.

"You would have knelt before my brother!" Amunhotep cried. "Tell me you wouldn't have knelt before Tuthmosis."

Horemheb remained silent and suddenly Amunhotep's fist lashed out, connecting with the general's stomach. Horemheb sucked in his breath, but his legs didn't buckle. Amunhotep looked quickly at the soldiers around him, whose bodies went tense, ready to defend their general. Then he grabbed Horemheb's shoulder and whispered savagely, "You are relieved of this duty. Go back to my father. But you would do well to remember that when the Elder dies, I will be Pharaoh of Upper Egypt as well."

The crowds parted as Horemheb moved toward his chariot. Then the soldiers turned as one to look at Amunhotep.

"Resume the building!" Panahesi shouted. "Resume!"

Even though it was early in the morning, a fire crackled in the brazier inside my chamber. Nefertiti sat in a gilded chair nearest the heat, the light of the flames illuminating the lapis eye between her breasts. Our father sat back, his fingers under his chin. The rest of the palace was asleep.

"Is there nothing you can do to manage his temper?"

The fire snapped and hissed. Nefertiti sighed. "I do what I can. He hates the army."

"They are what keep him in power," my father said sternly. "Horemheb will not forget what he did."

"Horemheb is in Thebes," Nefertiti replied.

"And when the Elder dies?"

"That could be another ten years." She was using my words, even though I knew she didn't believe them.

"Without the army, Egypt is weak. You are fortunate that in Thebes there are still generals who prepare their soldiers for war."

"They will only be building for three seasons," she defended.

"Three?" My father rose in anger. "It was six and now it's three? How can an army complete a temple in a year?"

"I am with child!" Nefertiti clasped her stomach. "He *has* to be consecrated on the altar of Aten." My father glared at her. "It's Amunhotep's wish," she added. "And if I don't do it, then Kiya will. What if she gives him a son?" she asked desperately.

"She will be brought to bed within seven days," my father warned. "If it's a prince, he will celebrate. There will be feasting and processions."

Nefertiti closed her eyes, willing herself to be calm, but my father shook his head.

"Prepare yourself for it. These next few days must belong to Kiya."

I could see the determination in my sister's face. "I'm going with him this morning to the Arena," she declared. She turned to the closet where she kept her riding clothes and called for Merit.

"You're going to ride with him?" I exclaimed. "But you haven't ridden in days!"

"And now I will. It was a mistake to think I could settle comfortably into pregnancy."

She tore through her closet until Merit came. Even at this hour of the morning, her body servant's kohl was perfect and her linen crisp. Nefertiti said sharply, "My gauntlets and helmet. Quickly. Before Amunhotep's awake and wants to ride."

My father confronted Merit. "Is she endangering the child?"

Nefertiti glared at Merit from behind my father's shoulder, and Merit said immediately, "It's early, Vizier. Only a few months."

Nefertiti tightened the belt around her waist. "Perhaps if I ride my blood will quicken and make it a son."

▣ ▣ ▣

On the twenty-eighth of Thoth, Ipu came running into my chamber where Nefertiti and I were playing Senet.

"It's happening!" she cried. "Kiya is having the child."

We both scrambled out of our chairs and rushed down the hall to our parents' chamber. My mother and father were sitting together, speaking quickly in hushed tones.

"She is going to have a boy," Nefertiti whispered.

My father looked at me, as if I had told her something I shouldn't have. "Why should you say that?"

"Because I dreamed it last night. She is going to give birth to a Prince of Egypt!"

My mother stood up and shut the door. The palace was overrun with messengers who were waiting to make a proclamation to the kingdom.

Nefertiti panicked. "I can't let it happen! I *won't* let it happen."

"There's nothing you can do," my father said.

"There's always something I can do!" she proclaimed. Nefertiti added calculatingly, "When Amunhotep returns, tell him I'm not well."

My mother frowned, but my father saw what game she was playing at once. "How unwell?" he asked quickly.

"So unwell . . ." Nefertiti hesitated. "So unwell that I could die and lose the child."

My father looked to me. "You must confirm her story when he asks." He spun around and instructed Merit. "Take her to her room and bring her fruit. Don't leave her side until you see Pharaoh."

Merit bowed. "Of course, Vizier." I thought I saw a smile at the edge of her lips. She bowed to Nefertiti. "Shall we go, Your Highness?"

I remained at the door. "But what should I do?"

"Tend to your sister," my father said meaningfully. "And do as she asks."

We walked in procession to Nefertiti's chamber, slowly, so that if anyone should see us, they would know something was wrong with the queen. In her room, Nefertiti lay like an invalid. "My sheath," she said. "Spread it for me."

I gave her a long look.

"Across my legs and over the sides of the bed."

"This is terrible, what you are doing," I told her. "You've already displaced Kiya in Amunhotep's affections. Isn't that enough?"

"I'm sick!" she protested.

"You're taking the only time that she has!"

We looked at each other, but there was no shame in Nefertiti's gaze.

I sat by her bed while Ipu stood guard outside the door, harassing servants for news from Kiya's birthing chamber. We waited all evening. Then, finally, Ipu came running, and when she opened the door her face was grave.

"Well? What is it?" Nefertiti sat forward in her bed. "What is it?"

Ipu lowered her head. "A prince. Prince Nebnefer of Egypt."

Nefertiti sank back on her pillows, and now her face became truly pale. "Send word to Pharaoh that his Chief Wife is ill," she said immediately. "Tell him I may die. That I may lose the child."

I pressed my lips together.

"Don't look like that," she commanded.

⧈ ⧈ ⧈

When word reached Amunhotep, he came at once. "What is it? What's wrong with her?" he cried.

I thought that the lies would stick in my throat, but they tumbled out quickly when I saw his fear. "I don't know, Your Highness. She took ill this morning, and now all she can do is sleep."

Terror darkened his face and his joy at having a son was gone. "What did you eat? Was it prepared by your servant?"

Nefertiti's answer was soft and weak. "Yes . . . yes, I'm sure it was."

He pressed his hand to her cheek and turned to me. "What happened? You must know. The two of you are thick as thieves. Just tell me what happened!" I saw that he was not trying to be cruel. He was afraid. Genuinely afraid for his wife.

My heart raced. "It might have been the wine," I said quickly. "Or the cold. It's very cold outside."

Amunhotep glared across the room at the windows, and then at the linens on the bed. "Give me blankets!" he bellowed, and women came running. "Blankets and wool. Find the Vizier Ay. Have him bring the physician."

"No!" Nefertiti sat up.

Amunhotep brushed the hair from her brow. "You are unwell. You must see a physician."

"Mutny is all that I need."

"Your sister is not a physician!" Then he leaned across her bed and grabbed her arm desperately. "You *cannot* be ill. You *cannot* leave me."

She closed her eyes, her dark lashes fluttering against her high pale cheeks. "I hear you have a son," she said quietly and smiled, resting her small hand on her stomach.

"You are the only thing that matters to me. We are going to build monuments to the gods together," he swore.

"Yes. A temple to Aten." She smiled weakly, playing her part so well that tears welled in Amunhotep's eyes.

"Nefertiti!" His cry of anguish was so real that I felt sorry for him. He threw himself across her bed and I panicked.

"Stop it! Stop it or you will hurt the child!"

There was a knock on the door, and my father appeared with the physician at his side. Nefertiti passed him an anxious glance.

"Don't be afraid," my father said meaningfully. "He can only help."

Something passed between them, and she allowed the physician to draw blood from her arm. He swirled the dark liquid in a pan to see its color, and we all stood and waited for him to read the signs. The old man cleared his throat. He looked once at my father, nodding briefly, then at Pharaoh.

"What is it?" Amunhotep demanded.

The physician lowered his head. "I am afraid she is very ill, Your Highness."

The color drained from Amunhotep's face. His champion, his wife, his most ardent supporter, sick now with his child. Amunhotep stole a glance at his beloved Nefertiti, whose hair spilled over the pillows like black ink. She looked beautiful and eternal, like a sculpture in death. He turned on the physician. "You will do *everything possible,*" he commanded. "You will do *everything* in your power to bring her back."

"Of course," the man said quickly. "But she must have rest. Nothing must disturb her with the child. No terrible news, no—"

"Just heal her!"

The physician nodded vigorously and rushed to his bag, producing several bottles and a vial of ointment. I peered closer, to see if I could recognize them. What if they were dangerous? What if they truly made her sick? I passed a look to my father, whose face remained expressionless, and I realized what it must be. Rosemary water.

The physician administered the draft and we waited the rest of the night with my sister, watching her drift into sleep. My mother came, then Ipu and Merit brought fresh juices and linens. As the night wore on, my mother returned to her heated chamber while Amunhotep, my father, and I remained. But as I watched her repose,

I grew resentful. If she wasn't so selfish, my father and I wouldn't have to partake in such a charade. We wouldn't have to stand like sentinels around her bed, warming our hands by the fire while she tucked herself neatly into her covers and Amunhotep caressed her cheek. When even my father left, he turned and said significantly to me, "Watch her, Mutnodjmet." He closed the door, and Amunhotep went to stand over Nefertiti's bed.

"How ill is she?" the king of Egypt demanded. His face was long and angular in the shadows.

I swallowed my fear. "I am afraid for her, Your Highness." It wasn't a lie.

Amunhotep looked down at his sleeping queen. She was a perfect beauty, and I knew in my own life I would never be loved with such obsession. "The healers will bring her back," he vowed. "She is carrying our child. The future of Egypt."

Before I could stop myself, I had asked him, "What about Nebnefer, Your Highness?"

He looked at me strangely, as if he had forgotten about Kiya's heir. "She is Second Wife. Nefertiti is my queen, and she is loyal to me. She understands my vision of a greater Egypt. An Egypt that is guided by the Almighty Aten. Our children will embrace the sun and become the most powerful rulers the gods have ever blessed."

My voice caught in my throat. "And Amun?"

"Amun is *dead,*" he replied. "But I will resurrect my grandfather's dream of Pharaohs who aren't cowed by the power of the Amun priests. I will honor his name and be remembered forever for what I've done. What *we've* done," he said forcefully, looking down at Nefertiti, his battle consort, his staunchest ally. For any advance Kiya made, Nefertiti was there suggesting a new statue, a new courtyard, a glittering new temple.

He remained at her bedside the entire night. I watched him, wondering what would possess a man to destroy the gods of his people and raise in their place a protector no one had heard of. *Greed,* I thought. *His hatred of everything his father believes in, and his greed for power. Without the Amun priests, he will control everything.* I sat on a thickly cushioned chair and watched him caress my sister's cheek. He was tender, brushing his hand across her face, inhaling the lavender scent of her hair. When I fell asleep, he was still beside her, praying to Aten for a miracle.

When I awoke the next morning, my eyes felt like small weights in my head. Already at the door was a messenger with news from Thebes, dressed in lapis and gold. Yet Amunhotep would hear none of it. "No one is to disturb the queen," he said forcefully.

Panahesi appeared behind the messenger. "Your Highness, it is about the prince."

Amunhotep crossed the chamber. "What is it? The queen is ill."

Panahesi frowned, stepping into the room. "I am sorry to hear that Her Highness has taken ill." He peered across the antechamber to my sister's bedroom and narrowed his eyes. "Queen Tiye and the Elder have sent their blessings to your son," he continued. "The Birth Feast, with His Highness's permission, shall be tonight."

Amunhotep looked toward Nefertiti's chamber. Her door was open, and Panahesi could see her lying on the bed, Merit and Ipu fluttering around her.

"Go," my sister encouraged from the next room. "He is your son."

Amunhotep crossed back to her chamber and rested his hand on Nefertiti's. "I will not leave you."

"The gods have given you a son." She smiled wanly. "Go, give thanks." She beamed at him, all beauty and munificence, and I realized how craftily she had set up this scene: She was the one giving him permission to go, rather than Pharaoh telling her he would be gone in celebration. "Go," she whispered.

"I will think of you all night," he promised.

In the antechamber, Panahesi studied me. "I am so sorry to hear of the queen's illness. When did it happen?"

I felt my cheeks warm with shame. "Last night."

"About the same time as the prince's birth," he remarked.

I said nothing. Then Amunhotep emerged from Nefertiti's chamber and Panahesi tried a smile. "Shall we go to the feast, Your Highness?"

"Yes, but I am in no mood for celebration," he warned.

As soon as they were gone, Nefertiti sat up in her bed.

"Panahesi knows," I told her.

"Knows what?" she asked cheerfully, standing up and brushing her hair.

"He knows that you are lying."

She turned so quickly that the hem of her robe spun around her ankles. "Who says that I'm lying? Who says that I'm not ill?"

I remained silent. She could fool the entire court of Memphis, but she could never fool me. I watched her change into a fresh sheath and call on Merit for fruit. "How long will you keep this up?" I demanded.

A smile began at the edges of her lips. "Until the novelty of a new prince has worn off." She shrugged lightly. "And I am the center of Egypt again."

The novelty didn't last long—not with the building of the temple to Aten taking precedence over everything. And in three days, Nefertiti was miraculously well. The physician came and claimed it was a miracle. My father brought her *shedeh* from the winery and my mother squeezed out a few tears for the occasion. I was beginning to think we were more like entertainers than the ruling family of Egypt.

"What is the difference?" Nefertiti asked when I shared this thought with her. "Both require masks."

"But it's a lie. You lied. Don't you love him at all?"

She stopped in the courtyard, where the chariots were waiting to take us to the building site of the new temple. The cobra on her crown, nestled in her dark hair, glinted in the sun. "I love him as much as any woman ever will. You don't understand. You're only fourteen. But love means lying."

Amunhotep appeared through the arches, escorting my mother on his arm. They were laughing together, and I paused in shock.

"Your mother is a very charming woman," Amunhotep said warmly, and Nefertiti gave my mother her widest smile. *My mother.*

"Yes," she agreed. "The gods have blessed me in my family."

Pharaoh helped my mother into my chariot and she flushed with pride. Then he held out his arm for Nefertiti, and the procession began. A heavily armed cavalcade rode alongside us as we made for the site, the cool wind of Phaophi billowing their kilts. I wanted to lean over and ask my mother what Amunhotep had said to make her laugh. Then I thought that perhaps it was better I didn't know.

We began our ascent up a hill, far above the Nile and the naked sweep of earth. Amunhotep wanted the best vantage point to see his building, and when the chariots rolled to a sudden halt, armed guards fanned out in a circle around us. We descended and my mother whispered incredulously, "Great Osiris."

I stood frozen, stunned by the sprawling landscape dotted with pillars that pierced the sky. "They must never stop." Thousands of builders groaned under the weight of heavy columns, hoisting them up with ropes. The columned courtyard of Aten's temple had been completed, as well as a sanctuary and a granite altar. This time, because such heavy work was being done, Amunhotep didn't demand obeisance.

Panahesi appeared and bowed very low. "Your Highness." He smiled, flattering as always. He turned to my sister. "My queen," he said with less enthusiasm. "Shall we tour the god's temple?"

Nefertiti passed Amunhotep a triumphant glance, as if this had been her present to him, and we descended the small hill to stroll through the chaos. Nefertiti wanted to look at every pillar, every mosaic, every cut stone.

In the artists' quarters, Amunhotep stopped. "What is this?" he asked coldly.

A worker stood up and wiped the sweat from his brow. He was built like a charioteer, with thick arms and a wide chest. "We are working on statues of Your Highness." He bowed.

Amunhotep bent closer and saw the chiseled features of Pharaohs that artisans had been drawing for centuries. The perfect jaw, the long beard, the eyes rimmed in sweeps of kohl. He straightened and his face grew dark. "This isn't me."

The man faltered. He had depicted Pharaoh the way all Pharaohs had been depicted for the past thousand years.

"That isn't me!" Amunhotep shouted. "My artwork should reflect me, should it not?"

The artisan stared at him in horror, then went down on one knee, bowing his head. All around him work had come to a stop. "Of course, Your Highness."

Amunhotep whirled to face Panahesi. "Do you think I want the gods to confuse me with my father? With *Tuthmosis?*" he hissed.

Nefertiti stepped forward. "We shall have the rest of the sculptures done in our likeness," she commanded.

Panahesi inhaled. "The artisans use grids. They will have to—"

"Then do it," Nefertiti directed. She wrapped her arm around Amunhotep's, and Pharaoh nodded in agreement. Then she led him away through the dirt and stone. Panahesi glowered after her. Then he looked down at the man with the thick arms.

"Fix it!"

"But how, Your Holiness?"

"Go and find the best sculptors in Memphis," he shouted angrily. *"Now!"*

The artist looked between himself and the other men. "But we are considered the best," he replied.

"Then you will all be fired!" Panahesi raged. "You will find me an artist who can sculpt Pharaoh as he wishes or you will never work again."

The man panicked. "There *is* a sculptor in the city, Your Holiness. He is well renowned. He is flamboyant, but his work is—"

"Just find him and bring him to me," Panahesi seethed. He looked down at the image of Amunhotep as a Pharaoh no different in appearance than any other and lashed out with his foot, sending the carving toppling to the ground. "Don't ever depict His Highness like this again. No one is like him. No other Pharaoh in Egypt can compare."

I hurried to where Nefertiti and Amunhotep were walking. Men were working on an outer courtyard, raising pillars with carvings of the sun god etched into the yellow stone. So much work was being done by so many men. I stared across the courtyard—at the farthest end stood General Nakhtmin. He was staring back at me. Then Amunhotep moved toward him and his gaze flicked away. *What was he doing in Memphis? He belonged with the Elder in Thebes.* My mother, with her sharp eyes, had missed nothing.

"Was the general staring at you?" she asked.

I shook my head quickly. "No. I don't know."

She looked into my face. "General Nakhtmin is not liked by the king."

"So I've been warned."

"Do not think of falling in love with a soldier."

I looked down sharply. "Of course, I'm not in love!"

"Good. When the time comes, you will marry a nobleman who has Pharaoh's approval. It's the price we all pay for the crown," she said. I stared at her resentfully, thinking of her laughing with Amunhotep, and I wanted to say, *We?* But I shut my mouth firmly.

The next morning, Amunhotep burst into the Audience Chamber, startling the viziers and emissaries from Mitanni who had arranged themselves around my father's table. Panahesi and Nefertiti followed on his heels, and Nefertiti passed our father a warning look. He stood at once.

"Your Highness, I thought you were riding in the Arena."

The viziers and emissaries rose quickly to bow. "Your Highness."

Amunhotep swept up the dais and sat on his throne. "The horses from Babylon have not arrived and I'm tired of Egyptian steeds. Besides, the High Priest of Aten has found us a sculptor." He glanced across the room, at the foreign dignitaries with their curling beards. "What is this?" he demanded.

My father bowed. "These are the emissaries from Mitanni, Your Highness."

"What do we care about Mitanni? Dismiss them."

The men looked among themselves, passing nervous glances at one another.

Amunhotep repeated loudly, "Dismiss them!"

Immediately, the men rose to file out, and my father whispered calmly, "We will meet again."

Amunhotep settled comfortably into his throne. Now that Pharaoh was present, a crowd had gathered in the Audience Chamber: the daughters of viziers and troupes of musicians. Panahesi, who had come from the building site to present the new sculptor to Pharaoh, stepped in front of the dais. "Shall we fetch the artist, Your Highness?"

"Yes. Bring him in."

The doors of the Audience Chamber were thrown open and the entire court turned. The sculptor entered. He was dressed like a king, with a long wig of golden beads and more kohl than was usually deemed proper for a man. He came before the dais and swept a low bow.

"Your Most Gracious Highnesses." He was beautiful in the way a woman is beautiful in her best jewels and henna. "The High Priest of Aten has said that your palace is in need of a sculptor. My name is Thutmose, and if it so pleases Your Majesties, I shall render your images famous through eternity."

There was an excited murmuring throughout the court and Nefertiti sat forward on her throne. "We want them to be like no one else's," she cautioned.

"They will not be like anyone else's," Thutmose promised. "For no other queen has ever possessed your beauty, and no Pharaoh has shown such courage."

I could see that Amunhotep was wary of this man who was prettier than him. But Nefertiti was taken. "We want you to sculpt us today," she announced, and Amunhotep added icily, "Then we shall see if you are as good as your reputation."

The court rose, and Panahesi sidled up to Amunhotep as we walked through the halls of the palace. "I think Your Highness shall find him the best sculptor in Egypt," he predicted.

A makeshift studio had been prepared for Thutmose's coming. Panahesi held the doors open to the studio, with its open windows and tables cluttered with paints and clay. There was every tool of an artist's trade available: reed pens and papyrus, bowls of white powder and crushed lapis for dye. An elaborate dais had also been built.

Thutmose proffered his hand to Nefertiti and escorted her up to her throne. The viziers whispered at this familiarity, but there was none of a man's flirtatiousness in it. "What shall we do first, Your Highness? A carving into stone"—he flicked his free hand—"or a painted sculpture?"

"A sculpture," Nefertiti ruled, and Thutmose nodded agreeably.

Nearly fifty members of the court took seats as if preparing to witness a troupe of dancers or a songstress with her lyre. The artist turned inquisitively. "And how would Your Highnesses like to be portrayed?"

There was a moment's hesitation, then Amunhotep replied, "As Aten on earth."

The sculptor hesitated. "As both life and death?"

"As both female and male. As the beginning and the end. As a power so great none can touch its divinity. And I want them to know my face."

Thutmose paused. "Just as it is, Your Highness?"

"Stronger."

The court whispered. For a thousand years, whether a Pharaoh was fat or short or old, he had been depicted on temples and on tombs as young and slender, his kohl perfectly drawn, his hair immaculately coiffed. Now Amunhotep wanted his own face staring into the ages, his slanted eyes and narrow bones, his full lips and curling hair.

Thutmose inclined his head thoughtfully. "I will sketch you on papyrus. When it is finished, you can determine whether you approve of the likeness. If His Highness is satisfied, I shall carve him into stone."

"And for me?" Nefertiti pressed eagerly.

"For you I shall be faithful to life." Thutmose smiled. "Since nothing could ever improve Her Highness."

Nefertiti settled back in the throne that had been prepared for this day and looked satisfied.

We watched as the sculptor's reed pen worked the papyrus, two dozen eyes critiquing his movements on the wide bronze easel at the center of the chamber. As we waited for a figure to emerge on the paper, Thutmose entertained us with the story of his life. It began with a dreary boyhood in Thebes, a life of toil. His father was a baker, and when his mother died he took her place at his father's ovens, pressing loaves and kneading dough. The women who came in stared at the boy with dark hair and green eyes, and the men looked, too, especially the young priests of Amun. Then one day a renowned sculptor came into his father's bakery, and when he saw Thutmose at the ovens, he saw his next model for Amun.

"The famous sculptor Bek asked if I would model for him. He would pay me, of course, and my father said go. He had seven other sons. What did he need with me? And when I arrived at his studio, I found my calling. Bek trained me as his apprentice, and in two years I had my own studio in Memphis."

He stepped back from his papyrus, and we all saw that he was finished.

The viziers at the front leaned forward as one, and I craned my neck to see what he had drawn. It was an image of Amunhotep's face, his leonine features half covered in shadow. His eyes were bigger than they truly were, his chin longer and more threatening. There was a quality about his face that made him seem both female and male, both angry and merciful, both ready to pronounce and ready to listen. It was a haunting face, powerful and striking; the face of a man with no equal.

Thutmose turned the easel toward Pharaoh, who sat forward on his throne, and we held our breaths to hear his pronouncement.

"It's magnificent," Nefertiti whispered. Amunhotep looked from the image on the easel to the face of the young sculptor who had sketched it.

"I can begin filling the image in with paint, if that would please Your Highness."

"No," Pharaoh said firmly, and the court held its breath. We looked to Amunhotep, who had risen from his throne. "There is no need to paint. Carve it into stone."

There was an excited murmur in the studio, and my sister ordered jubilantly, "A pair of busts, and we shall place them in the Temple of Aten."

Chapter Thirteen

Peret, Season of Growing

WHEREVER NEFERTITI WENT, Thutmose was made to follow. He was told to sketch the royal couple in every aspect of their lives, and my mother thought it was shocking how he was even allowed to sit next to the dais in the Audience Chamber.

My father demanded, "How do we know that we can trust him?"

Nefertiti laughed. "Because he's an artist. Not a spy!"

Even Pharaoh was entranced by this slight young artist. With his scrolls always at his lap, Thutmose studied Amunhotep while the king played at Senet or careened around the tracks of the Memphis Arena. I watched from the tunnel of the Arena as Thutmose seated himself near my mother, and she smiled as he complimented her eyes.

"Is there anywhere he isn't permitted?" I challenged, and Nefertiti followed the direction of my gaze. Merit strapped a pair of leather greaves to my sister's legs, though she was several months pregnant.

"Only our chamber," Nefertiti admitted. "But I think Amunhotep will change his mind."

"*Nefertiti!* You aren't serious?"

She smirked a little.

"In your *chamber?*"

"Why not?" she asked brazenly. "What is there to hide?"

"Then what is there that's private?"

She thought a moment, then put on her helmet. "Nothing. Nothing is private in our reign, and that is why we shall be remembered until the last days of Egypt."

I followed my sister through the tunnel to the Arena. A chariot was waiting for her, already fastened to two massive steeds. Thutmose held out his arm to help me up into the tiers. I hesitated, then grasped his hand. It was smooth for an artist who worked with a chisel and limestone.

"The Sister of the King's Chief Wife," he remarked, and I thought he would go on to compliment my eyes, but he remained silent, studying me. For once, there weren't two dozen ladies surrounding him. Amunhotep had wanted to ride early this morning, and the rest of the court was tucked warmly in their beds. I shivered, and Thutmose nodded.

"So you came to watch His Highness as well." He looked meaningfully around at the empty tiers. "You are a dedicated sister."

"Or a foolish one," I mumbled.

He laughed, then leaned closer and confided, "Even I wondered whether I should leave my bed this morning."

We both looked at Amunhotep in his dazzling chariot, racing Nefertiti and his trained Nubian guards. Their shouts of joy could be heard over the snorting of horses and the pounding of hooves, and the sounds carried high above the walls of the Arena. Our breaths fogged the chill morning air and a chariot came to a sudden halt before the low wall next to Thutmose. Amunhotep shouted joyously, "This morning I want a sketch of myself in the Arena!" He took off his helmet and his dark curls pressed wetly against his head. "We will carve this morning's image into a limestone relief."

Thutmose picked up a papyrus sheaf and stood quickly. "Of course, Your Highness." He indicated the lofty columns of the Arena. "I will sketch your chariots gilded in the rays of the winter's sun. See where it filters between the columns to make an ankh?"

We all turned, and for the first time I noticed the rough shape of an ankh on the dusty floor of the ground.

Amunhotep gripped the side of his chariot. "Eternal life," he whispered.

"Etched in the sand. The gold of electrum chariots," Thutmose envisioned, "and beneath them, the blazing ankh of life."

I stared at Thutmose, who was not all flattery and talk. I looked again at the symbol of eternal life created by the interplay of shadows and sun and couldn't imagine why I hadn't noticed it before.

In the Great Hall that night, Thutmose was placed at the royal table, and Kiya sat next to him with her gaggle of ladies, women who had been raised in the comfort of the Elder's harem. Nefertiti and Amunhotep watched with satisfaction as the court fussed over their sculptor, who lived now in the palace simply to serve them.

"May we see what you sketched today?" the women entreated. But Kiya's mood at the table was dark.

"Why did no one tell me they were going to the Arena?"

Thutmose placated her. "It was too early, my lady. You would have been cold."

"I don't care about a little cold," she snapped.

"But it would have paled your cheeks, and their color is too lovely for that." He appraised her intimately. "Skin the rich tones of the fertile earth."

Kiya settled a little. "So where are these sketches?"

While we waited for our body servants to bring food, Thutmose produced the sheaf of papyrus I had seen in the Arena. New among the drawings was an image of Pharaoh, shaded to reveal the ankh of life beneath him as he reined in his powerful horses. Thutmose passed the sketches around the table, and there was a short silence even among the viziers and my father.

Kiya looked up. "These are very good."

"They are excellent," my father complimented.

Thutmose bowed his head, and the beads from his wig clinked musically. "Their Majesties are easy subjects to render."

"I think it is your skill," my father replied, and a warm glow colored Thutmose's cheeks.

"It is my pleasure. And yesterday His Highness gave me permission to use my studio for other commissions as well."

There was a sudden surge of interested questions, and Kiya said grandly, "Then I will commission you to do a bust of myself and the first son of Egypt."

There was an uncomfortable moment at the table. My father glanced at my mother. Then Thutmose said tactfully, "Any child of His Highness will make a fine bust."

"And you?" my mother asked at my side. "Should we commission a portrait for you? It could be a bust, or even a relief for your tomb. You should begin to think about how the gods will remember you."

Thutmose was inundated with requests and everyone was talking at once, even the viziers. In the midst of the cacophony, Thutmose saw my silence and smiled at me.

"Perhaps later," I said to my mother. "Perhaps later I might like a painting of a beautiful garden."

▣ ▣ ▣

The women of the court fluttered around Thutmose like newly released butterflies to a bloom. Even after two months in the palace, Thutmose was like a new guest, being invited to every feast and shown around the gardens.

"I don't know why they bother," Ipu said, braiding my hair one morning. "It's not as if he's interested in women."

I stared at her, uncomprehending. "What do you mean?"

Ipu took up a jar of frankincense and glanced sideways at me. "He likes men, my lady."

I sat still on the edge of my bed and tried to fathom this. "Then why do all the women like him so much?"

Ipu applied the oil to my face with wide sweeps. "Probably because he's young and handsome and his skill with limestone can't be found anywhere else. He complimented my work," she added smugly. "He said he'd heard of me even in Memphis."

"Everyone's heard of you," I replied.

She giggled. "All of the ladies want him for their portraits. Even Panahesi commissioned one."

There was a fire in the brazier. The weather had turned, and we all wore long kilts and robes now. I huddled against the warm fur of my cloak, considering this new addition to Amunhotep's court. "Well, everywhere Nefertiti goes, he follows," I replied. "Suggesting places he can engrave her image. He'll be there this morning at the Arena, I'm sure."

"Does he go every morning?"

I sighed. "Like the rest of us." But this morning I didn't want to go see Pharaoh ride. I knew what it would be like in the stadium, with the viziers and Panahesi and Kiya all crowded around each other for the benefit of Amunhotep, watching him ride with Nefertiti even though she was five months with his child. I knew the wind would be chill and that even if the servants warmed *shedeh* and brought it to us, I'd still be freezing. And my mother would be silently worrying that Nefertiti shouldn't be riding in her condition, that it was the future of Egypt she was carrying in her belly, yet no one would say anything, not even Father, because he understood that this was how she kept him from Kiya.

"Ready." Ipu put her brush and kohl away. But when I went out into the hall, my feet didn't make their way toward the courtyard. If I was going to spend my time freezing, I decided, then I would do it in the gardens. Perhaps in the commotion I would be forgotten and no one would notice that I was gone.

I took a seat beneath an old acacia and then heard Nefertiti's sharp voice calling for me.

"Mutny? Mutny, are you out here?"

I pulled my feet up onto the bench and remained silent.

"Mutnodjmet?" My sister's voice grew more urgent. "Mutny?" She rounded the lotus pond and saw me sitting. "What are you doing? We're going to the Arena." She stood over me, her black hair brushing the sides of her cheeks.

"I thought I'd stay here."

Her voice rose dramatically. "And not watch me ride?"

"I'm tired today. And it's cold."

"It's cold here, too!"

"Ipu can go," I offered. "Or Merit."

Nefertiti hesitated, debating between continuing the argument and letting it go. "Thutmose finished the busts," she said instead. She would allow me then to remain in the gardens. "He's painting them now."

I lowered my feet. "How long will he remain in the palace?"

Nefertiti gave me a strange look. "Forever."

"But what will he paint all day?"

"Us."

"All the time?"

"He is free to hire out his services to courtiers as well." She turned. "Can you see it?" she asked me, moving sideways so I would notice the little belly on her, protruding over her belt of golden scarabs. "He's already growing."

I hesitated. "What if it's a she?"

"Amunhotep will love whatever child I give him," she said heatedly.

I frowned, knowing her better. "Will you?"

She pressed her lips together, worrying them with her bottom teeth the way I often did. "If it's a girl, Kiya will be mother to Egypt's eldest prince."

"But she's Second Wife. If you give the Pharaoh a son, even if it's next year, he will still come to be Pharaoh."

Nefertiti looked out into the distance, beyond the lotus pond, as if she could see all the way to Thebes. "If I don't have a boy, Nebnefer will have more time to gather support."

"He's only four months old!"

"But not forever." She leaned forward. "You will help me, won't you? You will be there with me when it's time. And you will pray to the goddess to make it a boy."

I laughed, then stopped short at the look on her face. "Why would the goddess listen to me?"

"Because you're honest," Nefertiti replied. "And I'm . . . I'm not like you."

Nefertiti moved through the palace with her hand on her belly, and no one dared speak a word about the four-month-old prince suckling at Kiya's breast in the Great Hall, even though everybody saw him. And he was a sweet little prince, even if his mother was sour as a lemon. Amunhotep helped Nefertiti over every step, into every chariot, even onto her throne. He fussed over her and praised her growing baby even as he ignored the one already born.

In the month of Mechyr, Amunhotep announced in official scrolls and on public buildings that Aten was the god who reigned in Memphis. A proclamation was sent forth that Egyptians would bow down before the priests of Aten as they had for the priests of Amun.

For Aten embraces Egypt. He is all powerful.
He is most beautiful. All knowing and all wise.

The scroll did not end with the word *Amun*. No official scroll in Egypt had ever ended without the word *Amun*. Now none in Memphis ever would again.

My father lowered the scroll onto his lap. "This is blasphemy, and the Elder will hear of it! He will *not* be pleased." He glared at my sister and Nefertiti shrugged. She didn't shrink away as I would have done.

"Blasphemy is whatever Pharaoh says it is," she replied.

"And your husband is not the only Pharaoh!" My father stood and flung the scroll into the brazier. "The Elder still lives. And mark me, Nefertiti, mark me well. If your husband is not careful, do not be surprised if my sister sends men to assassinate him."

I covered my mouth and Nefertiti turned white.

"Amunhotep already wears the atef crown! She wouldn't!"

My father said nothing to her.

"You wouldn't let that happen!"

"It has gone too far."

"But I'm carrying his child!"

He moved toward her. "Listen and listen very carefully. There could very well be an assassination. Be sure the men you've hired to protect you are willing to die."

The color drained entirely from Nefertiti's face. "You must stop her! She is your sister!" she cried.

"She is also Queen of Egypt and I am only a vizier."

Nefertiti looked sick. "But you will protect me, won't you?"

He didn't answer.

"Won't you?" she whispered. She looked so small and frightened that I wanted to cross the room and wrap her in my arms.

Our father closed his eyes. "Of course, I will protect you."

"And my child? And Amunhotep?"

"I cannot promise that. You must hold him back. You must find a way. Or no protection of mine will ever be enough."

We lived like cats, sniffing our food before we ate it, even when it had been tasted by servants, and keeping one ear pricked at night for the sound of intruders. Ipu began to worry for my health.

"All night you toss and turn. It isn't good for you, my lady."

"I've heard news, Ipu, that makes me worried."

My body servant stopped folding my linen so that she could look at me. "Bad news?"

"Yes," I admitted, putting my hands under my legs. "You would tell me if there was talk in the palace?"

Ipu's dimples disappeared. "What kind of talk, my lady?"

"Of assassination."

Ipu recoiled.

"It's not so shocking," I whispered. "Amunhotep has made enemies. But you would tell me if you heard of something, wouldn't you?"

"Of course," she assured me, and I could see the earnestness in her face.

Nefertiti took me aside that afternoon before we rode to the site of the new temple. "I think I heard something last night," she confided.

I froze. "Did you tell Father?"

"No, I wasn't sure that I heard it. It was outside the window."

A chill went up my spine so violent that I shook. "Have you told the king?"

She shook her head, her hand on her stomach. "No, but I want you to sleep with me tonight."

Then I remembered it was Amunhotep's night with Kiya, and I stepped back to take her measure.

"What?" she cried violently. "Do you think I would lie?"

I watched her for a moment, wondering.

"Please," she said firmly, and there seemed to be real fear in her eyes. "Not just for me. For the baby."

The child six months in her womb.

That evening, she moved over in the large bed she shared with Amunhotep, and I hesitated.

"Come."

"But it's the king's bed."

She narrowed her eyes. "Not tonight. Tonight he's left me alone."

But I refused to lay there.

"Stop wasting time and get in," she snapped. Pregnancy was making her irritable.

"No. Come to my bed," I replied.

She looked at me sharply, her hand on her belly. "I'm *pregnant*."

"It will be safer," I encouraged.

She paused, and I knew I had won her. She tossed back the linens and held out her hand. I took it, helping her across the chamber. Inside my room, she maneuvered carefully onto my cushions.

"Your bed's not as comfortable as mine," she complained.

"No, but it's a whole lot safer." I smiled, content in my triumph, and she didn't say anything. I arranged the pillows behind her back.

"Do you really think someone would try to kill me?" she whispered.

I laughed uneasily. "Not if they have to get past the twelve Nubians standing outside my door." I tried to speak lightly to calm her fears, but Nefertiti's mood was dark and she persisted.

"But why would someone want to kill me?" she asked.

I shivered to think about it. "Because you are married to Pharaoh and carrying his child. What better way to get to Amunhotep than through you?"

"But the people *love* me."

"The people," I replied. "Not the priests. Not the men whose lives are dedicated to Amun and whose temples you are about to destroy—"

"That's *Amunhotep's* idea," Nefertiti said sharply. Then there was the sound of footsteps in the hall and we both froze. The person outside must have decided to retreat, because the footsteps immediately pattered away. I held my breath.

"I can't take this anymore!" Nefertiti exclaimed. "I'm afraid of everything."

"Well, it's a bed of your own making," I said cruelly. But I was still holding her hand, and that night we fell asleep with the lamps still burning. In the morning, both of us awoke at dawn, curled around each other like cats.

Chapter Fourteen

Shemu, Season of Harvest

NEFERTITI'S CHILD WAS to come in the month of Pachons. She refused to give birth to the heir of Egypt in the same pavilion that Kiya had used, so Amunhotep ordered the workers from the temple to begin construction on a birthing pavilion near the lotus ponds.

"There should be windows facing all four directions." My sister spread her hands so the workers could see what she envisioned, a palace of light and air. "Windows from ceiling to floor," she instructed. The soldiers bowed obediently and the sculptors set to work, carving leaves into the bedposts and painting fish onto the tile that spread blue and green across the floors.

When she wasn't directing the construction of her pavilion, she and Amunhotep rode out to the temple to see its progression, which was slower now that the workforce had been divided. "Mutny, find your cloak," she'd call. "Mutny, we're going out to the temple."

I saw General Nakhtmin on the temple grounds, instructing the builders, and I wondered again what he was doing in Memphis when he'd been so adamant about staying in Thebes. He smiled when I passed and I looked away, so Nefertiti wouldn't think there was anything between us, but Ipu, who rode in my chariot, whispered softly, "Pharaoh has made an offer the soldiers won't turn down. Twenty deben of silver a month for building in Memphis."

I turned to her in shock. "General Nakhtmin came here for silver?"

She looked out to where the general was standing and gave a dimpled smile. "Or something else."

Then one morning my sister was too ill to ride, and she wanted me to go in her place. "I don't want Amunhotep going with Kiya," she said spitefully. "I can just imagine her riding out to the site and writing a poem to his shining new building. And he would probably inscribe it for her on the wall of the temple."

I might have laughed, but what she was asking for frightened me. "You want me to go to the temple site? *Alone?*"

"Of course not alone. You'll take Ipu."

"But what will I do?"

She placed her hand on her belly, weary with my ignorance. "You will do as I've always done," she snapped. "You will establish your presence at the temple to make sure the builders aren't lazy. You will be sure that the workers aren't stealing gold, or alabaster, or limestone."

"And if they are?"

"They won't," she said flatly. "They wouldn't dare with you watching them."

While the Master of the Horse prepared my chariot, Ipu asked, "Where is Pharaoh? Isn't he coming?"

"My sister is ill and she wants him by her side."

"So we're to go alone? With no guards?"

"None at all."

When the Master of the Horse was finished, we rode beyond the palace to the site of the temple building. The soldiers were breaking rock and carving into stone. None looked to be pilfering alabaster, but several men waved cheerfully to Ipu as we passed. I raised my eyebrows and Ipu smiled.

"I have friends in strange places, my lady. And because you cannot make friends among the soldiers, I make them for you."

I followed her gaze to a man in the street who halted our chariot with an outstretched arm. The horses stopped as if they'd been commanded, and Nakhtmin smiled up at the two of us.

"General." I nodded formally.

"My Lady Mutnodjmet," he said. Ipu grinned.

"And how is the work going on the temple?" I asked. I made a show of supervising his men. They were grunting in the heat, heaving a heavy stone column into place.

A smile played at the edge of the general's lips. "As you can see, they are working hard for His Highness's great ambitions. But aren't you going to ask why I'm here?" The sun had turned the general's skin a deep shade of bronze, darker than his long hair and light eyes.

"I already know why you are here," I replied. "Pharaoh made an offer no soldier could resist. Twenty deben of silver a month."

General Nakhtmin blinked against the merciless sun. "Is that what you think? That I sold out for a handful of silver?"

I stared at him plainly. "Why else would you come?"

He stepped back and his face grew thoughtful. "When I was a boy, I saved the gold that I earned in the army to buy a farm in Thebes, and when my father died I inherited his land. So no, I did not come for a handful of deben."

I felt I had offended him somehow, and he continued staring at me until I was forced to reply, "Then why have you come?"

He glanced at Ipu. "Perhaps you can explain it, my lady. As for myself, I must return to my soldiers before they begin stealing limestone." He gave a quick smile. "Or sand."

I watched him walk away, then rounded on Ipu. "Why does he enjoy playing with me?"

"Because he's interested in you. He's interested in you, and he is not sure that you are interested back."

I was silenced.

"Only don't let your sister see you looking like that," Ipu warned me. "Or there will be more trouble in the palace than whether the queen gives Pharaoh a prince."

The Temple of Aten was completed early, in time for Nefertiti to give birth. The child was weighing heavily on her, and she sat in a special pavilion decorated with images of Hathor and Bes, her feet propped on feather pillows while harpists played music in the antechamber. Fan bearers stood at every corner of the room. My sister reigned as Queen of the Bedside, snapping at anyone who was near, even our father.

"Why didn't anyone tell me Kiya's been going with him to see the construction? Has she taken my place now?" Her voice rose with indignation. *"Has she?"*

"Shut the door, Mutnodjmet," my father ordered. He looked down at my sister. "For a few days, you will simply have to bear it. There's nothing you can do."

"I'm Queen of Egypt!" She struggled to sit up, and her body servants moved quickly to be at her side. "Send for Amunhotep!" she commanded. The young girls looked at our father. "I said send for Pharaoh!" Nefertiti's voice grew sharp.

My father turned to the nearest woman and nodded. The girl scurried out. "You'd do better to concern yourself with the state of affairs in this kingdom," he said. "Have you even bothered to find out what is happening in Thebes?"

Nefertiti shrugged. "Why should I?"

My father's face darkened. "Because the Elder is ill."

The servants did their best not to look at one another, but they would be gossiping come night. Nefertiti sat forward on her pillows. "*How* ill?"

"There is news that Anubis may take him soon."

Nefertiti struggled to sit up. "Why haven't I heard of this?"

"Because you haven't heard of anything unless it concerns the Temple of Aten," my father reproached. "When is the last time Amunhotep visited his Audience Chamber? Or corresponded with the princes of foreign nations? Every day *I* sit beneath the Horus throne and wield the power of a king."

"Isn't that what you want, the Kingdom of Egypt stretched before you?"

"Not when your husband plays Pharaoh for a day and sends statues plated in gold to his allies instead of real gold. Then I am the one who must make his amends. I am the one who must explain to the mayor of Qiltu why the army is not ready to come to his defense because the Hittites have attacked his kingdom."

"There is an army in Thebes. Let him send them to the Elder."

My father's ire rose. "How long until Amunhotep uses *them* as workers, too? What next? A palace? A *city*?" I looked quickly at Nefertiti. "There is division in Egypt," he warned. "The priests of Amun are preparing for rebellion."

"They'd never rebel!" Nefertiti hardened her jaw, a seventeen-year-old queen.

"Why not?" my father challenged. "With Horemheb at their side?"

"Then Horemheb would be a traitor and Amunhotep would have him killed."

"And if the army joined with him? What then?"

Nefertiti recoiled, her hands on her stomach, as if to protect her child from such news. Then the door to Nefertiti's birthing chamber opened and Amunhotep arrived.

"The most beautiful queen in Egypt!" he proclaimed.

"The *only* Queen of Egypt," Nefertiti said sharply. "Where were you?"

"At the temple." Amunhotep smiled. "The altar is ready."

"And did you consecrate it with Kiya?" she hissed.

Amunhotep froze.

"Did you?" she shouted. "Now that I'm Pharaoh's heifer, about to birth a prince, I'm not of interest anymore?"

Amunhotep looked around the chamber, hesitating, then moved quickly to her side, placing his hand on hers. "Nefertiti—"

"It is *my* likeness that looks down over the people of Egypt. *I* am the one who watches over this kingdom. Not Kiya!"

Amunhotep knelt swiftly. "I am sorry."

"You will not go with her again. *Say* you won't go with her."

"I promise—"

"A promise is not enough. Swear it to me. On Aten."

He saw the seriousness in her face and said it. "I swear it to you on Aten."

My father and I exchanged glances, and my sister raised him from the ground. "Did you know your father is ill?" she asked, settling back on her pillows, creating the illusion beautifully: When she was happy, everything unfolded in Amunhotep's favor.

At once he stood up. "The Elder is ill?" He looked at my father. "Is it true?"

My father bowed. "Yes, Your Highness. There is such news from Thebes."

Amunhotep tossed his glance around the chamber, and for the first time he seemed to notice the women. "Go!" he shouted. Ipu and Merit hustled the women out. Amunhotep turned to my father. "How long until he is dead?"

My father stiffened. "The Pharaoh of Egypt may live another year."

"You said he was ill. You said there was word."

"The gods may preserve him for longer."

"The gods have abandoned him!" Amunhotep cried. "It is *me* they look after, not a decrepit old man." Amunhotep crossed the chamber in two strides, then opened the door and spoke to the guards. "Find me the builder Maya," he commanded. Then he turned to my father. "You will go back to the Audience Chamber and draft a letter to the princes of every nation. Warn them that within the season I shall be Pharaoh of Upper Egypt."

The color in my father's cheeks revealed his temper. "He may not die by then, Your Majesty."

Amunhotep came so close to my father that for a moment I thought he would kiss him. Instead, he whispered in his ear, "You're wrong. The Elder's reign is finished."

He stepped toward the door and summoned the guards again. "Find Panahesi!" He turned back to my father. "The High Priest of Aten is making a trip to Thebes," he announced. "Go now and draft a letter to the kings of foreign nations."

He indicated the door, and my father and I were led into the hall. Then he barred it shut behind us. Immediately, muffled voices could be heard from within, high pitched and excited. I followed the angry slap of my father's sandals to the Per Medjat.

"What is he doing?"

"Preparing." My father seethed.

"Preparing for what?"

"To hasten the Elder's trip into the Afterlife."

I sucked in my breath. "Then why did you allow Nefertiti to tell him?"

My father didn't stop walking. "Because someone else would have."

"The queen is giving birth!"

A servant found me in the palace gardens and her words tumbled out breathlessly. At once I was up, pressing through the crowd around Nefertiti's chamber. Messengers and court ladies stood seven thick outside the pavilion, covered by sunshades, gossiping about what should happen if Nefertiti produced a son. Would Nebnefer be sent to live in another palace? What if it was a girl? How soon might the queen become pregnant again? I entered the birthing chamber, shutting the door and the gossip behind me.

"Where were you?" Nefertiti cried.

"In the gardens. I didn't know it had begun."

My mother shot me a look, as if I should have known.

"Bring me juice," Nefertiti moaned, and I rushed to the nearest servant and told her to find it. "Quickly!" I turned back to my sister. "Where are the midwives?"

She gritted her teeth. "Preparing the birthing chair."

Two midwives appeared. "It is ready, Your Highness."

Nefertiti's chair had been painted with the three goddesses of childbirth. Hathor, Nekhbet, and Tawaret held out their arms across the ebony throne. My sister's body was straining to release the heavy burden in her womb. Her breath was growing labored.

The women eased her onto the padded seat with its hole in the middle for the child to make its descent into the world. My mother placed a cushion behind her and Nefertiti reached out her hand for mine, screaming loud enough to wake Anubis. The chattering outside the pavilion stopped and all anyone could hear were Nefertiti's cries. My mother turned to me instead of the midwives. "Isn't there anything else we can give her?"

"No," I said honestly, and the midwives nodded.

The eldest woman shook her graying curls. "We've already given her *kheper-wer*." She had inserted the mixture of *kheper-wer* plant, honey, and milk into my sister to induce birth. Now the old woman spread her palms. "It's all we can do."

Nefertiti groaned. Her brows were drawn and sweat coursed from her neck, causing her hair to stick to her face. I ordered one of the women to pull it back. Ipu and Merit carried a dish of hot water to the birthing chair, placing it between my sister's legs so that the steam would help ease the delivery. Then Nefertiti tilted her head back and gripped the chair.

"He's coming!" my mother cried. "The Prince of Egypt!"

"Push harder," the old midwife encouraged.

Merit pressed a cool cloth to Nefertiti's head and the midwife was beneath the chair at once, her hands reaching for the crowning head of the baby. My sister arched back with a cry of agony, then her little body shuddered and the child came in a rush of water.

"A princess!" the midwife cried, searching for any deformities. "A healthy princess."

Nefertiti stared up from her chair. "A girl?" she whispered, gripping the arms. "A *girl?*" Her voice grew shrill.

"Yes!" The midwife held up the little bundle, and my mother and I exchanged glances.

"Someone go tell Vizier Ay," my mother rejoiced. "And send a message to the king."

Ipu rushed out to announce to the palace that the queen had survived. The bells would toll twice for a Princess of Egypt. The midwives bundled Nefertiti back into her bed, and her womb was packed with linen to stop the bleeding. "A princess," she repeated. She had been so sure it would be a prince. She had been so certain.

"But she's healthy," I replied. "And she's yours. Your own little link to eternity."

"But, Mutny . . ." Her eyes grew distant. "It's a girl."

The midwife came over and presented my sister with the First Princess of Egypt. Nefertiti shifted the child in her arms. My mother's eyes grew moist. She was a grandmother now. "She looks like you," she told Nefertiti. "The same lips and nose."

"And so much hair," I added.

My mother caressed the soft, downy head. The child gave out a piercing wail, and the gray-haired midwife came rushing over.

"She must be fed," the midwife announced. "Where is the milk nurse?"

A tall plump woman was let into the birthing chamber. The midwife squinted into the young woman's round face. She was not much older than Nefertiti. Seventeen or eighteen, and she was hearty looking and strong.

"Are you the one Vizier Ay chose?"

"Yes," the girl replied, and it was clear from her swelling breasts that she, too, was a new mother.

"Then come sit by the queen," the midwife instructed.

A seat was arranged and the new mother exposed one of her breasts. We all watched the little princess suck greedily, and Nefertiti studied the miniature reflection of herself in the milk nurse's arms.

The midwife smiled. "As beautiful as you, Your Majesty. Pharaoh must be pleased."

"But not a son." Nefertiti looked down at the princess she had birthed: the princess who was supposed to have been a prince.

"What will you name her?" I asked.

"Meritaten," Nefertiti said at once.

My mother started. "Beloved of Aten?"

"Yes." Nefertiti straightened and her face grew determined. "It will remind Amunhotep of what is important." My mother frowned, and Nefertiti replied heatedly, "Loyalty." Bells were tolling in the distance, twice so that Memphis would know a princess had been born. Nefertiti gripped the edge of her linens. "What is that?"

"They are the bells," my mother began, but Nefertiti cut her off.

"Why are they only ringing twice?"

"Because the bells toll three times for a prince," I said, and Nefertiti flew into a rage.

"*Why?* Because a daughter is less important than a prince? The bells tolled three times for Nebnefer and the bells will toll three times for Princess Meritaten!"

My mother and I looked at each other, and Princess Meritaten began to wail.

Merit broke the silence. "Shall we take you to the baths, Your Highness?"

"*No!* Someone must stop the bells," Nefertiti ordered. "Bring Amunhotep!"

"First have your bath, then you can see Pharaoh and tell him," my mother encouraged.

"Nefertiti, you can't see anyone like this," I pleaded. Her sheath was stained, and though her legs had been wiped clean and her hair brushed back, she was not a Queen of Egypt. She was a woman who had just given birth, reeking with the stench of blood. "Bathe quickly, then we'll call Pharaoh and tell him."

She did as I suggested, and there was silence in the birthing chamber as she was wrapped in fresh linen and taken away.

"She birthed a beautiful child," my mother said finally. The milk nurse continued to feed the princess while the midwife went about removing the birthing chair. It would be another year before there might be a prince. Perhaps longer.

"Do you think he will listen to her?" I asked.

My mother pressed her lips together. "It's never been done."

"Neither has a queen living in a Pharaoh's chamber."

When Nefertiti returned, bathed and dressed in white, my mother nodded. "Much better," she said, but Nefertiti was in no mood for flattery.

"Bring in Amunhotep."

Merit opened the door to the birthing chamber and called for Pharaoh. He came at once, and Nefertiti assailed him as soon as he appeared.

"I want the bells to ring three times," she commanded.

He rushed to her bedside, putting a hand on her cheek. "Are you well? Are you—"

"The bells must ring three times today!"

"But the birth . . ." He looked down at the sleeping Meritaten. "Look how beautiful—"

"I'm talking about the bells!" Nefertiti cried, waking the princess, and Amunhotep hesitated.

"But the bells only ring—"

"Is our princess any less important than a prince?"

Amunhotep looked down into the face of his daughter, real tears coming down his cheeks. She had inherited his dark eyes and curling hair. Then he looked at Nefertiti, her face set with conviction, and turned to Merit. "Instruct the men to ring the bells three times. The princess . . ." He glanced at Nefertiti.

"Meritaten has been born," Nefertiti said, and Amunhotep seated himself at her side.

"Meritaten," he repeated, looking into his daughter's face. "Beloved of Aten."

Nefertiti raised her chin proudly. "Yes. After the great god of Egypt."

"A princess." Amunhotep picked up the wailing infant from the milk nurse's arms and held her to his chest.

My father came in and looked poignantly at my mother. "A girl," he said quietly.

"But still an heir," my mother whispered.

My father stayed long enough to hold his granddaughter, the First royal Princess of Egypt, then left to address a message to the kings of foreign nations.

I studied Nefertiti in her bed. She looked drawn and pale, putting on a cheerful show for Amunhotep when she should have been sleeping. "Do you think she looks well?" I asked my mother.

"Of course not. She's just given birth."

Then Merit appeared at Nefertiti's side, armed with her great ivory box of cosmetics. Dutifully, my sister sat up, though if I had been her I would have ordered everyone out of my chamber. I looked down at Princess Meritaten, pressed firmly against my sister's breast, and I felt a pain in my heart that was probably envy. Nefertiti had a husband, a kingdom, a family. I was fifteen, and what did I have?

▣ ▣ ▣

The Birth Feast was held at the end of Pachons. Beautifully crafted vessels of precious metals were sent from foreign kingdoms and arranged on a table that spread from one end of the Great Hall to the other. There were statues of sculpted gold and ebony chests. The king of Mitanni sent a pack of hounds, while silver and ivory bracelets arrived from noble families in Thebes.

In Amunhotep's chamber, Nefertiti asked me which gown she should wear to the feast. "The open front, or something that cuts off at the neck?"

I studied her hennaed breasts, which were large and flattering. Her stomach was so small that it was impossible to think she had given birth only fourteen days ago. "The open front," I said.

I watched her body as it filled out her tiny gown and was fascinated with the way she looped two golden earrings through her double piercings. I thought, *I will never be that beautiful.* Then we looked at ourselves in the mirror: the Cat and the Beautiful One.

In the Great Hall, no man could take his eyes off her. "She is stunning," Ipu said as my sister swept between the columns and up the painted dais. Birth had filled out the hollowness of her cheeks and brought color to her face. Hundreds of candles wavered in her path, and there was a momentary hush as she took her throne.

It seemed that every member of the Egyptian royal court had come to celebrate Meritaten's birth. I walked outside to where my father was standing with my mother, enjoying a moment's peace before the food was served and we would all have to sit. I looked again at the people crowding the courtyard, floating in and out of the Great Hall with cups of wine, dressed in the finest linen and gold. Only Panahesi was absent.

"How come there are so many people?" I asked. Even the nobility from Thebes had come to celebrate, beginning the journey on the Nile a month earlier when news of Meritaten's impending birth had arrived.

"They have come to pay homage to the new Pharaoh," my father said. I didn't understand, so my father explained, "The Elder is dying."

I stared at him. "But he was supposed to live another season! You told me—" I stopped myself and realized what my father must be saying. I leaned forward and my voice dropped to a whisper. "He wasn't poisoned?"

My father said nothing.

"It wasn't poison?" I pressed, but my father's face was a mask. I reeled back. "Is that where Panahesi has been?"

My parents exchanged looks and my father stood up. "Whatever has happened in Thebes, the Elder won't last the month."

A bell rang from inside the Great Hall, summoning the guests to dinner. My father took my mother's arm and disappeared into the crowd while I stood, still gaping at his words.

"By the look on your face, we're either going to be invaded or you've just tasted something particularly sour."

I turned, and General Nakhtmin held out a bowl of wine.

"Thank you, General. It's nice to see you, too."

He laughed and indicated the Great Hall with his hand. "Shall we?"

We walked together through the arched doors of the Great Hall with its magnificent columns and hundreds of guests. He would sit at the table for the military elite, I with the royal family. But before we reached the dais, I stopped him. "Tell me, General. Have you heard anything about the Elder in Thebes?"

Nakhtmin regarded me thoughtfully, then drew me away from the tables to an alcove where we could speak with more privacy. "Why do you ask?"

I hesitated. "I . . . I just thought you might know."

Nakhtmin regarded me suspiciously. "He will probably pass into the arms of Osiris very soon."

"But he's only forty! He could live another ten years." I whispered, "It wasn't poison?" and searched his face for honesty.

He nodded gravely. "There's been talk. And if there's talk in the king's own family—"

"There isn't," I said quickly.

He studied me.

"But if . . . if the Pharaoh dies . . ."

"Yes?"

"Well, what then?"

"Then your sister becomes Queen of Egypt and the Dowager Queen will bow down before her daughter-in-law. And who knows," Nakhtmin added conspiratorially, "she may even be Pharaoh before it's over."

"Pharaoh?" I repeated dismissively.

"Is that so surprising?"

"No, that's foolish. Only a handful of women have ever ruled Egypt."

"And why not her?"

We both looked through the forest of columns at my sister, a thick golden signet pulling her glossy hair away from her face, enlarging her eyes. She commanded a view of the entire hall from her throne, but it was Amunhotep she watched.

"He trusts her with everything," Nakhtmin added. "They even share chambers."

"Who told you that?"

"I'm a general. It's my business to know. Even if I were a servant in a minor palace, I should know something so trivial."

"But she would have to become a widow before she would become Pharaoh." I glanced at him and he didn't argue the point, as if he wouldn't be surprised if Amunhotep should die. I felt a chill go up my spine and settle as a coolness on my back, despite the warm night. Guests were taking their seats, and laughter echoed beneath the ceiling of the Great Hall. The Birth Feast would last all night, but I might not get a chance to speak with the general again. I hesitated. "I thought you would stay in Thebes and live a quieter life than this."

"Oh, it's not quiet in Thebes. Anywhere there's a palace it's never quiet. But someday I hope to find someone who might share a quiet life with me. Away from Thebes or Memphis or any city with a royal road."

We both looked into the hall and I nodded, understanding that desire.

"But now that the temple is finished, the soldiers wonder what will happen next. Pharaoh is afraid of the army. He won't send us to war even though the Hittites encroach on our territory with every season that passes and Egypt offers no resistance. With Panahesi serving Aten and Amunhotep building temples to glorify Aten's reign, your father ascends the throne of Egypt. Perhaps not literally, but in every other way he is Pharaoh, *miw-sher.* Now is the time to decide what you want in this life. Your name etched in sandstone for eternity or happiness?"

"And how do you know I'm not happy here?"

"Because you're standing in a corner speaking with me while your sister sits on the Horus throne and your father smoothes her way. If you were content, you'd be there." He indicated the table for the royal family, presided over by my mother and father, the two of them surrounded by bald-headed men in fine linen. "So where does that leave you, little cat?"

"As the handmaiden to Nefertiti," I said sharply.

"You could always change that." Nakhtmin regarded me with interest, then added meaningfully, "By marrying someone."

"Mutny, would you find me my robe?"

I looked up from my Senet game but remained in my chair. "Where's Merit? Can't she get you a robe?"

Nefertiti watched me with her large painted eyes from where the milk nurse was feeding Meritaten. Sitting next to the woman, she stroked the princess's downy hair. "I can't leave Meritaten. Won't you get it? It's just in the other room."

"Go ahead, Mutny," my mother said. "She's busy."

"She's always busy!"

My mother gave me a look that told me simply to do it, and I returned with my sister's robe. I paused over Meritaten's tiny face. She had her mother's coloring, the light hue of sand, but her eyes were olive, like Amunhotep's. It was impossible to tell whether she would have her mother's jaw or her father's height. But her nose was slender and long like Nefertiti's. "She looks like you," I said, and my sister smiled.

My mother's shoulders tensed. "Did you hear that?" she asked quickly, tearing her gaze from the Senet board.

We all froze, even the milk nurse with Meritaten in her arms. I could hear what she was referring to. It was the sound of wailing women and temple bells.

Nefertiti rose up. "What is it?"

Then the door to the chamber swung open and Amunhotep's grin was so wide that we knew. My mother covered her mouth with her hand.

"He's gone to Osiris," Nefertiti whispered.

Amunhotep embraced her. "The Elder is dead. I am Pharaoh of Egypt!"

My father entered the room with Panahesi on his heels. In her joy, Nefertiti didn't even notice that men were in her birthing chamber. My father bowed. "Shall we prepare for the move to Thebes, Your Highness?"

"There will be no move to Thebes," Amunhotep announced. "We will begin building the city of Amarna at once."

There was a sudden silence in the birthing chamber.

"You will move the capital of Thebes?" my father asked.

Amunhotep exulted, "For the glory of Aten."

My father glared at Nefertiti, who wouldn't meet his gaze.

Chapter Fifteen

THEBES

1349 BCE

fifteenth of Thoth

AMUNHOTEP PACED. "MY mother is in the Audience Chamber. She is wearing the Queen of Egypt's crown. It is yours now. Shall I take it for you?"

We sat in a circle in the richest chamber of Malkata: my mother, my father, Ipu, and I. We had sailed to Thebes for Pharaoh's burial, and now the Elder's room belonged to Amunhotep IV. We watched while Merit painted Nefertiti's eyes. She was beyond us now. More powerful than Tiye. More powerful than our father even. When the Elder had been alive, there had always been the possibility of appealing to him for help if there was trouble. Now, there was only Nefertiti.

"Let her keep the crown," my sister ruled. "I will wear a crown that no Queen of Egypt has ever worn. Something *I* have created." She looked over at Thutmose, who went wherever we did.

But Amunhotep wasn't satisfied. "We should take the crown," he insisted cruelly. "She could be dangerous to us."

My father's gaze found Nefertiti's, who stood up at once. "It's not necessary," she replied.

"She was my father's wife!" Amunhotep rejoined, his voice full of menace.

"And she is *my* father's sister. He will watch her for you."

Amunhotep studied my father, then shrugged, as if his mother was a matter he was willing to let go. "I want to move from this city as soon as we can find a place to build."

"We will," Nefertiti promised, going to him and caressing his cheek. "But we must put things in order."

"Yes," he agreed. "We must rid ourselves of the Amun priests before they can try assassination—"

"Your Highness," my father interrupted.

"I won't have them disturbing my sleep!" he raged. "I dream about them at night. They're in my *dreams*. But I will send the priests to the quarries."

I gasped, and even Nefertiti froze at the suggestion. These were men who had never toiled a day in their lives, representatives of Amun who spent their time praying. "Perhaps we should just send them away," she offered.

"So they can plot somewhere else?" Amunhotep demanded. "No. I will send them all to the quarries."

"But they will die," I blurted before I could stop myself.

Amunhotep turned his dark gaze on me. "Very good."

"And what about the ones who will bow to Aten? They can be saved," Nefertiti implored.

Amunhotep faltered. "We will offer them the chance. But those who refuse will be shackled and sentenced." He left the room, shouting at his guards to keep seven paces back.

"The Elder has not been a month in his tomb and you are planning the destruction of Thebes?" my father asked furiously. "The people will see that this is against the laws of Ma'at. They will never forget this."

"Then we will give them something else to remember," Nefertiti swore. Her eyes were painted and around her throat was the golden symbol of life. "Bring me my crown." Thutmose disappeared. Then Nefertiti took off her wig and those of us in the room let out a cry.

"What have you done?" my mother exclaimed.

Nefertiti had shaven off her hair. The beautiful black tresses that had framed her face were gone. "I had to shave it for the crown."

My mother placed a hand over her heart. "What kind of crown is it?"

"The crown that will come to be associated with Egypt," she said. As she did, I realized that even without her hair, Nefertiti was still beautiful. She was threatening and powerful and stunning. She looked at herself in the mirror as Thutmose came up behind her. He raised the flat-topped crown so all of us could see it, then fit the burden tightly around Nefertiti's head. No one else could have worn it. It had been designed for her, tall and slender with an asp ready to spit poison into her enemies' eyes. Nefertiti turned around, and if I had been a peasant in the fields, I would have thought I was staring into the face of a goddess.

▣ ▣ ▣

The Audience Chamber was filled to bursting. Scribes, merchants, courtiers, diplomats, viziers, and priests stood elbow to elbow in the magnificent room with its sweeping mosaics and towering windows. The Audience Chamber of Thebes put the chamber in Memphis to shame. There was a gasp of awe as we entered the room. Nefertiti swept up the stairs to her throne and Queen Tiye, on the second step of the dais, was no longer the reigning queen in Egypt. Now she would be Dowager Queen. I heard whispers as I took my place on the third step next to my father, for no one knew what my sister's crown meant. Was Nefertiti queen? A king-queen? A coregent? To whom should the people address their petitions? The viziers looked from Amunhotep to Nefertiti to my father. We were the most powerful family in Egypt. In the world.

General Nakhtmin stood in full regalia at the side of Horemheb. They were watching the Nubian guards behind our thrones with critical eyes. I knew what they were thinking: Amunhotep distrusted his army so much that he had hired foreign men to protect him. And I knew what even they did not. That now Amunhotep would announce the building of a new capital city called Amarna. There would be no war with the Hittites as they encroached on our territories. Instead, the army would build cities for Aten.

Panahesi stood from his chair and announced, "The Pharaoh of Egypt has declared that Aten shall be praised above all other gods in Egypt!"

There was an angry murmur among the priests.

Panahesi raised his voice to speak over them. "Aten shall have temples in every city, and the priests of Amun shall bow down before him or they shall be taken from Thebes and sent to the quarries."

There was a cry of outrage.

"The quarries," Panahesi continued, "of Wadi Hammamat."

The murmur rose and Amunhotep stood from his throne. "From this day forth," his voice echoed across the chamber, "I shall be known as Pharaoh Akhenaten. *Beloved of Aten.* And Thebes shall not be where Aten's Pharaoh reigns. I will build Aten a bigger city, a greater city, and this city shall be called Amarna."

Now chaos erupted in the Audience Chamber: shock that Amunhotep would change his name, and that a new capital would be built to replace the greatest city in the East. Akhenaten looked to Panahesi, who demanded silence. But the crowd had grown violent. The priests were shouting, the viziers were trying to calm the priests, and the merchants who had supplied the temples of Amun with costly herbs and gold were making deals with the new priests of Aten. I looked at my mother, whose face had gone white beneath her wig.

"Guards!" the newly proclaimed Akhenaten shouted. "Guards!"

Two dozen armed Nubians swept into the crowd. Akhenaten stood and took Nefertiti's hand in his. He turned to the generals of the army and shouted above the noise, "You will empty every temple and turn the statues of Amun, Isis, and Hathor to gold. You will give the priests and priestesses one chance to turn to Aten." Akhenaten looked at Nefertiti and she nodded. "If they refuse, chain them and send them to Hammamat."

At the word *chain,* the room fell silent. Guards stood poised at every window and entrance in case further trouble should erupt, only now the people in the chamber understood. Akhenaten didn't want to elevate Aten over Amun: he wanted to tear down every statue of the gods and goddess who had protected Egypt for two thousand years.

A vizier stood from his seat below the Horus throne. "But the Amun priests are nobility. They are the foundation upon which Egypt rests!" he cried.

There was a murmur of consent in the room.

"The Amun priests," Akhenaten said slowly, "will be given one chance. They may become priests of Aten or they may give up their lives for a god who no longer rules in Egypt. Is Pharaoh not the mouthpiece of the gods?"

The old man stared at him, at a loss for words.

"Is Pharaoh not the mouthpiece of the gods?" Akhenaten repeated, shouting.

The old man fell to one knee. "Of course, Your Highness."

"Then who knows better the will of the gods, *them* or me? We shall build Aten a city that shall be greater than any city that has come before it."

Queen Tiye shut her eyes and General Horemheb stood forward. "The Hittites have taken control of Qatna and the governor of Kadesh has requested three times that we come to his aid. His letters have not been answered by anyone but Vizier Ay, who can do nothing without Pharaoh's consent." He glared up at Akhenaten. "If we fail to send men this time, Your Highness, we will lose the territory the Elder won with the lives of three thousand Egyptian soldiers."

The blood rushed to Akhenaten's face. He scanned the room to see who agreed. "You say you wish to fight the Hittites?" he asked.

General Horemheb heard the threat in Pharaoh's voice. "My wish is to protect Egypt from invasion and to save the territories that my father and I fought so hard to procure."

"Who here agrees with the general?" Akhenaten shouted.

No one moved in the Audience Chamber.

"*Who?*" he bellowed.

Five charioteers stepped out of rank and looked around them. Akhenaten smiled widely. "Very well. Here is your army, General." The Audience Chamber shifted, not sure what game Akhenaten was playing. Pharaoh turned to my father. "Send them to the front lines of Kadesh, for this is the army that will save Egypt from the Hittites! Who else would like to join this war?" he asked menacingly.

I held my breath, wondering if Nakhtmin would volunteer.

Akhenaten grinned. "Five warriors then. Let's all rise for the heroes who will defend Kadesh from the invading Hittites." He began to clap in mock approbation, and when no one clapped with him, he clapped louder. The Audience Chamber erupted with nervous applause. "Your heroes!" Akhenaten turned to his Nubian guards. "Take them away. Take them all the way to the fronts of Kadesh!"

The courtiers who filled the chamber watched in stunned silence as General Horemheb and his five men were led away. No one moved. I don't think anyone even dared to breathe.

Panahesi straightened his cloak. "Pharaoh will now receive petitions."

Panahesi marched in to the holiest of holies with his army of Nubians and the great temples of Thebes were stripped of their statues.

Images of Isis were shattered or burned. Hathor was toppled from her place above the river and Amun was defaced. People cowered in their homes and the priestesses of Isis wept in the streets. Akhenaten's new army of Nubian guards ripped the robes from the chests of Amun priests and new robes were issued adorned with the sun. Those who refused them were sent to certain death.

And before the Elder was even cold in his tomb, Akhenaten and Nefertiti knelt before the altar that had once been Amun's, and Panahesi anointed them Pharaoh and Queen of all Egypt. I sat in the first row in lapis and gold, and while choirs of boys raised their sweet voices to the sun, all across Thebes Pharaoh's army defaced images of our greatest gods.

That night, Nefertiti called a meeting. We sat in a circle around my bed, keeping our voices low. I had a new room in Thebes. Princess Meritaten had my old room next to Pharaoh. I let my father into my chamber, expecting him to be outraged, but a deadly calm had settled over him.

"Say something," Nefertiti commanded.

"What is it that you want me to say?" my father asked quietly. "You called this meeting."

"Because I wanted your advice."

"What do you need my advice for? You don't take it."

"What am I supposed to do?" she demanded.

"Save Amun!" he lashed out. His eyes were blazing in the firelight. "Save *something*. What will be left of Egypt when he is through with it?"

"You think I don't know this?" Her voice broke a little. "He is building a city and he wants it in the *desert*."

"In the desert?"

"Between Memphis and Thebes."

"No one can build there. It's desolation—"

"That's what I told him! But Panahesi has convinced him it is Aten's will." Her voice rose hysterically. "You gave him the job of

High Priest of Aten and now *Akhenaten* thinks that Panahesi is the mouthpiece of the god."

"Better the mouthpiece of the god than treasurer. In the end, it will not be Akhenaten who decides the next Pharaoh of Egypt. If death should strike your husband, it will be the people and their advisers who choose. Panahesi may control the temple, but I control its gold, and gold will win more hearts than a god no one can see."

"But Akhenaten wants to choose the site by the end of Aythyr. And he wants to take Kiya!"

My father glanced at her. So here was the real crisis. Not that the city would be in the midst of desert, but that Akhenaten would take Kiya to help choose where it should be.

Nefertiti's panic rose. "What will I do?"

"Let him."

"Let Akhenaten take Kiya to choose our site?"

"There is nothing you can do."

"I am Queen of Egypt," she reminded.

"Yes, and one of two hundred other women that Akhenaten inherited from his father's harem."

"Akhenaten will have nothing to do with *them*. They were his father's women."

"So anything his father ever touched is tainted now? Including this city?"

Nefertiti sat silent.

"How will he find workers to build Amarna?" he asked her.

"The army."

"And how will we defend our foreign territories when they are invaded by Hittites?"

"Hittites! Hittites! Who cares about the Hittites? Let them take Rhodes or Lakisa or Babylon. What do we want with them?"

"Goods," I interrupted, and everyone looked at me. "We get pottery from Rhodes, caravans of gold from Nubia, and every year a thousand baskets of glass arrive on Babylonian ships."

Nefertiti narrowed her eyes. "How do *you* know?"

"I listen."

She stood up and directed her words at our father. "Send messages in Akhenaten's name and threaten the Hittites with war."

"And if they still invade our territories?" he asked.

"Then we'll tax the temples and send them the gold to raise an army!" she retorted. "Akhenaten has already sworn that our army will build the city of Amarna. He thinks it will write our name in eternity. There's nothing I can do to stop it."

"And you?" my father asked shrewdly. "Do you think it will write your name in eternity?"

She paused over the brazier, the rage gone from her face. "It could."

"Has Akhenaten met with Maya?" my father asked.

"Maya said it will take six years. They will build a main road and the palace first. Akhenaten wants to move by Tybi."

"So *soon?*" my father demanded.

"Yes. We'll set up tents so we can watch the progress and be there for every phase."

We both stared at her. "You?" I asked, brutally frank. "You, who like all the comforts of the palace?"

"And what about the old?" my father asked her. "What will they do when it begins to grow cold during Inundation?"

"Then they can stay behind and come when the palace is finished."

"Good. And so shall I."

Nefertiti stared. "You *have* to come. You're treasurer."

"And will there be a treasury? A secure-enough holding to keep safe all that gold?"

Nefertiti bridled. "Akhenaten won't like your staying behind at the treasury," she warned. "And not just you, but his mother."

My father stood up. "Then he'll simply have to learn to accept it," he said and stormed from the chamber.

Chapter Sixteen

Peret, Season of Growing

THE ROYAL BARGES were readied for the journey north. Panahesi and Kiya were given their own boat, the *Dazzling Aten,* in which to sail. I stood on the quay and asked my sister how Akhenaten would know the right spot for the building.

"Obviously, it will be near the Nile," she snapped. "Between Memphis and Thebes on land upon which no other Pharaoh has built."

She was angry with me because I'd refused to go, and my father hadn't made me.

As the barges set sail, the king's pennants with images of Aten whipped back and forth in the wind. Hundreds of soldiers and workers were going. They'd be left in the desert to begin building Amarna. I waved at Nefertiti from the quay and she stared back, refusing to raise her hand to me. When the barges slipped over the horizon, I went into the gardens, wondering about seeds. Gardens for the new city would have to be started . . .

A palace worker watched me from the shade beneath a sycamore.

"May I help you, my lady?" The old man came over, his kilt stained with soil. His nails were full of earth. A true gardener. "You are the Sister of the King's Chief Wife," he said. "The one the women go to for remedies."

I glanced at in him surprise. "How did you—"

"I have seen the herbs you grow in pots," he admitted. "They are all medicinal."

I nodded. "Yes. Once in a while women come to me for help."

He smiled, as if he knew that it was more than once in a while; that sometimes different women came six and seven times a day for the plants that Ipu procured for me in the markets. My pots weren't big enough to fit all the herbs I would've liked to have planted, but she found the rest among the busy vendors on the quay. I looked across the royal gardens and sighed. There would be no green in the wide stretch of desert between Thebes and Memphis. And who knew how long it would be before markets sprang up that would sell raspberry leaf or acacia? I looked down at the goldenrods and moringa. In Amarna, there would be only weeds and tamarisk plants for company. "May I take some cuttings with me when I go?"

"To the new city of Amarna, my lady?"

I stood back, to get a better look at this servant. "You hear a lot in these gardens."

The old man shrugged. "The general likes to walk here at times and we talk together."

"General Nakhtmin?" I asked quickly.

"Yes. He comes from the barracks, my lady." He turned his eyes south, and I followed his gaze to a row of squat buildings. "He likes to sit here beneath the acacias."

"Why? What does he do?"

"Sometimes I think he is looking." The old servant fixed his sharp eyes on mine, as if he knew something he wasn't saying. "But not so much lately. The general has been very busy lately."

Busy shutting down the temples of Amun, I thought, and wondered if that's what the gardener meant. I studied his face, but a lifetime of practice had made it unreadable. "What is your name?" I asked the old man.

"Ahmose."

"And do you know where the general is now?"

Ahmose smiled widely at me. "I believe the general is with his soldiers, my lady. They are standing outside the palace leading in the petitioners."

"But Pharaoh is gone."

"The petitioners are seeing the great vizier Ay. Would my lady like me to take her to see them?"

I thought for a moment, imagining Nefertiti's response if she knew I'd been to see the general. "Yes, take me to see them."

"And the cuttings?" he asked.

"You can leave them with Ipu, my body servant."

The gardener put down his tools and led the way to the gates of Malkata. We approached a large arch at the end of the garden, and when we emerged it looked like the bird market back in Akhmim. Every variety of petitioner had come to ask a favor of the new Pharaoh. There were women with children, old men on donkeys, a boy playing grab-me with his sister, weaving in and out of the sun-wearied crowds.

I stood back in surprise. "Is it always like this?"

The gardener patted the dirt off his kilt. "More often than not. Of course," he added, "there are more petitioners now that the Elder has passed." We crossed the busy courtyard and saw that there were people as far as the eye could see, including wealthy women with gold bracelets that made music on their arms and poor women in simple rags who muttered unkindly at children as they scampered around them. Ahmose led us to a shady corner beneath the palace roof where the misbehaving sons of noblewomen were wrestling each other into the dirt. They paid no heed to us. One boy rolled over my sandal, smearing it with dust.

Ahmose cried out, "Your dress, my lady!"

I laughed. "I don't mind."

The gardener stared, but I wasn't Nefertiti. I shook off the dirt and studied the courtyard. "Why are the wealthy in one line and the poor in another?"

"The poor want simple things," Ahmose explained. "A new well, a better dam. But the wealthy are asking to keep their positions at court."

"Unfortunately, Pharaoh will still dismiss most of them," someone said in my ear.

I turned, and the general was standing behind me. "And why would he dismiss them?" I asked earnestly.

"Because all of these men once worked for his father."

"And he can't abide anything that was once his father's," I reasoned. "Not even his father's capital."

"Amarna." Nakhtmin watched me intently. "The viziers say he wants the new palace built within the year."

"Yes." I bit my lip so I wouldn't say anything against the ambitions of my family, then stepped closer. "And what is the news from the temples?" I asked quietly.

"The temples of Amun all across Egypt have been sealed."

I tried to imagine it: temples that had stood since the time of Hatshepsut boarded up and their holy waters left to dry. What would become of all the statues to Amun and the priests who'd once paid obeisance to them? How would the god know we still wanted his guidance? I closed my eyes and sent a silent prayer to the god who had watched over us for two thousand years. "And the temples of Isis? And Hathor?" I asked him.

"Destroyed."

I covered my mouth. "Were many killed?"

"Not by me," he said firmly as a soldier came toward us.

"General," he called, and when he saw me his eyes lit up with surprise. He executed a hasty bow. "Lady Mutnodjmet, your father is in the Audience Chamber. If you are looking for him—"

"I am not looking for him."

The soldier passed Nakhtmin a curious look.

"What did you need?" Nakhtmin asked the soldier.

"There is a woman who claims to be a cousin of the Elder's, but she's wearing neither gold nor silver and has no cartouche to identify herself. I placed her in line with the others, but she says she belongs—"

"Place her with the nobility. If she is lying, she will pay the price when her petition is revoked. Warn her of that before you move her."

The soldier bowed. "Thank you, General. My lady."

He left, and I noticed that Ahmose the gardener was gone.

"Shall I take you back to the palace?" Nakhtmin asked. "A hot, dirty courtyard full of petitioners is no place for the Sister of the King's Chief Wife."

I raised my brows. "Then what is my place?"

He took my arm and we walked together in the shade of the gardens. "With me." We stopped beneath the acacias. "You are tired of being handmaiden to your sister. Otherwise, you would be with her now. Choosing the site for Amarna."

"There can be no future for us, General—"

"Nakhtmin," he corrected me, taking my hands, and I let him.

"We're going to the desert soon," I warned. "We'll be living in tents."

He pulled me toward him. "I have lived in tents and barracks since I was twelve years old."

"But there will not be the freedom we have here."

"What?" He laughed. "Do you think I just want to meet you for secret trysts?"

"Then what do you want?"

"I want to marry you," he said simply.

I closed my eyes, enjoying the warmth of his skin against mine. In the gardens, there was no one to see us. "She will never let me go," I warned him.

"I am one of the highest-ranking generals in Pharaoh's army. My ancestors were viziers, and before that they were scribes. I am no common mercenary. Every Pharaoh has married his sisters and daughters to generals in the army as a way of protecting the royal family."

"Not this Pharaoh," I said, thinking of Akhenaten's fear of the army. "This royal family is not like any other."

"Then you don't belong with them." His lips brushed against mine, and far behind us the hundreds of petitioners disappeared.

We didn't leave the gardens until the sun had nearly set, setting the sky ablaze in violet and red. When I was late returning to my chamber, Ipu was in a state.

"I nearly sent the guards after you, my lady!"

I grinned, tossing my linen cloak onto the bed. "Oh, there was no need for that." I met her glance.

"My *lady*. You weren't with the general?"

I stifled a giggle. "Yes." Then I lost my enthusiasm, realizing what this would mean.

Ipu whispered, "What of Pharaoh?"

"Nefertiti will have to convince him," I said.

Ipu found a fresh robe in one the baskets and draped it over my shoulders, watching me with concern.

"I'm fifteen already!"

Ipu kept watching. She sat down on the edge of a gold and ebony chair, folding her hands in front of her. "I am thinking this will not go well, my lady."

I felt some of the color drain from my face, remembering Nakhtmin's strong arms around me. "I can't be her handmaiden *forever!*" I exclaimed. "She has a husband and a family and a hundred doting servants! She has endless noblewomen waiting for her appearance so they can run off and copy her robes, her hair, her latest earrings. What does she need *me* for?"

"She will always need you."

"But it isn't what I want! I don't *need* this!" I flung my arm to encompass the heavy woven tapestries and bright ivory lamps. "No." I shook my head. "She will have to accept it. She will have to convince him."

Ipu's face tightened. "Be careful. Think of the general's position."

"We will wait until the move is complete. Then I will tell her."

"And if he is dismissed?"

If he was dismissed, then I would know where I stood in my family.

When Nefertiti returned to Thebes, she was furious. She paced my chamber, kicking at a stray piece of coal from the brazier and enjoying the dark streak it left along the floor. It was Akhenaten's time with Kiya and he had not come back early, as he usually did.

"He wants to build her a palace," she seethed.

"So then you will let him," my father replied. He steadied her with his sharp blue eyes.

"A palace!" She turned. "An entire palace?"

"Let him build her a palace," my father said. "Who says it has to be in the city?"

Nefertiti's eyes grew wide. "It could be to the north. It could be outside the city even."

"But inside the walls," my father clarified.

"All right. But the walls will be wide," she warned. She collapsed into a chair and looked into the brazier's glowing flames. "The army is being sent to Amarna," she said casually.

My breath caught in my throat. "*What?* When do they leave?"

There was too much haste in my voice, and Nefertiti regarded me suspiciously.

"Tomorrow," she replied. "As soon as the servants pack, we will leave after them. I don't trust Panahesi. I want to see that every coin in the treasury is going into the building and not into his pocket."

"Then Tiye and I will be staying behind in Thebes," my father said. "We can't hear petitioners—"

"Dismiss the petitioners! I need you there with me."

"Impossible. Do you want a nation wealthy enough to build a new city or a nation on the brink of starvation?"

Nefertiti stood up. She wore her crown indoors, even with us, her own family. "Egypt will never be on the brink of starvation. Let the petitioners wait. Let the foreign governments find us in Amarna if they want us so badly."

My father shook his head and Nefertiti sank ungracefully into the chair.

"Then who will I have?" she bemoaned.

"You'll have your servants. You'll have Mutnodjmet."

She glanced at me. "Did you see the plans for the villas? One will be for you," she said. "Of course, you'll spend most of the time in the palace. I'll need help. Especially now." She looked down at her belly with tenderness. "Now that a son is on its way."

My father and I stood up at once and I exclaimed, "You are pregnant?"

Nefertiti lifted her chin proudly. "Two months. I've already told mother. Even Akhenaten knows." She narrowed her eyes. "He can go to Kiya every night of the month, but *I* am the one who is pregnant with his son. Two children. And all Kiya has given him is one."

I looked at my father, who said nothing about Kiya, even though I was sure I'd heard whisperings among the servants of how strange it was that since our family had come to court, Kiya had not fallen pregnant again. But my father's face showed nothing but pleasure.

▣ ▣ ▣

Senet boards and heavy thrones, cedar tables with dozens of chairs and lamps—all were loaded onto heavily weighted barges that floated north toward the city that wasn't even a city. I stood and watched Malkata stripped of its most glorious treasures and tried to imagine what my aunt must be feeling, watching the rooms she and her husband had furnished emptied on a young Pharaoh's whim. She stood with my father on the balcony of the Per Medjat, and they both surveyed the chaos in silence; her blue stare unnerved me.

"You won't be coming north then, Your Highness?"

"No. I won't be sleeping in a tent waiting for a palace to be built from the sand. Your father can go."

I was surprised. "You'll be coming with us then?" I asked my father.

"Only to see what's been done so far," he replied.

"But it's only been a month."

"And there are thousands of workers already building. They will have cut the roads and built houses by now."

"When you have the entire army at your disposal," my aunt said sharply, "it's amazing what can be done."

"And the Hittites?" I asked fearfully.

Tiye glared at my father. "We will simply have to hope our new queen will show my son the wisdom in defending our territories." It was clear from her tone that she expected no such thing.

Nefertiti has not done what she was supposed to, I thought. *Instead of risking her place as Chief Wife to sway Pharaoh, she's protected it by goading him on.* All three of us looked down on Akhenaten, instructing his Nubian guards, and I heard my aunt heave a heavy sigh. I wondered how much of it was regret over choosing Nefertiti as Chief Wife the day she'd come to visit us in Akhmim. She might have chosen any of the palace girls. Even Kiya. My father turned toward me.

"Go," he suggested. "Go and pack, Mutnodjmet."

I returned to my chamber and sat on my bed, looking at my windowsill where my little pots of herbs had been. They had been so many places with me. First in Thebes, then Memphis, then back to Thebes, and soon to the desert city of Amarna.

The site that Akhenaten had chosen for his capital was surrounded by hills. There were overhanging cliffs to the north and copper-colored dunes to the south. The Nile ran along the western edge of our new city, where goods from Memphis and Thebes could be brought. In the midst of the endless stretches of sand, a road had been built, big enough to fit three chariots side by side. It was the Royal Road, Nefertiti said, and when it was completed it would run through the center of the entire city. It was a road unlike any ever created, just as this would be a city unlike anything that had ever come before it, a jewel on the east bank of the Nile that would write our family's name in eternity. "When future generations speak of Amarna," she vowed, "they will speak of Nefertiti and Akhenaten the Builder."

The workmen's village was to the east. As my father had predicted, there were hundreds of workers' houses already built, and the barracks for the soldiers had been placed at the edge of the city. To the south, the villas of the nobility were being constructed around the beginnings of a palace, and in the midst of it all, surrounded by palms and giant oaks, lay the half-built Temple of Aten. An avenue of sphinxes led to its gates, where my sister would travel by chariot every morning to do obeisance to Aten. Even with the help of the army, I didn't see how it had all been done.

"How could they have done this in such little time?"

"Look at the construction," my father said tersely.

I squinted. "Cheap?"

"Mud brick and sandstone *talatat*. And instead of taking the time to create raised reliefs, they've cut them into the rock."

I turned, holding my robe down in the wind. "And you allowed it?" I asked him.

"What is to allow with Akhenaten? It's his city."

We looked down over the building and I said thoughtfully, "No, it's all our city now. It is with him that our names will be remembered."

My father didn't reply. Tonight he would sail the Nile toward Thebes and return only when the palace was finished. And who knew when that might be. Five months? A year?

Our procession of viziers, followed by nobility and a thousand court servants, turned into the walled City of Tents. Then we crossed on foot over the rolling landscape to the brightly colored pavilions of the royal court. The soldiers' tents were set up outside the wall in rings, three tents deep, and as we passed through the gates I wondered which was Nakhtmin's. We stopped before the Great Pavilion where the court of Amarna would dine.

"So what do you think?" Nefertiti asked at last.

"Your husband has large aspirations," our father said, and only I knew what he really meant. That it was a cheap, quick city, a pale shadow of Thebes.

Two soldiers parted the curtains of the Great Pavilion. Newly polished tables stretched over rugs and tiled flooring. The walls had been covered with tapestries. At the longest table, Akhenaten was pouring himself wine. He was smug in his confidence as he raised his cup. "So how does the great vizier find the new city?"

My father was the perfect courtier. "The roads are very wide," he replied.

"Three chariots can ride abreast," he boasted, seating himself. "Maya says if we push, the palace will be done by the beginning of Mesore."

My father hesitated. "You'll get poor quality and half finished monuments."

"What does it matter," he hissed, "so long as the temple and the palace are built to last? The workers can rebuild their houses. I want this city before I die."

My father pointed out, "Your Highness, you are only nineteen—"

Akhenaten brought down his fist on the table in front of him. "And I am hunted at every hour! Do you really think I'm safe among the soldiers? Do you think General Nakhtmin wouldn't try to turn my men against me if he were given the chance? And then the priests of *Amun*," Akhenaten continued. "How many might escape the quarries to come hunt me in my sleep? In my own pavilion? In the halls of my own palace?"

Nefertiti laughed nervously. "This is foolishness, Akhenaten. You have the best guards in Egypt."

"Because they are *Nubians!* The only men who are loyal to me are outside of Egypt!" Akhenaten's eyes flashed and I looked to my father. He had dropped his perfect courtier's mask and I could see what he was thinking. The Pharaoh of Egypt had become insane. "Who can I trust?" Akhenaten demanded. "My wife. My daughter. The High Priest of Aten and you." He whirled on my father. "Who else?"

My father met his gaze. "There's an army of men waiting for you to lead them. They trust you and believe in your will to conquer and keep the Hittites at bay. They will do whatever you ask."

"And I am asking them to build the greatest city in Egypt! Nefertiti tells me you are returning to Thebes. When?"

"Tonight. Until the palace is finished, it is the wisest thing, Your Highness."

Akhenaten set down his wine. "Isn't my mother in Thebes?"

Nefertiti glanced at my father.

"I don't like the idea of the two of you there," Akhenaten admitted. "In the former capital of Egypt. Alone."

Nefertiti moved quickly around the side of the table. "Akhenaten, it is better this way. Do you want foreign leaders to send their ambassadors to meet us in pavilions? What will the ambassadors think?

If they come to Amarna before it's finished, imagine what they will report back home to their kings."

Akhenaten looked at his wife and then at his trusted vizier. "You're right," he said slowly. "No dignitary must see Amarna before it's finished." But his dark eyes met my father's. "You will not be taking Mutny."

My father smiled easily. "No," he replied. "Mutny stays here."

Akhenaten was afraid my father would take me to Thebes as his heir, and then crown himself Pharaoh to reign with Tiye. *So I am to be his hostage,* I thought. Nefertiti colored at the idea that my father would ever choose me over her. She swept past Akhenaten, hooking her arm through our father's and said sharply, "Come. I will see you off."

Akhenaten rose to join us, and Nefertiti leveled him with her gaze.

We stood on the quay and my eyes filled with tears. It was possible that my father would be gone for months, and suddenly I found myself wishing as much as Akhenaten did that the palace would be finished.

"Don't be sad, little cat." My father kissed the top of my head. "You have your mother and sister."

"And you will come back," my mother's voice was constricted, "just as soon as the palace is finished?"

He cupped her chin in his palm, brushing her hair from her face with his thumb. "I promise. It is business I'm going for. If I didn't have to—"

Nefertiti stepped forward, interrupting their moment. "Good-bye, Father."

My father gave a parting look to my mother, then turned to Nefertiti. He embraced her. "Your time will be near when I return," he said.

She rested her hand on her stomach. "An heir for the throne of Egypt," she said proudly.

We watched the ship set sail. As the barge disappeared over the horizon, Akhenaten came to stand next to me. "He is a loyal vizier." He put his arms around my shoulders and I tensed. "Isn't that right, Mutnodjmet?"

I nodded.

"I hope so," he whispered. "Because if he should try to make a move for the crown, it wouldn't be my wife who would suffer the consequences."

⊡ ⊡ ⊡

"My lady!" Ipu cried. "My lady, sit down. You are shaking."

I took a seat on my bed and put my hands beneath my legs. "Would you make me some tea?"

Ipu lit the brazier. Once she'd boiled a pan of water, she poured it into a cup with leaves. "You look ill," she said quietly, bringing me the tea and inviting my confidence.

I lifted the cup to my lips and drained it. "It's nothing," I said. Only an empty threat. My father was no traitor. "Was anyone here to visit today?" I asked her.

"Like the general?"

My eyes flew to the door and she lowered her voice.

"No. I'm sorry. Perhaps he can't get through the royal camp with so many guards."

A shadow lengthened outside the door of our pavilion. Someone pushed back the flap and Merit appeared.

"My lady, the queen wishes to see you," she said. "The young princess has an earache and the queen is ill. Pharaoh has asked for a physician, but she's said she'll only have you."

"Tell her I'm coming," I said at once. Merit disappeared, and I rummaged through my boxes. I took out mint for Meritaten. But what for Nefertiti? "I don't know why she should be sick," I mumbled. She was only two months. She had carried Meritaten for five months before ever feeling ill.

"Perhaps it is a son," Ipu said. I nodded. Yes. Perhaps that was the sign. I took out the fenugreek, shoving the dried herbs into several pouches.

The Nubian guards parted to let me inside the Royal Pavilion where the royal couple slept. At the bed, Akhenaten was standing over Nefertiti, holding her while she heaved into a cup. It was a strangely tender scene—this man, who thought nothing of sending men to their death, hovering over his queen while she was sick.

"Mutny, the herbs." Nefertiti groaned.

Akhenaten watched me unwrap the herbs. "What are they?"

"Fenugreek, Your Highness."

He snapped his fingers twice without taking his eyes from my face and two guards entered into the pavilion. "Test them."

I gaped at Nefertiti, who said sharply, "She's my sister. She's not going to poison me."

"She's a rival to the crown."

"She's my *sister* and I *trust* her!" Nefertiti's voice brooked no argument. "And when she's done, she will go to the nurse's tent for Meritaten."

The guards stepped back. Akhenaten said nothing as I boiled water, steeping the herbs to make a tea. I brought it to my sister and she drank it completely. Akhenaten watched us from across the pavilion. "You don't have to watch us," Nefertiti snapped. "Go find Maya and look over the plans for the villa."

Akhenaten passed me a look of deep hatred, then swept through the tent flap and was gone.

"You shouldn't shout while I am here," I told her. "He'll think it's me that makes you angry with him."

"It's his obsession with assassination that makes me angry. He suspects everyone."

"Even your own sister?"

She heard the criticism in my voice and said defensively, "He is

Pharaoh of Egypt. No one faces the danger that he does, for nobody's visions are grander than his."

I raised my brows. "Or more expensive."

"What is expense? We're building a city that will last through eternity. Longer than you or I ever will."

"You are building a city of cheap material," I replied. "A city as cheap as it is quick."

"Is this Father talking?" she demanded. "Does he think this city is cheap?"

"Yes. And what if we're invaded? Where will the gold come from to defend ourselves?"

She sat up. "I won't hear of this. I am carrying Egypt's future in my belly and you are going on as if it's doomed to failure! You're just jealous! You're jealous that I have a beautiful little girl and a son on the way, and you are nearly sixteen and Father has not even decided who you shall marry!"

I stepped back, stung. "He hasn't decided who I shall marry because of *you*. He wants me here with *you*, waiting hand and foot on *you*, giving advice to *you*. If I had a husband, none of that would be possible. *Would* it?"

We stared at one another.

"Am I dismissed?" I asked her.

"To go to Meritaten. Then you will have dinner with us," she replied.

It wasn't a question. It was a command.

⊡ ⊡ ⊡

"What are you looking for, my lady?"

"My cloak. I'm going out."

"But it's nearly nighttime. You can't go out now," Ipu cried. "It could be dangerous."

"My sister has plenty of guards. I'll take one of them." I picked up my basket for collecting herbs and Ipu trailed after me. "Shall I come instead?"

"Only if you feel like a walk." I didn't look behind me to see whether she had come, but I could hear her footsteps. She caught up to me at the gates. "You can't go into a man's camp—"

"I'm the Sister of the King's Chief Wife," I retorted. "I can do what I want."

"My lady," Ipu's voice was desperate. "My lady." She put her hand out to stop me. "Please, let me go instead. Let me give him a message."

Outside the walls, fires were being lit in the soldiers' camp. One of those fires belonged to the general. I stopped and wondered what message I should give him. "Tell him . . ." I bit my lip and thought. "Tell him that I accept."

"What do you *accept?*" she asked cautiously.

"Just tell him I accept and to come tonight."

Ipu's eyes grew wide as cups. "To your *pavilion?*"

"Yes. He can say he is coming to see Pharaoh."

"But won't they know?" Ipu glanced at a nearby soldier.

"Perhaps. But the guards at the gate are his men and they *despise* Akhenaten. They will turn their heads the other way. That I promise."

Amun must have been watching over me that night, because the fanfare and music accompanying our regular meals was mercifully short. Nefertiti ignored me while everyone laughed, telling stories about Memphis and what Amarna would be like once it was finished. Nevertheless, I walked Nefertiti back to the Royal Pavilion, and as we stepped into the chill night she shivered. Four guards stood back and two held open the flap leading into the Royal Pavilion. I walked Nefertiti to her large bed hung with linen. "Come and rub my back," she requested.

I took off my cloak and began with her shoulders. They were tense, even for a woman with child.

"I wish Father was here," she complained. "He'd understand how difficult this all is. The building and planning. He understands me."

"And I don't?"

"You don't know what it's like to be queen."

"So Father does?"

"Father rules this kingdom. Even without the crook or flail, he is Pharaoh of Egypt."

"And I'm just a handmaiden to my sister," I said sharply.

She tensed. "Why are you so bitter?"

"Because I'm almost sixteen years old and no one has planned *my* future!" I stopped rubbing the oil into her back. "Your future is all laid out. You're queen. Someday you'll be a mother to a king. And what will I be?"

"The Sister of the King's Chief Wife!"

"But who will I love?"

She sat up, taken aback. "*Me*."

I stared at her. "And what about a family?"

"*I'm* your family." She lay down again, expecting me to rub. "Warm the oil. It's cold."

I closed my eyes and did as I was told. I wasn't going to complain, not when it would only prolong my time in the Great Pavilion. I waited until Nefertiti fell asleep, then I washed my hands and crept outside into the cool Phamenoth night. In my own pavilion, Ipu was waiting. She stood up as soon as she saw me.

"Are you sure about this?" she whispered. "Do you still want him to come?"

I had never been more certain. "Yes."

Ipu's hands flew around her in excitement. "Then I should braid your hair, my lady."

I sat down on my feathered cushion and couldn't sit still. I had already told Ipu what the general had said. Now I told her that I wanted a quiet life. "A life away from any palace in a place where I can tend my herb garden and—"

There was the crunch of boots on gravel and we both turned. Ipu dropped my braids in her hands. "He's here!"

I grabbed the mirror to check my appearance. "How do I look?"

Ipu searched my face. "Like a young woman ready to meet her lover," she said with slight consternation. "If your father—"

"Shh," I remonstrated. "Not now!" I dropped the mirror. "Open the tent."

Ipu went to the door and the general's voice came softly through hangings. "And you are sure that she sent for me?"

"Of course. She is waiting for you inside."

Nakhtmin showed himself in. Then Ipu disappeared as I had instructed, and I held my breath. The general stood before me and bowed. "My lady."

Suddenly, I was very nervous. "Nakhtmin."

"You sent for me?"

"I have thought over your proposal," I replied.

He raised his eyebrows. "And what has my lady decided?" he asked.

"I have decided that I am done being the handmaiden to Nefertiti."

He stared at me in the firelight. In the glow of the flames, his hair was like copper. "Have you told your father this?"

My cheeks warmed. "Not yet."

He thought of Nefertiti. "And I suspect the queen will be angry."

"To say nothing of Akhenaten," I added. I looked up into his face and he wrapped his arms around me, grinning. "But what if we are banished?" I asked him.

"Then we will go back to Thebes. I will sell the land I inherited from my father and we will buy a farm. One that is all ours, *miw-sher,* and we'll have a quiet life away from the court and all its entanglements."

"But you will no longer be a general," I warned.

"And you will no longer be Sister to the King's Chief Wife."

We were quiet, clasping hands by the fire. "I wouldn't mind that."

I found I couldn't tear my gaze away from his, and he stayed until the early hours of the dawn. It was the same throughout that entire month of Phamenoth and into Pharmuthi: The guards would look the other way and smile as he made his way to my tent. Sometimes when he came, we talked by the brazier, and I asked him what the men thought of Akhenaten.

"They stay because they are paid so well," he said. "It's the only thing that keeps them from revolt. They want to fight. But they're willing to build so long as the gold keeps coming."

"And Horemheb?"

Nakhtmin heaved a heavy sigh. "I suppose that Horemheb is far to the north."

"Killed?"

"Or fighting. Either way"—he stared into the flames of our small fire—"he is gone and Pharaoh has what he wanted."

I was quiet for a moment. "And what do the men say about my sister?"

He glanced sideways at me, to gauge how much I really wanted to know. "They are under her spell the same as Pharaoh."

"Because she is beautiful?"

He watched me carefully. "And entertaining. She goes into the workers' villages and tosses deben of silver and gold into the streets. But she would do better to toss them bread, for there's little to buy, even with all the gold in Egypt."

"Is there a shortage?" I asked.

He glanced at me.

"I didn't know." In the royal camp, there was plenty of everything: meats, fruits, breads, wines.

"Until the population of Thebes moves north, there will always be a shortage. There are few bakers and no place to house them even if there were more."

A shadow appeared outside the tent and Nakhtmin rose. His hand flew to his sword.

"My lady?" It was only Ipu. She pushed aside the flap and looked at Nakhtmin, blushing although he was fully clothed. "The queen is asking for you, my lady. She wants her tea."

I looked at Nakhtmin. "She doesn't want tea. She only wants to gloat that they've nearly finished the palace."

"She could be an ally to us," he said practically. "Go," he suggested, "and I will see you tomorrow." He stood up and my eyes filled with tears. Nakhtmin said kindly, "It's not forever, *miw-sher.* You said yourself the palace is nearly finished. In a few days, then, your father will be here and we will go to him."

Nefertiti wasn't due to give birth until Thoth, but she walked through the camp as if the child might come any day. Everyone had to stand three paces back when they were near her, and work in the city stopped when she went past, so that the noise of the hammers wouldn't disturb the unborn child. She was convinced that it would be a prince, and Akhenaten catered to her every need, ordering her wool from Sumer and the softest linen from the weavers of Thebes. Then she tested her power by demanding that he stop visiting Kiya in the pavilion across the road, in case her worry should hurt the child.

"Could it happen?" Akhenaten came upon me at the well. Though we had servants for fetching water, I enjoyed the musty scent of the earth. I lowered my bucket and shaded my eyes.

"Could what happen, Your Majesty?"

He looked across the lotus pond that had been built in the midst of our camp. "Could she lose the child if I were to upset her?"

"Anything could happen, Your Majesty, if she were upset enough."

He hesitated. "How upset?"

He misses Kiya, I thought. *She listens to his poems and draws him into her quiet world while Nefertiti's world never stops.* "I suppose it depends on how fragile she is."

We both looked at Nefertiti, her small powerful body moving across the camp, trailed by seven guards.

She came up to us and Akhenaten grinned, as if he hadn't been talking about visiting Kiya. "My queen." He took her hand and kissed it tenderly. "I have news."

Nefertiti's eyes glittered. "What is it?"

"Maya sent word this morning."

Nefertiti let out a little gasp. "The city is finished," she guessed.

Akhenaten nodded. "Maya has sworn that within days the walls will be painted and we shall leave our pavilions behind."

Nefertiti gave a small cry, but I thought at once of Nakhtmin. How would we meet once we moved? He would live with his men in the barracks and I would be trapped inside Akhenaten's palace.

"Shall we go and see it?" Akhenaten asked eagerly. "Shall we reveal our city to the people?"

"We'll take everyone," Nefertiti decided. "Every vizier, every noblewoman, every child in Amarna." She spun around to face me. "Has there been word from Father?"

"Nothing," I replied.

She narrowed her eyes. "He hasn't written to you secretly?"

I stared at her. "Of course not."

"Good. I want to be the one to tell him Amarna is finished. When he sees the palace"—her face was exultant—"he will realize that Akhenaten was right. We have built the greatest city in Egypt."

At noon, the announcement was made: The gates would be opened and Amarna would be unveiled to the people at last. A palpable excitement passed through the camp. By orders of Pharaoh, only workers and noblemen had been allowed inside the gates to see the construction. Now the palace would be revealed, along with hundreds of villas crouched against the towering ridge behind it. By evening, the long procession of chariots swept through the desert, carrying viziers and noblemen, foreigners and commoners. Riding beside me in my chariot, Ipu gasped as the gates were drawn open to the city of Amarna.

The magnificent temple, with its glittering quay and its tightly packed villages, had been finished. Hundreds of white villas had been built for the nobility, and they sheltered like pearls in the folds of the hills. Everywhere was construction, everywhere were workers, but the city itself shone lustrous and white.

The procession went first to the Temple of Aten. Beneath its pillared courtyard, priests were making sacrifices to the sun. The men bowed in obeisance to Pharaoh and my sister, and they fanned away the smoke so we could see how beautifully the courtyard had been done. Moringa and pomegranate trees trimmed the wall, but most brilliant were the safflowers, yellow and cheerful in the fading light of the open court. Light had obviously been important in the design, and Akhenaten announced proudly that he was the one who had instructed Maya to build the clerestory windows inside.

"What are those?" I whispered.

Nefertiti smiled slyly. "Come see."

We passed from the courtyard to the inner sanctum, where the evening light streamed down from the ceiling, filtering through long windows. I had never seen anything like it.

"He is a genius," Ipu said wonderingly.

I pressed my lips together, but there was no denying it. Nothing like it had ever been built.

Viziers and nobility walked into the temple, studying the tapestries and large mosaics while the rest of the procession waited in the courtyard.

Nefertiti was triumphant. "What do you think Father will say?" she asked.

That this is the most expensive temple ever built. But I replied, "That it is magnificent."

She smiled; I had said what she wanted to hear. But I would never tell her that it was worth Amun's gold, or worth Egypt's security and her vassal states. Akhenaten came up beside us.

"Maya shall be rewarded richly," he announced. He surveyed the fluted pillars of his temple, the wide stairways leading up to balconies where smaller sanctuaries were bathed in light. Warm air floated up from the river, wafting through the courtyard. "When the emissaries return to Assyria and Rhodes, they will know what kind of Pharaoh reigns now in Egypt."

"And when they see the bridge"—Nefertiti opened a heavy wooden door—"they will know that a visionary planned this." The door swung back to reveal a bridge that arched over the Royal Road, connecting the Temple of Aten to the palace. It was higher than any bridge I had ever seen, wider and more elaborate. As we walked its expanse, I had the feeling I was crossing into the future, that I was seeing my grandchildren's lives and what their world would look like after I was gone.

In the palace, no expense had been spared. Windows swept from ceiling to floor and perfumed fountains tinkled musically in sunlit corners. There were chairs of ebony and ivory, beds inlaid with precious stone. I was shown to the room that I would have, and the chamber my parents would take, with blue glazed tiles and mosaics of hunting scenes.

"We have named it Riverside Palace," Nefertiti said, taking me to see every corner and niche. "Kiya's palace has been built to the north."

"Outside the walls?" I asked warily.

She smiled. "No, but far."

We walked through the water garden with its alabaster fountain, and I was amazed at what had been done. I couldn't imagine how they had built it all so quickly, or how much gold it had taken. Nefertiti kept walking, pointing out statues that I should notice and brightly painted walls where her image stared back at us. The court followed jubilantly behind us, whispering and exclaiming among themselves. "And this is where the royal workshop shall be," my sister said. "Thutmose will sculpt every part of our lives."

"In a thousand years, our people will know what we ate and where we drank," Akhenaten vowed. "They will even see the Royal Robing Room." He pushed open the door to a chamber with plush red cushions and boxes for wigs. There were kohl pots, copper mirrors, silver brushes, and perfume jars arranged on cedar stands, waiting to be used. "We will offer them a glimpse into our palace, and they will feel as if they have known the rulers of Egypt for a lifetime."

I surveyed the opulent chamber and wondered if I knew them myself. Nefertiti had spent Egypt poor for a city in the desert. It was new and it was breathtaking, but it was the sweat of soldiers that had built these walls, and painted these murals, and erected the colossal images of Akhenaten and Nefertiti so that the people would know they were always watching.

"When Thutmose is finished," Nefertiti swore, "Egypt will know me better than any other queen. In five hundred years, I'll be alive to them, Mutnodjmet. Living on the walls, in the palace, across the temples. I'll be immortal not just in the Afterlife, but here in Egypt. I could build a shrine where my children and their children would go to remember me. But when they are gone, what then? This"—and Nefertiti looked up, touching the brightly painted walls—"will last until eternity."

We passed through the doors of the Audience Chamber, and I noticed there were no images of bound Nubians on the tiles. Instead, there were images of the sun, its rays reaching down to Nefertiti and Akhenaten, kissing them in blessing. Akhenaten strode to the top of the dais and spread his arms. "When Thebans come," he proclaimed, "every family will be given a home. Our people shall remember us as the monarchs who made them wealthy, and they will bless the city of Amarna!"

"My lady, are you ill?" Ipu ran to fetch a bowl while I held my stomach and emptied its contents two, then three times. I groaned, resting my cheek against the soft leather of my padded stool. Ipu put her hands on her hips. "What have you eaten?"

"I've had nothing since the tour of the palace. Goat's cheese and nuts."

She frowned. "And your breasts?" She tugged at the corner of my shirt. "Are they darker"—she pressed her finger against my flesh—"tender?"

My eyes went wide and a sudden fear welled up inside me. These were Nefertiti's symptoms. This couldn't be happening to me. Not after all the help I'd given women in this very camp. Ipu shook her head and whispered, "When was the last time you bled?"

"I don't know. I don't remember."

"What about the acacia?" she demanded.

"I've been taking it."

"All the time?"

"I don't know. I think. So much has happened."

Ipu gasped. "Your father will be furious."

My lip trembled and I buried my head in my hands, for, instinctively, I knew it was true. I had missed my blood. "And I'm my mother's only daughter," I explained. "She will be so upset, so lonely if—" I began to cry and Ipu took me in her arms, stroking my long hair.

"It may not be so bad," she comforted. "No one knows better than you that there are ways to be rid of it."

I looked up sharply. "No!" I clasped my hands across my stomach. *Kill Nakhtmin's child?* "Never."

"Then what else? If you have this child, your father will never make you a marriage!"

"Good," I said wildly. "Then the only man who will want me is the general."

But Ipu's voice grew desperate. "And what about Pharaoh?"

"I have done enough for Nefertiti. It's her turn now. She will have to convince him."

Ipu's look was incredulous, as if she didn't believe it would happen.

"She *has* to," I said.

I paced the tent all afternoon. Two women came for acacia and honey, and my insides turned as I handed the mixture to them, thinking of how careless I had been. Then Merit appeared; the queen was asking for me.

"She wants to know if you will be coming for dinner?"

"No," I said, too ill with regret to face my sister. "Go and tell her that I am sick."

Merit disappeared, and several minutes later Nefertiti parted the curtains without announcing her arrival.

"You are always sick lately." She strode to a chair and sat down, studying me. I was sorting my herbs, and my hands trembled when they came to the acacia. "Especially at night," she added suspiciously.

"I haven't been well for several days." I didn't lie.

She watched me closely. "I hope you haven't been taken with that general." The color must have drained from my face because she added harshly, "This family cannot trust anyone in the army."

"So you've said."

Nefertiti studied me. "He has not come to visit you?" she demanded.

I lowered my gaze.

"He has come to visit you?" she shrieked. "In the camp?"

"What does it matter?" I snapped shut my herb box. "You have a husband, a family, a child—"

"*Two* children."

"And what do I have?"

She sat back as if I had slapped her. "You have me."

I looked around my lonely pavilion, as if she could understand. "That's it?"

"I am Queen of Egypt." She stood swiftly. "And you are the Sister to the King's Chief Wife! It is your destiny to serve."

"Says who?"

"It is Ma'at!" she exclaimed.

"Is it Ma'at to tear down the temples of Amun?"

"You will not say that," she hissed.

"Why? Because you're afraid the gods will be angry?"

"There is no greater god than Aten! And you had better learn to accept that. In a month, the Temple of Aten will be finished and the people will worship Aten the way they worshipped Amun—"

"And who will collect the money they give as offerings?"

"Father," she replied.

"And who will he give the money to?"

Nefertiti's face grew dark. "We built this city for the glory of our reign. It is our right."

"But the people don't want to move to Amarna. They have homes in Thebes."

"They have *hovels* in Thebes! Here, we will do what no Pharaoh has ever done before! Every family that moves to Amarna will be given a home—"

I laughed meanly. "And have you seen those homes?" Nefertiti fell silent. "Have you *seen* the homes? You visited your palace, but you didn't see that the homes of the workers are made of mud brick and *talatat.* Come Inundation, they will crumble to the ground."

"How do you know?"

I didn't answer her. I couldn't tell her it was because Father said they would, or that Nakhtmin had said the same when we'd lain in bed together.

"You don't know that," she triumphed. "Come. We are eating."

A command. Not a request.

Then, before she left, she said over her shoulder, "And we will not discuss the general again. You will remain single and in my service until Father or I choose a husband for you."

I bit my tongue against a sharp retort.

"And when is the last time you visited the princess?" she demanded.

"Yesterday."

"You are her aunt," she pronounced. "It goes without saying that she wants to see more of you."

You mean you want to see more of me. She disappeared, and I sat down and looked at my little belly. "Oh, what in this world will your father say when he hears about you, little one? And how will Nefertiti convince Akhenaten that you are no threat to his reign?"

Dinner in the Great Pavilion lasted forever and I wasn't in the mood for Thutmose, with his talk of henna and hair and the unfashionable beards on the emissaries from Ugarit. All I could think was how, in a few days, Nakhtmin wouldn't be able to visit my pavilion. He would have to sneak into the palace, if that was even possible, and who knew how long that would last before he was caught?

I looked across the table at Nefertiti; her child would be a prince. Without my father's consent or the king's, mine would be the fatherless heir to nothing. A bastard child. I watched as the servants catered to Nefertiti, and a deep longing welled up inside me when Akhenaten put his arms around her shoulders and whispered softly, "My little Pharaoh," staring down at her round stomach.

I stood up and asked to be excused.

"Now?" Nefertiti snapped. "This early? What if I have pains? What if—" She saw my expression and changed tactics. "Just stay for a game of Senet."

"No."

My sister pleaded. "Not even one game?"

The courtiers in the pavilion turned to look at me.

I stayed only for a single game in Nefertiti's pavilion, which my sister won and not because I let her.

"You should try," she complained. "It's not fun to win all the time."

"I do," I said flatly.

She laughed, getting up and stretching her back. "Only Father and I are a real match," she said, moving to the brazier. The firelight cast her shadow across the walls of the pavilion. "He's coming soon," she said lightly.

"You've had word?"

Nefertiti heard the eagerness in my voice and shrugged. "He will be here in six days. Of course, he won't see us move into the palace . . ."

But I wasn't listening to her. In six days, I would be able to tell him about his grandchild.

"A child, my little cat. *Our* child!" Nakhtmin was beside himself with joy. He drew me into the folds of his arms and pressed me tightly to his chest, but not so tightly as to crush the baby. "Have you told the queen?" he asked, and when he saw the ashen look on my face he frowned. "But she must be happy for you?"

"That I will be pregnant at the same time she is, sharing in my father's attention?" I shook my head. "You don't know Nefertiti."

"But she will accept it. We will marry, and if Pharaoh is still angry, we will leave the city and buy a farm in the hills."

I looked at him doubtfully.

"Don't worry, *miw-sher.*" He pressed me close to him. "It's a child. Who can resent a child?"

The next morning, I went to Nefertiti. She would be angry, but she would be furious if I told our father before her. She was in the Royal Pavilion, the morning light filtering through the walls and illuminating the chaos all around her: servants moving baskets, men packing heavy chests, and women gathering armfuls of cosmetics and linens.

"I need to speak with you," I said.

"Not there!" she cried. Every person in the pavilion froze. She pointed wildly at a servant with linens in his arms. "Over there!"

"Where's Akhenaten?" I asked.

"Already at the palace. We are moving tonight. You should be ready," she said, which made my need more urgent. Once we moved, Nakhtmin couldn't wander into my tent. The palace would be guarded. There would be gates and Akhenaten's Nubian men, who were jealous of the army.

"Nefertiti."

"What?" She didn't take her eyes off the commotion. "What is it?"

I looked around to see who was listening, but the servants were making too much noise to hear us, so I said it. "I am pregnant."

She was very still for a moment, so still I thought she hadn't heard me. Then she dug her nails into my arm and pulled me painfully to the side. "You are *what?*" The cobra on her crown glittered at me with its red eyes. "It is not the general's child," her voice was threatening. "Tell me it's not the general's child!"

I said nothing and she pulled me farther away into her chamber, separated from the antechamber by hanging cloth. "Does Father know about this?" she whispered savagely.

"No." I shook my head. "I came to you first."

Her eyes filled with venom. "Pharaoh will be outraged."

"We are no threat to him. All we want to do is live together and be married—"

"You have bedded a common soldier!" she shouted. "You take a man to your bed without my *permission?* Do you think to insult me?"

She moved threateningly close. "What you do is for *this family,* and now you have put this family in danger."

"This is only a child. *My* child."

"Who will come to be a threat to the throne. A royal baby. The son of a general!"

I stared at her in shock. "Our grandfather was a general, and he kept the army readied and loyal to Pharaoh. Only your husband could see it as a threat. Generals have always married into the royal court!"

"Not in *Amarna,"* Nefertiti seethed. "Akhenaten will *never* have it."

"Please, Nefertiti, you have to convince him. This child is no threat—"

She cut her hand through the air. "No. You got yourself pregnant and you will get yourself out of it. You of all people know perfectly well how to do it."

I stared at her with wide-eyed horror. My hands flew protectively to my stomach. "You would make me do that?" I whispered.

"You are the one who made the problem with your eyes wide open. And your legs," she added spitefully. "I should have known to keep you closer."

I drew myself up to my fullest height. "You have a husband, a daughter, and a second child on the way, and you deny me one? *One* child?"

"I have denied you *nothing!"* She was wild with rage, and now there was only the faintest sound of moving and packing coming from beyond the cloth. "I married Akhenaten to give you *everything,* and you throw it all away on a *commoner.* You are the most selfish sister in Egypt!"

"Because I dared to love someone other than you?"

The truth was too much. She stalked across the room toward the curtains, then said over her shoulder, "You will be at the banquet tonight in the palace."

I bit back my pride. "Will you tell him we want to get married?"

She stopped, making me ask her again.

"Will you?"

"Tonight you may have your answer," she said. The curtain twitched closed behind her, and I was alone in the king's inner chamber.

I went back to my pavilion and was sick to my stomach, wondering if I should find Nakhtmin at the building site and warn him.

"Of what, my lady?" Ipu asked sensibly. "And how will you get there?" She put her hands over mine. "Wait for the queen's decision. She will ask for you. You are her sister and you've served her well." Ipu handed me my clothes for the night's celebration. "Come," she encouraged. "Then I will see that your things are brought to the palace."

"I want to see my mother first," I told her. "I want you to bring her here."

Ipu stood for a moment to measure my resolve, then nodded quietly and left.

I put on the long tunic and golden belt, then fastened a beaded necklace around my neck, rehearsing what I would say when my mother came. Her only daughter. The one child Tawaret had seen fit to give her. I studied my reflection in the mirror, a young girl with dark hair and wide green eyes. Who was she, this girl who would allow herself to become pregnant with a general's child? I exhaled slowly and saw that my hands were shaking.

"Mutnodjmet?" My mother cast her eyes across my pavilion with disapproval. "Mutnodjmet, why haven't you packed? We are moving tonight."

"Ipu said she will do it while we're gone." I moved over on the leather bench so that she could sit next to me. "But first I want you to sit here." I hesitated. "Because . . . because I have something I must tell you right now."

She knew what I was going to say before I spoke. Her eyes traveled down to my midriff, and she covered her mouth. "You are with child."

I nodded, and my eyes filled with tears. "Yes, *mawat*."

My mother was very still, the way Nefertiti had been, and I wondered if she was going to strike me for the first time in my life. "You have slept with the general." Her voice was flat.

My eyes pooled with tears. "We want to be married," I said, but my mother wasn't listening.

"Every night I watched him come into the camp and I thought that Akhenaten had beckoned him. I should have known. When has Pharaoh ever been interested in the army?" My mother searched my face. "So the guards looked the other way for you?"

Shame colored my cheeks. "It would have happened without them. We love each other—"

"*Love? Commoners* marry for love. And they divorce just as quickly! You are the Sister of the King's Chief Wife! We would have married you to a prince. A *prince,* Mutnodjmet. You could have been a princess in the land of Egypt."

"But I don't want to be a princess." My tears flooded over. "That's Nefertiti's dream. I'm pregnant, *mawat.* I'm pregnant with your grandchild and the man I love wants to carry me across the threshold of a new house to marry me." I looked up at her. "Isn't there any part of you that is happy?"

She pressed her lips together. Then her resolve crumbled and she took me in her arms. "Oh, Mutnodjmet, my little Mutnodjmet. A mother." She wept tenderly. "But to what kind of a child?"

"A beloved one."

"One that will frighten Pharaoh and outrage your sister. Nefertiti will never accept it."

"She must," I said firmly, pulling away. "I'm a woman. I have the right to choose my husband. This is still Egypt—"

"But it's Akhenaten's Egypt. Maybe if you were in Akhmim . . ." My mother spread her palms. "But this is the king's city. The choices are his."

"And Nefertiti's," I stressed. "By the time Father arrives, the villas will be finished. Nefertiti can convince Akhenaten to let us live there."

"She will be angry."

"Then she will have to learn to accept it."

My mother picked up my hand and squeezed it. "Your father will be shocked when he returns. Two daughters, both carrying children."

"He will be happy. Both of his daughters are fertile."

My mother's smile was bitter. "He would be happier if you had married a prince."

That night there was feasting throughout the new city of Amarna. Everywhere was the sound of laughter, and as I helped my mother into a chariot I thought, *Nefertiti has done this on purpose. She's told me she will give me an answer tonight hoping I won't reach her among all these people.*

The courtyards outside the palace were filled with servants bearing platters of honeyed nuts, plump figs, and pomegranates. Thousands of men from the army drank in the streets with total abandon, singing about war and sex and love. I looked for Nakhtmin as we entered the palace, scanning the crowds for his broad shoulders and bright hair.

"He won't be here," my mother said. "He will be with his men."

I flushed to realize that my thoughts were so transparent. A servant took us to the Great Hall, where table after table was filled with feasting viziers and the flirting daughters of wealthy men, all imitating my sister in the way they dressed in the sheerest of linens, hennaing their hands and feet and breasts. But the two Horus thrones on the dais were empty.

"Where is the queen?" I asked, taken aback.

"In the streets, my lady!" cried a passing servant. "They are throwing out gold!" He grinned. "To *everyone.*"

"Come." My mother guided me by the arm.

I followed her to the table of honor before the dais. Panahesi was there with Kiya. So was the sculptor Thutmose and the builder Maya, and I wondered when they had become family. An old man with gold rings on his fingers called to my mother from across the hall and she changed course to go toward him. A servant pulled out an armed chair and Kiya's ladies watched me with quiet menace from under their wigs. As I took my seat, Kiya announced brightly, "Why, Lady Mutnodjmet, how nice to see you. I thought you might have missed the celebration."

"And why would I have done that?" I asked.

"We thought you were sick."

The color drained from my cheeks and the viziers passed questioning glances among themselves.

"Oh, there isn't any need to be modest. You must share your good news with everyone." Kiya announced to the table, "Lady Mutnodjmet is pregnant with the general's child!"

It was as if time had suddenly halted. Two dozen faces turned toward me, and the painter Thutmose's eyes grew large as cups. "Is it true?" he asked.

I smiled, lifting my chin. "Yes."

For a moment, there was a shocked silence among the viziers, then there was a flurry of frenzied whispering.

Across the table, Kiya smiled complacently. "Sisters, and pregnant at the exact same time. I wonder"—she leaned forward—"what Pharaoh had to say?"

I didn't respond.

"You mean"—Kiya gasped—"he doesn't know?"

"I am sure he will be happy," Thutmose interjected.

"Happy?" Kiya cried, losing all sense of decorum. "She has bedded a general! A *general!*" she shrieked.

"I should think Pharaoh would be proud," Thutmose assumed. "It is a chance to win the general over to his cause, since Osiris knows Nakhtmin's heart isn't in the building."

Kiya's voice was flat. "Then where is it?"

Thutmose thought. "In the north with the Hittites, I suppose."

"Well, perhaps he can go and join Horemheb then."

Kiya's ladies laughed, and Thutmose put a placating hand over hers. "Come now, no one wishes for Horemheb's fate." Kiya's features softened and the sculptor turned toward me. "Tawaret protect you," he said quietly. "You have helped enough women at court to have earned some happiness for yourself."

My mother returned and the trumpets blared, announcing my sister and Akhenaten's arrival. They cut a glittering path through the Great Hall, smiling as they went, but when my sister came to me her gaze shifted and she wouldn't meet my eyes. I heard Kiya's voice in my head. *Sisters, and pregnant at the exact same time.*

All night dancers swirled across the Great Hall of Amarna in ripples of linen and netted dresses of bright beads. Fire throwers had come to entertain Akhenaten, but all he had eyes for was my sister. It must have burned Kiya to her very core to see the way women crowded around Nefertiti when she descended the dais, deigning to talk to one or another of the noblewomen. I found my sister speaking with Maya's wife.

"Excuse us," I said, taking Nefertiti's arm.

"*What* are you doing?" The color rose in her cheeks.

"I want to know if you've spoken with Pharaoh."

Her temper rose. "I warned you about him. I told you not to—"

"Have you spoken to him?" My voice grew louder. My mother, at the table beneath the dais, looked over at us. Nefertiti's face grew hard.

"Yes. Nakhtmin has been sent north to fight the Hittites with Horemheb."

If she had struck me across the face, I would have been less shocked. My breath stuck in my throat. "*What?*"

Nefertiti flushed. "I warned you, Mutnodjmet. I said not to go near him—" She cut herself off as Akhenaten appeared. He must have known what we were talking about because he came to me with his brightest smile.

"Mutnodjmet."

I turned to him accusingly. "You sent the general to fight the Hittites?"

His smile faltered. "Playing with fire will only get you burned. I am sure your father taught you that, little cat." He reached out to caress my cheek and I flinched. Then he bent close and whispered, "Perhaps next time you shall choose a more loyal lover. Your general asked to go."

I stepped back, refusing to believe it. "Never!" My gaze switched to Nefertiti. "And you did nothing?" I demanded. "You did *nothing* to stop it?"

"He asked," my sister said weakly.

"He *never* asked," I said viciously, implicating Pharaoh in my truth, not caring how dangerous my words were. "I am pregnant. I am pregnant with his child and you let him be sent off to his *death!*" I cried. Conversation in the Great Hall had stopped.

I banged through the double doors into the night. But I had nowhere to go. I didn't even know where my chambers were in the palace. I wept, clutching my stomach. *What am I going to do?* My knees buckled and suddenly I felt ill, unable to stand.

"Mutny!" my mother cried. She turned to Ipu; they had both followed me out of the Great Hall. "Find her a physician! Now!"

There were more voices than I could name, all shouting instructions. I was very ill, someone said, and they should move me to the temple where the priestesses could pray for my life. Another voice asked if this would be the temple of Amun or Aten. I drifted into darkness, and I could hear someone talking about the healing powers of the priests. I heard the name *Panahesi* and my mother's sharp retort. Linens came, and I felt a heaviness between my legs. My stomach cramped. There was water. Lemon water and lavender. Someone said my father had arrived. Had entire days passed? When I awoke, it was always to darkness, and Ipu was constantly by my side. When I moaned, I remember feeling the cool hands of my mother across my forehead. I asked for her many times. I recall that clearly. But I never recall asking for my sister. I learned later that for days I drifted in and out of consciousness. The first thing I remember clearly is waking up to the smell of lotus blossoms.

"Mutnodjmet?"

I blinked against the morning light and frowned. "Nakhtmin?"

"No, Mutnodjmet."

It was my father. I pushed myself up on my elbows and looked around. Reed mats were rolled up above the windows, letting in the morning sun, and the tiled floors gleamed red and blue. Everything was large. The cross-legged stools of animal hide, the jeweled caskets and wig boxes, the onyx lamps with turquoise embedded into their columns. But I was confused. "Where is Nakhtmin?"

My mother hesitated. She sat down on the corner of my bed, exchanging looks with my father. "You've been very sick," she said at last. "You don't remember the feast, my love?"

And then it came back to me. Nakhtmin's death sentence, Nefertiti's selfishness, my sickness outside the palace. My breath came faster. "What happened? Why am I sick?"

My father took a seat next to me and placed his large hand over mine.

My mother whispered, "Mutnodjmet, you've lost the child."

I was too horrified to speak. I had lost Nakhtmin's baby. I had lost the only thing that bound me to him, the piece of him I was to keep with me forever.

My mother pushed my hair away from my face. "Many women lose their first child," she comforted me. "You are young. There will be others. We must be thankful the gods spared you." Her eyes welled. "We thought you were gone. We thought you were—"

I shook my head. "No, this isn't happening," I said, pushing away the covers. "Where is Nefertiti?" I demanded.

My father replied solemnly, "Praying for you."

"In *Aten's* temple?" I cried.

"Mutnodjmet, she is your sister," he said.

"She is a jealous, selfish queen, *not a sister!*"

My mother recoiled and my father sat back.

"She sent the general away!" I cried.

"That was Akhenaten's choice."

But I wouldn't let my father defend her. Not this time. "And she allowed it," I accused. "One word from Nefertiti and Akhenaten would have overlooked anything we'd done. We could have shamed Amun in the streets, and if Nefertiti had wanted it, he would have let it happen. She's the only one he listens to. She's the only one who can control him. Your sister saw it, you saw it. And she allowed Nakhtmin to be sent away. She allowed it!" I shouted. My mother put a placating hand on my shoulder, but I shrugged it off. "Is he dead?" I demanded.

My father stood up.

"Is he dead?" I said again.

"He is a strong soldier, Mutnodjmet. The guards will have brought him north to the Hittite lines and left him there. He will know what to do."

I closed my eyes, imagining Nakhtmin thrown to the Hittites like meat to wild dogs. I felt the tears, warm and bitter, coursing down my cheeks, and my father's placating arm around my shoulder. "You have suffered great loss," he said softly.

"He will never return. And Nefertiti did *nothing.*" My grief overcame me and the tightness in my stomach came back again. *"Nothing!"* I shrieked.

My mother held me, rocking me back and forth in her arms. "Shh, there was nothing she could do," she swore.

But that was a lie.

My father went to my bed table and held up a most exquisite chest, inlaid in lapis and pearl. "She's been here every day. She wanted you to have this for your herbs."

I studied the chest. It looked like something Nefertiti would have chosen. Elaborate and costly. "She thinks she will buy me off with a box?"

There was the sound of shuffled feet outside my chamber, then a servant swung open the door. "The queen is coming!"

But I would never forgive her.

She swept into my bedchamber, and the only thing I could see was the round belly beneath her linen. When she saw that I was awake, she stopped, then blinked quickly. "Mutny?" She had come with a turquoise ankh, probably blessed in the Temple of Aten. "Mutny?" She ran to me, embracing me in her tiny arms, and I could feel her tears on my cheeks. My sister, who never cried.

I didn't move, and she leaned back to see my face.

"Mutny, say something!" she pleaded.

"I curse the day the gods decided to make me your sister."

Her hands began to tremble. "Take it back."

I watched her and said nothing.

"Take it back!" she cried, but I turned away from her.

My parents looked at one another. Then my father said softly, "Go, Nefertiti. Give her some time."

My sister's jaw dropped. She turned to my mother, and when no defense came, she spun away and shut the door in her wake.

I looked up at my parents. "I want to be alone."

My mother hesitated. "But you've been so sick," she protested.

"Ipu's here. She will take care of me. For now, I want to be alone."

My mother glanced at my father and they left. I turned to face Ipu, who hovered over me, unsure what to do. "Will you bring me my box for herbs?" I asked her. "The *old* one," I said. "I want my chamomile."

She found the box for me and I lifted the heavy lid. I froze. "Ipu, has anyone been in this box?" I asked quickly.

She frowned. "No, my lady."

"Are you sure?" I sifted through the packages again, but the acacia was gone. The linen-wrapped seeds of acacia were gone! "Ipu." I struggled to stand up. "Ipu, who could have been in here?"

"What do you mean?"

"The acacia!"

Ipu glanced at the box, then covered her mouth. Her eyes wandered to my midriff, understanding. I grabbed the box and threw open the double doors to my chamber. My long hair swayed wild and loose behind me, my linen tunic was unbelted. "Where is Nefertiti?" I cried. Some of the servants backed away. Others whispered, "In the Great Hall, my lady, dining with the viziers."

I clenched the box tighter, in a rage so dark that I couldn't even see the people in the hall when I threw open its doors, startling the guards.

"Nefertiti!" I shouted. The chatter in the room went silent. The musicians below the dais stopped playing and Thutmose's mouth fell slightly open. Nefertiti's ladies gasped.

I held up the box so that everyone in the hall could see. "Who stole my acacia?" I advanced on the dais, looking at my sister. Panahesi made a noise in his throat and my father stood up. "Someone stole the acacia seeds and poisoned me with them to rid me of my child. Was it you?"

Nefertiti had gone white as alabaster. She looked at Akhenaten, her eyes wide, and I turned my attention to Pharaoh. "You?" I shrieked. "Did you do this to me?"

Akhenaten shifted uncomfortably.

My father took me by the arm. *"Mutnodjmet."*

"I want to know who did this to me!" My voice echoed in the hall, and even Kiya and her ladies went silent. If it could happen to me, it could happen to any of them. Who were their enemies? Who were mine?

"Let's go," my father said.

I let myself be led out, but at the doors to the Great Hall I turned. "I will never forgive this," I swore, and Nefertiti knew it was meant for her. "I will never forgive this so long as the sun still sets on Amarna!" I screamed.

My sister sat back in her chair, looking as though someone had robbed her of her kingdom.

Chapter Seventeen

AMARNA

twenty-eighth of Payni

"I'M AFRAID SHE will stay here tending her herb garden for the rest of her life. Without a husband, without children . . ."

I could hear my body servant's words from the garden. Three months ago, on the day I'd discovered that someone had poisoned me to kill Nakhtmin's child, I had found this villa myself, newly built and sitting empty in the golden terraces overlooking the city. No family had purchased it yet from the palace, so I moved into its rooms and claimed the villa as my own. No one would dare to suggest I be removed.

It had taken three months of seeding and planting, but now I reached down to feel the leaves of a young sycamore, warm and soft. My body servant's voice grew closer to the garden. "She's outside, where she always is," she said, sounding worried. "Tending to her herbs so she can sell them to the women."

I felt her presence behind me like a pillar of stone. I didn't need to hear her voice to know who it was. Besides, I could smell her scent of lily and cardamom.

"Mutnodjmet?"

I turned and shaded my eyes. I never wore a wig since leaving the palace. My hair grew long and wild. In the sun, Ipu said my eyes were like emeralds; hard and unyielding. "Your Majesty." I made a very deep bow.

Queen Tiye blinked in surprise. "You have changed."

I waited for her to tell me how.

"You seem taller, darker, I think."

"Yes. I spend more time in the sun where I belong." I put down my spade and she studied the gardens while we walked.

"It's very impressive here." She noticed the date palms and blooming wisteria.

I smiled. "Thank you."

We entered the loggia and my aunt took a seat. I had changed, but she was still the same: small and shrewd, her mouth pinched, her blue eyes cunning. I sat across from her on a small feather pillow. She had arrived in Amarna with my father, leaving behind the city of Thebes at his request, working with him in the Per Medjat until all hours of the morning, studying scrolls, writing letters, negotiating alliances.

Ipu placed hot tea between us and the queen took it in her hands. "I have not come to try to bring you back," she said.

"I know. You are too judicious for that. You understand that I am done with the palace. With Nefertiti and her statues and her endless scheming."

Queen Tiye smiled thinly. "I always thought I chose the wrong sister."

I blinked in surprise that anyone would want me over Nefertiti. Then I shook my head firmly. "No. I would never have wanted to be queen."

"Which is why you would have made such a fine one." She put down her cup. "But tell me, Mutnodjmet, what would you suggest for an old woman whose joints are aching her?"

I glanced at her questioningly. "You have come for my herbs?"

"As you said, I've not come to convince you to come back. I am far too judicious. Besides, why would you leave this villa?" She looked around her, at the wandering vines and high painted columns. "It's a peaceful sanctuary, away from the city and from my son's foolish politics." She tilted her head so that the jewels around her neck, heavy lapis and gold, clinked musically. Then she leaned forward intimately. "So tell me, Mutnodjmet, what do I use?"

"But your court physicians—"

"Are not as well versed in herbal knowledge as you." She looked out the open doors to my cultivated garden, row upon row of senna and chrysanthemums, their leaves flashing green and yellow in the sun. There was juniper for headaches, wormwood for cough. For women who wanted it desperately, I still ground acacia. Even knowing that my herbs had killed my own child, I wouldn't deny them. "The women say you've become quite a healer. They call you Sekem-Miw," she said, meaning powerful cat, and at once I thought of Nakhtmin and my eyes became clouded. My aunt studied me with a critical expression, then reached out and patted my hand. "Come. Show me the herbs."

Outside, the warm sun dappled the garden. The dew on the plants would dry as the day grew warmer, and I inhaled the heady scent of the earth. I bent down and plucked a green unripe berry from the juniper plant.

"The juniper would be good." I handed her the berry. "I can make you a tea, but you would have to have it twice a day."

She crushed the berry between her forefinger and thumb, then brought her fingers to her nose. "It smells of letters from Mitanni," she mused aloud.

I looked at her in the light, forty years old and still making alliances with foreign nations, conspiring with my father on how best to run a kingdom.

"Why do you still do it?" I asked, and she knew at once what I meant.

"Because it's Egypt." The sun reflected in her bright auburn eyes and the gold around her wrists. "I was the spiritual and physical leader of this land once. And what has changed? So I have a foolish son who is sitting on the throne. They are still my gods, my people. Of course, had Tuthmosis been Pharaoh . . ."

She sighed and I asked quietly, "What was he like?"

My aunt looked down at her rings. "Intelligent. Patient. A fierce hunter." She shook her head at a regret that only she knew. "Tuthmosis was a soldier and a priest of Amun."

"Both things that Akhenaten can't abide."

"When your sister married him, I wondered if she was too fragile." My aunt laughed sharply. "Who knew that Nefertiti, little Nefertiti, would be so . . ." She searched for the word, her gaze falling across the city below us, a white pearl against the sand.

"Passionate," I responded.

My aunt nodded ruefully. "It wasn't what I planned."

"Nor I." My lip trembled and when my aunt saw the tears she took my hand. "Ipu thinks you are lonely."

"I have my herbs. And my mother comes in the mornings with bread. Sesame bread and good *shedeh* from the palace."

The queen nodded slowly. "And your father?"

"He comes, too, and we talk about news."

She arched her brows. "And what has he told you recently?"

"That Qatna has sent pleas for help to defend themselves against the Hittites," I said.

Tiye's face grew stern. "Qatna has been our vassal for a hundred years. To lose her now would tell the Hittite kingdom we are not willing to fight. It is the second of our vassal states to ask for help. I write letters of peace, and behind my back my son sends requests for more colored glass. They want soldiers"—her voice rose—"and he asks for glass! When our allies have fallen and there is no buffer between us and the Hittites, what then?"

"Then Egypt will be invaded."

Tiye closed her eyes. "At least we have our army in Kadesh."

I was horrified. "Of one hundred men!"

"Yes, but the Hittites don't know that. I would not underestimate the power of Horemheb or Nakhtmin."

I refused to think that Nakhtmin could return. I sat in the garden under the sunshade and thought, *If he returns, they will have been victorious in Kadesh, and that will never happen.* I dropped a chamomile leaf into my morning tea. Even after so many months, I never slept well, and when I thought of Nakhtmin, my hands wouldn't stop shaking.

"My lady!" Ipu appeared on the terrace. "A gift has arrived from the palace."

"Then send it back like the others," I said. I would not be bought off. We weren't little girls anymore; she couldn't break my favorite toy and give me one of hers later. She still thought that this was nothing, that Nakhtmin was just one man and that there would be others. But I wasn't like her. I couldn't kiss Ranofer one day and leave him the next.

But Ipu was still watching me. "This may be something you'd like to keep."

I scowled, but I put down my tea and went into the house. There was a basket on the table. "Great Osiris, what's in it?" I exclaimed. "It's moving."

Ipu grinned. "Look."

At Ipu's prompting, I lifted the lid. Crouching inside, tiny and scared, was a small spotted kitten, a breed only the wealthiest nobles in Egypt could afford. "A *miw?*" The little creature looked up at me, crying for its mother, and against my better judgment I took her out.

She was small enough to fit in the palm of my hand, and when I brought her to my chest she began to purr.

"You see?" Ipu said, proud of herself.

I put the kitten down. "We're not keeping her."

"It's a *him*. And why not?"

"Because it's a gift from my sister, and she thinks that a kitten can replace a child."

Ipu lifted her palms. "But you're lonely."

"I'm not lonely. Every day I have clients. And my parents." I put the kitten back into the basket, placing the lid carefully on top. Its little voice echoed through the weaving and Ipu stared at me coldly.

"Don't look at me that way. I'm not killing it. Only sending it back."

She was silent. The only sound was the kitten's pitiful mew.

I rolled my eyes. "All right. But *you* can take care of it."

When my father arrived with my mother in tow, their serving lady had a basket filled with luxuries from the palace I didn't need. He frowned at the sight of Ipu crouched by the divan, dangling a string and calling softly to something underneath.

"What is she doing?" he asked.

The serving woman put the basket on the table, and the three of us turned to look. There was the flash of a gray paw, then a startled scream as the string disappeared. "The naughty creature won't come out!" Ipu cried.

"What is it?" My mother peered closer.

"Nefertiti sent me a kitten," I said flatly. My father studied my expression. "I only took it because Ipu wanted it," I said. The kitten scampered down the hall.

My mother grinned. "Have you named her?"

"Him. His name is Bastet."

"The patron of felines," my mother said approvingly.

My father looked at me in surprise.

"It was Ipu's idea."

My mother began unpacking various linens from the basket, and my father and I strolled out into the garden.

"I heard my sister came to visit you yesterday."

"She thinks there is a chance of success in Kadesh," I told him, waiting for his response.

He put his hand on my shoulder. "It's possible, Mutnodjmet. But it's nothing I would wait for. He is gone. We have all lost loved ones to Osiris."

I fought back tears. "But not like this!"

"Nefertiti didn't know," my father explained. "She is beside herself. The child is due at the end of Thoth, and the physicians say if she doesn't get rest and begin to eat she will lose it."

Good. Let her lose it, I thought. *Let her know what it's like to wake up robbed of everything she holds dear.* Immediately, however, guilt overwhelmed me. "I hope she finds peace." I bowed my head. "But even if she didn't know about the herbs, she allowed Nakhtmin to be taken."

My father said nothing for a while. Then he warned, "She will want you at the birth."

I bit my tongue. My father knew the irony of what he was asking. "When the time comes," I whispered.

Queen Tiye visited me for a second time. She swept up the steps of the villa with seven ladies in tow, each of them carrying large willow baskets.

"Ipu, find Bastet!" I shouted. "We can't have him running around attacking the queen's ankles." This was Bastet's new game. He would find a piece of furniture under which to hide, and then run out to bite the ankle of anyone who passed. "Bastet," Ipu wailed. "Come here, Bastet."

I could hear the queen's ladies drawing closer. "Bastet!" I commanded, and the little ball of fur pranced out from his hiding place, marching up to me as if to demand what I wanted with him. "Ipu, take him into the back room." I pointed.

He looked at Ipu and gave a plaintive cry.

"How come he comes for you and not for me?"

I looked down at the proud little kitten. Even though Ipu was the one who fed him, it was my chair he sat under and my lap he curled up on in front of the brazier. *Arrogant miw,* I thought.

A knock resounded throughout the house, and Ipu rushed to open the door. Outside, two servants held a peacock sunshade over my aunt's head to protect her from the sun.

"Queen Tiye." I bowed. "It is a pleasure to see you."

My aunt held out her hand so that I could escort her inside. The rings on her fingers were dazzling, great chunks of lapis set in gold. She took a seat on a feather pillow in the loggia, studying the torn tapestry on the wall. She fingered the loose threads. "The kitten from Nefertiti?" She smiled at my surprise. "There was talk in the palace when it wasn't returned."

At once my ire rose. "Talk?" I demanded.

"Someone suggested that all might be forgiven." She watched me carefully while color darkened my cheeks.

"And did *someone* suggest that a gift won't buy a child? Won't buy back a man's life?"

"Who would say that to your sister? No one challenges Nefertiti. Not I, not even your father."

"Then she does what she pleases?" I asked her.

"The same way all queens have. Only with a greater passion for building."

I gasped. "There can't be more building?"

"Of course. There will be building until the army finds a leader who will lead them in revolt."

"But who could be powerful enough to revolt against Pharaoh?"

Ipu brought in tea with mint. My aunt raised the cup to her lips. "Horemheb," she said frankly.

"Which is why Horemheb was sent to Kadesh."

My aunt nodded. "He was too popular. Like Nakhtmin. My son saw danger where he should have seen advantage. He is too much a fool to see that with Nakhtmin in your bed, he would never have revolted."

"Nakhtmin would never have led a revolt," I said quickly. "With or without me."

Tiye raised her sharp brows.

"He wanted a peaceful life."

"He didn't tell you that in Thebes, when Akhenaten was ready to take his brother's crown, soldiers came and asked him to lead a rebellion? And that he agreed?"

I lowered my cup. "Nakhtmin?"

"There were viziers and soldiers who convinced him that a rebellion was the only way to achieve Ma'at once Prince Tuthmosis was killed."

I stared at my aunt, trying to determine whether she was truly saying what I thought she might be. That Tuthmosis had been killed not by a fall from his chariot, but by his own brother's hand. She saw my question and stiffened.

"I hear servants' gossip as well as anyone else."

"But his chariot fall—"

"Might have killed him regardless. Or he might have recovered. Only my living son and Osiris now know the truth."

I shuddered. "Only there was no revolt."

"Nefertiti arrived and the court believed she would be Egypt's salvation from my son."

I sat back. "Why are you telling me this?" I asked her.

My aunt put down her tea. "Because someday you will return to the palace, and either you will return with your eyes wide open or you will be buried with them shut."

Twenty days later, Tiye was sitting on an ivory stool between the rows of my garden, quizzing me about plants, wanting to know what other uses the licorice root had besides sweetening tea. I told her that when it was used instead of honey, it prevented tooth decay, and that eating onions instead of garlic would do the same. My father came upon us between the feathery green herbs; I hadn't even heard Ipu greet him at the door.

My father looked first to her, then at me. "What are you doing?"

My aunt stood up. "My niece is showing me the magic of herbs. A very clever girl, your daughter." She shaded her face with her hand. I couldn't tell whether the look in my father's eyes was one of pride or displeasure. "And what brings you here?"

"I came to find you." My father's voice was grave, but my aunt had lived through many grave times and wasn't moved.

"There is trouble in the palace," she guessed.

"Akhenaten is planning a burial in the east."

Tiye glanced at him sharply. "No Pharaoh has ever been buried in the east."

"He plans to be buried where the sun rises beyond the hills and wants the court of Amarna to leave any tombs they've already cut in the west."

My aunt's voice deepened with rage. "Leave tombs we have already built in Thebes? Move the tombs from where they have always lain at the feet of the setting sun to be *buried in the east?*" It was the angriest I'd ever seen her. "He will never do it!"

My father spread his palms. "We can't stop him. But we can build a second tomb and keep the tombs we've built in the Valley—"

"*Of course,* we will keep them. I will never be buried in the city of Amarna," she vowed.

"Nor I," my father said, and his voice was also low.

They both turned to me. "You must be the keeper of this," Tiye instructed me. "If we die, you must make sure we are buried in Thebes."

"But how?" How would I go against Akhenaten's wishes?

"You will use your cunning," my father said swiftly.

When I saw that he was serious, I was stricken with fear. "But I'm not cunning," I worried. "That's Nefertiti. She could do it."

"But she won't. Your sister is building a tomb with Akhenaten. They have abandoned our ancestors to risk burial in the east." My father stared at me in earnest. "You are the one who must make sure this happens."

My voice rose with fear. "But how?"

"Bribery," my aunt replied. "The men who work as embalmers are as easily bribed as the next." When she saw that I did not understand, she gazed into my face as if no girl could be as ignorant as I was. "You have never heard of women who give up their children to the infertile wives of the nobility? They tell their husbands the child has died and the embalmers take a monkey and wrap it up like an infant." I shrank back in horror and Tiye shrugged, as if everyone knew about this. "Oh, yes, they can work miracles in the City of the Dead. For a price."

"If it should ever come to that," my father said, "you would bribe the embalmers to place a false body in the city of Amarna."

My hands began to shake. "And take you to Thebes?" It didn't seem real. It didn't seem possible. My father and the queen would never die. But my father patted my shoulder as if I were a child.

"When the time comes—"

"*If* it comes," I stressed.

"If it comes." He smiled tenderly. "Then you will know what to do." He glanced at Tiye. "Shall we meet here tomorrow?"

"In my garden?" I exclaimed.

My father replied, "Amarna has become a court infested with spies, Mutnodjmet. If we wish to speak, it will have to be here. Akhenaten trusts no one, and Panahesi's women are everywhere, flitting through the palace and reporting back to him. Even some of Nefertiti's ladies."

I thought of Nefertiti alone in the palace, surrounded by false friends and spies. But I refused to feel sorry for her. *It's a bed of her own making.*

I was commanded to the palace at the end of Epiphi. A herald arrived with a letter that bore my father's heavy seal, pressing it into my hand with urgency.

"The queen, my lady, is already in labor."

I opened the letter and saw it was true. Nefertiti was about to give birth. I pressed my lips together and folded the sheets, unable to bear the sight of the news. The herald continued to watch me. "Well, what do you want?" I snapped.

The boy didn't flinch. "I want to know if you will be coming, my lady. The queen has asked for you."

She had asked for me. She had asked for me knowing that while she was birthing her second child, my first had been murdered! I crumpled the folded papyrus in my hand, and the herald watched me with widening eyes.

"There is a chariot waiting." The boy's voice grew pleading.

I studied him. He was twelve or thirteen. If he failed to bring me, it might end his career. His eyes remained wide and hopeful. "Wait, and I will get my things," I told him.

Ipu hovered in the kitchen. "She has physicians. You don't have to."

"Of course I do."

"But why?"

Bastet arched his silky body against my calf, as if to comfort me. "Because it's Nefertiti, and if she dies, I would never forgive myself."

Ipu followed me into my chamber, trailed by Bastet. "Do you want me to come?" she offered.

"No. I'll be back before night." I took my box of herbs, but as I went to leave Ipu pressed my hand.

"Remember, you're going there for the child."

I swallowed bitterly. "Which should have been mine."

"She said she had nothing to do with it," she reminded.

"Maybe," I replied. "And maybe she sat by and said nothing while it was done."

The herald took me to his chariot. He snapped the whip and the bright chestnut horses galloped along the Royal Road. On every pillar, at every crossroads, there were statues of my sister. In painted images, she raised her arms over the desert city she and her husband had built, dressed in the dazzling clothes of Isis, and where the gods should have been on the temple gates there was her face with Akhenaten's.

"Amun, forgive their arrogance," I whispered.

▣ ▣ ▣

As in Memphis, a birthing pavilion had been built. I could see Nefertiti's hand in the design: the floor-to-ceiling windows, the padded seats, the vases spilling over with plants, particularly lilies, her favorite kind. There were dozens of chairs arranged around the room for the ladies of the court, nearly all of them occupied.

"The Lady Mutnodjmet," the herald announced, and the talking and laughing that filled the chamber stopped.

"Mutny!" Nefertiti shooed her women away, and the viziers' daughters who clustered around her bed all parted, their eyes wide and envious.

I stopped before her bedside. She was healthy and beautiful, propped up on a pile of cushions without any sign of pain. The color rose in my cheeks. "I thought you were in labor."

"The physicians all say it will be today or tomorrow."

A storm crossed my face. "Your messenger said it was urgent."

She turned to her ladies, who were studying my hair, my nails, my face. "Leave us," she commanded. I watched them flutter away like so many moths, girls I didn't even know. "It is urgent. I need you."

"You have dozens of women to keep you company. Why do you need me?"

"Because you're my sister," she said sharply. "We're *supposed* to be with each other. Watching out for each other."

I laughed meanly.

"I didn't take your child!" she cried.

"But you know who did."

She didn't say anything.

"You know who poisoned me. You know who was too afraid that I should give birth to a son, a child of a general . . ."

She covered her ears. "I won't hear any more!"

I stood silent, watching her.

"Mutny," she pleaded. She looked up at me with her dark plaintive eyes, as black and wide as pools, thinking her charm would get her what she wanted. "Be with me when I have this child."

"Why? You look happy enough."

"Should I go around with the fear of death on my face, frightening Akhenaten so he won't give me more children? So that the ladies of my court can run back to Panahesi and tell him that the Queen of Egypt has grown weak? What better time for Kiya to rise up than when I'm down? What else am I supposed to look but happy?"

I marveled that she could think of these things even when she was about to give birth.

"Stay with me, Mutny. You're the only one I trust. You can be sure of what the midwives are giving me."

I stared. "You don't think they would poison you?"

She looked up at me with a wearied expression.

"The physicians would discover that you were poisoned," I pointed out.

"After I am dead! What good is it then?"

"Panahesi would be risking his own life to do such a thing."

"And who would be there to prove it? Who do you think Akhenaten would believe? A tattling midwife or the High Priest of Aten? And then there are the Amun priests," she said fearfully, "who would give their lives to see that Akhenaten never produces an heir."

I thought of someone poisoning her the way I had been poisoned. I imagined her contorted in pain, crying out as Anubis crept closer because I had refused to be with her during her child's birth. "I will stay. But only for the birth." She smiled, and I sat down grudgingly. "So, what will you name it?"

"Smenkhare," she said.

"And if it's a girl?"

She looked sharply at me from under her long lashes. "It will not be a girl."

"But if it is?"

She shrugged. "Then Meketaten."

▣ ▣ ▣

Though Nefertiti was impossibly small, Nekhbet must have blessed her womb, because all of her children seemed to come without difficulty. The midwife caught the tiny bundle in her arms, bloodied and crying, and the other midwives in the room pressed forward to peer at the sex. Nefertiti sat forward.

"What is it?" she gasped.

The midwife looked down. My mother clapped her hands with joy, but as the servants helped Nefertiti back to her bed, I saw that the color had drained from her face. Her eyes met mine from across the room. *Another princess.* I let out my breath and thought spitefully, *I'm glad it's not a son.* I gathered my basket and moved toward the door.

My mother grabbed my arm. "You must stay for the blessing!"

The room grew more crowded. A herald arrived, followed by

Thutmose, as servants flitted around Nefertiti to wash her body and fit her crown. My mother took my elbow and led me toward the window. Bells were ringing, announcing the new princess's birth. Three tolls for a Princess of Egypt, same as a prince. "At least wait until she is named," my mother begged.

Nefertiti looked over and saw the two of us together. "Isn't my own sister going to come to wish me a long life and good health?"

The entire room turned. I could feel my mother's hand on the small of my back, pushing me forward. If my father had been allowed in the birthing chamber, he would have set his jaw sternly against my disrespect. I hesitated, and then moved forward. "May Aten smile upon you."

Everyone backed away as Nefertiti opened her arms to embrace me. The milk nurse was in the corner of the cheery pavilion, already giving suck to the little princess. "Come, be happy for me, Mutny." Everyone was smiling. Everyone was exultant. It wasn't a boy, but it was a healthy child, and she had delivered successfully. I held up my basket.

"For you," I said.

She peered into it eagerly and her eyes grew bright. She looked from the basket to me, then back again. "Mandrakes?"

"Only a few grew well this season. Next season should be better."

Nefertiti glanced up. "*Next* season? What do you mean? You're coming back."

I didn't answer her.

"You *have* to come back to the palace. Your family is here!"

"No, Nefertiti. My family was murdered. One in my womb and the other in Kadesh." I turned away before she could rebuke me.

"You will be there for the blessing," she shouted. It was not a request.

"If that is what you want." I left the birthing chamber, letting the doors swing shut behind me.

Outside the palace, villagers throughout Amarna were feasting. The birth of a royal heir meant a day of rest, even for the tomb builders high above the valley. I walked to the outer courtyard, where royal charioteers stood waiting to take dignitaries in and out of the city. "Take me to the Temple of Hathor," I said, and before the charioteer could say he did not know of any such forbidden temple, I placed a deben ring of copper in his hand. He nodded quickly. Once we were there, we both stared at the columned courtyard carved into the side of the hill.

"Are you sure you want to be left here, my lady? It's abandoned."

"A few women still tend Hathor's shrine. I will be fine," I said.

But the royal charioteer was young and concerned. "I can wait," he offered.

"No." I gathered my basket and descended. "There's no point. I can walk home if I need to."

"But you are the Sister of the King's Chief Wife!"

"And like many other people, I possess two legs."

He chuckled and was gone.

On the hill amidst the outcroppings of rock and carved stone, there was silence. The few women who kept Hathor's hidden shrine would be feasting in the villages below, pouring out libations to the new god of Egypt in thanks for the delivery of a new princess. "But not all of us have forgotten you." I knelt before a tiny statue of Hathor on the hill, placing an offering of thyme beneath her feet. Although shrines to Amun were forbidden in Amarna, on the outskirts of the city women had secretly commissioned small temples like this. And in homes like mine, her statues were often hidden in secret niches where oil and bread could be placed so the goddess would remember our ancestors and children that never were.

I bowed in obeisance. "I thank you for delivering Nefertiti safely.

Though she offers you up no wine or incense, I do so in her name. Protect her always from the hands of death. She is thankful for the gift of new life you bring her, and for a healthy recovery in childbed." I arranged the herbs next to a jug of oil another woman had brought and heard the crunch of gravel behind me. Someone spoke.

"Do you ever pray for yourself?"

I didn't turn. "No," I replied. "The goddess knows what I want."

"You can't do this forever," my aunt said. A hot wind blew the edges of her skirt behind her. "At some point, you must let the child's *ka* rest. He's not coming back."

"Like Nakhtmin."

My aunt's eyes were solemn. She took my hand in hers, and we stood on the topmost tier of the temple, looking out over the desert to the reeds of River Nile. White-kilted farmers threshed in the fields and oxen pulled the heavy carts of grain behind them. A hawk wheeled overhead, the incarnation of the soul, and the Dowager Queen sighed. "Let them both rest."

Chapter Eighteen

1348 BCE

Shemu, Season of Harvest

DAY AFTER DAY, village women sent for my herbs, and sometimes I delivered them personally. In the city that sprawled beneath the white pillars of the palace, I would wind my way through the narrow streets, and often I would find myself in houses where women had just given birth and there was no hope that the mother would survive. I would bend over her sickbed to inspect her womb and make a special tea with the oil of nettle. And the women would rub their forbidden amulets to Hathor and whisper prayers to the goddess of motherhood. The first time I saw these forbidden amulets I was surprised, and a servant in the house explained quickly to me, "She has protected Egypt for a thousand years."

"And Aten?" I asked curiously.

The servant tensed. "Aten is the sun. You cannot touch the sun. But Hathor can be held and made obeisance to."

So, at seventeen years of age, they called me Sekem-Miw, and I came to know all the villages in Amarna better than Pharaoh himself.

"Where are we going today, my lady?"

It was the charioteer from the palace. He was not on duty, and I had reached the end of the long road from my villa. He smiled down at me, and I tried to stop myself from thinking of Nakhtmin.

"To collect seeds," I replied, walking faster, ignoring the rapid beat of my heart.

"Your basket looks heavy. Wouldn't you rather ride?" He slowed, and I debated. I had no guards. I had insisted on having none when I'd left Nefertiti and her palace. But without guards, I had no charioteer, and it was a long way to the quay. The charioteer saw my hesitation. "Come." He held out his hand and I took it, stepping up into his chariot. "I'm Djedefhor." He bowed.

Djedefhor began to appear every morning.

"Do you wait out here for me each day?" I demanded.

Djedefhor grinned. "No, not each day."

"You shouldn't," I said earnestly.

"Why not?" He lent me his arm and we rolled toward the quay, where I searched out new herbs from among the foreign sellers every few days.

"Because I am the Sister of the King's Chief Wife. It is dangerous for you to be seen with me. I'm not a favorite of Pharaoh."

"But you're a favorite of the queen's."

When she wants something, I thought, and my lips thinned into a line. "If you value your place in Pharaoh's house," I said sternly, "you will not be seen with me. I can be of no use to you."

"Very well, then, because I am not looking to use you. Just escort you to the market and back again."

I flushed. "You should know the man I love is in Kadesh."

It was the first time I had spoken of Nakhtmin to anyone outside of my family.

Djedefhor bowed his head. "As I said, I want nothing from you. Just the pleasure of escorting you back and forth again."

The first time Ipu saw me with Djedefhor, her eyes grew wide. She followed me around the house, as bad as Bastet, and tried to get me to speak about him. "Where did you meet him? Does he drive you every day? Is he married?"

"Ipu, he isn't Nakhtmin."

Ipu's smile faded. "But he's handsome."

"Yes. He's a handsome, kind soldier. That's all."

Ipu hung her head. "You're too young to be alone," she whispered.

"But it's how my sister wants it," I replied.

"The Hittite regime is growing in the north. The mayor of Lakisa sent for help this morning." My father produced a scroll from his belt, and Tiye held out her hand to read it.

My house had become a place of meeting. I was allowed to listen while Tiye and my father debated how to rule the Kingdom of Egypt. And while the Hittite king Suppiluliumas swept through Palestine, creeping closer to Egypt, Akhenaten and Nefertiti commissioned statues and rode through the streets arrayed like gods, tossing copper from their chariots into the crowds.

My aunt lowered the scroll to her lap. "Another of Egypt's territories in danger." I knew she was thinking that the Elder would have forfeited his *ka* to Ammit before he saw Hittites on Egyptian land. "Just like Qatna." She looked at my father. "But we cannot send help."

"No," my father said, and took back the scroll. "At some point, Akhenaten will discover that gold is being drawn from the treasury to defend Kadesh and—"

"Gold is being drawn from the treasury to defend Kadesh?" I interrupted.

"To draw more to defend Lakisa would be dangerous," Tiye agreed, ignoring my outburst.

My father nodded, and I wondered what Akhenaten might do if it was ever discovered that Egypt's highest vizier was siphoning gold to defend Egypt's most important stronghold against the Hittites. My father was taking a risk, ruling Egypt the way he believed the Elder would have wanted the world's most powerful kingdom to be ruled, but it was Akhenaten's crown, not his, not even Nefertiti's. When the Elder had built his army, Egypt had extended from the Euphrates into Nubia. Now her land was being eaten away, and Akhenaten was allowing it. My sister was allowing it. And had it not been Nefertiti, had it been Kiya or another harem wife, Tiye and Ay would have struck her down—murder, poison, an unfortunate fall. But Nefertiti was Ay's daughter. She was Tiye's niece and she was my only sister, and we were supposed to forgive her anything.

Tiye rearranged her linen. "So what will we do with Kadesh?" she asked.

"Hope the gods are with Horemheb and he will achieve victory," my father said. "If Kadesh falls, every other city will fall in her wake, and there will be nothing to stop the Hittites from marching south."

The next month when I went to the market, Djedefhor insisted on coming with me through the crowded stalls along the quay. "It's not safe for the Sister of the King's Chief Wife to walk by herself," he said.

"Really?" I smiled slyly. "And yet I have been doing it every other day since Mesore."

I thought he was flattering me, but then he stepped forward and said seriously, "No. It is not safe for you to be alone right now."

I glanced about me, at the bustling market with its foreign goods baking in the heavy heat. Everything was as it normally was. Only the children paid me any attention, staring at my sandals and the gold bracelets around my arms. I started to laugh, then was checked by the look on his face. He took my arm and led me through the crowd. "Pharaoh has done a foolish thing today," he confided.

I looked at him askance. "Is my family in danger?"

He drew me into the shade where two pottery merchants had

erected a pavilion. "He's answered the mayor of Lakisa's plea for troops with monkeys in soldiers' garb."

I studied him to see if he was joking. "You're not serious."

"I am very serious, my lady."

I shook my head. "No! No. My father would never have allowed it."

"I doubt your father even knows of it yet. But he will, when angry Lakisans begin marching on the palace."

I looked around me, and now I could see that none of the dark-skinned Lakisans were at their stalls. Suddenly, the heat became overwhelming.

"My lady!" Djedefhor reached out his hand to steady me, then withdrew it quickly.

"Take me to my villa," I said quickly, and as we rolled through Amarna I realized how many builders there were, on the streets, around Akhenaten's half-built temples, and all of them were soldiers. All of them were men who, in the Elder's time, had been defending our vassal states, keeping the Hittites at bay in Qatna, Lakisa, and Kadesh. As soon as we were at the gates to my villa, Ipu came running and my heart leaped into my throat.

"The Vizier Ay was just here!" she cried.

I jumped from the chariot. "What did he say?"

"There is going to be trouble today. He sent soldiers to the market to find you."

I looked at Djedefhor, feeling rising panic.

"I'll find them," he promised. Then he turned around. "Don't worry, my lady. They will not harm your sister. The soldiers will stop them at the gates!"

▣ ▣ ▣

I had not been in the palace since the birth of Princess Meketaten eleven months before. Now, the sound of my sandals slapping against the palace stones drew the servants out to stare. There would be gossip all throughout the kitchens tonight. Even the children peered around the columns at me. My mother tightened her hold on my arm, as if she was afraid I might turn and run away. "Your sister has made very foolish decisions. But we are bound to Nefertiti. In life and in death, her actions will speak for all of us."

Two Nubian guards opened the doors to my father's rooms and I saw that Nefertiti was already inside, pacing the tiles and clenching the scepter of reign. When she saw me, the guards moved swiftly to shut the doors behind us. She turned an accusing look on our father.

"Ask Mutnodjmet what the people think," he commanded.

Nefertiti glared at me, and I was surprised at how Meketaten's birth had changed her. The angles of her face had softened, but there was still a sharp determination in her eyes. "Well," she said. "Tell us all what the people think."

I wasn't afraid of her disapproval anymore. "They think Aten is something too distant to be worshipped. They want gods they can see, and touch, and feel."

"They can't feel the *sun?*"

"They can't touch it."

"No god should be touched," she retorted.

My father added hastily, "That's not all the people think."

"They are afraid of the Hittites," I added, commanding myself not to think of Nakhtmin. "They hear news from merchants who tell them that the Hittites are sweeping through the north, taking women as slaves and slaughtering men, and they wonder how soon before it happens here."

"In Egypt?" she cried, and she turned to see if our father agreed. "The people of Amarna think the Hittites will invade?" When his face was hard against her, she looked at me. "We have nothing to fear from the Hittites," she said smugly. "Akhenaten has made a treaty with them." My father dropped the scrolls he'd been carrying, and Nefertiti shifted defensively. "I think it is a wise decision."

"A treaty with *Hittites?*" my father roared.

"Why not? What do we care about Lakisa or Kadesh? Why should we pay to defend them when we could spend—"

"Because the blood of Egyptians bought those territories!" My father was shaking in his rage. "This is the most foolish thing you have ever done! Of all the poor decisions you have let your husband make, this—"

"It was the decision of both of us." She stood tall, her black eyes proud and defiant. "We did what we thought was right for Egypt." She reached out her hand. "I thought you of all people would understand this."

My father looked at me to see my reaction.

"Don't look at Mutnodjmet!" Nefertiti shrieked.

My father shook his head. "Your sister would never have been foolish enough to bargain with Hittites. Handing them Kadesh!" My father's eyes blazed. "What next when they have taken Kadesh? Ugarit, Gazru, the Kingdom of Mitanni?"

My sister lost some of her confidence. "They wouldn't dare."

"Once Kadesh has fallen, why not? The Kingdom of Mitanni will be theirs for the taking. And when they've raided Mitanni's land, raped her women, and turned her men into slaves, what's to stop them from marching south to Egypt? Kadesh is the last stronghold saving Mitanni. When Mitanni falls"—my father's voice rose, and I wondered how many servants could hear him through the door—"then so does Egypt!"

Nefertiti walked to the window and looked out over Amarna, a city of sun and light. How long would it last? How long before the Hittites came to the borders of Egypt and contemplated attacking the most powerful kingdom in the world?

"Build up the army," my father warned.

"I can't. To do that would be to stop building Amarna. And this is our home. In these walls, we will achieve immortality."

"In these walls, we will be *buried* if we do not stop the Hittites."

Nefertiti opened the window and stepped out onto the balcony. A hot breeze pressed the soft linen of her dress to her body. "We have signed a treaty," she said with resolution.

The next morning, the markets were calm, but I sensed a tenseness when I walked through the stalls, like the sharp eyes of a crocodile watching just below the surface of placid waters.

"This treaty with the Hittites is all everyone is talking about," Ipu confided.

And Nefertiti's belly, I thought bitterly. Only eleven months after Meketaten and Nefertiti was with her third child.

Ipu stopped walking to glance across the market. "Djedefhor's not here," she observed.

I looked around. Djedefhor usually patrolled the quay, but today the soldiers were all strangers. From across the square, the meat seller recognized Ipu and called out to her.

"Good morning, my lady! Has the Sister of the King's Chief Wife come to buy gazelle?" We made our way over to his crowded stall, where apprentice boys were using palm leaves to keep away the flies.

"No gazelle today." But Ipu smiled and leaned across the counter, inviting the man into her confidence. "The market is quiet."

The meat seller raised his thick eyebrows and nodded, cleaning his knife. "There are rumors," he said. "Rumors of—" He was cut off by the sound of children shouting. Their cries filled the streets. Women began rushing from the stalls, calling to their husbands, and the meat seller dropped his knife in excitement.

"What's happening?" I exclaimed.

But the meat seller had dropped his linens and begun shutting up his stall, searching for his apprentice. When he found the boy, he shouted excitedly, "Take care of everything. I'm going to see."

"See what?" Ipu cried. But the meat seller disappeared. Hundreds of people surged around us. She dropped her basket and grabbed my arm, but we were carried away by the swell of the crowd. I had never witnessed anything so wild or chaotic. Sellers abandoned their stalls, leaving their daughters behind to mind them. Women began tearing branches from dwarf palms and running into the street, shouting out praises as if the gods themselves had descended upon Amarna.

"What's going on?" I shouted above the din.

A woman next to me pointed wildly. "Horemheb and his men are coming! They've defeated the Hittites in Kadesh!"

Ipu looked at me, and I felt my eyes go wide as saucers. She took hold of my hand and pushed me toward the front of the crowd. Riding through the streets in chariots of gold, as the woman had said, were Horemheb and his men, still dressed in their armor.

"Is he there?" I cried.

Ipu pushed us farther in front, so close that we could reach out and touch the men's horses. And then we both saw him. "He is here, my lady!" She was screaming. "He is here!"

The procession passed and I shouted out his name, but the people were cheering too loudly. Their sons were coming home; Egypt's soldiers had been victorious. They were heroes. Then I thought of Akhenaten.

"Ipu! We have to go. We have to get to the palace!" But the crowd was moving. It swelled and swayed. Children ran after the horses and women threw flowers at Horemheb's feet, following the soldiers down the Royal Road. "We have to go! Akhenaten will kill them!"

We pushed our way out and at the edge of the crowd, his eyes searching frantically, was Djedefhor. "My lady!" he shouted.

"Djedefhor!" I almost cried in relief. "How did they do it? How did they defeat them?"

"General Nakhtmin is a great tactician. With Horemheb's training, the Hittites were slaughtered! Horemheb has brought back the head of the Hittite general."

I stepped back in shock. "The head?"

Djedefhor nodded. "To lay at Pharaoh's feet."

I imagined Horemheb riding triumphantly into the palace, his soldiers following on his heels as he burst into the Audience Chamber, tossing the general's head at Akhenaten's sandals. I could imagine the horrified look on Akhenaten's face, and the dark glare of Nefertiti, who would neither shudder nor look away. Then I imagined Akhenaten's anger filling the halls, ordering death for every soldier returning from the fronts of Kadesh. My voice rose with fear. "Djedefhor, can you take me to the palace?"

He took my arm and led us through the crowds. Then I gathered my skirts and we ran like thieves through the back alleys of Amarna until we came upon the gates of the palace, guarded by two dozen of Akhenaten's Nubian men. The procession was only a few blocks behind us and the noise could now be heard even in the courtyard where Akhenaten's trees grew in manicured rows. "Open the gates!" I cried, thrusting my ring with the insignia of Nefertiti under the guards' noses.

The guards passed looks among themselves, and then the tallest one grunted his approval. Grudgingly, the soldiers opened the gates. "Come!" I shouted to Djedefhor and Ipu, but a tall Nubian stepped in front of me.

"They remain outside."

I looked at Djedefhor, and he nodded to Ipu. "She should go to your villa, and I will wait here in the courtyard," he said.

"I'll return," I promised. But with what kind of news, I didn't know.

I heard my father's voice in the Audience Chamber even before the guards pushed opened the heavy doors. Inside, Nefertiti was with the princesses Meritaten and Meketaten. Akhenaten was standing before the Horus thrones. He was dressed in gold armor and carried a spear. He threw open the doors to the balcony, and the cheering of the crowd echoed from below.

"HOR-EM-HEB! HOR-EM-HEB!"

The wind blew the chants up to the Audience Chamber, and the veins in Akhenaten's neck grew thick. "Arrest them!" he commanded. His white cloak swirled around his ankles. "Arrest them and make sure that none of those men see the light of day!" He stalked from the balcony, his eyes as hard as coal. I don't think he saw me when he passed. I don't think he saw anyone. "The people want heroes?" Akhenaten sneered. "Ay!" he shouted. "Bring a chest of gold from the treasury."

"Your Highness—"

"Now!"

My father bowed and went away to do Pharaoh's bidding.

Akhenaten turned on my sister. His eyes glittered, cold as an adder's, and he gripped Nefertiti's shoulders so hard that I gasped. "When your father returns, we will go to the Window of Appearances. Then the people will remember who loves them. They will remember who built a city out of sand for the glory of Aten."

There was a commotion outside, and I saw that beneath the balcony Horemheb was standing on a block of granite. Nubian guards surrounded him, waiting to see what he would do. Then the people began to cheer, and Horemheb held up the bloodied head of the Hittite general he had killed. I gasped, and Nefertiti pressed closer to the balcony.

"He's brought back the head," she said in a horrified whisper. "He's brought back the head of the general!"

Akhenaten rushed to the balcony. In the courtyard below, Horemheb held the severed head high to the cheering crowds. Then the general turned and recognized Akhenaten. He tossed the bloody trophy over the balcony, where it rolled against Akhenaten's white sandals. Akhenaten reeled backward. It was the closest he had ever come to battle, and it was the closest I had come to such gruesome death. I covered my mouth as blood splattered across Akhenaten's legs. Panahesi rushed forward to draw Pharaoh away and the doors to the Audience Chamber swung open. My father had returned with seven men, six of whom carried a chest laden with gold.

Akhenaten grabbed Nefertiti's arm. "To the Window of Appearances!"

He stalked through the palace, the entire court on his heels. My father studied the blood on Akhenaten's feet and said to me, "Stay close and say nothing."

We swept through the halls to the bridge between the palace and the Temple of Aten. From there, the Window of Appearances looked out over the same courtyard as the one where Horemheb stood with his men. But unlike the balcony from the Audience Chamber, the Window of Appearances was official. When the window opened, all of Egypt stopped to listen. We entered the chamber, and Panahesi rushed to throw open the window. At once, the chanting stopped below. Akhenaten looked at Nefertiti for guidance. She stepped forward, raising her arms.

A thousand Egyptians dropped to their knees.

"People of Egypt," she called. "Today is a day of celebration. For today Aten has given mighty Pharaoh a victory over the Hittites!"

A cheer went up throughout the crowds.

Nefertiti continued. "Aten looks on Pharaoh with pride, and the blessings of Aten are bestowed upon us!" Akhenaten dug his hands deep into the wooden chest, tossing armfuls of coins out to the people. Women began to shriek and children cried with laughter; men leaped into the air. No one noticed the guards fanning out around the soldiers, marching them away to the dungeons of Amarna.

I surged forward, but my father held me tightly. "There is nothing you can do for Nakhtmin," he whispered. I wrestled my arm away. Suddenly, Tiye was there, speaking quietly but sharply.

"Don't be foolish. This is not the time."

"But what will happen to him?"

"The people will either rise up," she predicted with brutal honesty, "or every one of those soldiers will be executed."

We stood back and watched as Akhenaten tossed handfuls of gold over the balcony. In the crush to reach the glittering coins, the soldiers had been forgotten. Guards ordered the men to drop their weapons, and directed them to step clear of the crowd and to follow them into the palace. Every one of them complied.

Even Horemheb. Even Nakhtmin.

"Why aren't they resisting?" I cried, pressing closer to the Window of Appearances.

"It is a hundred of them and five hundred Nubian guards," Tiye said.

My father turned to me. "Go now," he said quickly. "Go to Nefertiti's chamber and wait for her there."

Light flickered from two dozen oil lamps and illuminated the paintings on Nefertiti's walls. An artist had painted Nefertiti and Akhenaten raising their arms to embrace Aten, and the rays of sun ended in tiny hands whose fingers caressed my sister's face. The pair of them together looked like gods, while Aten was unknowable, untouchable, a disk of fire that disappeared every night and reappeared at dawn. I looked around the room, but none of the gods that had made Egypt great had been rendered. Not even the goddess Sekhmet, who had brought Egypt victory in the land of Kadesh.

I took one of Nefertiti's figurines in my hand and there was a sharp intake of breath from behind me. My look silenced the guards, but they continued to watch me, wondering what I was doing in Pharaoh's quarters. I stared at the miniature carving in my hand and held it up to the oil lamps. When the light revealed its feline face, I gasped. No other god besides Aten had been given a place in these chambers, but here was the cat-goddess, Lady of Heaven, counterpart of Amun, the great mother Mut. I pressed my lips together. *I have been cruel to Nefertiti. I have accused her without truly knowing if she knew of Akhenaten's plans.*

The door opened and a tall figure appeared silhouetted in the light of the passage. *Akhenaten?* My heart jumped and the guards stretched out their arms in obeisance. "Your Highness." At once, I let out my breath. Her crown had made her taller in the evening light.

"Mutnodjmet?" She saw me and came closer, hesitating.

I put the statuette on a chest as she stepped into the room. "What is happening to Nakhtmin?"

Her eyes fell on the ebony statue. She pointed to the goddess Mut. "My replacement."

"For what?" I didn't like how she changed the subject.

"For you." Nefertiti turned to the guards and barked, "Go!" They moved out, and when the door had shut, she turned back to me. "I am pregnant for the third time and none of my children know their aunt, and now I wonder if they ever will."

My eyes filled with tears. She was pregnant again, but I refused to be drawn in. "Nefertiti, where is Nakhtmin?"

She took the statue of Mut and placed it back on the table. "Do you remember when we were young," she said, "and we laughed that someday we would raise children together and you would be the firm mother and I would be the one to give them everything?" She cast her eyes around the room, taking in the paintings and murals. "I miss those days."

I repeated, "Where is Nakhtmin, Nefertiti?"

My sister averted her gaze. "In prison."

I took her hands. They were cold. "You *have* to get him out. You *have* to."

She watched me sadly. "I have already made arrangements for his release. The others will be executed; only Nakhtmin shall be spared."

I blinked in shock. "How?"

"How?" she repeated. "I told Akhenaten to let him free. He refuses me *nothing*, Mutnodjmet. *Nothing*. Of course, he went running off to Kiya's chamber. But so what? *I* am the one who's pregnant with his child. *I'm* Queen of Egypt, not her." She looked like a little girl singing out loud in the dark to convince herself that she wasn't scared. I embraced her tightly, and the two of us stood in the light of the oil lamps, leaning into one another. "I will miss you," she whispered. "I wanted to be the only one that mattered to you." She stepped back to look at me. "But I would *never* have poisoned your child," she whispered. "I never—"

I squeezed her hand, looking over at the small feline goddess. "I know," I said. I leaned into her shoulder and squeezed again.

She nodded. "*Go*. Go tonight."

▣ ▣ ▣

"Djedefhor, isn't there any other way?"

"This is the only way up the hill, my lady."

The streets teemed with people. Chariots shared the road with jostling carts and dozens of soldiers milled about. "What is everyone doing?" I asked him.

"Talking," he replied. "They have heard that General Nakhtmin has escaped."

"Escaped? But he hasn't. My sister—"

Djedefhor raised a gloved hand and lowered his voice. "The people want an escape. And it won't be long before the soldiers go to him, asking him to lead the army against Pharaoh and take the Horus throne."

"He would never do that," I said firmly.

Djedefhor said nothing and the chariot rolled toward the hills and my villa.

"He would never do that," I repeated.

"Perhaps not. But Pharaoh will send men tonight."

Assassins. That was why Nefertiti said her children would never know their aunt. Why she pushed me out of her chamber and told me to hurry. "Do you really think they will come tonight?" I leaned closer so that Djedefhor could hear me above the wind.

He nodded. "I *know* they will, my lady."

I held my breath as the chariot rolled toward the villa that I had made into my home. We stopped in the courtyard that I had seen so many times in the sun, but in the waning light it suddenly seemed dark and threatening. Djedefhor took my hand, and together we rushed into the forecourt. But when he threw open the door to the villa, I stepped back. Dozens of soldiers occupied my loggia. And Nakhtmin was there. He turned, and the entire room went quiet.

"Mutnodjmet."

My eyes welled with tears as he took me in his arms. In a room full of strangers, we held each other close. He smelled of heat and dirt and battle. I drew back to study his face. He was dark from the sun, and there was a scar across his cheek that had not had time to heal. I thought of the sword that had cut him there and fresh tears came to my eyes. "There is no child," I wept.

He looked into my face, brushing the tears away. "I know." Akhenaten had stolen our child and imprisoned him. His gaze found Djedefhor's, and his look was threatening.

"What?" I panicked. "What are you going to do?"

"Nothing."

"My sister is queen. You won't rebel against her?"

"Of course I won't. Nor will anyone else," he swore loudly, and the soldiers shifted uneasily in their armor. "The gods saw fit to put Akhenaten on the Horus throne, and there he will stay."

"Until *what?*" one of the soldiers shouted. "The Hittites overrun Egypt?"

"Until Pharaoh sees the fault of his actions." My father swept in from the back of the atrium, his white cloak brushing the tiles. "Daughter." He took my hand.

I looked around my villa and realized that the men were dressed for battle. "What are all of these men doing here? In my house?"

"They came to convince Nakhtmin to take the Horus throne," my father said. "I had Nakhtmin brought here for his safety, and these men came to find him. If they know where he is, then so does Pharaoh." My father stepped toward me. "The time has come for you to make a choice, Mutnodjmet."

My mother appeared at my father's side, and suddenly, my throat felt tight. I could see Ipu at the edge of the kitchen, and Bastet surveying the room from his perch on a pillar. I turned to Nakhtmin.

"I will have to leave Amarna," he warned. "And unless my safety is guaranteed by Pharaoh, I will never come back."

"But Nefertiti released you. *She* could ensure it."

My father shook his head. "Your sister has done what she can tonight. If you choose this life, if you choose to marry Nakhtmin, you must leave Amarna."

I looked first at Ipu, then at Bastet, then out to my beautifully cultivated garden.

"Tiye will tend it until you can return," he promised.

Panic swelled in my chest, imagining a life without my parents. "But when will that be?"

My father's eyes shone the color of bright polished lapis, imagining a time when his daughter would be Pharaoh of Egypt in all but name. Perhaps even in name. The ultimate ascension for our family. "When Nefertiti grows powerful enough to order you back with or without her husband's consent."

"But then again, it could be never," Nakhtmin warned.

I looked at my parents and Nakhtmin. Then I slipped my hand in his. I felt his shoulders relax, and I turned to my mother. "You will visit?" I whispered.

My mother nodded quickly, but her tears still came. "Of course."

"And Nakhtmin will be safe?"

"Akhenaten will forget about him," my father predicted. "He will not risk Nefertiti's wrath to pursue him from city to city. Nefertiti is the one the people follow," he said. "And Akhenaten will not risk her anger."

Ipu shoved handfuls of linen into baskets and the servants rushed into action. The soldiers were gone, and my mother and father took Nakhtmin aside, whispering with him about Thebes. Fear and excitement welled in my stomach. Tiye watched from the garden as the donkeys were laden with my belongings, then came and held out a lotus flower for me to take.

"The sister who should have been queen," she said.

"No, I could not do what Nefertiti has done."

"Make a treaty with the Hittites, birth two girls in succession, and erect statues of herself at every crossroads?" My aunt turned to Nakhtmin. There were signs of battle still on his kilt, the blood of enemies he had slain. "You have been fortunate in your destiny," Tiye said. To me she added, "Maybe you are the lucky sister. The one who will have peace in this life."

In the city below us, tension hovered like a cloud. As the evening cool settled across the villages, women opened their shutters and men took to the Royal Road.

"The men are taking to the streets." I panicked, peering over the balcony.

"They have heard my son plans to execute Horemheb and his men. Certainly, they are."

"Then why did Horemheb return? He must have known that Pharaoh would imprison him."

Tiye looked to Nakhtmin and guessed, "Perhaps he hoped for rebellion."

"I don't know," Nakhtmin admitted, his voice softening. "Perhaps it was pride. Horemheb is full of lofty ambitions. I only know what I came for."

I felt heat creep into my cheeks. Beyond the balcony, I could see the swelling of people in the streets. My aunt saw the direction of my gaze and raised her brows.

"So it begins."

I glanced at her. "Aren't you afraid?"

Tiye tossed her head, a gesture I had seen Nefertiti make a hundred times, and at once a deep regret overwhelmed me, that I could steal away in the night like this, leaving my sister forever.

"It is the price of power, Mutnodjmet. Someday you may come to understand that."

"No. I would never want to be queen."

When the sun descended, Nakhtmin and I mounted horses. Djedefhor was to sail a bark full of servants behind us while we went on. "We will visit when we can," my mother swore, standing at the edge of the villa. Ipu came forward. Her eyes were red as she embraced various members of my household: the cook, the gardener, the boy who cleaned the lotus pools. Then she stepped toward Djedefhor, since she'd be sailing with him.

"You don't have to come with us," I told Ipu again. "You can stay here and keep Bastet."

"No, my lady. My life is with you."

Nakhtmin fastened his bow behind him. "We must go," he said tensely. "It will be dangerous tonight."

My father pressed my hand in his.

"What if they storm the palace?" I asked him.

"Then the soldiers will beat them back."

"But the soldiers are not on Akhenaten's side."

"They're on whatever side has silver and gold," he said, and I understood suddenly why my father had not opposed my marriage with Nakhtmin. With the general on our side, the soldiers had no one to rally behind. As long as Horemheb remained in prison, our family was safe on the throne of Egypt.

We rode out under the cover of darkness, and as we sped through the streets, we could see the beginnings of rebellion. Men with sticks and rocks marched in the streets, demanding the release of the soldiers who had thwarted King Suppiluliumas and defeated the Hittites. The chanting grew louder as we rode through the city, then there was the clash of weapons. Fire swept up the mountainside where my villa and its herb garden stood, and I turned around on my horse and looked back into the night.

"The fire will not reach it," Nakhtmin promised, slowing to a canter as we came upon the gates that would lead us out of the city of Amarna. "Say nothing," he instructed. He held out the scroll my father had given him; I could see Vizier Ay's seal in the torchlight, as dark as dried blood with the sphinx and Eye of Horus pressed into it. The guard looked at us, nodding his assent for the gates to be opened.

And suddenly, we were free.

Chapter Nineteen

THEBES

eleventh of Payni

OUR NEW HOUSE stood on the banks of the Nile, perched on a cliff like a brooding heron. The building looked cold and empty in the middle of the night, and the owner was curious when we appeared at his door, inquiring about buying his house on the shore.

"It was built for the daughter of the mayor," he explained, "but she said it was too small for Her Highness's tastes." He appraised my jewels and the cut of my linen, wondering if it wouldn't be too small for me. Then he said, "Strange time of night to be buying a house."

"We'll take it all the same," Nakhtmin replied.

The owner raised his eyebrows at us. "How did you know it was for sale?"

Nakhtmin produced a scroll and the man held it up to the lamplight. Then he looked at the both of us anew. "The vizier's daughter?" He peered at it again. "*You* are the Sister of the King's Chief Wife?"

I straightened my shoulders. "I am."

He held up the candle to see me better. "You do have cat eyes."

Nakhtmin frowned and the owner laughed. "Didn't you know that I went to school with Ay?" He rolled up the scroll and gave it back to Nakhtmin. "We both grew up in the palace at Thebes."

"I didn't know that," I said.

"Udjai?" he replied. "Son of Shalam?"

I blinked naively.

"*What?* He never told you about our boyhood adventures? Pulling pranks on the Elder's servants, running naked through the lotus gardens, swimming in the sacred pools of Isis?" He saw my scandalized look and said, "Ay has changed, I see."

"I cannot imagine Vizier Ay running kiltless through lotus gardens," Nakhtmin admitted, scrutinizing the old man.

"Ah." Udjai patted his belly and laughed. "But those were our younger days, when there was less hair on my stomach and more on my head."

Nakhtmin grinned. "It is good to know you are a friend, Udjai."

"Of Ay's daughters, always." He looked as though he wanted to say more, but he turned and motioned with his hand. We followed him into a hallway where a dog pricked its ear at our approach but didn't bother to move. "I am guessing you are in need of discretion," he said. "At this time of night, with no baskets or servants . . . It can only mean you have angered Pharaoh." He looked at Nakhtmin's kilt with its golden lion. "Which general are you?"

"General Nakhtmin."

Udjai stopped in his tracks, turning fully around. "General Nakhtmin who fought against the Hittites in Kadesh?"

Nakhtmin smiled wryly. "News travels fast."

Udjai stepped forward and there was the deepest respect in his voice. "You are all the people will talk about," he said. "But you were imprisoned."

I stiffened. "And my sister set him free."

Understanding dawned on Udjai's face: why we were there in the dark of night, why we'd come without baskets or linens or even a day's worth of food. "Is it true, then," he whispered, "that Pharaoh will execute the great general Horemheb?"

Nakhtmin stiffened. "Yes. It is only by Lady Mutnodjmet's grace that I am free. Horemheb has no such luck."

"Unless the gods are with him," Udjai replied, glancing up at a mural of Amun. He saw my look and shifted. "The people don't forget the god who gave them life and made Egypt great." He cleared his throat tactfully, as if he'd said too much to the daughter of Ay. "Do you think to hide from Pharaoh, then?" Udjai asked.

"No one can hide from Pharaoh," Nakhtmin said. "We've come to raise a family and make a new life far away from court. By tomorrow, they will know where we have gone. But Pharaoh will not send men after us. He is too afraid of rebellion."

And Nefertiti, I thought.

Udjai produced a key from a golden box. "Payment due once a month, beginning on the first. Or you can pay me outright."

"We will pay you outright," Nakhtmin said at once.

Udjai bowed. "It is an honor to do business with a general who would have made the Elder proud."

We walked up the stone path, and I shivered in the chill that had settled over the desert. But there was warmth in Nakhtmin's hand and I didn't let it go. Inside the empty house, he lit the brazier and shadows moved across the ceiling.

My eyes welled with tears. We had crossed the threshold of an empty house together, and in every family of Egypt this meant the same thing. I held back my tears. "We are married now," I said. "Only a few days ago I thought you were dead to me, and suddenly in the darkness of night we are together as husband and wife."

Nakhtmin pressed against me, smoothing my black hair. "The

gods have protected us, Mutnodjmet. There is destiny in our being together. My prayers to Amun have been answered." He kissed me, and I wondered if he had been with another woman; he would have had his choice of any woman in Kadesh. But I looked into his eyes, and his urgency told me otherwise. He lifted my gown and we made love near the warmth of our small fire, over and over again. Toward morning, Nakhtmin rolled on his side to look at me.

"Why are you crying?"

"Because I am happy." I laughed, but there was sadness and bitterness in it, too.

"Did you think I wouldn't return?" he asked seriously.

My linen gown lay at the foot of the brazier, so he wrapped me in a fold of his cloak. I pressed my cheek against its warmth and nodded.

"They told me to forget you," I whispered. My throat tightened, thinking of the night when I'd lost our child. "And then the poison . . ."

My husband clenched his jaw, wanting to say something violent, but tenderness overcame him. "There will be other children," he promised, putting a hand to my stomach. "And no force of Hittites, however strong or numerous, could keep me from you."

"But how did you defeat them?"

He told me the story of the night that Akhenaten's Nubian guards had ordered him onto a barge with seven other men bound for the front at Kadesh. "I don't doubt Pharaoh thought it was suicide, but he overestimated the Hittite forces. They are scattered throughout the north, and there weren't enough of them to break through a coordinated defense. They'd chosen the city because they'd gambled that Akhenaten wouldn't send soldiers to defend it. But they were wrong."

"Only because he thought those he was sending were going to their *death*."

"But the Hittites didn't know that. The mayor of Kadesh didn't know that. We have saved Egypt from a Hittite invasion," he said, "but they'll try again."

"And next time, there will be no one to save Kadesh, and when it falls, their march to Mitanni and then to Egypt will be unstoppable."

"We could fight them," he said, sure of himself, remembering the fear Egypt's army had instilled during the time of the Elder. "We could stop them now."

"But Akhenaten will never do it." I conjured an image of Akhenaten, the white leather of his sandals and his pristine cloak that would never see battle. "Akhenaten the Builder," I said contemptuously. "While the Hittites march south, Egypt's soldiers will be busy sanding stone for his eternal city to Aten."

Nakhtmin paused, considering his next words. "When we rode into the city, the soldiers were shocked to see your sister on every temple," he confided. "Her image is everywhere."

"She is reminding the people who rules in Egypt," I said defensively.

Nakhtmin watched me, and his look was guarded. "There are some who say that she has raised herself even above Amun."

I was silent, and when he saw that I wasn't going to speak against her he sighed.

"Either way, I am glad our children will know what it's like to till the earth and fish the Nile and walk through the streets without being knelt to as if they were gods. They will be humble."

"If I have a son"—I measured my words—"Nefertiti will never forgive me."

Nakhtmin shook his head. "That's over now."

"It's never over. So long as Nefertiti is alive and we are sisters, it will never be over."

The next morning, the sun had risen well into the sky before we rolled off our pallet and looked around us. There was a commotion outside. "Soldiers?" I tensed.

Nakhtmin's hearing was sharper. "Djedefhor. And from the sounds of it, Ipu."

Now I, too, could hear my servant's incessant chatter. We dressed in a hurry and I opened the door.

"Ipu!" I exclaimed.

"My lady!" She set down a basket. "What a place," she cried. "It's so large. Not as nice a garden, but look at the view." The basket toppled over and an angry Bastet marched out with an injured air. When he saw me, he leapt into my arms.

"Oh, Bastet. Was the river ride so terrible?" I chucked him under the chin.

"I have no idea what *he's* complaining about. Djedefhor caught two fish and gave them both to him."

I turned to Djedefhor.

He bowed. "My lady."

Nakhtmin embraced him warmly. "I never had to chance to thank you," my husband said. I glanced at Nakhtmin. "I asked Djedefhor to watch over you while I was gone," he explained.

I covered my mouth and Ipu stifled a giggle.

Djedefhor shrugged. "It wasn't difficult. A few trips into the village."

"A *few*? You came every day!" I looked again at Nakhtmin, and my heart filled with a sudden, overwhelming love. Even as he was being sent away by my own family, he had thought to find someone to watch over me. I went to Djedefhor and took his hands. "Thank you," I said.

Djedefhor flushed. "You're welcome, my lady." He studied the house and said with admiration, "You've found a beautiful place up here." He passed his hand over the smooth walls. "Real construction. Not mud brick and *talatat*," he added.

"Yes. A real city of limestone and granite," I said.

We unloaded the baskets that had come on the barge and spent the afternoon laying rugs and washing linens. Neighbors peered through our window, curious to see who had moved into the house that had been meant for the mayor's daughter.

Ipu rolled her eyes. "That is the third person who has come here looking for lost cattle. Has everyone in Thebes lost their cow today?"

I laughed, spreading cushions for them in the front room. When it was time for Djedefhor to go, we stood on the shore and waved farewell. I put my arm around Nakhtmin's waist and asked if he thought we'd ever see him again.

"Djedefhor?" he asked. "Of course."

I hesitated. "You are no longer part of Pharaoh's army, Nakhtmin."

"But the winds will blow and the sands will shift. Akhenaten won't be Pharaoh forever."

I stiffened in his arms.

"It's nothing against your sister, *miw-sher,* but no one is immortal."

"My family has *always* been on the throne of Egypt."

Nakhtmin pressed his lips together. "Yes, and that is what worries me."

We walked back into the house and I followed him into the loggia. "What do you mean?"

"Only that should our Royal Highnesses die, what link will there be left to the throne? Akhenaten has no legitimate siblings." He looked over at me. "It's only you, *miw-sher.*"

Only me. I realized that it was true, and I shivered. If something should happen to Nefertiti, if Akhenaten died, the new Pharaoh would need a link to the throne to legitimize his claim. He would have to marry into it. And what royal woman would be of age to marry if something should happen now? Not Nefertiti's little girls. Only me.

"You've never thought about it?" he asked.

"Of course I have. But not . . ." I hesitated. "Not seriously."

"If Akhenaten dies without a son, one of his generals is in a prime position to take the reins of Egypt," Nakhtmin explained. "Why, even right now people could be whispering that I married you for a claim to Egypt's throne."

I watched him carefully. "So, did you?"

He wrapped me in his arms. "What do you think?" His kisses traveled downward and I closed my eyes.

"I think it was for love." I stopped his hands from going any farther and we retired to our chamber.

Ipu knew better than to disturb us.

* * *

For the first month in Thebes, we did nothing but enjoy the quiet of a life near the water. We listened to the gulls as they searched for food along the sand, and the brassy ring of bells that farmers tied around the necks of their cattle, which grazed at the banks of the River Nile. We went to the market and picked out baskets for our new home, enjoying our anonymity. Although I wore linens and gold, I was no different from the daughters of the priests or scribes whose wrists jangled with bangles and glass.

Twice, men in soldiers' garb from Amarna came up to Nakhtmin and whispered with him. Each time they bowed very low, even though Nakhtmin was no longer a general. "This is Lieutenant Nebut," Nakhtmin said the second time we were approached.

The lieutenant shaded his eyes with his hand and smiled. "Did you know your husband is all they talk about back in Amarna?"

"They better not talk too loudly, then," I told him, "or they will endanger both of our lives."

The lieutenant nodded. "Of course, my lady. None of the men have forgotten what happened to Horemheb." He lowered his voice. "But there is a rumor that Pharaoh will not execute him after all."

I glanced quickly at Nakhtmin. "What will they do then?"

"Keep the men in prison," my husband replied.

"Yes. Until the people forget. But they have chanted outside the palace gates for a month. Pharaoh's guards beat them back, but the crowds don't stop coming. His own city has turned against him." His voice dropped nearly to a whisper. "The night I left, he declared any man chanting against him to be a traitor. They have put a dozen men to death already."

Nakhtmin was shaking his head.

"Now the people stand at the gates as a silent mob."

I imagined Akhenaten's rage as he watched the angry mobs from his Window of Appearances, Panahesi next to him, whispering platitudes in his ear.

"He will have to resolve it soon," Nakhtmin predicted.

"Oh, he will," I promised. "Pharaoh will declare a Festival to Aten. He will throw gold from his chariots and the people will forget."

A Festival to Aten was declared the next day.

My heart sank, knowing that men like Nebut must think I was just like my family, cunning and ambitious to have guessed at her plan. I knew as well that in the halls of eternity, my name would echo with Nefertiti's, and that if the gods were to obliterate her name from the scrolls of life, they would obliterate mine, too.

All of Thebes was in the streets, and we walked through the city to watch the festivities. Dancers and acrobats crowded the quay, along with merchants selling baked catfish and pheasant. I watched men make obeisance to an image of the sun on a pillar.

"I only wonder what the gods must be thinking." Nakhtmin spoke my thoughts, studying women making offerings to the sun.

The festivities carried on long into the night, and from our villa perched above the Nile we could hear the sounds of singing and the ringing of party bells. We went to sleep with the cries of drunken revelries in our ears, and I thought, *This is how you make a people forget. Free wine, free bread, a day off from labor, and suddenly Horemheb is a name buried in the sand.*

The next day, a messenger from Amarna arrived.

"From Vizier Ay," the boy said expectantly.

I read the scroll, then went into the garden to read it aloud to Nakhtmin. "News from Amarna," I said. I unrolled the papyrus and read it to him.

> I hope this letter finds you well, Mutnodjmet, and that you have been wise enough to protect your new husband from village gossips and women at the wells. I do not need to say how your mother misses you. But there is rebellion in the city, silent rebellion that eats away at Pharaoh until only Queen Neferneferuaten-Nefertiti can calm him.

"Queen Neferneferuaten-Nefertiti?" Nakhtmin asked.

"Perfect Are the Beauties of Aten," I said disbelievingly.

> Should the Hittites invade, neither you nor Nakhtmin would be safe. Akhenaten is no fool. At the first sign of real rebellion, he will execute Horemheb, then send men to Thebes. Do not think that because you live away from court that you are safe. Should there be an uprising, Udjai will give warning and you will flee to Akhmim. Write nothing to us and send nothing to Pharaoh's city until the tide of unrest has washed over Amarna. These are only precautions, little cat, but though your heart may belong to your husband, your duty is to family should Akhenaten ever fall.

Nakhtmin looked up at this. "Your father does not mince words."

I let the scroll fall onto my lap. "He is only being honest."

Chapter Twenty

1347 BCE

first of Mechyr

THERE WAS NO rebellion in Amarna, though we expected it with every message that came from my father. Horemheb had been forgotten, and the people tolerated their heavy taxes for the glory of Aten the way they did throughout the rest of the kingdom. They ate less, they worked harder, and more women sought out acacia and honey. Fewer mouths to feed meant less food to buy. But as they watched Akhenaten's buildings rise pillar by pillar, they met in secret to pray to Amun. In Thebes, we set up our own shrine, hidden beneath a bower of jasmine. And this is how the late days of summer passed, and all of autumn. I knew my sister must be growing heavy with child. Then, one day as I was sitting by Ipu's side, explaining to her the uses of foreign herbs, the message I knew would come arrived.

I had expected to see my father's seal on the scroll, his two sphinxes rearing with the symbol of eternal life between their claws. But it was my mother who had written.

The month of Mechyr has arrived and your sister has summoned you to Amarna. She cannot, however, promise Nakhtmin's safety. Horemheb still sits in prison and Pharaoh's fondest wish is that he will die on his own. Your father has told him that if he raises his hand to strike Horemheb down there will be civil war. But all this is insignificant if Nefertiti produces a prince. Your father asks that you come as well. He will send the royal barge for you.

"You must go," Nakhtmin said simply. "She is your sister. "What if she dies in childbirth?"

I recoiled. Nefertiti was strong, she was relentless. She wouldn't die. "But you can't come," I protested. "If the people should see you and rise up, Pharaoh would have you killed."

"Then I'll stay here and wait for your return. Take Ipu. I will be fine," he promised. "And besides, there is the matter of our tomb."

Yes. We were married now, and work should begin on our tomb. I thought back to the tomb of Tuthmosis, the dank and heavy darkness, and shivered. I didn't want to choose the site of my own burial chamber. It would be better to let him find our resting place in the hills of Thebes without me. He could choose a rocky outcropping near the sleeping Pharaohs of Egypt, in the valley near my ancestors and his. I looked at my husband in the shifting light, and a feeling of great tenderness overwhelmed me. He was waiting for me to say something, and I nodded. "I will go."

I left on the royal barge with Ipu, early enough to escape the prying eyes of neighbors, who would have wanted to know why the barge was there, who was leaving in it, and where it was going. We traveled downriver, and I thought of how much had changed in the eight months since I had left Pharaoh's city in the desert. I was a married woman now, with a house and my own land. I had sheep and chickens, and I didn't need to stand in Nefertiti's shadow anymore. I didn't need to fetch her linen or make her juice to know that she loved me. We were sisters, and as I looked out across the River Nile, I realized that that should be enough.

My mother and father met us in the Great Hall, and when my mother saw me she gave a sharp cry and threw up her hands, kissing my cheeks, my hair, my face. "Mutnodjmet."

My father smiled and kissed my cheeks warmly. "You look well." He turned to Ipu. "As do you."

"Tell us everything!" my mother exclaimed, and she wanted to know a hundred things at once. How I was living, what my villa was like, and if the Nile there was full this Season of Growing. Thutmose, hearing that I had arrived, came in and swept a great bow to me.

"The lady that Amarna won't stop talking about." He smiled. "And Ipu, the finest beautician in Thebes. Everyone will want to see you," he promised.

Ipu giggled. "What? Don't they have any other fodder for gossip?"

"Only Pharaoh's Arena."

I threw a sharp glance at my father and he said ruefully, "His new gift for the people."

I paused in the Great Hall of Amarna. "But there are no more builders," I protested.

My father raised his brows. "Which is why he hired Nubians."

"Foreigners to work alongside soldiers?" I asked, shocked. "But they could be spies!"

"They certainly could," my father said as we began our walk to the Audience Chamber. "But Panahesi convinced Akhenaten that he could have an Arena immediately and cheaply if Nubians were employed."

"And you allowed this? Couldn't Tiye try to stop him?"

My mother and Thutmose exchanged heavy looks.

"Tiye has been banished from the palace," my father said. "She stays in your villa."

"Like a prisoner?" My voice echoed in the hall and I checked myself. "Like a prisoner in her own son's city?"

He nodded. "Panahesi has convinced Akhenaten that his mother is dangerous; that if given the chance, she will take back the throne."

"And Nefertiti?"

"What can Nefertiti do?" my father asked. We arrived at the Audience Chamber, then he turned to warn me. "When you go in, do not be surprised." The guards threw open the doors, sweeping low bows before us, and the herald announced our names to the court.

Servants were dressed in golden pectorals, their wrists cuffed in bands of lapis and gold. The women who sat like statues around Nefertiti's throne wore dresses of netted beads and nothing else, playing harps and writing poems and laughing. Pharaoh's nearly completed Amarna shone like a polished jewel, and I was shocked. I walked into the chamber and felt like a foreigner in a different land.

"Mutny!"

Nefertiti was helped to her feet, and as she came down the dais the room parted before us. I inhaled the familiar scent of her hair, realizing suddenly how much I had missed her. Above us, Akhenaten cleared his throat.

"Sister," he greeted. "How nice to see you."

"It is always a pleasure to be in Pharaoh's city," I said flatly.

"Is that why you ran off so quickly to Thebes?"

The court went very quiet.

"No, Your Highness." I smiled my sweetest court smile. "I ran because I thought I was in danger. But, of course, being here now in the arms of my sister, all such feelings disappear."

Rage flushed Akhenaten's face, but the look Nefertiti shot her husband shrank him back onto his throne. I was the not the same girl who'd run away to Thebes. I was a married woman now.

The silence that had stolen over the Audience Chamber turned at once to nervous conversation. Nefertiti embraced me. "You know you have nothing to fear," she promised. "This is my home. *Our* home," she corrected. She hooked my arm in hers, and the court watched us move toward the double doors of the Audience Chamber. My sister pressed her cheek against my shoulder, and I could feel Akhenaten's eyes boring into our backs. "I knew you would come. I knew you would," she swore.

The court made its way through the glittering hall, following us, talking and laughing while my father spoke with Pharaoh.

"There is news of Hittites in Mitanni, Your Highness."

But Akhenaten didn't want to hear any news. "Everything is taken care of!" he snapped.

Nefertiti turned and Pharaoh smoothed his face, laughing nervously. "Your father thinks I have underestimated the Hittite power."

We entered the Great Hall and Nefertiti said sharply, "My father loves you. He is trying to protect our crown."

"Then why does he think I am less powerful than King Suppiluliumas?" Akhenaten whined.

"Because King Suppiluliumas is greedy and you are satisfied living a life that serves your people and the glory of Aten."

They ascended the dais and I took my old seat at the royal table with my father and mother.

"The wandering sheep returns," Kiya said, and looked down at my waist. "Not in foal?"

"No, but then neither are you." I lowered my voice. "I hear Pharaoh visits your chamber only twice a *renpet* now. Is that true?"

One of Kiya's ladies said quickly, "Don't listen to her. Come." They rushed away to greet guests across the hall.

"So tell us about Thebes," my mother pressed brightly.

"And Udjai," my father added.

I told them that Udjai had grown fatter than he had been in my father's boyhood days.

"No, he was always large," my father said. "And now he is a landowner." He nodded approvingly. "He has carved a good life for himself. But no children?"

"Three," I replied. "And a wife from Mitanni. She cooks perch with cumin and Bastet sneezes whenever he comes back from their garden."

My mother laughed. I had forgotten how beautiful it sounded. "And your house?"

"It's mine." I smiled with satisfaction. "No one else's but mine. We've planted a garden and expect a harvest in Pachons. Ipu has arranged an entire room for me where I can work, and Nakhtmin has promised to watch the garden till I return."

My mother reached across the table to squeeze my hand while cheerful music played around us. "You have had the blessings of the gods," she said. "Whenever I cry, your father reminds me that you have what you've always wanted."

"I do, *mawat*. I am only sorry we are so far away."

I rubbed the soles of Nefertiti's feet with coconut oil, smoothing it into her small, rough heel as she lay in her bath. "What do you do, go barefoot all day?" I asked her.

"When I can," she admitted, stretching her back. A great copper tub had been built in the royal rooms and was perfumed with lavender. "You just don't know what it's like to carry a child," she complained.

My eyes met hers and she sat up quickly. "I didn't mean it that way," she said at once.

I rubbed the oil over her feet. "I have been trying for eight months," I told her. Her eyes traveled to my waist. "Nothing. I don't think I will ever have a child."

"You can't know that," Nefertiti replied hotly. "It's up to Aten."

I set my jaw, and she laid her head back in the tub and sighed. "Why don't you tell me about Thebes? What is it you do all day?"

I would have answered, but we were interrupted by the squeals of children and the heavy sound of an adult woman chasing after them.

"Meritaten, Meketaten!" My sister laughed. The two girls scrambled into Nefertiti's wet arms, and my story was forgotten. The nurse was not laughing, however, though she made a short bow when she entered Pharaoh's chamber.

The younger girl was crying, holding her forelock. "Meri pulled my hair," she wept.

"I didn't touch her hair. You can't believe her!"

I let Nefertiti's foot drop, and both children immediately stopped what they were doing to look up at me with wide, interested eyes. The older girl came up and stared into my face with the confidence Nefertiti had owned as a child.

"Are you our aunt Mutnodjmet?" she asked.

I smiled at Nefertiti. "Yes, I am."

"You have green eyes." She narrowed hers, trying to determine whether she liked me or not. Then Meketaten began to wail again.

"What's wrong?" I asked the little princess, holding out my arms, but she clung to her mother's hand.

"Meri pulled my hair," she sobbed.

I looked at Meri. "You wouldn't do such a thing, would you?"

She batted her dark eyes. "Of course not." She looked up winningly at her mother. "Otherwise, *mawat* won't let us ride."

I stared at Nefertiti.

"Chariots," she explained.

"At *two* and *three*? But Meketaten is too small—"

I thought I caught a satisfied nod from the nurse, who was standing at the door watching over her two charges. "Nonsense," Nefertiti said as a servant helped her from her bath and brought her a robe.

"They ride as well as any boy their age. Why should my children be denied just because they are girls?"

I stared at her in amazement. "Because it's dangerous!"

Nefertiti bent down to Meritaten. *So Meri's the favorite,* I thought. "Are you frightened when you ride in the new Arena?" she asked, and the scent of her lavender soap filled the bath.

"No." The older princess shook her black forelock and the ponytail came to rest as a curl beneath her chin. She was a pretty child.

"You see?" Nefertiti straightened. "Ubastet, take the girls to their lessons."

"No, *mawat.*" Meritaten let her shoulders go limp. "Do we *have* to?"

Nefertiti put her hands on her hips. "Do you want to be a princess or an uneducated peasant?"

Meri giggled. "A peasant," she said naughtily.

"Really?" Nefertiti asked. "Without horses or paints or pretty jewels to wear?"

Meritaten trudged out but hesitated at the door, wanting some consolation before she left. "Will we be going to the Arena tonight?" she pleaded.

"Only if it pleases your father."

In the Royal Robing Room, Nefertiti held up her arms. The servant moved to get her dress, but she said, "Not you. Mutny."

I took the linen gown and pulled it over her head, envious of the way it fit her body, even in pregnancy. "You allow them to ride in the Arena at night? Is there anything you *don't* allow?"

"When we were children, I would have given half of Akhmim to live the kind of life my daughters are having."

"When we were children, we understood humility," I said.

She shrugged and sat before her mirror. Her hair had grown. She handed me her brush. "You always do it so much better than Merit."

I frowned. "You could write to me once in a while," I told her, taking the brush and pulling it gently through her hair. "Mother does."

"It was your choice to go running off with a soldier. Not mine." My fingers tightened around the brush and Nefertiti's eyes flew open.

"Mutny, that hurt!"

"I'm sorry."

She settled back in her ebony chair. "Tonight we'll go to the Arena," she decided. "You haven't even seen the crowning jewel of this city."

"I thought that was you."

She ignored my wry humor. "I think I have accomplished it," she said. "I think I have built something that will stand until the end of time."

I stopped with her hair. "Nothing is forever," I said cautiously. "Nothing lasts."

Nefertiti studied her reflection in the mirror and grinned brazenly. "Why? Do you think the gods will punish my overreaching?"

I replied, "I don't know."

In a noisy throng of guards and jeweled chariots we moved down the Royal Road to the towering Arena. It was the first time I had seen the Royal Road in completion, and it stretched impossibly wide, threading through the city like a long white ribbon. Thutmose, who had become as important as any vizier at court, rode in my chariot, and I caught him watching me in the evening light.

"You look more like your sister than I remember," he said. "The same cheeks, the same lips . . ." The artist in him hesitated. "But not the same eyes." He peered closely at me as we rode. "They have changed."

"They have grown more like my father's. Wary and cunning." I stared out ahead of me. "And Nefertiti?" I asked. "Has she changed since you first came to the court of Memphis?"

We both looked at Nefertiti in the chariot before us. Her crown glinted in the pale evening light and her long silver cloak whipped in the wind. Thutmose said proudly, "No, the queen is exactly the same."

Still a spoiled child, I thought. But the people loved her. As we rode toward the Arena, they crowded in the streets, chanting her name and throwing lotus blossoms before her. As word spread that the queen was in the city, the chanting grew more fervent. Her Nubian guards made a circle around her in their polished chariots, warding off the crying people with their shields. "Stand back!" they shouted. "Stand back!" But crowds crushed against each other on the Royal Road, begging my sister to intervene with Aten to bring them happiness. "Please," they cried out. *"Please, Your Majesty!"*

I glanced at Thutmose. "Is it always like this?"

"Always, my lady. They would walk to the quarries of Aswan for her. They line up at the palace gates just to see her pass by the window of her chamber. Every statue in Amarna is her shrine."

"So she's a *goddess?*"

"Of the people."

"And Pharaoh?" It was difficult to see him. He was surrounded by a thick press of Nubian guards.

Thutmose leaned close to me and said, "I would think he would be jealous. But she guides their love to him, and they praise him because she does."

The horses turned sharply into the entrance of the Arena and the cries of the people fell behind us. I gasped. It was grander than anything I had ever seen. Thutmose gave me his arm to help me out of the chariot. "Look at the crown." He drew my eyes to the top of the open Arena, where images of Nefertiti and Akhenaten had been painstakingly carved, their arms raised to the rays of Aten.

I gaped. "You did all of this?"

"With Maya's direction. And in only seven months."

Each of the sandstone statues had been painted and gilded. Their united hands formed the top of the Arena. It was a magnificent sight.

A building to rival the temples of Thebes. We walked inside, and the stillness of night settled across the empty colonnades. Our voices disturbed the silence, and our long procession filled the Arena.

"What do you think?" Nefertiti searched my face.

"It's magnificent," I told her. "Thutmose is truly gifted."

There were portraits of all the royal court on the Arena walls, riding in chariots, striking blows at the Hittites, but I searched in vain for Kiya and Prince Nebnefer. My sister had already erased them from Amarna. She knew that to speak the name of the dead was to make them live again, and that someday, when the Gods returned to Egypt, they would find no trace of Kiya's existence.

"Shall we take her to the new horses?" Meri asked eagerly. "They're Assyrian."

Akhenaten led the way to the stables, and Nefertiti watched my awe at the lavishness of it all with satisfaction. I imagined all the letters my father must have written to procure so many breeds.

"That is the pair from Assyria." Nefertiti pointed. "Akhenaten purchased two for Meri and Meketaten. And now who knows? Soon we may need one for a little son. It's the greatest Arena in Egypt, isn't it?"

"It must have taken a great deal of labor."

"Three thousand Nubians," Nefertiti replied.

"I would have thought you would have been wary of them as spies," I said cautiously.

"The Nubians are more loyal than half of Egypt," Akhenaten sneered. "They are loyal not just to me, but to the glory of Aten. There is only one god of Egypt." He looked to Nefertiti. "The god who granted us the Horus crowns."

Nefertiti had total sway over him now. *Us.*

She leaned her head against his arm and rested her hand on her belly.

ꕥ ꕥ ꕥ

It was an easy birth, like the first and the second, and I wondered how many more I would attend before I crossed the threshold of my own birthing pavilion. I told myself that I was going to leave as soon as the child came, but I couldn't be jealous of my sister's happiness when I saw the little infant pressed against her breast.

A third princess. Three girls in a row.

The herald announced the child's name. Ankhesenpaaten, meaning "She Who Lives for the Glory of Aten," and when I saw the tears of joy in Akhenaten's eyes, I could not stop the bitter voice that asked why he deserved a child and Nakhtmin did not.

"What are you thinking?" my mother asked quietly.

I watched Nefertiti surrounded by her family. Akhenaten, Meritaten, Meketaten, and now the infant princess Ankhesenpaaten. All of them named after the god of the sun, a god no one understood but them. "You can guess," I replied, pressing my lips together.

"It will only eat away at you."

My father and Tiye came up behind us, embracing me sympathetically.

"Aren't I the one who just had the child?" Nefertiti exclaimed. "What did she do besides sit and watch?"

Tiye passed me a look, then went to see the new Princess of Egypt. "Great Osiris." My aunt looked over at me. "She has Mutnodjmet's color. And the same shape of her eyes."

My mother and father moved quickly to the bedside to see whether this was true, but I stayed where I was, too upset to see anything.

"She does," my mother exclaimed.

Nefertiti beamed proudly at me. "Come. She looks just like you," she said.

Pharaoh clenched his jaw as I bent over his third child and peered into her face. Then I smiled up at him. "Yes, just what my own daughter might have looked like. Had she not been killed."

"He is furious with you." The anger on her face froze the guards in their positions. But I refused to care.

"Then let him be furious!"

Nefertiti sat up and hissed, "You should never have said that! No one in Amarna believes such a thing."

"Because no one in Amarna is foolish enough to tell you the truth. But I will not lie! I am going home."

"To Thebes?" she cried, scrambling out of bed in the birthing pavilion. I shouldn't have let her. She held on to my arm to pull me back. "Don't go. Please don't go, Mutnodjmet. You can't leave me like this."

"Like *what?*" I demanded. For a moment, I thought she wouldn't answer.

Then she replied, "So vulnerable. Akhenaten never goes to see Kiya when I'm pregnant. He will go to her now."

I couldn't do this anymore. Be her spy, play her games, want what she wanted. I moved to go again.

"Mutnodjmet, please!" She scrambled so that her legs became twisted in the linens. "I can't do this without you."

"What exactly do you do?" I asked scornfully. "You don't till the land, you don't fish the Nile, you don't fight to keep the Hittites at bay the way Tiye did when this was truly an *empire.*"

"No! I play the goddess to the people!" she cried. "I play the savior of this kingdom when the soldiers want to revolt and are stopped only when I can convince them that Aten has spoken through me and assured them of prosperity. *I* am the one who must hold the puppet strings in this play, and only Father"—her lower lip began to tremble—"only Father knows how hard and tiring that is."

She closed her eyes and the tears hung suspended on the edge of her lashes. "Please. Stay with me. Just for a while."

"Not forever," I warned her.

"But a little while."

As soon as Nefertiti knew that I would stay, she did her best to make sure I thought very little of my husband in Thebes as he was working on our tomb, carving our likenesses into the stone so that the gods would know us when they returned. She made sure she was full of laughter and praise, showering me with gifts: emerald pendants to match my eyes, golden cuffs for my ankles, even turquoise beads for my hair, which was thick and lustrous—the only feature I possessed that Nefertiti ever envied. Every morning we rode to the Temple of Aten, where she made obeisance to the sun and Akhenaten shook the sistrum to the holiest of holies.

"You can't stand and do nothing while we worship," Nefertiti admonished.

But Pharaoh didn't argue when I refused, for I was the one who reined in Nefertiti's vicious temper, playing Senet with her, reading myths to her, bouncing the precocious Meritaten on my knee, while for three nights he went to see Kiya. So I stood in the cool shadows of the columns and watched. I would not worship a disk in the sky. Hidden in my chests, I had brought my own statues of Hathor and Amun to Amarna, and those were the gods I bowed to every morning.

"What?" A voice echoed across the empty hall as I watched. "The Sister of the King's Chief Wife doesn't worship Aten?" Panahesi emerged from the shadows. "Aten is the god of Egypt," he said warningly.

But I wasn't afraid of Vizier Panahesi anymore. He was nothing more than the father of the king's second-favorite wife. "So you believe in a faceless god?" I demanded.

"I am the High Priest of Aten."

My eyes lingered on his jewels. He caught my meaning and stepped closer to me.

"You know that Pharaoh has been to visit Kiya for three nights now," he hissed. "He went to her as soon as the princess was born. I thought you'd be interested to know, *little sister,* that Kiya is certain she is pregnant. And this time, like the last, it will be a son."

I studied Panahesi's deceptive face and challenged him. "How do you know that she is pregnant? A woman can't tell for two months, even three."

Panahesi turned his eyes to the courtyard where Nefertiti and Akhenaten were kneeling. He grinned. "I have been given a sign."

⧈ ⧈ ⧈

I did not tell Nefertiti what Panahesi said, but I went to my father, who counseled me to say nothing. "She is recovering from birth. Do not disturb her with gossip. There is enough to think about with the Hittites so close to war in Mitanni."

"But Akhenaten has been to her palace for three nights," I complained.

My father started at me as if he didn't understand the problem.

"For three nights!"

"And he must have sons. Even in his foolishness, Akhenaten knows that. If Nefertiti cannot produce one, then he will turn to someone else."

I looked at my father in horror.

"It's not disloyal." He read my thoughts. "It's the way of the gods." He put his hand on my shoulder to placate me, and I noticed how many scrolls were unrolled on his table, waiting to be answered. Many of them bore the Mitanni seal.

"Will there really be war in Mitanni?" I asked, studying the parchments.

"Before the month is out."

"And then?"

"Then if Egypt sends no soldiers to their aid, Mitanni will fall and we will be next."

We watched one another, both understanding what this meant for Egypt. Our army was not ready; our greatest generals had either been imprisoned or sent away. We were a kingdom great in our history and in our gold, but in might, we would be crushed.

I went back to Nefertiti in the small studio Akhenaten had built for the princesses. Pharaoh was there, and they were arguing. As soon as Nefertiti heard the door open, she beckoned me angrily. "Ask her," she demanded.

Akhenaten looked at me with loathing.

"Ask her!" Nefertiti demanded louder this time, and Akhenaten replied that he didn't need to ask me how many nights he had been to see Kiya in the Northern Palace. She stormed past me toward the door and Akhenaten sped after her.

"Wait! I'll be with you tonight," he promised.

"I should hope you would be!" Nefertiti seethed. "Or have you forgotten you are *their* father, too?" She jerked her chin toward Meritaten and Meketaten, who had stopped playing with their paints to watch the scene.

"I won't return to her palace," Akhenaten apologized.

Nefertiti hesitated at the door. "Will we ride out tonight?" she asked him, already knowing his answer.

"Yes, and we can take Thutmose with us," he said.

"Good." Her gaze softened.

"And will we be going, too?" Meritaten asked.

I held my breath, waiting to see how Akhenaten would react to being questioned by a child, but Pharaoh swept Meri up into his arms. "Of course, you will be coming, my little princess. You are the daughter of Pharaoh. Pharaoh does not go anywhere without his precious ones."

The family filed out. Nefertiti pressed me to join their expedition into the city, but I refused.

"I'm tired."

"You're always tired," she complained. "You would think you were queen the way you drag yourself around."

I threw a sharp look at her and she laughed, wrapping her arm around my waist. "I'm only playing."

"Who rubs your feet, who makes you juice, who brushes your hair?"

She rolled her eyes. "But you're eighteen years old. What will you be like at forty?"

"Probably dead," I said acerbically, and her dark eyes narrowed.

"Don't say such things. You want Anubis to hear you?"

"I thought there was only Aten."

Fifteen days later, my sister shrieked. "A festival for *what?*"

The doors to the Audience Chamber had been shut to everyone; only our family was in attendance. Akhenaten muttered, "A festival in honor of Kiya's second child."

Nefertiti threw her scepter of reign across the dais, listening to it clatter against the tile floors. She exploded with rage. "Does that mean you will be eating *as well as* sleeping in the Northern Palace tonight?"

Akhenaten hung his head. "It's a feast in her honor, and it can't be refused. But you are Queen of Egypt." His reached out to her. "You are welcome, of course."

For a moment, I thought she would say she would go. Then she stood violently and moved past him. The double doors to the chamber swung open, and with a commanding look in my direction she was gone. As the doors banged shut, I glanced at my mother.

"Go," she said immediately.

I ran after Nefertiti and found her in the antechamber leading to the Window of Appearances. She was looking down over the city of Amarna. The temples of Aten reared up in the distance, their columns like dark sentinels in the dusk. I was afraid to disturb her, but she'd already heard my footfalls.

"*I* am the one they want," she said.

I moved closer to see who she was talking about. Below, wealthy foreigners in jeweled turbans stood staring up at the palace, as if they could see her shape in the window. But the dark of night shielded her from their view. "They love him because of *me*," she said.

"He has to go to Kiya," I replied. "He has to have sons."

She spun around. "And you think I can't give him one?"

I stepped closer so that we were both looking down over the city. "If you don't, would he stop loving you?"

"He adores me," she said heatedly. "Who cares that Kiya is pregnant? He's only going tonight because it's Panahesi who called him. He *thinks* Panahesi is loyal." She stiffened. "So while Father slaves away procuring ships and avoiding war, Panahesi whispers into Akhenaten's ear, and it's as if Aten himself has spoken. And his influence is growing."

"Not above Father's?"

"*Never* above Father's. I make sure of that." She looked down at the people who couldn't see her. They moved across the city carrying baskets of harvested grain on roads that twisted like white ribbons. "Only Hatshepsut ever had such influence as I have. And Kiya is not a queen. She could have five sons and never be queen." The rage returned to Nefertiti's eyes. "I should attend," she said viciously. "I should attend this feast and ruin it for her." And I could see by the look on her face that she meant it.

There was a noise behind us and Father entered the antechamber. "Come, Nefertiti." He drew my sister away from the Window of Appearances and they conversed in low tones. While they spoke, I passed my fingers over the paintings that decorated the walls of the palace. I wondered what Nakhtmin would think if he could see the gold from the temples staring back at him in gilded images of my family, myself in some of them, all faces that Thutmose had drawn from memory.

I studied one of the engravings, an image of my father receiving golden necklaces from Pharaoh. It was symbolic, of course, since my father had never received such gifts and would have only needed to raise his hand to command them. But in the scene, Nefertiti had her arm around his waist, her other arm resting on Akhenaten's shoulders. The two princesses were there, and someone had begun painting a third child held in a nurse's arms. Tiye and I stood off in the distance. Our arms were not raised to Aten the way everyone else's were. We were dressed in open kilts, and the sculptor, Thutmose, had emphasized the green color of my eyes. We were everywhere, my family, and only the absence of Panahesi and Kiya was conspicuous in Amarna. If the Northern Palace ever fell, their tombs would be the only testament to their existence.

"Are you coming?" Nefertiti demanded.

I looked around. "Where's Father?"

Nefertiti shrugged slyly. "On business."

Her smug silence warned me. "What's happening?" I asked her. "What's going on?"

"We're going to the feast," she said simply.

"Nefertiti—"

"Why not?" she exclaimed.

"Because it's cruel."

"Power is cruel," she retorted, "and it will either be mine or hers."

My sister watched herself in the mirror. "I want to be as beautiful as Isis tonight. Unearthly beautiful."

She stood, and the netted dress she was wearing arched over her breasts and fell down her back. The silver on her lashes and across her thighs caught the torchlight. She had replaced her crown with silver beads in her hair that moved when she did. I almost felt sorry for Kiya. But Kiya was just as cunning as my sister, and if Nefertiti never gave Akhenaten a prince, our family would bow to Kiya when her son took the throne. It was this that made me sit and endure the painful plucking and careful painting of my cheeks and lips. The thought of our family serving a man like Panahesi . . . I shook my beaded head. It must never be.

In the open courtyard, Nefertiti's ladies were waiting, talking and giggling like girls. We walked between them, and I had the impression that we were silver rain droplets in a field of lotus blossoms. The ladies parted, and I realized that they were all girls I didn't know, the daughters of scribes and Aten priests whose job was to keep my sister entertained. From the stables, a throng of guards had appeared. A lieutenant took Nefertiti's hand and helped her up into her chariot. She took the whip from him.

"You're going to drive?" I exclaimed.

"Of course. To the Northern Palace!" she cried.

Nefertiti flicked the whip and the chariot lurched forward toward the white beacon in the night. The guards scrambled to chase after her, and I could hear the wild laughter of the women racing in their chariots from behind.

"Not so fast," I shouted, petrified of turning over, but the wind drowned out my words as the chariot sped north. "We will die, Nefertiti!"

My sister turned to me in triumph. "*What?*"

As the chariot reached the palace gates, she tugged on the reins and the horses dropped back. I was stunned at the majesty of Kiya's palace. Its delicate reflection wavered on the Nile, a white bastion constructed out of love and dedication. Every column had been carved into a lotus blossom, springing upward as if to embrace Aten. From the wide opening of the palace's pillared front, I could see into its courtyards and torchlit gardens. Kiya's guards assembled themselves in a frenzied panic when they saw who we were, falling over one another to lead the way and bow before us.

"Your Majesty, we didn't know you were coming."

"Announce our arrival," Nefertiti commanded.

The servants in gold kilts rushed toward the hall as we made our slow and purposeful progression between the oil lamps that lined the limestone stairs. Guests bowed down before us, whispering to each other. When we reached the Great Hall, the trumpeters reassembled.

"Queen Nefertiti and the Lady Mutnodjmet," the herald declared.

We swept inside and the Great Hall burst into chatter. Nefertiti's ladies followed us closely; they fanned out, finding food and seating appropriate for a queen. The silver of our necklaces and bangles caught the light, and I knew that we were more beautiful than anyone there, even the proud and pretty daughters of the palace viziers and scribes. Kiya turned sharply, talking quickly to her husband to draw his eyes away, but his gaze was fixed on my sister, a silver fish flashing in an illuminated pond.

"Take me to the table of honor," Nefertiti said, and we were taken across the hall to the table where Akhenaten and the pregnant Kiya were sitting. Nefertiti sat down at the opposite end. Between us sat all of Kiya's closest ladies. I knew I could never have the courage to do what Nefertiti had just done: sweep into a lion's den like the head of the pride.

Panahesi, on the right side of Akhenaten, grew red with fury. At Kiya's own feast, Nefertiti called for music, and everyone laughed and sang and drank. Kiya was caught; at any other time, all of her ladies would have snubbed my sister. But now, in the Northern Palace, none of them dared to snub Nefertiti in Akhenaten's presence, so they were fawning and kind, telling her stories, exchanging gossip, and as the wine-fueled laughter heightened, so did Kiya's rage.

"What is it?" Akhenaten said, worried.

Kiya glared back at him from under her lashes. "This is *my* feast, not hers!"

Akhenaten looked around to be sure Nefertiti wasn't near him, then promised, "I will make it up to you."

"How?" she cried shrilly.

Akhenaten tore his gaze away from my sister, who threw back her head and laughed at one of Thutmose's jokes. "I will have Thutmose sculpt you," I heard him say.

"And if we have another son," Kiya pressed her advantage, "will Nebnefer finally be declared your heir?"

I leaned closer to hear how he would respond.

"That is up to Aten."

I thought triumphantly, *To Aten and our family.*

When the feast was over, I could see the strain of what Nefertiti had done in her eyes. Her voice brooked no argument when we reached her chamber and she said, "Stay with me until he returns."

I climbed into her bed and stroked her hair comfortingly.

"The Hittites are at Mitanni's gates and I am playing seductress to my own husband," she seethed. Then her voice broke, "She *cannot* have another son."

"She might not. It might be a princess."

"But why can't I have a son?" she cried. "What have I done to anger Aten?"

What have you done to anger Amun? I thought, but said nothing. "Have you been taking the honey?"

"And mandrakes."

"And have you gone to the temples?"

"Of *Aten?* Of course."

I let my silence speak.

Nefertiti asked quietly, "Do you think I should seek out Tawaret?"

"It couldn't hurt."

She hesitated. "Will you come? Akhenaten can't know."

"We can go tomorrow," I promised, and she squeezed my hand tenderly. She turned over and pressed the covers to her chest. When she'd fallen asleep, I lay awake, wondering where in Amarna we'd find a shrine to the hippopotamus goddess of birth.

Early the next morning, before the sun was up, Merit had an answer for me. She told me that some of the women in the village kept their own statues to Tawaret for when their daughters went to the bricks to bear a child. I asked her to take us to the house with the largest shrine, and even before Akhenaten awoke, bearers carried our covered litter up the hills into the cluster of wealthy villas.

The rising sun in the sky was warm. Below us the city was waking in shades of cardamom and gold. I parted the linens and inhaled the scents of a woman cooking date bread and mulling wine.

"Close the curtains," Nefertiti snapped. "This should be done quickly."

"You're the one who wanted to come," I said sternly.

"Have you ever prayed to Tawaret?" she asked.

I knew what she was asking. "Yes."

At the top of the hill, the bearers lowered the litter and a servant came to greet us. "Your Majesty." The girl bowed deeply. "My lady is waiting inside."

We swept up the steps, Nefertiti, Merit, and I. The litter bearers remained in the courtyard, ignorant of why we had come, and a woman in fine linen came to greet us.

"Thank you for gracing my humble home. I am Lady Akana." But Nefertiti wasn't listening. She was looking around for the statue of Tawaret. "Our goddess is this way," Lady Akana whispered. "Hidden from public view." Her eyes shifted nervously from Nefertiti to me.

We walked to a room at the back of the villa where the reed mats were lowered. The white walls had been painted with bold images of the hippopotamus goddess. Lady Akana felt the need to explain. "Many people keep images like this, Your Majesty. Only public shrines have been forbidden. Many people keep their private shrines hidden."

Not well hidden enough to escape Merit's attention, I thought, and Nefertiti nodded silently.

"I shall leave you, then." Lady Akana retreated. "If you have need of anything, you have only to call."

Nefertiti, as if woken from a dream, turned around. "Thank you, my lady."

"Do you want me to go as well?" I asked.

"No, I want you to pray with me. Merit, leave the offering and shut the door."

Merit left the incense and lotus blossom on a stool, then retreated the way Lady Akana had gone. We were left alone in the chamber. The hippopotamus goddess smiled at us, her big belly of polished ebony gleamed blue in the rays filtering through the reed mats. "You go first," Nefertiti prodded. "She knows you," she explained.

I went to the goddess, kneeling before her with a handful of lotus blossom. "Tawaret," I murmured, "I have come before you asking to be blessed with a child."

"We're here for me," Nefertiti said sharply. I scowled over my shoulder at her.

"I have *also* come on behalf of the Queen of Egypt." I pressed the lotus blossoms to Tawaret's feet. "I have come to ask that you make her fertile."

"With a son," Nefertiti clarified.

"Can't you do this yourself?" I demanded.

"No! She might not listen to me!"

I bowed my head again. "Please, Tawaret. The Queen of Egypt is in need of a son. She has been blessed by three princesses, and now she asks that you send her a prince."

"And not Kiya," Nefertiti blurted. "Please make it that Kiya does not have a son."

"Nefertiti!" I cried.

She stared blankly. "What?"

I shook my head. "Just light the incense."

She did as she was told, and we stared at the hippo goddess, enshrouded in smoke. She seemed to smile benevolently on us, even when what Nefertiti had asked for was malicious. I stood up, and Nefertiti stood with me.

"Are all your prayers like that?" I asked.

"What do you mean?"

"Never mind. Let's go."

▣ ▣ ▣

The next morning, a messenger arrived in the Audience Chamber.

"The Great Wife Kiya is ill."

Immediately, I thought of Nefertiti's prayer and paled. My father glanced at me and I began to confess. "Yesterday—"

But my father's hand cut through the air. "Go find your sister and Pharaoh in the Arena!"

I brought Akhenaten and Nefertiti, and though Nefertiti kept asking me what had happened, all I could whisper was "Your prayers have been answered." We burst into the Audience Chamber. It had been emptied of servants and petitioners. My father stood at once. "This messenger has news for Pharaoh," he said.

The messenger bowed low. "There is news from the Northern Palace," he reported. "The Great Wife Kiya is ill."

Akhenaten froze. "Ill? What do you mean? How ill?"

The messenger's eyes fell to the ground. "She is bleeding, Your Highness."

Akhenaten went very still and my father came toward him. "You should go to her," he suggested.

Akhenaten turned to Nefertiti, who nodded. "Go. Go and make sure the Great Wife gets well." He hesitated at her kindness and she smiled sweetly. "She would want you to go for me," she said.

I narrowed my eyes at Nefertiti's cunning, and when Akhenaten was gone, I shook my head sternly. "What's happening?"

Nefertiti shrugged off her cloak. "Tawaret answered my prayer, just as you said."

My father frowned. "Nothing's done yet."

"She's ill," Nefertiti said quickly. "And she's certain to lose the child." I stared at her in horror, and then Nefertiti smiled. "Would you find me some juice, Mutnodjmet?"

I froze. "*What?*"

"Find her some juice," my father said, and I saw what was happening. They wanted me gone so they could speak in private. "Pomegranate," Nefertiti called out after me, but I was already out the doors of the Audience Chamber.

"My lady, what happened?" Ipu stood quickly. "Why was everyone dismissed from chambers?"

"Take me to my old villa," I replied. "Find me a chariot that will take me to Tiye."

We rode the entire way in silence. When we arrived, the house looked the same as when I had left it. The broad loggia and rounded columns shone white in the sun, the cornflowers a dazzling blue against them.

"She planted more thyme," Ipu observed quietly. She went to the door and a servant answered. Then we were shown in to what had once been my home. There were more tapestries in the hall and several new murals depicting a hunt. *A lifetime of rule and this is what the Dowager Queen of Egypt is left with.* We turned into the loggia, and the queen stepped forward to embrace me. She had heard of our coming.

"Mutnodjmet." Heavy bangles made music on her arms, and her golden pectoral was rich with pearl. She held me at arm's length to take in my face. "You are thinner," she noticed. "But happier," she added, looking into my eyes.

I thought of Nakhtmin and felt a deep contentment. "Yes, I am much happier now."

A servant brought us tea in the loggia and we sat on thick pillows stuffed with down. Ipu was allowed to stay. She was family now. But she remained silent.

"Tell me all of your news," my aunt said happily. She meant about Thebes and my garden and my villa. But I told her about Nefertiti's birth and Kiya's pregnancy. Then I told her about the feast and Kiya's illness. "They say she will lose the child."

Tiye passed me a calculating look.

"I'm sure my father would never have a child killed," I said swiftly.

"For the crown of Egypt?" She sat back. "For the crown of Egypt, all that has been done and worse. Just ask my son."

"But it's against Amun," I protested. "It's against the laws of Ma'at."

"And do you think anyone worried about that when you were poisoned?"

I flinched. No one mentioned that anymore. "But there's Nebnefer," I warned.

"Who's only seen his father every few months, when Nefertiti lets Akhenaten out of her sight. And do you really think that Akhenaten would let a son rule? He, who knows better than anyone else the treachery a son can bring?"

We were interrupted by my aunt's old herald. He bowed at the waist. "A letter from the general Nakhtmin. To Her Lady Mutnodjmet."

I glanced at Tiye. The servants still called my husband "general." I hid my satisfaction and replied, "But how did this come to be here?"

"A messenger heard where you were and came looking." He bowed himself out, and my aunt watched my face as I read.

"Our tombs are finished. They've carved them and have already begun painting."

My aunt nodded encouragingly. "And the garden?"

I smiled. She had become a great lover of gardens. I skimmed the papyrus for news of my herbs. "Doing well. The jasmine is in bloom and there are grapes on the vines. Already. And it's not even Phamenoth." I looked up and saw the yearning on Tiye's face to have a real home of her own. Then a thought came to me. "You should leave Amarna and come and see them," I said. "Leave Amarna and return to Thebes."

At once, my aunt grew very still. "I doubt I shall ever leave Amarna," she replied. "I will never return to Thebes except in my coffin."

I stared at her, aghast.

She leaned forward and confided, "Just because I am not in the palace doesn't mean my power there has vanished. Your father and I work hard never to have our influence seen." She smiled ruefully. "Panahesi has succeeded in turning Akhenaten against me. But he'll never rid Egypt of your father. Not so long as Nefertiti is queen."

I stared at Tiye in the light of the windows. Where did the strength come from to do what she did? To remain in Amarna and be the power behind the throne while her spoiled, arrogant son sat on the dais?

"It's not as hard as it seems," she replied to my unspoken question. "Someday you may understand this."

▣ ▣ ▣

"Where have you been?" Nefertiti crossed the chamber in several strides.

"In my villa."

"You don't have a villa," she challenged.

"I was visiting Tiye."

My sister reeled back as though I had hit her. "While I was waiting for news, you were visiting Tiye? While Kiya was ill"—her voice rose with fury—"you *left* me?"

I laughed. "What? Did you need support for the shocking news that Kiya was sick? That she might lose her child?"

She stood immobile. I had never spoken to her this way before. "What is that?" She was looking at the scroll in my hand.

"A letter."

She tore it from me and began reading.

"It's a letter from my husband!" I reached out and took it back.

Nefertiti's face darkened. "Who delivered it here?"

"How should I know?"

"When did it come?"

"While you were with Father."

Then I realized what she was saying and my voice rose with indignation. "Why?" I exclaimed. "Have there been others?"

She said nothing.

"Have there been more?" I shouted. "Have you hidden them from me? Nakhtmin is my *husband!*"

"And I am your *sister!*"

We glared at one another.

"I will come to dinner. After that," I swore, "I am leaving for Thebes."

She stepped in front of me. "You don't even know what happened to Kiya—"

"Of course I know what happened to Kiya. Just what you said. She lost the child."

"Panahesi will be suspicious—"

"Of course he'll be suspicious. But you will have to watch him alone."

"You can't leave me!" she cried, and I turned to face her.

"*Why?* Because no one else can? Because everyone else is too awed by your beauty? You have fifty other women at court who will follow you like lapdogs. Have one of them watch out for you."

I went to dinner as I promised, and Nefertiti tried to test my loyalty by ordering me to find her a special fruit she knew was only kept in the back of the kitchens. I stood up and told the nearest servant to bring my sister a plate of jujube.

"It could be poison!" she cried. "I want *you* to go."

I gave her a long look, then swept across the Great Hall in a fury. When I returned, my sister was surrounded by a throng of young courtiers. She tossed her head back and smiled when she saw the platter of fruit in my hands. "Mutny, you brought it."

As though she'd doubted I would.

The women parted so that I could give her the fruit. Nefertiti swore, "You're the best sister in Egypt. Where are the musicians?" She clapped. "We want music!"

While the girls took their seats, I sat with my mother at the base of the dais, and servants came with roasted gazelle and honeyed lamb.

"It's how she shows she loves you," my mother offered.

"What? By making me her servant?"

The music began, and Nefertiti clapped as the dancers emerged, clad in bright linens and bangles with bells. Half a dozen ladies were watching the way Nefertiti drank, holding their cup the way she did, between forefinger and thumb. "How long do I have to stay?" I demanded.

My mother frowned. "Until the dancing is over."

My father said, "I hear you visited Tiye."

"I told her what happened to Kiya," I replied.

He nodded. "Of course."

"And she wasn't surprised."

He stared at me strangely, and I wondered for a moment if there had been any poisoning at all, or if it had just been a happenstance of fate. Nefertiti looked down at us and her sharp brows lowered. She crooked her finger at me.

My father motioned with his chin. "She wants you."

I got up, and Nefertiti patted an empty chair on the dais where guests were allowed to sit and converse. "I hope you weren't talking to Father about Kiya," she warned.

"Of course not."

"It's a dead subject."

"Like her child."

Nefertiti's eyes widened. "Don't you let Akhenaten hear you," she warned. Akhenaten turned to see what we were saying. She smiled for him and I stared back expressionlessly. She turned back to me. "Look at this feast I had to arrange just to take his mind off her."

"How kind of you," I replied.

Her temper flared. "Why are you so angry with me?"

"Because you're endangering your immortal *ka* and going against the laws of Ma'at," I retorted. "And for what?"

"For the crown of Egypt," she replied.

"Do you think there won't be a single vizier who hasn't wondered whether Kiya was poisoned?"

"Then they'd be wrong," she said firmly. "I didn't poison her."

"So someone else did on your behalf."

There was a lull in the music and our conversation stopped. Nefertiti smiled brightly, so that Akhenaten would think we were talking of inane, sisterly things. When the music started up again, she leaned over and said briskly, "I need you to discover what Kiya's ladies are saying."

"No," I replied, and my answer was resolute. "I am returning to Thebes. I told you I'd leave. I told you that even before Ankhesenpaaten was born." The musicians still played at the other end of the hall, but those nearest the thrones could overhear what we were saying. I walked to the bottom of the dais and she sat forward on her throne.

"If you leave me, then you can never come back!" she threatened. The court turned to look at me and she was aware of an audience. She flushed. "Make your choice!" she shouted.

I saw Akhenaten's eyes widen with approval. Then I turned to look at my father at the royal table. His face was a perfect vizier's mask, refusing to reveal what he thought of his two daughters fighting it out in public like cats. I inhaled deeply. "I made my choice when I married Nakhtmin," I replied.

Nefertiti sat back on her throne. "Go," she whispered. "Go and never come back!" she shrieked.

I saw the determination in her face, the bitterness that had set there, and I let the doors of the Great Hall swing shut in my wake.

In my chamber, Ipu had already heard what had happened. "We'll leave, my lady. We'll leave on the first royal barge tonight. You're already packed."

My chests lay readied on the bed, and I was shocked by the immediacy of it all.

I had been banished.

Then, suddenly, my mother was there. "Mutnodjmet, rethink what you've done," she pleaded. My father stood like a sentinel at the door. "Ay, please! Say something to your daughter," she cried. But he would not try to convince me to stay.

I went over to my mother and held her face in my hands. "I'm not dying, *mawat.* I am simply returning to my husband, to my house, to my life in Thebes."

"But you have a life here!" She looked at my father, who took her hand in his.

"It's what she has chosen. One daughter reached for the sun and the other is content to feel its rays on her garden. They are different, that is all."

"But she can never come back," my mother cried.

"Nefertiti will change her mind," he promised. "You were good to have come here at all, little cat."

I embraced my father, then held my mother tightly as the servants moved the chests, balancing them one on top of another.

"We will come twice a *renpet,*" my father promised. "I will arrange a meeting with the Mitanni king while we are there."

"If Akhenaten lets you."

My father said nothing, and I knew he intended to do it with or without Pharaoh's permission. Then I heard a noise and turned, catching two little girls peeking around the columns at me. I beckoned them with my finger.

"Are you leaving?" the older one asked.

"Yes, Meri. Would you like to walk to the quay and bid me farewell?"

She nodded, then began to weep. "But I want you to stay."

I was touched. She had only known me for a month.

"You haven't even seen all my horses. I wanted to show them all to you."

I blinked at her selfishness, then bent down and kissed her forehead. "Someday I will return and see them," I promised.

"Even my temple?" Meri managed between sobs.

"Even your temple," I said, biting my lip against such indulgence. *Her own temple to Aten? What kind of queen would this little child become if she was permitted every luxury? How would she come to know restraint or patience?*

I walked with my mother down to the quay and cried despite myself when the ship was ready. Who knew what might happen once we said farewell? I could die in childbirth or my mother could succumb to any pestilence that flourished near the Nile. We held each other's hands, and I felt keenly how much I'd failed her. I had brought her only sorrow when a daughter was supposed to bring a mother joy.

"I'm sorry," I told her. "If I'd been a better daughter, I would have married a man who was acceptable to Pharaoh and stayed close to you. I would have given you grandchildren to bounce on your knee and be thankful for. Instead, all I have given you is heartache."

"You have lived the life that Amun destined. There is nothing to regret."

"But you are lonely," I argued.

She bent close to whisper so that my father wouldn't hear. "And I am consoled every night by the reminder that of my daughters, you are the one that eternity will smile upon. Even without gold, or children, or a crown."

She kissed the top of my head, and even my father looked moved when I waved farewell to the towering city of Amarna, a jewel my family had created from the sand. She was only a cheap rival to Thebes, full of new glitter and gold, yet when I left her, there was a sense of loss, too: that this was my family's legacy and I'd left it forever.

Chapter Twenty-One

THEBES

fourteenth of Phamenoth

MY HUSBAND WAS at the quay as soon as the ship sailed into port. He took me into the house and laid me down on our bed. I looked up at the walls that had shone white and lusterless when we'd arrived. Now they were bright with river scenes and faience tiles. "Who did all of this?" I asked him.

"I hired a painter from the city. He did it all in three days."

I appraised the painter's work. It was pretty. Not anything as grand as Thutmose would have produced, but beautiful all the same. The colors he had chosen for the river were deep and varied.

"So tell me," he said.

I sighed, telling him the story of Ankhesenpaaten's birth, then of Kiya, and of my banishment from Amarna. He wrapped his arms around me and squeezed. "What is it about you, *miw-sher,* that makes people so obsessed? I thought about you every day and wondered if your sister would hatch some plan to send assassins, then marry you off to someone else when I was dead."

I gasped. "*Nakhtmin.*"

"You are everything to her," he said soberly.

"And you are everything to me. Nefertiti understands that. And if she so much as heard a whisper against your name, she would stop the hand of Pharaoh—"

"She has become that powerful?"

"You should see the people at the Arena and in the streets. They would do anything for her."

"And for him?"

"I don't know."

He caressed my cheek with his hand. "Let's think of other things now."

We made love that afternoon. Later, Ipu brought us lunch, figs and almonds with slices of fish and fresh barley bread. We ate and talked, and Nakhtmin told me about our tomb in the hills of Thebes, how solidly it was built and how beautiful the workers had already made it. "I found the workers Pharaoh fired before moving to Amarna. Now they are hiring out their services to any nobleman who is willing to pay. Pharaoh was foolish not to take them."

"Pharaoh is foolish about many things," I said. The door creaked open and Nakhtmin's hand flew to his knife. I looked down and laughed. "It's only Bastet! Come here, you big *miw.*"

Nakhtmin frowned.

"And look how big he's grown!" I lifted Bastet onto my lap and he purred, pleased with my attention. "I'm surprised he's not angry with me for leaving."

Nakhtmin raised his brows. "Oh . . . He did his share of moping while you were gone."

I looked down at Bastet. "Were you a naughty *miw?*"

"Ask your favorite linen sheath."

I paused. "The one—"

Nakhtmin nodded.

"You tore my good sheath?" I cried, and Bastet's ears flattened against his head, as if he knew exactly what I was talking about.

Nakhtmin said, "I doubt he understands you."

"*Of course* he does. He ruined my favorite sheath!"

"Maybe that will teach you to leave home," Nakhtmin added playfully. We wrapped ourselves in our light linen covers and Bastet curled up at the foot of our bed. Then Nakhtmin listened while I described Amarna to him, the Northern Palace and the Arena that had taken thousands of men to build. Eventually, when evening fell, we opened the doors and sat on the balcony, watching the moon rise over the river. Across the water, large houses glittered with a hundred winking lamps.

"How could he think Amarna would ever compare to this?" I asked, and I was so thankful to Amun to be alive and sitting with the man I loved on a balcony overlooking the greatest city in Egypt.

▣ ▣ ▣

The next morning when I returned to my garden, I complimented my husband on the job he had done to keep the mandrakes watered and the hibiscus fed. Even Ipu was impressed with his skill while we'd been gone.

"I thought for certain we'd return to dirt and weeds," she confided.

We both laughed, and Nakhtmin demanded to know what we were laughing about.

"Only your prowess in the garden!" I said.

It was not difficult to return to my life in Thebes. The Nile rushed, the birds sang, the herons mated, and Bastet stalked through the house like the Master of Egypt.

Ipu and I went to the market to buy fish for Bastet, and I was reminded yet again what a magnificent city Thebes was. The blush of the hills and deep gold of the rocks was bright and fresh in the early morning light. Between the stalls old women were arranging their wares, chewing on betel nuts as they gossiped to one another. The winter's sun glinted gold off the river, where men with heavy nets carried cargo from merchant ships. We walked through the crowds and the men looked first at me, attracted by my gold and silver cartouches, but their eyes lingered longest on Ipu, who swayed through the stalls, smiling at all the men's jokes.

Paser, the carpenter, wanted to know whether Pharaoh was satisfied with the box he had made him seventeen years ago.

"It's still in his chamber, accorded the most prominent place," Ipu told him.

The old seller reeled back, clapping his hands. "You hear that? Paser the Carpenter's work in the Riverside Palace."

I glanced at Ipu, who gleamed at her lie. Paser leaned forward. "I could have worked on the tombs. I bet they would have taken me if I had gone to Amarna, and I could have carved *ushabti* for Pharaoh's journey into the afterlife."

"But what would your daughter have done without you?" she asked.

"She could have come, too," he said excitedly, and then he gave a heavy sigh. "Ah, but these are just an old man's dreams."

"Not so old," Ipu flattered, and the carpenter grinned.

We moved on, and I reminded Ipu of the fish for Bastet.

"We'll go to Rensi's stall," she promised. "He always has the best."

"It's for Bastet. I doubt he will know the difference."

Ipu passed me a look. "He knows everything, that *miw*." She strode purposefully to the last stall in the market, then came up short at the sight of a young man in Rensi's place. He was tall and well built with hands that didn't belong to a fish seller.

"What can I get for you, my ladies?"

"Where is Rensi?" Ipu demanded.

"My father has business in Memphis these next two months. Until then, I'll be tending his stall."

Ipu put her hands on her hips. "Rensi never told me he had a son."

"And my father never told me he had such lovely customers." He looked between us, but I could see that his compliment had been meant for Ipu.

"Well, then, we want perch. Fresh perch. Nothing you caught two days ago and rubbed over with thyme."

The son looked taken aback. "Do you think I would really sell a days-old fish?"

"I don't know. Is the son of Rensi as reputable as his father?"

He handed her a wooden bowl with perch already cut. "You take this home and tell me if it's not the finest fish in Thebes."

"I'm afraid she won't be able to tell you that," I said flatly. "It's for a *miw*."

The son looked at Ipu as if she was insane. "Perch for a *cat?*" he rejoined, and reached out to take the fish back.

"You sold it," Ipu exclaimed. "Too late!"

"That's the finest fish in Thebes!" He looked to me to try to find some reversal.

"And I'll be giving it to Thebes' finest *miw*," Ipu promised.

"You can't give perch to a *miw!*"

"What is your name?" she demanded.

The fish-seller frowned. "Djedi."

"Well, Djedi, when your father returns"—she tucked the wrapped perch neatly under her arm—"my lady here will be sure to commend you to him."

He stared openmouthed as Ipu marched away, then looked to me. "I've seen her before. Is she always so impertinent?"

I smiled. "Always."

▣ ▣ ▣

In the unseasonable warmth of Pachons, I began pruning withered leaves and crushing eggshells to enrich the garden soil. Our house became flush with bright canna lilies and flowering hibiscus several months early, but when I reached down to pluck the lotus blossoms I thought of Nefertiti and loss overwhelmed me. In my anger, I had refused to apologize, and now I imagined my mother sitting alone in her chamber while my father shut himself away in the Per Medjat, sending spies and writing scrolls to determine how far the Hittites had advanced in the Kingdom of Mitanni. As I sat on my balcony, Ipu came to me and said, "You wanted it this way, my lady."

I nodded sadly. "I know."

"You've left them before," Ipu pointed out, not understanding my distress.

"But never like this. Now we are separated because Nefertiti is angry, and my mother will be worried, and my father will need me if she becomes difficult, only I won't be there." I looked over the balcony. *If I had children, it would all be different,* I thought. I would be taking care of a son or teaching a daughter the ways of the soil. I would never find a wet nurse for my child. He would be all mine. He would be everything to me. And I wouldn't play favorites between my daughters. But I wasn't the one that had been blessed by Tawaret. The goddess had chosen to smile on Nefertiti.

"Come." Ipu tried to distract me from my gloom. "We'll go to the market and watch the fire eaters."

"In the sun?"

"We can take a shade," she offered.

We went into the market for the second time in seven days and lost ourselves in the busy sprawl. We had nothing to buy, but somehow Ipu's fish merchant managed to find us. He held out two packages wrapped in papyrus, blowing the hair from his eyes in the heat.

"For the loveliest ladies in Egypt," he said.

"That's very kind." Ipu glanced at the fish. "But you know the Sister of the King's Chief Wife can't accept food from strangers." She handed the fish back, and he played at being deeply offended.

"And who says I am a stranger, my lady? I've seen you here twice.

And before you left Thebes I saw you once. You may not have noticed a simple, unmarried man like myself, but I noticed you."

Ipu stared back at him.

I laughed. "It seems you have left Ipu without words," I congratulated. "I believe this is a first."

"Ipu," the fish merchant repeated her name thoughtfully. "The Friendly One." He placed the fish back into her hands. "Take it. It isn't poison."

"If it is, I will return from the Afterlife to find you."

Djedi laughed. "There will be no need for that. I will be eating fish from the same catch tonight. Perhaps you will come tomorrow and tell me how it was?"

Ipu tossed her hair coyly over her shoulder and the beads made a hollow music together. "Perhaps."

When we left the market, I turned to Ipu at the bend in the road. "He is interested!" I exclaimed.

"He's only a fish merchant," she said dismissively.

"He's more than that. Look at the gold on his fingers."

"Then perhaps he's a fisherman."

"With rings like those?" I shook my head. "Haven't you said you wanted a husband with a little wealth? What if this is him?"

We stopped at the path that led up to my garden and Ipu grew serious. "Please tell no one about this," she said.

I frowned. "Such as who?"

"Such as any of the women who come to buy your herbs."

I stepped back, offended. "I never spread gossip."

"It is only because I want to be cautious, my lady. He could be married."

"He said—"

"Men say many things." But there was a gleam in her eyes. "I only want to be careful."

回 回 回

I didn't go with Ipu into the market the next day, but I saw her leave and whispered to Nakhtmin that her dress was finer than usual.

"Do you think she is going to see him?" he asked, hugging me to his chest.

"Of course! We have plenty of meat and no need for fish. Why else would she go?" I smiled, thinking of Ipu finally in love.

Now that my return to Thebes had become known, women began appearing at my door again. Most of my business was for acacia and honey, a mixture that women in the villas of Thebes were afraid to send to their physicians for. So servants crept up my pathway at first light, always careful to conceal their lady's name, arriving with purses full of deben rings in exchange for the certainty that trysts with lovers or unhappy marriages would not produce a child. I tried not to see the irony in this, giving women herbs to stop children when that was all that I prayed for.

Sometimes the women came for other drugs, plants that could cure warts or heal wounds that had been inflicted in ways they did not tell and I did not ask about. One such woman showed me bruises and whispered, "Is there anything that can cover these?"

I flinched to touch the raised bruise on the woman's small arm. I moved across the room that Nakhtmin had furnished with wooden shelves to hold my glass jars and vials. I took down my book of patients and flipped through the pages. "You came six months ago for acacia and honey. Now you return for something to cover the bruises?"

She nodded.

I said nothing; I only went to the polished cedar shelf where I kept my oils. "If you wait, I will mix you some rosemary oil with yellow ocher. You will have to apply it with a brush in several layers."

She sat near my table and watched me work with the pestle to grind the powder. I could see by the tone of her skin she would need a yellow copper, and I was proud of myself when she reached out her arm and the bruise disappeared under my paste. She paid with a deben of copper, and I looked at the gold around her neck and asked her if his riches were worth it.

"Sometimes," she replied.

Servants came all afternoon—some that I knew, others that were strangers. When the house was quiet, I went outside to watch Nakhtmin in the open courtyard of our villa, where the river winked blue and silver between the columns. His shirt was off, and in the warm sun his golden torso glistened with sweat. He turned and saw me watching and smiled. "All the customers gone?" he called.

"Yes, but I haven't seen Ipu since morning," I worried.

"Perhaps she developed a sudden interest in fish."

I thought how strange it was, my helping Ipu dress for her dinner with Djedi—who owned not just one merchant ship, but three. I placed my best wig on her head, and each tress was threaded with golden tubes and scented with lotus. She wore a smooth-fitting tunic and my fur-lined cloak. The braided papyrus sandals on her feet were mine, and when I looked at her in the mirror I was reminded of Nefertiti and all the times I had dressed my sister for dinner. I embraced Ipu and whispered encouragement in her ear, and when she left, I thought selfishly, *If she marries, I will have no one except Nakhtmin.* Every night I placed oil at the feet of my little shrine to Tawaret, and every moon my blood came. I was twenty years old without any children. I might never have any. *And now I won't have Ipu, either.*

At once I flushed, appalled that I could ever think like Nefertiti. *Perhaps we are more similar than I realized.*

I went into the kitchen and found the bread and goat's cheese that Ipu had left. "Ipu is dining with the fish merchant tonight," I told Nakhtmin.

But he was studying a scroll in the front room. He didn't look up at me.

"What is it?" I asked, bringing him food.

"A petition from men in the city," he said gravely. He held it up for me to take. It was from the men of Thebes. I recognized some of the names as men who had held positions of power before the Elder had died. Old friends of my father and former Amun priests.

I gasped. "They want you to take over Amarna!"

Nakhtmin said nothing, staring beyond the balcony to the River Nile.

"We must show this to my father at once—"

"Your father already knows."

I sat down, staring at him in the light that came through the lowered reed mats. "How can he know this already?"

"He knows everything, he watches everything. If armed men have not come here to slit my throat, it is because he has commanded that I remain safe. He trusts that I will not lead an army against Amarna because he knows that you are more important to me than any crown."

"But why wouldn't my father arrest these men? They are traitors!"

"Only if I lead them in rebellion. Until then they are friends, and if Amarna ever falls and Aten turns his back on Egypt, where will your father turn for help?"

I looked up slowly, realizing, "You. You will have the loyalty of the Elder's people." He nodded, and I felt a sudden awe of my father. "He is planning in case Akhenaten dies. In case the people turn. This is why my father let me marry you."

Nakhtmin smiled. "I should hope it was for more than that. So there is no need to send this to him." He took the scroll and crumpled it in his hand. "I will not lead the people in rebellion and he knows it."

"But Akhenaten doesn't."

"Akhenaten does not deal with anything outside his sphere of Amarna. All of Egypt could crumble, and if Amarna was left standing, he would be content."

I felt a heat creep into my cheeks. "My sister would never—"

"Mutnodjmet," he interrupted. "Your sister is the daughter of a Mitanni princess. Did you know that twelve nights ago Mitanni was attacked?"

My breath caught in my throat. "The Hittites *invaded*?"

"And Egypt did nothing," he said ominously. "But history will remember that we stood by and watched. If Mitanni falls, we will be next. If she survives, it is a kingdom that will never forgive us, Mitanni princess or no."

"Nefertiti never knew her mother. You can't blame her—"

"No one is blaming." His face looked sharp in the moonlight. "But the wars we shut our eyes to now may blind us in eternity." A night breeze stirred the curtains and he stood. "Would you care for a walk?"

"No," I said quietly, sick at heart. "You go."

He took my chin in his hand. "Amun watches over us. We will always have each other, no matter what happens in Mitanni or the palaces of Amarna."

He left. I went into my chamber, but I couldn't sleep. In the heat, all I could do was go to the balcony to sit and think. When Ipu returned, I got up to see how her night had been. At twenty-four years old, she looked young and radiant. Care sometimes made me forget we were both still young.

"Look!" she gushed. She held out her arm and showed me a bracelet. "He bought it for me. It's as if we have known each other all our lives, my lady. We grew up near the same town, near the same Temple of Isis. His grandmother was a priestess and so was mine!"

I motioned for her to sit with me on the balcony, and we talked into the night.

Chapter Twenty-Two

fourteenth of Pachons

"THERE'S A SURPRISE for you waiting at the quay," Nakhtmin whispered the next morning when I opened my eyes.

I sat up at once, blinking against the light. "What is it?"

"Get up and see," my husband teased.

I pushed Bastet off the bed and went to the window, then shouted, recognizing the blue and gold standards of my parents' bark. "Ipu!" I called, throwing on my good linen. "The Vizier Ay and my mother have arrived. Prepare the house and get out the good wine!"

Ipu appeared at the doorway to my chamber.

"What are you doing? Find the wine!" I exclaimed.

She exchanged a private smile with Nakhtmin. "It's already done."

I looked back at my husband, who was grinning like Bastet. Then I understood. "Did you know about this?"

"Of course he did," Ipu replied eagerly. "He has been hiding this surprise for more than ten days."

I stopped what I was doing, fastening a gold chain around my neck, and my eyes filled with tears.

"Go!" he urged me. "They're waiting!"

I ran out to meet my parents the way a child runs to meet her friends at the market. When my mother saw me, her face transformed. "Mutnodjmet!" she cried, throwing her arms around me. "You look well." She pulled back to inspect me. "Not so skinny anymore. And the house!"

"It's a handsome villa." My father appraised, studying the faience tiles and surrounding hills. The villa's reflection wavered in the Nile, and the rising sun splashed the water with gold. Already Thebans on both sides of the river were staring from their windows, recognizing the pennants on the bark as royal colors and wondering who had come to visit the city.

"Ipu! Find a sheet of papyrus and write that I will not be having customers today," I shouted. "Hang it on the door."

Servants stayed behind with the ship while I took my mother and father up through the gardens. My father greeted Nakhtmin solemnly. "So tell me what is happening in Thebes," he said.

I didn't listen to what they were saying. I already knew. And while they talked in the front room over roasted goose and spiced wine, my mother and I sat in the garden. My mother looked down the hill to the River Nile, comparing the land in her mind to Amarna. "It's richer here, somehow," she said.

"Thebes is older. There's less glitter and rush."

"Yes. Everything's a rush in Amarna," she agreed.

"And Nefertiti?" I asked, raising my cup.

My mother inhaled. "Still strong."

Still ambitious, she meant. "And my nieces?"

"They couldn't be more spoiled if they were the daughters of Isis. No horse is too fine or chariot too grand." My mother clicked her tongue.

"It's a bad way to teach them."

"I tell Nefertiti that, but she won't hear it." My mother's voice dropped, though there was no one in the garden to hear her but me. "You have heard about Mitanni?"

"Yes." I closed my eyes. "And we have sent no soldiers to help them," I guessed.

"Not one," she whispered. "It's why your father has come here, Mutnodjmet."

I sat back. "It wasn't to see me?"

"Of course to see you," she said quickly. "But also to speak with Nakhtmin. He's a hero to the people and valuable to us as an ally. You chose wisely in your husband."

"Because *now* he can help us?" I asked bitterly. At once, I regretted my tone of voice. My mother, who was no more cunning or pretentious than I would ever be, sat back in shock.

"Egypt will need him if Akhenaten's reign should ever crumble."

"And by Egypt, you mean our family."

She put down her cup and reached across the table, covering my hand with hers. "It is your destiny, Mutnodjmet. The path to the Horus throne was laid long before you were born, before Nefertiti was born. It was the destiny of your grandmother, and her mother, and her mother before that. You can accept it, or it can chase you down and wear you out with all the running."

I thought of my father inside, plotting with Nakhtmin, drawing him into the web that would ensnare us and bring us back to Amarna.

"Nefertiti will always be queen," my mother continued. "But she needs a son. She needs an heir to make sure that Nebnefer never rules in Egypt."

"But she's had only princesses."

"There's still hope," my mother said, and something about her tone made me lean forward.

"She isn't—"

My mother nodded.

"Three months after Ankhesenpaaten?" My lip trembled. Then surely this one would be a boy, and Nebnefer would be forgotten and our family would be safe. So Nefertiti was pregnant with a fourth child. *Four.*

"Oh, Mutnodjmet. Don't weep." My mother embraced me.

"I'm not weeping," I replied, but the tears came fast, and I rested my face against her breast. "But aren't you disappointed, *mawat*? Aren't you disappointed you will never have a grandchild?"

"Shh . . ." She stroked my hair. "I don't care if you have one child or ten."

"But I have none," I cried. "And doesn't Nakhtmin deserve a child?"

"It is up to the gods," my mother said resolutely. "It is not about deserving."

I wiped away the tears. Nakhtmin and my father came out into the garden, and both wore grave faces. "We'll be meeting with former Amun priests tomorrow night," my father said.

"In my house?" I exclaimed.

"Mitanni has been burned, Mutnodjmet," Nakhtmin said.

I glanced at my father in horror. "Then shouldn't you be in Amarna? The Mitanni king will ask for soldiers. Surely *now*—"

"No. It is better to be here, planning for a time when there might not be an Amarna."

I flinched. "Does Nefertiti know what you are doing?"

"She knows what she wants to," my father replied.

The next night, when the moon was a thin sliver cut into the sky, my parents' servants moved the long table from the kitchen to the middle of the open courtyard. Ipu dressed it with fine linen and laid out our best wine, lighting the brazier and throwing sticks of cinnamon onto the coals. I wore my best wig and earrings, and Nakhtmin left to stand watch at the bottom of our hill. Then men whose names I'd heard spoken with the deepest reverence as a child began to arrive in hooded cloaks and gilded sandals. Their bald heads shone in the light of the oil lamps. They were silent as they came to the door and addressed Ipu with respectful greetings from Amun.

"How many men are coming?" I asked.

My father replied, "Nearly fifty."

"And women?"

"Eight or nine. Most of these guests tonight were once Amun priests. They are powerful men"—his voice was full of meaning—"and they still practice in secret shrines."

There was no official welcome. When my father determined that everyone he'd summoned had arrived, he slipped off into the darkness to find Nakhtmin, then returned. Sitting cross-legged on a cushion, he announced, "Everyone here knows that I am the Vizier Ay. You know the former general Nakhtmin." My husband inclined his head. "My wife." My mother smiled softly. "And my daughter, the Lady Mutnodjmet."

Sixty silent faces turned toward me, searching out my eyes in the flickering light. I inclined my head, which felt heavy and cumbersome in its wig, and I knew they were comparing me to Nefertiti: my dark skin to her light, my plain features to her chiseled ones.

"We are all aware that Mitanni has been invaded," my father went on. "The Hittites have crossed the Euphrates and subdued Halab, Mukish, Niya, Arahati, Apina, and Qatna. No one here is under the assumption that Egypt will send soldiers to Mitanni's King Tushratta. These cities are gone." The men in the courtyard shifted. "But Pharaoh Akhenaten finds comfort in the treaty he has signed with the Hittite king."

There rose a clamor of voices.

"You have talked of rebellion," Nakhtmin addressed the men who looked to my father with alarm, "and the Vizier Ay is on our side. He *wants* to fight the Hittites, he *wants* to release General Horemheb from prison, he *wants* to turn back to the great god Amun—but now is not the time for rebellion."

A chorus of disapproval went up and dozens of shaved heads rose angrily.

"I have no desire to be Pharaoh, and my wife has no desire to be queen."

"Then raise the Vizier Ay!" one of the men said loudly.

My father stood. "My daughter is Queen of Egypt," he replied. "The people of Amarna support her possession of the crook and flail. And *I* support her."

"But who supports Pharaoh?" someone shouted.

"We all must. It is through him that Egypt will be given an heir. The queen," he announced, "is with child again."

"We must hope it is a son," Nakhtmin added quietly.

"*Hope* has gotten us nowhere," one of the men interjected. Two gold earrings pierced each of his ears. He stood up, and the cut of his linen was very fine. "In the Elder's time, I was High Priest in Memphis. When the Elder embraced Osiris, I *hoped* to return to my temple. I *hoped* not to lend out my services as a scribe to put food on my table, but hope has done me little. I am lucky that I saved and was a frugal man. But not all of these men can say that." He gestured with a bangled arm. "What Egyptian could have foreseen what would happen at the Elder's death? A new religion, a new capital. Most men here have lost everything. And Vizier, we are not a group without means," he warned. "We have sons in the army; we have daughters in Pharaoh's neglected harem. We hoped your daughter would bring sense to Egypt, but we are tired of hoping. We are *tired* of waiting." He sat down, and my father spoke directly to him.

"But wait you must," he said simply. "To meet here is treason"—his voice grew low—"to suggest removing Pharaoh is more dangerous still. To remove a Pharaoh is to risk setting a terrible precedent. The Queen of Egypt watches over her people."

"Yes, in *Amarna*. What about Thebes?" the former priest demanded.

"Thebes's time will come," my father promised.

"When?" An old woman stood up. "When I have embraced Osiris as well? By then it will be too late!" She steadied herself on her ebony cane and peered across the room. "Do you know who I am?"

My father nodded respectfully.

"I was Prince Tuthmosis's nurse. I tended him even to his deathbed. And there is no one here who doesn't know the story of what I saw that night." There was an uneasy shuffling. "A prince surrounded by tangled sheets," she went on, "a pillow cut with teeth marks!" I shot a terrified look at my father, who allowed the old woman to continue with her fratricidal tale. "Akhenaten cast me out of Malkata Palace as soon as his brother was buried. He might have killed me, too, but he thought I was old and useless. And now what family will hire me," she cried, "the nurse of a dead prince?"

She sat down, and a shocked silence filled the courtyard. I held my breath. The old woman had just accused Pharaoh of murder.

"All of us have deeds that will weigh heavy with Osiris, some heavier than others," Nakhtmin replied. "We have all been wronged. We have all struggled since the Elder's death, and we have all been called here to be reminded that destinies are decided by the gods, not by former Amun priests. We must wait for a prince to be born to the queen, and Vizier Ay will train him to be a soldier worthy of Egypt."

"That's not for fifteen years!" several men cried.

"Perhaps," my father conceded. "But know that I am with you, that my daughter, Queen Neferneferuaten-Nefertiti, stands by you as well. Amun will not be lost to Egypt forever." He stood up, and it was clear the meeting was over.

Our hooded guests bowed with respect to my family. When they had left, I whispered to Nakhtmin, "I don't see how this meeting will stem rebellion."

"These men won't be so quick to want war against Pharaoh now that they know Amun has not died in the heart of Akhenaten's closest adviser," he replied. "Egyptians are a patient people in the end. The worst is over. Now they have only to wait for change." Nakhtmin squeezed my shoulder. "Don't worry, *miw-sher.* Your father knows what he is doing. He wanted to calm their fears, to tell them that the future is not as bleak as it seems so long as he is there to mold it. And to see you there, his second daughter, with a former general willing to fight against the Hittites, it sends a powerful message."

"And what is that?"

"That not all Egyptians have fallen under the spell of Amarna. There is hope within the royal family."

My parents stayed through the end of Pachons, and when it was time for them to go I bit my lip and swore I wouldn't cry, even when I knew they would not be coming again soon.

Chapter Twenty-Three

1346 BCE

Peret, Season of Growing

NEWS OF NEFERTITI'S confinement came in the first month of Peret, only this time I was not commanded to attend. If my sister died, I would not even be there to say good-bye.

I went into my shop and Nakhtmin followed. He sat on the bright-orange cushion for customers, watching me take down a box of cinnamon bark that would keep away head lice and perfume a home. It was for a woman who came every ten days at this time, the daughter of a well-respected scribe who could afford such luxuries from the land of Punt.

Nakhtmin kept staring and I turned around.

"I rarely see you at work," he explained. "I'm always outside." His skin was dark because of his practice with local soldiers, and the contrast with his hair and eyes was stunning. I believed there was no man more beautiful. He stood up and took me in his arms. "I'm glad you won't be going to Amarna," he admitted, kissing my neck. "I miss you when you're gone."

▣ ▣ ▣

While we waited for word from Amarna, other news came one evening as Nakhtmin and I walked along the Nile. We were discussing how stalwart the soldiers of Mitanni must be to keep fighting the Hittites though half of their cities were lost. The waning sun shimmered on the water, and every so often the sound of fish cut the still evening air. Then Ipu came running down the riverbank, dressed in her finest linen. Holding up her middle finger, she cried, "I am getting married!"

The three of us stopped. Nakhtmin was the first to congratulate her, embracing my body servant and promising we would throw her the grandest feast in all of Thebes.

I took her hand to examine the ring. A thick golden band. It must have cost three months' worth of wages. "When did this happen?"

"This afternoon!" Ipu's cheeks were flushed. "I went to his stall and he gave me a little boat he had carved himself. He said someday we would sail in one just like it. Then he told me to look inside the miniature cabin and there it was."

"Oh, Ipu! We shall have to begin planning the feast at once. When will you move?"

"At the end of Tybi."

"That's soon," I exclaimed.

She smiled. "I know. But I won't be leaving you."

"That's not my—"

"But I won't. His home is not so far away. I'll come every morning and leave when he returns from the fish stall at night," she promised.

Ipu's marriage feast was held on the tenth of Tybi, an auspicious day. On that evening, I dressed her in Thebes's finest linen, painting her eyes and lending her one of my golden pectorals studded with turquoise. Blue faience earrings pierced her ears, and her hair was swept back by a blue Nile flower. Women came to henna her hands and breasts, and when Nakhtmin appeared at the door to our chamber he gave a low whistle. "A bride to rival Isis," he complimented.

Ipu stared at herself in the polished bronze. "I wish my mother could see me," she whispered, putting down the mirror and holding up her arm, letting her jewels catch the evening light.

"She would be proud," I told her, taking her hand. "And I am sure her *ka* is watching over you."

Ipu choked back her tears. "Yes, I am sure it is."

"Now come, Djedi is waiting."

In the glitter of a torchlit night, barks sailed along the River Nile. Three hundred people watched the ships from our courtyard, the triangular sails like white moths in the dusk, and I marveled that Ipu knew all of these guests, men and women, children and grandmothers. Lamps burned along the pathway down into the garden, and people came and went all evening long, bringing gifts of gold and spices for the new couple, kissing Ipu's forehead and rubbing her stomach to bless her womb. I watched the proceedings and I felt like the scales of Anubis, my happiness going both up and down.

"Do you wish you'd had this?" Nakhtmin asked me during the celebration. We were surrounded by tables of roasted goose in garlic, lotus flower dripping in honey, and barley beer. Wine had been flowing all night and women danced to a chorus of flutes.

I smiled, reaching across the table to take his hand. It was rough, not like my father's hand, but there was strength in it. "I wouldn't trade you for all the gifts in Thebes."

Ipu and Djedi appeared, their hair decked with flowers and their faces filled with the wonderful contentment of a newly joined couple. "To the hosts of this feast," Djedi shouted above the din, and hundreds of guests raised their cups to us, and the musicians struck up a happy tune. "Come and dance!" Ipu cried.

I held out my hand to Nakhtmin, and then we crossed the courtyard to where men and women were clapping, shaking sistrums, and watching the young dancing girls from Nubia, their skin like polished ebony in the torchlight, bending backward and leaping in unison to the men's cries.

If a stranger stood across the Nile, he would have seen a hundred golden torchlights flickering like stars against an indigo palette, rising in tiers and casting illuminations across the villa belonging to the Sister of the King's Chief Wife. The celebration disappeared in the early morning hours, when litters arrived bearing the most important guests back to their villas along the water. When the courtyard was empty at last, I spent the first night since my childhood without Ipu.

The next morning, a servant from Amarna arrived. He held out a scroll that I didn't wait to read. "What does it say?" I held my breath, and the young man's face grew bleak.

"The queen has given birth to the Princess Neferuaten. They both survived."

A fourth princess.

Chapter Twenty-Four

1345 BCE

seventh of Thoth

FOR EIGHT LONG months after the birth of Nefertiti's fourth daughter, Egypt knew only drought. A hot wind blew over the arid land, parching the crops and sucking the life from the River Nile. It began in the season of Peret. At first it was only a warm breeze at night when the desert chill should have arrived. Then the heat invaded the shadows, stealing into places that should have been cool, and old men began to go down to the river to stand in the water, splashing their faces in the withering sun.

At the wells, women began to gossip, and outside the city temples men whispered that Pharaoh had turned his back on Amun-Re, and now the great god of life had unleashed his anger, a drought that killed off half our neighbors' cattle and sent fishermen's children begging in the streets. Only Djedi seemed immune to the famine, telling Ipu that now was the time to sail, and that they could go upriver to Punt and bring back treasures far more valuable than any fish: ebony, cinnamon, and green gold.

"But Ipu's not a sailor," I cried. "She will die in Punt!"

Nakhtmin laughed at me. "Djedi is a talented man. He will hire sailors, and merchants will invest in his expedition."

"But Ipu wants children," I complained.

Nakhtmin shrugged. "Then she will have them in Punt."

The horror of the notion left me speechless.

"It's what she has chosen," he reminded, "and I would bid my farewell to her before morning."

I went to Ipu's home with a heavy heart; I was losing my closest friend. Ipu had been with me since I had first passed the threshold of Malkata Palace, and now she was sailing for a foreign land from which she might never return. I was quiet, watching my body servant who was more than a body servant stuff linen into baskets and wrap cosmetics in papyrus.

"I'm not leaving for the ends of the earth," Ipu remonstrated.

"Do you even know how they treat women in Punt? How do you know it's not like Babylon?"

"Because Egyptians have been there before."

"Egyptian *women?*"

"Yes. In Pharaoh Hatshepsut's time, Punt was ruled by a woman."

"But that was Hatshepsut's time. And besides, you've never really sailed. How do you know that you won't get sick?"

"I'll take ginger." She took my hand. "And I'll be careful. When I return, I will bring you herbs that no one in Thebes has ever seen. I will search the markets for you when I am there."

I nodded, trying to reconcile myself to what I couldn't change. "Be safe," I made her promise again. "And don't you dare bear a child on foreign bricks without me!"

Ipu laughed. "I will tell my child it must wait for its godmother."

She and Djedi, with their ship full of sailors and merchants, departed the next morning for a land we Egyptians imagined as far away as the sun.

"It's not so far as you believe," my husband told me, sharpening his arrows in the courtyard the following morning. "She'll be back before next Akhet," he predicted.

"In a *renpet?*" I cried. "But what will I do without her?" I sat down on the stump of a fallen palm, feeling sorry for myself.

Nakhtmin looked over and a slow smile spread across his face. "Oh, I can think of some things we can do while Ipu is away." I had the feeling he would be glad to be relieved of Ipu's incessant chatter for a time.

But every month, my moon blood came.

I grew mandrakes, I added honey to my tea, I visited the shrine of Tawaret in the city every morning, laying down the choicest herbs from my garden. I began to accept that I would never give Nakhtmin the children we wanted. I would never be fertile again. And instead of turning me aside the way many husbands might have, Nakhtmin only said, "Then the gods meant for you to make the earth fertile instead." He caressed my cheek. "I would love you the same with five children or none." But there was a fire in his eyes, and I was afraid. It was only for me, for my family, that he refused to rid Egypt of a man who should never have been Pharaoh. Yet he never said a word about the letters that arrived from soldiers in Akhenaten's army. He only took me in his arms and held me close and asked me if I wanted to walk along the river. "Before it disappears," he joked darkly.

"I hear the priestesses in the shrine talking among themselves," I told him. "They think this drought is the result of something that Pharaoh has done."

Nakhtmin didn't disagree. He opened the gate to the garden so we could pass through and walk the short distance to the water. "He has neglected Amun and every other god."

We both looked at the river. On the exposed banks, naked

children were playing, tossing a ball and laughing while their parents watched them, covered by sunshades. Three women nodded deferentially to us as we passed, and Nakhtmin said, "It's amazing how much Egyptians will tolerate before they rise and rebel." He turned to me in the setting sun. "I am telling you this because I love you, Mutnodjmet, and because your father is a great man forced to serve a false Pharaoh. The people won't always bow, and I want to know that you won't be crushed. You will be ready."

His words were making me afraid.

"Promise me you won't make foolish decisions," he pressed. "When the time comes, promise me you'll make decisions for the both of us, not just for your family."

"Nakhtmin, I don't know what you're talking—"

"But you will. And when you do, I want you to remember this moment."

I looked beyond him to the River Nile, the sun reflecting on its shrinking surface. I looked at Nakhtmin, who was waiting for my response. I replied, "I promise."

Chapter Twenty-Five

1344 BCE

Akhet, Season of Overflow

MY HUSBAND DIDN'T mention my promise on the river again, and before I knew it the seasons of Peret and Shemu passed and word arrived that Djedi's ship had come into the harbor. I put on my wig and brightest linen belt.

Nakhtmin raised his brows. "You'd think it was the queen who was arriving."

We rode to the port, where we found the ship to be as large and impressive as I remembered it. The scent of roasted cumin hung heavy in the air, and we pushed our way past the people who were packed like fish along the quay. Many of them had come to see their loved ones arrive. More than fifty sailors had left with Djedi that day in Thoth, and now their wives pressed against each other with flowers and lotus blossoms in their hair. When I spotted Ipu on the docks, I gaped. She was round with child!

"My lady!" Ipu made her way through the throng. "My lady!" She threw her arms around my neck, and I could barely reach mine around hers. "Look." She grinned, and indicated her round stomach. "He waited for you."

"How many months?" I gasped.

"Nearly nine."

"Nine," I repeated. It was impossible to believe. Ipu. My Ipu. With child.

She turned to Nakhtmin. "I thought about you when I was gone," she admitted. "On the shores of Punt, the soldiers carry weapons unlike anything in Egypt. My husband brought you back examples of their weaponry. All kinds. In ebony and cedar. Even one in a metal they call iron." She put her hand on her round stomach, looking healthier than I'd ever seen her.

Nakhtmin said gently, "Why don't you two go home? I can help Djedi here, and the two of you can talk. This is no place for a woman nine months with child."

I took Ipu back to the house she hadn't seen in nearly a year. As we walked, she told me about a land where the people were darker than Egyptians and lighter than Nubians. "And they wear strange ornaments in their hair. Bronze and ivory. The wealthier the woman, the more charms in her hair."

"And the herbs?" I pressed.

"Oh, my lady, herbs like you've never seen. Djedi has an entire chest of them for you."

I clapped my hands. "Did you ask the local women what they were for?"

"I wrote down most of it," she replied, but we had come upon her house and her footsteps slowed. She looked up in wonder at the two-story building, white with brown trim around the windows and doors. "I had forgotten how nice it is to be home," she said, holding her stomach, and a strange feeling of envy washed over me.

There was a deep sense of stillness when we opened the door, a quiet I could only remember from the tombs in Thebes. Ipu looked around at the statues of Amun, all standing in the same places that she had left them. Besides a thin layer of dust, nothing had changed. Except her. I was the first to speak. "We should roll up these shades and let in some light." I went about rolling up the reed mats while Ipu watched. Then I turned around. "What's wrong?" I asked her.

She sank down on a bench, putting her hands on her stomach. "I feel so badly that I'll be the one on the bricks. I wanted you to have a child so much."

"Oh, Ipu," I said tenderly, making her move over and embracing her. "It's the will of the gods. There's a reason for all of it."

"But what?" she asked bitterly. "What can it be? I prayed for you while I was there," she admitted. "To a local goddess."

I sucked in my breath. "Ipu."

"It couldn't hurt," she said firmly, and there was a seriousness in her tone I'd rarely heard before.

We looked at each other in the soft sunlight that filtered through the lowered mats, and I said, "You are a good friend to me, Ipu."

"As are you, my lady."

We talked and cleaned at the same time, dusting the wall hangings and scrubbing the tiles. She told me about all of her adventures on the Nile. They had begun by sailing upriver to Coptos, then, after leaving the ship in the care of a sailor, they traveled east by caravan through the Wadi Hammamat. When they arrived at the seacoast, Djedi bought three ships for all of the goods they intended to bring back, and then they hired more sailors and embarked on their voyage to the south. She recalled how one of the men was nearly killed by a crocodile when he went for a swim, and how the croaking of the hippos kept her up at night.

"Weren't you ever afraid?"

"Djedi was there, and fifty armed sailors. There was nothing to fear on the water besides the animals, and as we sailed farther south there were animals like you've never seen."

I lowered my dust linen. "Like?"

"Like snakes the length of this room and cats as big as . . ." Ipu searched about her. "As big as that table."

My eyes went wide. "Bigger than our statues at the Temple of Amun?"

"Much bigger."

Then she began to describe the magnificent herbs that she had found, and the cinnamon wood they had brought back by the chestfull. "We walked everywhere, my lady. There were no litters for women. Only donkeys to ride. And once I grew big, it was easier to walk than ride." Djedi had allowed her into the foreign marketplaces, where women sold dark-colored pods with a gingery-lemon scent, used to flavor honey cakes and bread. Ipu had seen grown men the size of children, and tall spotted beasts that ate leaves from the tops of trees. Women sold dry spices and flavored tea, and the colors in the marketplace were bright saffron yellow, earthy basil, and flaming red. "Like their garments."

"Do all of the people wear red?"

"Only the rich. It's not like in Egypt," she explained, where all classes wore white.

When Djedi returned from the quay with Nakhtmin, sailors trailed behind him carrying chests filled with goods. The smell of cedar filled the house, and we sat around looking through the exotic finds and listening to the stories each of them held. Some of the chests were gifts for us. There was an ivory box filled with the herbs that Ipu had searched out herself, and a wooden case with the weapons for Nakhtmin. Ipu brought back a dress in bright indigo for me as well. The rest were goods for the house and jewelry for the coming child. This would be its inheritance: ivory and gold from the land of Punt.

We ate well that night, and stayed up until morning listening to Djedi's hearty laugh when he retold the tale of a sailor who ate a local dish and couldn't leave his hole in the ground for a day, since in Punt, unlike Egypt, there was no such thing as toilets. Only Djedi could match Ipu's full laughter, and when we left, carrying my box full of herbs and Nakhtmin's new weapons, it was as if they had never been gone.

In Egypt, there is a saying: When good fortune looks down upon us, it does so in threes, one for each part of the Eye of Horus. His upper lid, his lower lid, and the eye itself. The morning after Ipu arrived nine months heavy with child, the drought ended. The rains came down in heavy torrents, splashing into the Nile and making puddles of mud across our fields. In the evening, while Nakhtmin took dinner by the brazier and I chatted with Ipu, a messenger from Amarna arrived, holding out a scroll with my family's seal. Djedi, who had opened the door to our house, handed it to me with wide, interested eyes. I don't think he had ever seen a vizier's seal; heavy golden wax on the finest papyrus grown in the Delta. I opened it at once and read it aloud.

> A new birth is weighing heavily with your sister and the priestesses of Aten hold hope it will be twins, or perhaps the sign of a prince. But she is sick often and summons you here. Nakhtmin is welcome.

Ipu gasped. "A *fifth* child?"

I knew what else she wanted to say. That only a queen blessed by the gods could be so fertile. Every year Nefertiti was with child no matter rain or drought. And suddenly, without warning, my eyes filled with tears.

Nakhtmin lowered his cup. "Oh, *miw-sher,*" he said tenderly.

I wiped the tears from my eyes, embarrassed. "You are to come," I said. "My father wouldn't let my mother send such a letter if he thought you were in danger. Will you come?" I asked him.

He hesitated, but when he saw the hope in my face he replied, "Of course I will. We will sail as soon as Ipu goes to the birthing pavilion."

I wrote back at once, telling my mother we would sail as soon as Ipu had given birth. "It will not be for at least fifteen days," I replied, and the letter that came swiftly in return five days later was in Nefertiti's own hand.

> You want to wait for the birth of your godchild when your nephews, the future Princes of Egypt, are about to be born? I am ill every morning and can't sleep through the night, but you want to stay in Thebes when I could be dead by Aythyr?

I could hear the blame in her voice. If she died and I was not there to bless her, my *ka* would never be at rest. I finished her letter.

> I know you would never abandon me, not with Anubis so close at my door, so I have sent a ship. When it arrives, it will take you with all speed to Amarna. And since I know you will not come without Nakhtmin, he is welcome, too. You may both stay in the guest rooms near the Audience Chamber.

I crushed the new scroll in my hand. "And so it begins again. She has sent a ship. But I'm not leaving," I vowed, "not until I have seen my godchild blessed."

Ipu shook her head. "This time your sister is right, my lady. When the ship comes, you must go. If she's carrying twins . . ." She spread her hands in sympathy.

Nakhtmin nodded. "I do not need to tell you how my mother died," he said softly. "And neither of my brothers survived."

There was no choice but to go back to Amarna, to return to the city from which I had been banished.

"But what if Ipu's birth ends badly?" I whispered, and Nakhtmin turned over in the darkness. The images of Tawaret that had been carved into the bedposts looked down at us benevolently in the moonlight.

"You know what the physicians say, Mutnodjmet." He put his thumb on my forehead to smooth away the care.

"They think Ipu will give birth within the next seven days. But they could be wrong." I worried my lip, thinking of Nefertiti's ship approaching Thebes. "What if the ship comes and Ipu isn't ready?"

I stayed up thinking of ways to stall the ship. Nefertiti wasn't due for months. She could wait. If Ipu's birth didn't happen for days . . .

But I needn't have worried. The next morning, Ipu went into the birthing pavilion that Djedi had built and attached to their home. All morning she pushed and screamed. Outside the carved door, Nakhtmin comforted Djedi, while Ipu gripped my hand and made me promise to look after the boy or girl, whichever it should be, if she should not survive.

"Don't be foolish," I told her, smoothing the thick hair away from her face, but she made me swear it. So I promised her, but for nothing. By evening, her ordeal was done, and Djedi was the father of a strapping son.

"Look how heavy he is!" I complimented, handing her the swaddled infant. His lusty cries pealed through the chamber. "What will you name him?"

Ipu looked down over the bloodied linens; outside, I could hear Djedi and Nakhtmin celebrating. "Kamoses," she said.

I spent the days waiting for Nefertiti's ship with Ipu, watching her with Kamoses and envying the way she bathed him and rocked him and studied his chest rising and falling in his sleep. And even though he was fussy, I felt a longing in my stomach watching him feed at Ipu's breast, his little face full of contentment.

In the evenings, I came home to Nakhtmin and we fell into bed together, spending the nights trying for our own son. On our last night in Thebes, Nakhtmin smoothed the hair away from my face. "If we never have a child, I will be at peace. But you won't, *miw-sher.* I can see that."

I blinked away the tears. "Don't you want a son?"

"Or a daughter. But it's a gift from the gods."

"A gift we sent back!"

"A gift that was stolen," he clarified, and his voice was dark.

"Sometimes I dream there will be a child," I said. I turned up my face to him and he wiped away the tears. "But do you think it means anything?"

"The gods give us dreams for a reason."

The next day, the barge came, but leaving Thebes was harder than it had been before. We waved to Ipu and Djedi on the docks, who were passing Kamoses between them with a new-parents' pride. They would care for our house while we were away, tending the garden and feeding Bastet. Ipu would serve the women who came for honey and acacia. She'd watched me with my herbs for nine years, and I had promised to pay her handsomely. "You don't have to do that, my lady." But I'd replied, "It's only fair. It may be several months before we return."

Standing on the prow of the ship, blinking into the fresh sunlight, I had no idea then how long we'd be gone, or under what circumstances we would return.

◙ ◙ ◙

We arrived in Amarna when the warm autumn's sun was setting. We stood on the ship's deck, and I was shocked by how big the city had grown, and how beautiful it appeared. Litters had been sent for us and we were carried through the city to the Riverside Palace, shielded from the fading sun by strips of linens. I parted the curtains, and on every new temple and shrine was Nefertiti's image: on the doors, across the walls, from the faces of crouching sphinxes. She was etched into every public space, her face engraved where the faces of Isis and Hathor should have been. And from the massive columns supporting the palace, in place of Amun peered the profile of Akhenaten. When the litter bearers put us down beyond the fortified gates, Nakhtmin stared up at the pylons, then looked out over the city. "They have made themselves into gods."

I put my finger to my lips as my father appeared.

"Mutnodjmet. Nakhtmin." He embraced my husband warmly. When he came to me, he lowered his voice in earnest. "It has been too long."

"Over two years since Thebes."

He smiled. "Your mother is waiting in the birthing pavilion."

"Nefertiti has already taken to her pavilion?"

"She is ill," he said quietly. "The birth is weighing heavily with her this time."

"At four months?"

"Some of the physicians say it could be six."

We were shown into Riverside, which looked the same as when I'd left. White limestone columns reached toward the heavens, and in every courtyard the sunlit gardens were in bloom. Someone had planted myrtle and jasmine, and the jasmine was overtaking the water gardens, dipping their fragrant tendrils in the pools. We passed the Great Hall and my father said, "Your rooms will be here," and he pointed to the guest rooms for foreign diplomats and messengers. I felt a sharp pang, but Nakhtmin nodded gratefully.

"Come," my father said. "I'll take you both to the pavilion."

I glanced at Nakhtmin. "But what about—"

"This is Amarna," my father said wryly. "Nefertiti allows everyone in. Men, women . . ."

We entered the birthing pavilion and a chorus of voices rose all at once. I glanced at the bed where Nefertiti lay and Akhenaten sat rigid, watching Nakhtmin with suspicious eyes. Then we were surrounded by jumping, laughing children who wanted to see their aunt Mutnodjmet and meet their uncle Nakhtmin. I counted back and realized that Meritaten was already five years old. Her precocious grin reminded me of Nefertiti. "Mother said you'd bring gifts," she said and held out her hand.

I looked at Nakhtmin, who raised his eyebrows and opened his bag. Each gift was wrapped in papyrus; Ipu had labeled them before we left. "Where is Meritaten?" he called.

"That's *me,*" said the eldest princess. When she had her gift tucked neatly under her arm, she gave Nakhtmin an introduction to her sisters. "That's Meketaten." She pointed to a plump girl with curly hair. "She's only one year younger than me. And Ankhesenpaaten." Meritaten indicated a beautiful child standing behind her sisters, waiting patiently for her gift. "She's two. And that's our baby sister, Neferuaten."

The baby toddled over to us, then each of the girls received their gifts. There was a frenzy of unwrapping while my mother came over to embrace me, kissing both of my cheeks. Then Meritaten's voice rang out.

"I've never seen anything like this," she announced, sounding ten years older than her age. *"Mawat."* She went to Nefertiti's bedside. "Have you ever seen anything like this?"

Nefertiti gazed at the ivory writing palette Nakhtmin had carved with help from a stonecutter working on our tomb. The princesses' names were engraved in hieroglyphs and both palettes held brushes and a shallow bowl for ink. My sister fingered the smooth edges and slender brushes, and there was a different look on her face as she raised her eyes to thank Nakhtmin.

"They are beautiful. We have nothing like this in the palace," she admitted. "Where are they from?"

"I want to see them," Akhenaten commanded. The girls brought their writing palettes over to their father. He inspected them casually. "Our workers can do better."

Nakhtmin lowered his head respectfully. "I worked on them with a stonecutter from Thebes."

"They are exquisite," Nefertiti complimented.

Akhenaten stood up and his face was flushed. "Meritaten, Meketaten! We are riding in the Arena."

"Will the general be coming, too?" Meritaten asked.

Akhenaten paused at the door and the rest of us froze. He turned, then looked down at Meritaten. "Who said this man was a general?"

"No one." Meritaten must have heard the danger in his voice because she knew better than to answer him with the truth, which must have been that the Vizier Ay still called him "general." "I saw his muscles and knew he must work outside."

Akhenaten narrowed his eyes. "Why couldn't he have been a fisherman or a painter?"

I'll never forget the answer Meritaten gave, for it showed her cunning even at five. "Because our aunt would never have married a fisherman."

There was a moment of tension, then Akhenaten laughed, sweeping Meritaten into his arms. "Let's go to the Arena and I will show you how a *warrior* rides. With a shield!"

"What about me?" Ankhesenpaaten cried.

"You're only two," Meritaten said sharply.

"You shall come, too," Akhenaten proclaimed.

When the four of them left, my father asked Nakhtmin, "Shall I show you to your chamber?"

"I think that would be best," my husband replied.

"And we should arrange for several body servants while you are here." My mother stood to go with them and Nefertiti called desperately, "But you'll be back for dinner?"

"Of course," my father said, as if it wouldn't be any other way.

I pulled up a stool to Nefertiti's bedside.

"Your husband is a handsome man," my sister admitted. "No wonder you'd rather be with him than me."

"Nefertiti—" I protested, but she raised her hand.

"Sisters can't be close forever. Merit and I have become friends; I made her father vizier this year. He was wasting his talents as scribe."

I glanced around the chamber.

"She's fetching me juice. She makes perfect jujube. And she doesn't want to marry," she added pointedly.

I sighed. "So how are you feeling?"

My sister shrugged. "As well as possible. They say it's heavy enough to be a son." Her dark eyes gleamed. "But others say it could be twins. Have you ever heard of a woman living through twins?"

I pressed my lips together so I wouldn't have to lie.

"Never?" she whispered fearfully.

"Twins are rare. There must be women who have lived through it."

She looked down at her stomach. "*Four* princesses, Mutnodjmet. I think Nekhbet has abandoned me." Her voice was heavy, and I wondered if this was the first time she'd confided her true fears since I'd last been in Amarna. Who else could she trust? My mother, who would assure her that everything would be fine? Our father, who would tell her to think of the kingdom? Merit, who knew nothing of childbirth and its pain? She took my hand, and suddenly I felt the terrible loss of living in Thebes, the terrible guilt of leaving her alone to her fears and ambition, though it was she who'd banished me. "Mutnodjmet, if I die in this birth, promise you will make Meritaten queen. Promise me that Kiya won't be made Chief Wife."

"Nefertiti, don't speak like this—"

Her grip tightened on my hand. "I *have* to survive this birth." She trembled. "I have to survive to see my son rule." She looked hopefully into my face and I didn't promise her that she would. Only Nekhbet knew. Only Tawaret could say.

Instead I asked her, "How many months are there left?"

She looked down at her swollen belly, small and shapely like all of the other times, but this time rounder, heavier somehow. "Three. Three months until it's over." She had never been this way with the others, so eager to have it done. "But you will help me, won't you?"

"Of course."

She nodded slowly, reassuring herself. "Because I thought"—her eyes welled with tears—"I thought you had abandoned me." She had completely forgotten my banishment, locking the memory away in a place where it couldn't haunt her, where she could be the one who'd been wounded.

"I have not forsaken you, Nefertiti. You can love two people at once, the way you love Meritaten and our father."

The look she gave me was one of deep mistrust.

"I will stay here until you have delivered your sons," I promised.

Chapter Twenty-Six

Peret, Season of Growing

A FEW MONTHS later, the pains came at dawn. It was the longest my sister had ever known labor, and in a corner the midwives passed worried glances among themselves, discussing rhubarb and rue.

"What are they saying?" Nefertiti cried.

"That you have never had so much pain before," I said truthfully.

"You would tell me if there was something wrong," she gasped. "If they knew something—"

"There's nothing," I cut her off, placing a soothing hand on her forehead, and she gripped the arms of her birthing chair.

"*Mawat,*" she screamed. "Where is Father? I'm in so much pain!"

"Push!" the midwives cried together, and Nefertiti strained against the padded seat, shrieking to wake Anubis, and then they arrived.

Not one child but two.

The midwives shouted, "Twins!" and Nefertiti demanded, "What are they?" She strained to see. "*What are they?*"

The midwives passed worried glances among each other. Then one of them stepped forward and replied, "Daughters, Your Highness."

The lusty wails of newborn children pierced the air. Nefertiti collapsed in the birthing seat. Five times she'd tried. Five times for six girls. There was crying and shouts of joy in the pavilion. My mother held one of the princesses aloft.

"Take me back to my bed," Nefertiti whispered, and no sooner was she dressed and put into bed than Akhenaten burst into the birthing chamber.

"Nefertiti!" He searched for his wife, and seeing that she lived, he searched for his children.

"Twins!" The midwives feigned joy, and the look on Akhenaten's face was triumphant. Then his peace grew disturbed.

"Sons?" he asked swiftly.

"No. Two beautiful daughters," the eldest midwife said, and it was strange, for no man could have looked more joyous.

Akhenaten was at Nefertiti's side at once. "What shall we name them?"

She smiled for him, though I knew her disappointment was bitter. "Setepenre," Nefertiti replied. "And—"

"Neferneferuaten."

"*No.* Neferneferure."

I glanced at Nefertiti, and the hardness in her eyes told me that she would not name her daughters after a god who had given her six princesses. I wondered whether Amun might have given her a prince.

Akhenaten picked up my sister's hand and pressed it to his chest. "Neferneferure," he conceded, "after the most beautiful mother in the world."

When my father heard the news, he sat down outside the birthing chamber and called for a drink. "Six girls," he said hollowly; he couldn't believe it. "He gives Kiya a son and your sister has *six girls.*"

"But he loves them. He's possessive of them."

He stared up at me. "He may love them more than he loves Aten, but it's what the *people* will think."

As the news spread through Amarna, I went into the gardens to find my husband.

"Did you hear?" I asked him, wrapping my cloak around my shoulders.

"Twins."

"Not just twins," I said softly, and my breath made a puff of air in the garden. "Girls."

"How did he take the news?" Nakhtmin asked.

I joined him on the bench near the lotus pond and wondered how the fish could swim when it became so cold like this. "Akhenaten or my father?"

"Your father. I can guess how Pharaoh feels. No son to be in competition with for Nefertiti's affection. No prince to be wary of when he's an old man. Panahesi may think he's holding all seven pawns. He doesn't realize how much Pharaoh fears Nebnefer."

"But Nebnefer's seven—"

"And when he's fourteen or fifteen?" my husband asked.

I watched the fish come to the surface of the pond, their round mouths searching for food. "Would you be jealous of a son?"

"Jealous?" He laughed. "I couldn't think of a greater blessing," he said earnestly. "Of course," he added, "if it never happens—"

I took his hand and squeezed softly. "But what if it did?"

He stared quizzically at me and I smiled. He leaped from the bench. "Are you—"

I nodded, my smile widening.

He pulled me off the bench and pressed me into his arms. "How long have you known? Are you sure? It isn't—"

"I'm three months already." I laughed deliriously. "I haven't told anyone. Not even Ipu. I waited to be sure it wasn't a false sign."

The joy in his face was deep and overwhelming. *"Miw-sher."* He pressed me to him and stroked my hair. "A *child, miw-sher."*

I nodded, laughing. "By Mesore."

"A harvest child," he said wonderingly. There was nothing more auspicious than a child at harvest. We stood with our hands clasped, gazing into the pond, and the air didn't seem so bitter.

"Will you tell your sister?"

"I will tell my mother first."

"We should tell her before we leave for Thebes. She will want to make arrangements to be there for you."

"If my sister doesn't demand I have the child here," I said. It would be just like Nefertiti to do such a thing. Nakhtmin glanced at me. "I will tell her no, of course. But we should stay another few months; the extra time will pacify Nefertiti, especially if it's a son."

"Must everything pacify Nefertiti?" he asked.

I looked down at the hungry fish and told him the truth, the way it had always been in my family. "Yes."

Nakhtmin came with me to tell my mother the news. She was with my father in the Per Medjat, warming herself by the brazier as he drafted a proclamation to the kings of foreign nations that the Pharaoh of Egypt had been blessed with two more heirs.

Guards opened the heavy doors, and when my mother saw the look on Nakhtmin's face she knew at once.

"Ay," she said warningly, standing up.

My father lowered his reed pen in alarm. "What? What is it?"

"I knew it!" My mother clapped loudly and came to embrace me. "I knew there would be!"

Nakhtmin grinned at my father. "There is going to be an heir for this family, too."

My father looked at me. "Pregnant?"

"Three months."

My father laughed, such a rare, precious sound, then he stood up and came over to embrace me as well. "My youngest daughter," he said, holding my chin in his hands. "About to be a mother. I will be a grandfather seven times over!" For a few golden moments, I was the daughter that had achieved something worthwhile. I was going to bring a child into the world. A legacy of their flesh and blood, and part of us that would last until the sands ran out. We stood as one happy, laughing family, then the door swung open and Meritaten was there, watching us.

"What's happening?"

"You are going to have a cousin," I told her, and with a knowledge well beyond her years she asked wisely, "*You* are pregnant?"

I beamed. "Yes, Meritaten."

"But aren't you too old?"

Everyone laughed and Meritaten flushed.

My mother tutted softly, "She is only twenty. *Your* mother is twenty-two."

"But this was her *fifth* pregnancy," Meritaten explained, as if we were all very foolish not to understand.

"Well, for some it takes longer than others to have a child."

"Is that because Nakhtmin went away?" she asked us.

There was an uncomfortable silence in the Hall of Books.

"Yes," my father said at last. "It is because Nakhtmin went away."

Meritaten saw she had said something she should not have, and came to embrace me. "Twenty isn't so old," she said seriously, giving me her permission. "Are you going to tell my mother now?"

I took a heavy breath. "Yes, I think I will tell her now."

Nefertiti was still in the birthing pavilion. I was prepared for rage or weeping or drama. A child would take me away from her. I wasn't prepared for her joy.

"Now you will have to stay in Amarna!" she cried happily. But it was a calculated happiness. The ladies in the birthing chamber watched me with interest. Over the soft music of the lyre, they could hear what we were saying.

"Nefertiti," I cut in sharply, "in the end I will go home to have my child."

My sister turned toward me with a look of deep betrayal, perfectly executed so that I would look like the one being unreasonable. "*This* is your home."

I gave her a long look. "And if I had a son, do you think he would be safe in Amarna?"

She sat straighter in her bed. "Of course he would be. *If* it's a son."

"I will stay for another two months," I promised.

"Then what? You will leave and take Mother with you?"

"Don't worry. Mother won't leave you alone," I snapped. "Not even to see me give birth to my first child."

She laughed, embarrassed by the truth in front of so many women. "Mutny! That's not what I'm saying." She moved over on the cushions, which loomed large and heavy around her tiny frame. "Come. Sit."

She wants to make up to me now, I thought.

"Did you know there will be a feast tomorrow?" she asked. "For three nights. And Thutmose will sculpt a new family portrait to go in the temple. To remind Panahesi."

He would have to endure it every time he walked past the altar of Aten. Nefertiti wearing the asp and crown. Nefertiti and her six beautiful children.

She lowered her voice. "Panahesi thinks that just because I've birthed two daughters there will never be a son now. He thinks that Egypt's crown will go to Nebnefer. But I'm going to change that," she swore.

I looked behind me. "How?"

"I don't know," she admitted. "But I will find a way."

On the third day of celebration, Nefertiti slammed the door to her chamber, blinded with an uncontrollable rage. Before I could calm her, she threw her brush against the wall and the tiles shattered. "I deliver him two daughters and now he's with *Kiya*?"

My father ordered a servant to pick up the pieces and added sharply, "Sweep it up, and then close the doors behind you."

We waited for the girl to do as instructed while Nefertiti fumed. When the girl shut the doors, my father stood.

"Have some control," he demanded.

"I have just birthed *two* children and that's not enough?"

"You have given him six *girls*."

"We must go to her again—"

"Absolutely not," my father said. "It's too dangerous now."

"This time Mutny can do it!"

My father looked hard at her. "You will not bring your sister into this."

I tried to convince myself that what they were saying had nothing to do with the loss of Kiya's second child.

"We leave it to the gods," my father said.

"But she will be pregnant within the month," my sister whispered. "And what if it's another heir to the crown?" Her panic rose. "One son might die, but *two*?"

"Then we will have to find another way to hold the throne. Six girls or no."

▣ ▣ ▣

Seven days later, on the first of Phamenoth, two priests arrived in the Audience Chamber and announced to the court, "Your Highness, our priests have had a great vision."

My father and Nefertiti exchanged glances. This was not a remedy that they had brewed together.

Akhenaten sat forward. "A vision?" he asked. "What kind of vision?"

"A vision for the future of Egypt," the old priest whispered mystically, and when Panahesi stood eagerly from his chair, we knew at once that this was his doing. He had been waiting for this moment from the time that Nefertiti had used the ruse of a dream to convince Akhenaten that Panahesi should become High Priest and not treasurer. Now he cried dramatically, "How come I haven't been told of this vision?"

The old priest bowed with a flourish of his hand. "It has only come this morning, Your Holiness. Two priests were blessed by a vision from Aten."

I looked over at Panahesi and the second priest, who had a round, kind face. *Not one priest, but two.* Panahesi had chosen his puppets beautifully.

"Beware of false prophets," Nefertiti warned from her throne. The court filled with expectant chatter.

"What was the vision?" Akhenaten pressed.

The younger priest stepped forward. "Your Highness, in the Temple of Aten today, we were given a revelation—"

"Where exactly?" Nefertiti demanded, and Akhenaten frowned at the hardness in her voice.

"In the courtyard beneath the sun, Your Majesty."

Better and better.

"We were honoring Aten with incense when a bright light came before us and we saw—"

The old priest cut in. "We saw a vision!"

Akhenaten was taken. "Of what?"

"Of Nebnefer, wearing the pschent crown."

Panahesi stepped forward eagerly. "Nebnefer? You mean His Highness's son?"

"Yes." The old priest nodded.

The entire court tensed, waiting for Akhenaten's reaction.

"A very interesting vision," my father said. "Nebnefer"—he arched his brows meaningfully—"wearing the crown of Egypt."

"Aten's visions are never wrong," Panahesi said sharply.

"No," my father agreed, "Aten never lies. And, of course, there were two. *Two* priests who saw the vision."

Panahesi shifted in his leopard-skin robes, disliking this new accord.

"A *son* to rule the throne of Egypt," my father went on. "And wearing the crown that rested once on his father's head. Didn't the Elder receive such a vision?"

The court realized what he was doing and Akhenaten paled.

My father added quickly, "But Nebnefer is loyal. I am sure he is a son who will serve His Highness well."

It was a twist Panahesi had not foreseen. "Of course Nebnefer is loyal," he stammered. "*Of course* he is."

Akhenaten looked down at my father, who shrugged cunningly. "It is a danger that all Pharaohs risk with sons."

And who knew that better than Akhenaten? I felt a victorious thrill, the triumphant feeling my father must experience whenever he outwitted an opponent.

Kiya turned red with rage. "No one can prove that the prince is disloyal!" she shrieked.

Akhenaten looked to the priests. "What was the rest of the vision?" he commanded.

"Yes!" Nefertiti stood, watering the seed our father had planted. "Was there bloodshed?"

The entire court looked to the priests and the younger one replied, "No, Your Highness. No bloodshed. No betrayal. Only great golden light."

Akhenaten glanced at the older priest for confirmation.

"Yes." The old man was swift to agree. "Nothing of violence."

Panahesi bowed deeply. "Your Highness, I can bring Prince Nebnefer now. You can test his loyalty."

"No!" Akhenaten looked at his princesses, arranged on their little thrones. "Come here, Meritaten."

Meritaten stood and went to her father's knee. The court watched with expectation.

"You will always be loyal to your father, won't you?"

Meritaten nodded.

"And do you teach your sisters to be loyal to their father?" he demanded.

Meritaten nodded again, and Akhenaten smiled the way a doting father might. "Does the court hear this?" he asked forcefully. He stood, displacing Meritaten. "The Princesses of Egypt are loyal," he swore. "None of my *daughters* would ever reach for my crown."

Kiya looked to Panahesi with desperation.

Panahesi started to say, "Your Highness, Prince Nebnefer would never—"

"Very well," Nefertiti announced, cutting off the vizier's plea. "We have heard Aten's vision and need nothing more." She dismissed the priests with her hand, and the court rose with her to adjourn itself.

Kiya moved briskly to Akhenaten's side. "All the priests saw was a simple vision," she said quickly. "A glow and the crown on Nebnefer's head. I have taught our son to be *loyal.* The way I am to you and to Aten."

Akhenaten's look was unforgiving. "Of course you are loyal. To be anything else would be foolish."

Chapter Twenty-Seven

AMARNA

ninth of Pachons

DESPITE OUR FATHER'S triumph over Panahesi, by the Season of Harvest Kiya was pregnant. Even after the disaster in the Audience Chamber, Panahesi swept through the halls barking orders as if he could already feel the heavy crown of Egypt in his hands.

One son might be ignored, but a nation could not ignore two princes, two heirs to the throne. If Kiya could do it, the ascension would be final.

Akhenaten found Merit in the Great Hall and instructed her to give Nefertiti the news. He was too much of a coward to do it himself. "Be sure to tell her that no child will ever take Meritaten's place in my affection. She is our golden child, our child of Aten."

I watched him as he led his girls away. His adoring princesses. The daughters he believed would never turn on him the way a son might, the way he had turned on his brother and father. *He doesn't understand girls if he thinks they can't be cunning,* I thought.

Merit looked at me with rising desperation. "How should I tell her?"

We reached the doors of the Audience Chamber. "Just tell her. She predicted it herself; it shouldn't be a surprise."

Inside, Nakhtmin was playing Senet with my mother. On the dais, my father's head was bent close to Nefertiti's; for once, my sister wasn't surrounded by ladies. They had all gone to see Akhenaten ride.

"You're not outside?" I asked her.

"I don't have time for the Arena," she snapped. "*He* can go riding around whenever he chooses, but I have to oversee plans for the walls. If there is an invasion, we'll have no defense against the Hittites, but Akhenaten isn't interested—" She interrupted herself, staring sharply between me and Merit. "What do you want?"

I nodded to Merit, and my father lowered the architectural plans to his lap.

"Your Highness," Merit began, "I have news that is not going to make you happy." She added as quickly as possible to get it over with, "There is word that Kiya is pregnant."

Nefertiti remained very still. When the silence stretched on, Merit continued uncertainly. "It is only Kiya's second child, Your Highness. You have six princesses, and Akhenaten wished me to tell you—"

Nefertiti sent scrolls rolling across the tiles as she stood. "My husband sent *you* to tell me?" she shrieked.

My father rose quickly to be at her side. "We must move now," he suggested. "Make him show all of Egypt that Meritaten is the one he intends to have reign over Nebnefer."

Something unspoken passed between them and I asked, "But how?" No one answered my question. "How can you do that?"

There was a strange glint in Nefertiti's eyes. "In the only way that's never been done," she said.

⁂

Akhenaten declared a Durbar in Nefertiti's honor. It was a festival to celebrate their reign together, and the change from jealous wife to victorious queen was immediate. Nefertiti said nothing more about Kiya, and Nakhtmin wondered how deep Amarna's coffers would be drained to create the largest Durbar in history.

"Mutny, come," my sister called brightly to me. I entered her Robing Room with its dozens of chests packed with bright linen. There were bronze-handled razors strewn about, and pots of kohl carelessly tipped over. "Which wig should I wear?" She was surrounded by hairpieces.

"The one that cost the least," I said immediately.

She continued to wait for an answer that pleased her.

"The short one," I replied.

She swept the other wigs into a pile for Merit to clean up later. "Father has sent invitations to every king in the East," she boasted. "When the princes of the greatest nations in the world are assembled here, an announcement will be made that will write our family's name in eternity."

I glanced sideways at her. "What do you mean?"

Nefertiti looked out over her city. "It's a surprise."

Chapter Twenty-Eight

Peret, Season of Growing

IT TOOK UNTIL Tybi to prepare for the coming of a dozen nations, princes and courtiers, minor queens with their traveling entourages, and thousands of nobles from Mitanni and Rhodes. The soldiers worked from dawn till dusk to swathe the Arena in gold cloth and to finish the images of Aten on every shrine. There were seven nights of festivals to plan, rooms to prepare for a thousand dignitaries, and wine to procure. The palace did not sit still for an entire month, and while everyone believed that the first Durbar in twenty years was a celebration of Nefertiti and Akhenaten's rule, only our family knew better.

My father stood in Nefertiti's doorway, watching her choose between sandals. "Is it true?" he demanded.

I had heard the rumor, too, that Akhenaten had drawn up a letter on his own, sending it to King Suppiluliumas of the Hittites and inviting our enemy to see the glory of Amarna.

My father stepped inside. "Is it true that your husband is welcoming Hittites? Hittites," he hissed, "in the midst of this city?"

Nefertiti drew herself up to her fullest height. "Yes," she declared. "Let them see what we have built."

"And shall we let them bring in plague?" my father shouted. "Black Death," he spelled out for her. "Shall we let that happen, too?" He thrust before her face the scrolls that he'd been carrying. She unrolled them fiercely, scanning their contents. "Plague throughout the north," he told her.

"Akhenaten already knows this." She pushed them away.

"Then the more fool he!"

They glared at one another.

"You know what I am about to do," Nefertiti said.

"Yes. You are about to bring death into this city."

"Everyone must see what is about to happen. They must all understand. Every kingdom in the East!"

I could see what my father wanted to say. That pride, the pride of the whole royal family, would be our undoing. Instead he replied, "Then invite the king of Nubia, but do not risk the Hittites. Do not risk bringing plague into this city."

"When was the last time there was plague in Egypt?"

"When the Elder was Pharaoh. When soldiers brought it home from the north," he said forebodingly.

My sister faltered. "Well, there will be no convincing Akhenaten to change his mind."

My father stared at her. "You have never seen the Black Death," he warned. "How a person's limbs turn black, how swelling begins under the skin to become huge black balls." My sister recoiled and my father drew closer. "We don't know what they're carrying in the north. Some sicknesses can take days to appear. They have to be stopped!"

"It's too late."

"It's never too late!" he declared, and Nefertiti shouted back.

"He won't change his mind! The Hittites will come, and they will disappear when the Durbar is over."

"Leaving *what* behind?"

Nefertiti grinned smugly. "Their gold."

My father went to Akhenaten, but there was no changing his mind, just as Nefertiti had said. "Why would Aten allow plague to touch this city?" he demanded. "This is the greatest city of Egypt."

My father went to his sister and she suggested that one last attempt be made. But Panahesi only laughed. "No one has seen plague in fifteen years," he sneered.

"But they have seen it in the north," my father said steadily. "Near Kadesh, hundreds of sailors have died."

"What is it, Vizier? Are you afraid the Hittites will come marching in and see how defenseless this city really is? That they will see how Pharaoh will need a strong son to lead his army if he ever hopes to defend it? None of your girls could lead men into battle. It's a matter of time before Nebnefer is made heir."

"Then you do not know Akhenaten," my father said, and I wondered if that was Nefertiti's great secret. If Meritaten would be declared heir when the Durbar began. "And if that is your reason for allowing Hittites into Amarna, then you are more foolish than I thought."

They arrived from every corner of the world: Nubians, Assyrians, Babylonians, Greeks. The women who came from far reaches of the deserts wore veils on their faces, while we wore hardly anything at all, with our breasts and ankles hennaed and our hair in beaded wigs that made music when the warm wind blew from the west.

The servants fluttered around my sister like butterflies, smoothing and painting and arranging her crown. Thutmose sketched her onto papyrus while she sat under Merit's care, used to all the fuss and pampering.

"Won't you tell me what the surprise is?" I asked. "You're not pregnant again?"

"Of course not. It's bigger than a son for Egypt. This *is* Egypt," she said bracingly.

Thutmose flashed a private smile at her, and I turned to the sculptor.

"*You* know?" I looked back at Nefertiti. "You told Thutmose and not your own sister?"

"Thutmose *has* to know." She raised her chin. "He must capture it all."

The trumpets blared and Merit stood back. Nefertiti was aglitter with the most precious jewels in Egypt. Not even her daughter, the posterity and keeper of her beauty, could rival her. Meritaten stepped forward.

"Will it be a good surprise, *mawat*?"

"It will mean your inheritance as well as mine," she promised, hooking one arm in her daughter's, then calling for me. Behind us trailed Meketaten and three-year-old Ankhesenpaaten.

"Where is Pharaoh?"

"At the Window of Appearances," she replied.

I could hear the cheers even from the inner courtyard of the palace, and when we arrived at the window where my parents spoke in quick tones with Akhenaten, I held my breath. Below us, two hundred altars had been erected and crowned with myrrh. Thousands of priests were gathered in front of them, and on every slab a bull was being slaughtered and offered to Aten; two hundred sacrifices to show the wealth and glory of the palace of Amarna. No expense had been spared for the Durbar that would live throughout history. Everywhere there glittered carnelian, lapis lazuli, and feldspar, on the necks of noblewomen and the ankles of scribes. The people stood beneath shades and canopies, drinking, feasting, and gazing upward in expectation of the god-on-earth who had brought this spectacle to them. The priests were clad in gold, from their ankles to their blazing pectorals, and before them, on the highest altar of all, was Panahesi.

"Impressed?" Akhenaten stood beside me, and I thought it was strange that he should want my opinion. I looked back down, listening to the blend of laughter and harps as the men sang songs to the great god Aten, the god who created so much gold and wine. Bull meat and myrrh wafted through the air to the heights of the palace, and there was the heady scent of beer in the wind.

"It will be remembered until eternity," I replied.

"Yes, eternity." Then Akhenaten took Nefertiti's hand in his and revealed himself in the Window of Appearances. "A Durbar for the greatest Pharaohs in Egypt," he declared and the people cheered. "Pharaoh Akhenaten and the Pharaoh Neferneferuaten-Nefertiti!"

I gasped.

"What does that mean?" Meritaten asked.

Nefertiti and Akhenaten remained at the window, united, and the people sent up a cry that might have deafened the gods.

"What does that mean?" Meritaten repeated, and my husband gave her an answer, for I was in shock.

"It means your mother shall do what no other queen has done before her. She's about to become Pharaoh and Coregent of Egypt."

It was unthinkable. For a queen to become a king. To be coregent with her husband. Even my aunt had not made herself Pharaoh. My father's expression was unreadable, but I knew what he must be thinking. It was higher than our family had ever reached.

"Where is Tiye?" I searched the chamber.

"With the emissaries from Mitanni," my father said.

"And Panahesi?" my husband asked.

My father used his chin to indicate a man who'd grown red with fury. Panahesi looked first to his right, then to his left, trying to find a way out of the courtyard among the chanting priests and thousands of dignitaries, but there was nowhere to go. Then he looked up at the picture our family created, perfectly framed in the Window of Appearances.

I stepped away. Next to me, Nakhtmin shook his head, his eyes bright with speculation, trying to determine what this would mean for a queen with no sons. But I already knew what it would mean. No one, not Kiya or Nebnefer or Panahesi, could pull our family down now.

"Mutnodjmet! Meritaten! Come," Nefertiti called.

We moved forward.

"Where is Nakhtmin?" Akhenaten demanded. He saw my husband at the back of the chamber. "You, too."

My father stepped forward quickly. "What is it that you need, Your Highness?"

"The former general is to stand beside me. He will stand beside me and the people will see that even Nakhtmin bows down before the Pharaohs of Egypt."

My heart quickened in my chest, knowing that Nakhtmin was going to refuse. I caught my husband's gaze, then my father stepped toward him and touched his arm, whispering something into his ear.

At the sight of Nakhtmin in the Window of Appearances, the men on the ground, soldiers and commoners alike, threw up such a cry that even Akhenaten moved back as if confronted by a vicious blow.

"Take my hand!" Akhenaten commanded. "They will love me the way they love you," he swore. He raised Nakhtmin's arm with his, and it seemed as if all of Egypt had begun to cry, "Akhen-aten." On his left was Nakhtmin. On his right stood Nefertiti. He turned to his Pharaoh-Queen and cried, "My people!" glowing with the love of commoners who'd been bought with bread and wine. "The Pharaoh Neferneferuaten-Nefertiti!"

The cheers became deafening when Nefertiti held up the crook and flail, the unmistakable sign of kingship in Egypt. I stood back, and Nefertiti shouted, "We welcome you to the greatest Durbar in history!"

"They will think you love him," I whispered to my husband during the procession to the temple. "All the soldiers will think you have bowed to Aten!"

"They will think no such thing." He pressed close to me. "They aren't fools. They know I am a believer in Amun who is only in Pharaoh's presence because of you."

I looked ahead at the procession of men in their soldiers' kilts and military belts. "They will also know that I am the reason you are no longer general."

"Horemheb is imprisoned; I would be there, too, if you hadn't loved me."

We stopped in a courtyard crowded with chariots. They were ablaze with electrum, turquoise, and copper. Then Panahesi stepped forward to carry Nefertiti to the destiny she had carved for herself without sons or history or precedent. His face was arranged in a smile, as if her ascension to Egypt's throne over his grandson was his greatest wish.

"Now he will have to hitch his star to hers or plot against two Pharaohs," my husband said.

"Even at the expense of his daughter and grandson?" I asked.

Nakhtmin spread his palms. "Whatever star is rising."

We were swept away into a sea of chariots and carried across the Courtyard of Festivals to the temple with its statues of Nefertiti and Akhenaten. Trumpets blared and a path to the gates was cleared. "You look as if you've swallowed something bitter." Nefertiti laughed musically, descending from her chariot. "What's wrong, Mutnodjmet? This is the greatest day we shall ever know. We are immortal."

No. We are surrounded by lies. Before she could be carried away by the priests into the inner sanctum of the temple to receive the pschent crown of Egypt, I said aloud, "These people are happy because they've free bread and wine. And there are *Hittites*. In the capital, Nefertiti. How do you know they haven't brought plague?"

My sister turned an incredulous face to Nakhtmin, then back to me. "Why are you saying this during my greatest triumph?"

"Shall I lie to you, the way everyone else will do when you are Pharaoh?"

Nefertiti was silent.

"Just don't touch them," I advised. "Don't let them kiss your ring."

"Touch who?" Akhenaten appeared behind Nakhtmin.

"The Hittite emissaries," Nefertiti said. "Do not let them kiss your ring," she told him, and Akhenaten sneered.

"No, they shall kiss my feet when they see what I have built."

Throughout the Durbar, there was nothing Akhenaten did not lavish on Nefertiti. She was his Chief Wife, his chief adviser, his partner in every plan, and now she was Pharaoh. And so that the world should never forget it, we traveled to the borders of Amarna, where he erected a pillar to her reign. He stood before the emissaries of the East and ordered Maya to read the inscription he had written for his wife, the Pharaoh-Queen of Egypt.

To the Heiress, Great in the Palace, Fair of Face,
Adorned with the Double Plumes, Mistress of Happiness,
Endowed with Favors, at hearing whose voice the Pharaoh rejoices,
The Chief Wife of the King, his beloved, the Lady of the Two Lands,
And now Pharaoh Neferneferuaten-Nefertiti,
May she live for Ever and Always.

No Pharaoh had ever granted the crook and flail to a woman. But when Nefertiti stood before the crowds to bless them, they pressed against each other and stood on stools simply to catch a glimpse of her face.

"They love me," she swore on the second day of the Durbar. "They love me more than when I was queen!"

"Because now you have greater power over them," I said.

But she ignored my cynicism. "I want the people to remember this forever," she answered. In the waning light of her Robing Room, the setting sun turned her skin to gilded bronze. "Mutny," she said, "find Thutmose. I want to be sculpted just as I am."

I crossed the palace to the artist's studio. The Durbar would last six days and seven nights, and already there were drunken men in the streets, while the wives of dignitaries went stumbling to their litters, reeking of scented oil and wine. Thutmose was in his workshop, laughing in the midst of a gaggle of young girls and handsome men. His eyes lit up when he saw me.

"A sculpture?" he asked breathlessly. "I'll be ready at once. When I saw her at the temple with the crook and flail," he confided, "the cobra rearing on her crown, I knew she would call for me. No queen has ever worn that crown with such grace."

"No one has ever worn it at all," I said dryly.

Thutmose laughed. "Tell Her Majesty she should come," he said grandly, then motioned with his hands. "Everybody must go!" The women pouted, trailing out the door with their wine cups and beaded skirts.

When the crowd was gone, I asked Thutmose, "Why is it that the women love you so much?"

He thought for a moment. "Because I can make them immortal. When I find the right model I might use her for Isis, and when the winds of time erase her memory from her house, there will still be her face looking down from the temples."

I thought of what Thutmose said when I went to tell Nefertiti that he was ready. She had changed, and I wondered if this was the way she would be remembered to history. She was wearing a linen so thin that it was perfectly transparent. On her wrists, at her ankles, from her ears and on her toes, thick gold and faience glittered. We walked through the halls of the palace together as we had done so many years before in Thebes, on the night when she had gone to

Akhenaten as a virgin. We could hear the crowds outside in the courtyards, laughing and dancing, but inside the palace it was cool and silent.

In Thutmose's studio, cushions had been placed where Nefertiti should sit. There was an armed chair for myself and when Nefertiti entered Thutmose executed a deep bow. "Pharaoh Neferneferuaten-Nefertiti."

My sister smiled at the sound of her new name. "I want a bust," she told him. "From my pectoral all the way to my crown."

"With the spitting cobra," Thutmose nodded approvingly, coming closer to study the rubies that made the snake's glittering eyes. Nefertiti sat a little higher on the cushions. "I shall do the bust in limestone," he announced. I stood up to go and Nefertiti cried, "You can't leave! I want you to see this."

So we spent the afternoon that way, and although my memory of the greatest Durbar in history is filled with images of drinking and dance, the memory that remains clearest to me is that of Nefertiti sitting forward on her ocean of cushions, the coral and turquoise from her golden pectoral catching the sun's last light, her black eyes like pools of obsidian. There was true tranquillity on my sister's face. At last, Nefertiti was convinced that she would never be abandoned, that a Pharaoh's crook and flail would mean that she would be remembered by eternity.

Chapter Twenty-Nine

sixth day of the Durbar

THE JACKAL-HEADED GOD descended on Egypt while there was still dancing in the streets and thousands of dignitaries in the palace. At first he stole through the alleys at night, snapping up workers in Pharaoh's tomb, then he grew bolder and stalked the Baker's Quarter by day. When panic finally spread to the palace, there was no one in Amarna who could deny what they had seen.

Anubis had arrived with the Black Death in his jaws.

My father came into the Audience Chamber on the sixth day of the Durbar to bring Pharaoh the news. In the open courts that looked out onto the river, there was still dancing. "Your Highness," my father said, and the gravity on his face stopped Nefertiti's laughter.

"Come forward." Akhenaten smiled widely. "What is it, Vizier?"

My father's face remained serious. "There is report of plague in the workers' quarters, Your Majesty."

Akhenaten glanced at Nefertiti. "Impossible," he hissed. "We sacrificed two hundred bulls to Aten."

"And eleven workers in the tombs have died."

Several dignitaries backed away from the dais and Nefertiti whispered, "It must have been the Hittites."

"I suggest quarantining yourself in the Northern Palace, Your Highness."

"To a Second Wife's palace?" Nefertiti cried.

"No. We stay here," Akhenaten was firm. He scanned the Audience Chamber. The horror of plague had frozen the court. The music played on in the outer chambers, but now the women's laughter went silent.

"Your Highness," my father interrupted. "Rethink whether it is wise to stay in this palace. The Hittites, at least, should be quarantined. Anyone from the north should be sent—"

"No one is to be sent away!" Pharaoh boomed. "The Durbar is not finished." Even the musicians fell silent. He turned and commanded, "Keep playing!"

At once they struck up a tune, and Panahesi moved quickly to the base of the dais. I had not even seen him appear. "We could make a special offering in the temple," he suggested.

Akhenaten smiled at him, snubbing my father. "Good. And Aten will protect this city."

"But seal the city gates," my father implored. "No one should be allowed in or out."

Nefertiti agreed. "We must seal the gates."

"And let our guests think that there is plague?"

My father said quietly, "They will know it soon enough. The Baker's Quarter has also been infected."

There was a moment of panicked silence, then dignitaries began talking at once. A surge of courtiers pressed against the dais, wanting to know what to do and where to go. Akhenaten stood from his throne, and my father gathered our family around him. Tiye, my mother, and Nefertiti were there. "You must all go back to your chambers," my father instructed the court. "Go back to your chambers and do not go outside."

"*I* am Pharaoh, and no ones goes back to their chambers!"

Nefertiti contradicted him. "Do as the vizier says!"

We swept as an entire family down the hall, and even Tiye's steps were brisk. We turned the corner to the royal rooms, but Akhenaten refused to go any farther. "We must prepare for tonight."

Nefertiti grew enraged, and I saw that it was fear that was making her shake. "During plague, you want to prepare for a feast? Who knows who could be sick? It could be all of Amarna!"

"And do we want our enemies to see us weak?" Akhenaten challenged. "To see trouble in the midst of our celebration?"

She didn't answer.

"Then *I* will prepare the feast and *no one* will forget why they are here. For the glory of Aten. This is what will be remembered in history."

Nefertiti watched him disappear into the Great Hall, and I was reminded of the boat ride many years ago when my father had remarked, "He is not stable." My sister looked up at the carvings of herself and her family and her eyes welled with tears. "It was supposed to be glorious."

"You invited the Hittites, and you knew they were tainted," I replied.

"And what could I do?" Nefertiti snapped. "Could I stop him?"

"You wanted it, too."

She shook her head. Her answer might have been a yes or a no. "The people will blame us," she said as we came upon her chambers. "They will blame our devotion to Aten." She closed her eyes, already knowing how the drama would play in the streets of Amarna and across the kingdom. "And what if it comes into the palace?" she asked. "What if it destroys everything that we've built?"

I thought of Ipu, who once told me that her father had used mint to keep rats away from the cellar and that none of his workers had ever died of plague. "Use mint," I told her. "Use mint and rue. Tie it around your neck and hang it over every door."

"You should leave, Mutnodjmet. You are pregnant." Nefertiti choked back her tears. "And you've wanted a child so badly."

"We don't even know if it's plague," I said hopefully.

My father gave me a long look before we entered the royal rooms. "It is plague."

Yet we feasted. The night was filled with harpists and lotus candles, and a hundred dancers glittered in the firelight, reflecting silver and gold. There was a tension among the guests, but no one dared to mention plague beneath the columns of the Great Hall of Amarna. The scent of orange blossoms floated on the night air between the pillars, and guests laughed high and nervous in the courtyard. Nakhtmin brought me a plate with the choicest meat, and we ate while below us Anubis roamed the streets. Women flirted and men played Senet and servants refilled cup after cup of red wine. By the end of the night, even I had forgotten the fear of death. It was only the next morning, when several hundred of the guests smelled a cloying sweetness in the air, that anyone thought to see what was happening in the city.

When the messenger returned, he reported what he'd seen to a filled Audience Chamber.

While we had been feasting, a thousand poor lay rotting in their beds.

"Seal the palace!" Akhenaten shouted, and the Nubian guards rushed to isolate Pharaoh's palace from the rest of the city.

"What about the servants on errands?" my father asked.

"If they're not in the palace, then they die in the streets."

Nakhtmin turned to me. "It's our last chance, Mutnodjmet. We can go back to Thebes now. We can escape."

I gripped the edge of my chair. "And leave my family?"

"It's their choice to stay." His eyes held me in their sway, reminding me of that evening by the river.

My father came up and spread his hands on my shoulders. "You are pregnant. You have a child to think of."

The staccato of hammers fell in the distance. The doors were being boarded, the windows shut. If the sickness crept in, it would spread to every chamber. I put my hands across my belly, as if I could shield my child from this terror. I looked at my father. "And what about you?"

"Akhenaten won't leave," my father's voice was solemn. "We stay with Nefertiti."

"And mother?"

My mother took my father's arm for support. "We stay together. It's unlikely that plague will come into the palace." But her eyes remained uncertain. No one knew why plague came, to what house, to what person.

I looked at Nakhtmin, and he already knew the choice I would make, the choice I would always make. He nodded in understanding, taking my hand. "It could be in Thebes as well."

We gathered quietly in the Audience Chamber. Every foreign dignitary, whether from Rhodes or Mitanni, had been turned onto the streets, and only three hundred people took shelter beneath the massive columns. Kiya and her ladies hovered in a corner while Panahesi whispered into Pharaoh's ear. Few people stirred. Nobody talked. We looked like prisoners waiting to be summoned to our execution.

I looked at the weeping servants. A scribe I had seen many times in the corridors of the Per Medjat was without his wife. I wondered where she had been when Pharaoh decided to seal the palace without warning. Perhaps she'd been away at the temple giving thanks or at home visiting with her elderly mother. Now they would wait out the plague in separate houses and hope that both were passed by Anubis. That, or they would reunite in the Afterlife. I squeezed Nakhtmin's hand and he squeezed back tenderly, looking into my face.

"Are you frightened?" I asked.

"No. The palace is the safest place in Amarna. It's above the city and apart from the workers' houses. The plague will have to come through two walls to find us."

"Do you think it would have been better in Thebes?"

He hesitated. "It's possible the plague has spread to Thebes as well."

I thought of Ipu and Djedi. They could be sick even now, boarded up in their own home with no one to bring them food or drink. And what of young Kamoses? Nakhtmin squeezed my shoulder.

"We will take your herbs and protect ourselves the best we can. I am sure that Ipu and Djedi are safe."

"And Bastet."

"And Bastet," he promised.

"Did the Hittites really bring this?" I whispered.

Nakhtmin's look was hard. "On the wings of Pharaoh's pride."

▣ ▣ ▣

As thousands outside the palace were dying, I was taken early to my birthing chamber.

The pavilion my sister had used was outside, so women rushed to fill a room with protective images of the sun, and as the pains began Nefertiti slipped an image of Tawaret into my hand, to hide beneath the pillows while I screamed. The midwives called for *kheperwer* and basil to help me push, and I knew later when they shouted for clove that this child had been a gift from Tawaret and there would probably be no more.

"He's coming!" the midwives cried, "He's coming!" and I arched my back to give a final push. When my son finally decided to enter the world, the sun was nearly set. Nothing about his birth was auspicious. He was a child of death, a child of the waning sun, a child born into the midst of chaos as outside the revelers of Pharaoh's Durbar died in the streets, first smelling the scent of honey on their breaths, then discovering a swelling in their armpits and groins, lumps that would turn black and ooze. But inside, the midwives pushed my child into my arms, crying, "A boy! A healthy boy, my lady!" He wailed loud enough to disturb Osiris, and my sister rushed out of the birthing chamber to tell my husband and my father that we'd both survived.

I caressed the thatch of dark hair on my son's head and pressed it to my lips. He was soft as down.

"What will you call him?" my mother asked, and as Nakhtmin burst into the birthing chamber I said, "Baraka." *Unexpected Blessing.*

For two days, I knew only the bliss of motherhood and nothing else. Nakhtmin was a constant companion at my side, watching over me in case I should show the first signs of fever or little Baraka should begin to cough. He went so far as to forbid any servants from having contact with us, in case they should be carrying plague. On the third day, when he thought we were well enough to be let out of our bed, he ordered us moved back into our room where he could protect us from the comings and goings of palace well-wishers.

The specter of Anubis was on every face. The servants crept around the halls of the palace in silence, and only the wail of Baraka pierced the stillness of the guest chambers. Nefertiti had ordered our room to be decorated in golden beads, the color of my son's bright skin, and the ladies of the court had collected beads from their hair and strung them together. It was something to occupy their time while we were prisoners inside the palace. Meritaten, Meketaten, and Ankhesenpaaten had painted happy images on the bottom of the walls with their pallets. Beads hung from every corner and across the wooden beams. Myrrh had been scattered on the braziers throughout the palace, and its heady scent filled the room when I entered it for the first time. My sister looked down at Baraka, and I thought I caught a glimmer of resentment in her eyes, but when she saw that I was watching her she flashed her brightest smile. "I have already found you a milk nurse who can milk him when your three days are finished."

"Who is she?" I asked warily. I had thought I would feed him myself.

"Heqet, the wife of an Aten priest."

"And you're sure she isn't carrying plague?"

"Of course I am."

"But how do I know her milk is good?"

"You aren't thinking of milking him yourself?" Nefertiti demanded. "Do you want your breasts to hang to your navel by the time he is three?"

I looked down at my son, at his puckered lips and deep contentment. He was my only child, and there would probably only ever be one. Why shouldn't I feed him, at least until the plague was over? Who knew what the milk nurse could be carrying inside of her when so many were dying? But there was something else to think of. If I spent myself giving him milk, what if the plague should come into the palace and I was too weary to fight it? Baraka would be motherless. Nakhtmin would be widowed to raise a son alone. Nefertiti was watching me. "Bring Heqet," I said. "I will stop feeding Baraka in two days." I traced his small nose with my fingertip and smiled. "I can see why you did this five times, Nefertiti."

My sister wrinkled her brow. "You enjoy it more than I did, then."

I glanced up from my bed. "But you were always happy," I protested.

"Because I had survived," Nefertiti said bluntly. "And I would live to try again for a son." Her eyes flickered over Baraka. "But now I will never need one. I am Pharaoh and Meri will be Pharaoh after me."

I sat up on my cushions, eliciting a sharp cry from Baraka. "Does Father know this?"

"Of course. Who else would he want it to be? *Nebnefer?*"

I thought of Kiya and Nebnefer on the other side of the palace. The entire court of Amarna—sculptors, priests, dancers, tailors—had flocked to the palace for shelter. Now they were crowded in the rooms around the Audience Chamber. Anyone who had influence or a job in the palace had been allowed to stay, but food was not infinite.

"What will we do if the plague outlasts supplies?" I asked slowly.

"We'll send for more," Nefertiti said lightly.

"You don't have to lie to protect me. I know there can't be many servants willing to leave the palace. Nakhtmin told me that a messenger came to the window last night to report the deaths of three hundred workers. Three *hundred,*" I repeated. "That's two thousand people since the Durbar."

Nefertiti shifted uneasily. "You shouldn't think about this, Mutnodjmet. You have a child—"

"And I won't be able to protect him if I don't know the truth." I sat straighter on my cushions. "What's happening, Nefertiti?"

She sat on a chair near my bedside. Her cheeks lost their color. "They are rioting in the streets."

I sucked in my breath, shifting Baraka in my arms until he cried.

"And there is nothing to stop them charging the prison and releasing Horemheb," she said. "The army is quarantined. There are only a few soldiers—"

"There'll be plague within the prisons. If there is plague at the tombs—"

"But they could break him free if he hasn't succumbed. And he would lead a revolt against our family. We would all be lost." She hesitated. "Except you. Nakhtmin would save you."

"Never, Nefertiti. The gods are with you. That would never happen."

She smiled wryly, and I knew she was thinking of the plague following so closely on the heels of the Durbar and her ascent to the ultimate throne in the land. If the gods had been with her, why was there plague?

"So what will we do?" I looked down at Baraka. His tiny, innocent life could be over before it even began. But why would the gods do that? Give me a child after so long only to take him away? "What does Father think we should do?"

"He thinks we should send messengers to Memphis and Thebes. To warn them."

"You haven't warned them?" I cried.

"We've stopped up the ports," she countered. "No one can leave. The gates are shut. If we send messengers to Thebes, what will the people think so soon after a Durbar?"

I stared at the boarded windows. "It's against all the laws of Ma'at not to warn them," I said.

"Akhenaten won't do it."

"Then you must," I told her. "You are Pharaoh now."

▣ ▣ ▣

Six men from the palace were paid in gold to carry messages to Memphis and Thebes, warning them of Amarna's plight: The Hittites had carried plague to Pharaoh's Durbar, and it had already claimed two thousand lives.

There were not enough tombs cut to hold all the dead; even the wealthy were tossed into mass graves, anonymous for eternity. Some risked death to place amulets with their loved ones in the earth so that Osiris could identify them. I had nightmares about these graves at night, and when I'd wake up crying, Nakhtmin would ask what was haunting me in my dreams.

"I dreamed Osiris couldn't find me, that I'd been lost to eternity, that no one cared enough to write my name on my tomb." My husband caressed my hair and swore it wouldn't happen, that he'd risk everything to press an amulet into my palm before I was buried. "Swear you wouldn't do that," I begged him. "Swear that if I were to die of plague, you would let them take my body, amulet or no."

His arms tightened protectively around me. "Of course they wouldn't take you without evidence for the gods. I would never let that happen."

"But you would have to let me go. Because if I were to die and you were to sicken, who would Baraka have to watch over him?"

"Don't speak this way."

"All of Amarna is dying, Nakhtmin. Why should the palace be immune?"

"Because we are protected! By your herbs, by our position on a hill. We are above the plague," he tried to convince me.

"And if the people were to break into the palace and bring it with them?"

He was surprised by my mistrust. "Then the soldiers would fight them because they're protected here and fed." Baraka's wail pierced the morning stillness, and Nakhtmin rose to get him. He looked tenderly at his son, placing him carefully at my breast. Tomorrow, our son would have a milk nurse.

"Nefertiti has sent word to Memphis and Thebes that there is a plague," I told him.

Nakhtmin watched me carefully. "Akhenaten will learn of it, once the plague has passed."

"How do you know it will pass?"

"Because it always does. It's simply a matter of how many Anubis will take with him before he goes."

I shuddered. "Nefertiti said they are rioting in the streets."

Nakhtmin looked sharply at me. "Why did she tell you this?"

"Because I wanted to know. Because I have never lied to her, and she knows I would want the same courtesy. You should have told me."

"For what good?" he protested.

"Imagine my shock if they broke into the palace. I wouldn't know what was happening. I might not know enough to hide our son."

"They won't break into the palace," Nakhtmin said sternly. "Pharaoh's army is just outside. They're eating the same food that we are and wearing the same herbs. For all of Akhenaten's foolishness, he knows better than to risk losing his army or his Nubian guards. We are safe," he promised. "And even if they came, I would protect you."

"What if they came with Horemheb?" I asked, and by his expression I could see it was something he had thought of, too.

"Then Horemheb would instruct them not to touch you."

"Because he is your friend?"

Nakhtmin set his jaw. He didn't like this line of questioning. "Yes."

"And Nefertiti?" I asked.

He didn't answer.

My voice dropped. "And my nieces?"

He still didn't answer. Instead, a messenger knocked and requested our presence in the Audience Chamber.

"More Senet," Nakhtmin guessed, but it wasn't this time. My father had called us to report that three thousand Egyptians were dead.

"From now on, begin stocking bread in your room," he told those gathered in the chamber. "And water in vessels. The plague will outlast our supplies."

In the hall, my father looked back at the unoccupied thrones and the ebony tables. In an hour, the chamber would be filled with dancing, and Akhenaten would command the emissaries to play Senet. "An empty husk," he said quietly. "They kissed his sandals just as he wished, and now his people will lie dead at his feet."

We knew Black Death had entered Riverside Palace when the cook ran screaming into the Audience Chamber, sweat beading on his face. "Two apprentices are sick," he cried. "There is death in the kitchens. Five rats and the wife of the baker are dead."

The Senet games stopped, and the harpist's fingers froze in horror at the fat man's labored words.

He might as well have unleashed Anubis in the palace.

Nakhtmin grabbed my shoulders. "Get back into our chamber. Bring Heqet and her child, then seal the door and let no one in until you hear my voice. I'm going for fresh water."

Women ran and men rushed to get away. Nefertiti met my glance, and I could feel her horror as Amarna slipped from her grasp. If there was plague in the palace, it was a death sentence for everyone inside. Akhenaten stood from his throne and summoned his guards, screaming that no one must leave him. But there was no controlling the panic as it spread. He turned to Maya at the bottom of the dais. "You will stay," he commanded.

Maya's face turned gray. His city, their city, once a tribute to life, was now a monument to death. Amid the panic, someone ordered the children to the nursery. Every child under the age of sixteen was to be protected in the most secluded chamber of the palace.

"Who will watch them? Someone must watch them," my father shouted. But the chaos was too loud. No guard stepped forward. Then Tiye appeared, her face ashen but calm.

"I will watch over the nursery."

My father nodded. "Order the guards to reseal the windows," he instructed Nefertiti. "Kill anyone who attempts to break free. They are risking our lives."

"What does it matter?" a woman shrieked. "There is already plague in the palace."

"In the *kitchens,*" my father snapped. "It can be contained."

But no one believed him.

"You!" Akhenaten shouted, pointing to a noblewoman who had pushed her child to freedom through a broken window and was herself preparing to break free. He grabbed one of his guards' bow and arrows. "Step farther and you will die."

The woman looked between herself and her child. Then she moved to bring the child back into the palace and an arrow twanged. There was a collective gasp, then silence in the Audience Chamber as the woman slumped forward and her child screamed. Akhenaten lowered his bow. "*No one* leaves the palace!" he shouted. Akhenaten drew back a second arrow and pointed into the midst of the suddenly silent crowd. Nefertiti came up beside him, lowering the weapon.

"No one else is leaving," she promised.

The people watched her with wide, frightened eyes.

Akhenaten stopped in front of one of the priests, who fell to the floor in obeisance. "*Anyone* who opens a window or slips a message under a door to the outside will be sent to the kitchens to die. Guards!" he commanded. "Kill every cook and baker's apprentice. Keep no one in the kitchens alive. Not even the cats." He looked for the man who'd delivered the news of plague and pointed. "Begin with him."

The guards were swift. The man was taken screaming through the doors of the Audience Chamber before he could even beg for his life. Our family looked as one to Nefertiti.

"Everyone return to their chamber," she said. "Anyone with sign of the plague is instructed to take charcoal from their brazier and mark the Eye of Horus upon their door. Meals will come once a day." She saw my father's approving nod, and her voice grew louder and more confident. "The servants will take food from the cellars, not the kitchens. And no one is to venture beyond their chambers until the palace is free from plague for a fortnight."

Panahesi stepped forward, eager to put himself in the center of things. "We should make a sacrifice," he announced.

Akhenaten agreed. "A platter of meat and a bowl of Amarna's best wine outside of every door," he declared.

"No!" I moved quickly forward to the dais. "We should hang garlands of mint and rue outside of every door. But that is all."

Akhenaten turned on me. "The Sister of Pharaoh thinks she knows more than the High Priest of Aten?"

Nefertiti's look was fierce. "She is wise with herbs and she suggests rue, not rotting meat."

Akhenaten's voice grew suspicious. "And how do you know she isn't trying to rid herself of a sister and brother-in-law? She could take the throne for herself and her son."

"Every door will have a garland of mint and rue," Nefertiti commanded.

"And the sacrifice?" Panahesi pressed the two Pharaohs of Egypt.

Akhenaten straightened. "For every chamber that wants protection from Aten," he said loudly. "Those who wish the great god's wrath"—his eyes found mine—"will go without."

The exit from the Audience Chamber was subdued. As the crowd broke up, Nefertiti touched my hand. "What will you do?"

"Go back to Baraka, then seal the door and let no one inside."

"Because we can't all be together, can we?" she asked. "To put all of our family in one chamber would be to risk everything." There was fear in her voice, and it occurred to me that this was the first time she would have only Akhenaten and no one else. Our parents would go to their chambers while Tiye watched over the children.

I reached out and touched her hand. "We may all survive this separately," I said.

"But how do you know? You could be dead of plague and I wouldn't discover it until a servant reported the Eye of Horus. And my daughters—" Her slight body seemed to grow even smaller. "I will be all alone."

It was her greatest fear, and I took her hand and placed it on my heart. "We will all be well," I promised, "and I shall see you in a fortnight."

It was the only time I ever lied to her.

▣ ▣ ▣

While Black Death swept through the palace, Panahesi placed offerings of salted meat at the doors of those who wished for Aten's blessing. In his leopard robes and heaviest golden rings, he moved through the halls, followed by young priests singing praises in their high, sweet voices to Aten. And while the young boys sang, Anubis ravaged.

When Panahesi came to our door, Heqet ordered him away.

"Wait!" I flung the door open to confront him. Both Nakhtmin and the milk nurse cried out. "I will hold a sprig of rue before me," I promised, then faced Panahesi. "Are you placing an offering at the nursery?" I asked.

He tossed aside his leopard cloak and moved to the next door.

"Are you placing an offering at the nursery?" I demanded.

He looked at me with condescension. "Of course I am."

"Don't do it. Don't place an offering there. I will give you whatever you want," I said desperately.

Panahesi looked me up and down. "And what would I want from the Sister of the King's Chief Wife?"

"The sister of *Pharaoh,*" I replied.

His lips curled. "My own grandson sleeps in the nursery. Do you think I would poison Egypt's hope for the throne to kill six meaningless girls? Then you are as foolish as I thought you were."

"Close the door!" Heqet cried from behind me. "Close the door," she begged, holding my son with hers. I watched Panahesi disappear down the hall with his bowls full of meat, then I closed us back inside, shoving springs of rue and mint beneath the door and sealing up the crack.

⁂

Two days passed, and there was no sign of the Black Death in the halls of the palace, no charcoal eyes of death on any door. Then, on the third night, just as we had begun to believe that the palace would be protected, Anubis paused to eat at every chamber that had an offering to Aten.

A servant girl's screams pierced the silent halls at dawn. She ran by the royal chambers, shouting about the Eye of Horus. "A boy next to the kitchens," she screamed, terrified. "And the Master of the Horse. Everyone who placed an offering to Aten! Two ambassadors from Abydos. And one from Rhodes. We can smell it from their chambers!"

"What now?" I whispered from behind our closed door.

Nakhtmin replied, "Now we wait and see, and hope death only visits those who placed offerings to Aten."

But when the people of Amarna saw the death carts rolling toward the palace, fury swept through the city. If Pharaoh's god wouldn't protect Amarna's palace, why would he protect its people? Despite the risk, Egyptians took to the streets, chanting to Amun and shattering Aten's images. They pressed against the palace gates and demanded to know if the Heretic Pharaoh was still alive. I moved closer to our boarded-up windows and heard the cries. "Do you hear what they're calling him?" I whispered.

Heqet's eyes were wide with fear. She replied, "The Heretic King."

"And do you hear what they are chanting?"

We listened to the sound of shattered stone and hammers. They were defacing Akhenaten's statues and chanting for the destruction of Amarna itself. "BURN IT DOWN! BURN IT DOWN!"

I took Baraka and held him to my chest.

When food came at noon, Nakhtmin opened the door and stepped back in shock. A different servant was carrying our food, trembling and crying.

"What is it?" Nakhtmin demanded.

"The nursery," the girl gasped.

I handed my son to Heqet and ran toward the door. "What about it?"

"They've all been touched," she cried, holding a basket out for us. "All the children have been touched!"

"Who? *Who* has been touched?" I shouted.

"The children. The twin princesses are gone. The Princess Meketaten is taken. And Nebnefer, my lady . . ." She covered her mouth, as if the words that would fall out must be held back in.

Nakhtmin gripped the girl's arm. "Died?"

The servant's knees grew weak. "No. But sick with plague."

"Give us our food and shut the door," he said quickly.

"Wait!" I pleaded. "Nefertiti and my parents. Do they have the Eye of Horus?"

"No," the girl whispered, "but our Pharaoh will wish she was dead when she hears that her six princesses are reduced to three."

I recoiled in horror. "She hasn't been told?"

The girl pressed her lips together. The tears came harder and she shook her head. "No one has been told but you, my lady. The servants are afraid of him."

Of Akhenaten. I steadied myself against the door: three princesses and soon the Prince of Egypt. And if there was plague in the nursery, what of Tiye? Of Meritaten and Ankhesenpaaten? Nakhtmin bolted the door and Heqet was on her feet at once.

"We shouldn't eat the food."

"It's not carried by food," Nakhtmin replied. "If it was, we'd all be dead by now."

"Someone must rescue the survivors," I said.

Nakhtmin stared fixedly into the room where our son was lying.

"Someone must rescue the queen and Meritaten," I repeated. "Ankhesenpaaten—"

"Is lost." My husband's eyes were grim.

"But she's still alive!" I protested.

"And there is nothing we can do for her. For any of them. If three princesses have already died, the nursery must be quarantined."

"But we can separate the healthy. We can place them in separate chambers and give them a chance."

Nakhtmin was shaking his head. "Pharaoh damned their chances by inviting the Hittites and listening to Panahesi."

We all knew when the news arrived that the twin princesses were gone, and the two-year-old Neferuaten and five-year-old Meketaten had also been taken.

Bells tolled in the courtyards and there were screams in the palace. Women were weeping and calling on Aten to lift the curse that had descended over the palace of Amarna. A servant came and told us that Nubian guards had been sent to rescue the remaining princesses and the queen, but that for Nebnefer it had been too late. I shut the door, and we listened to the chanting beyond the walls of the palace. It had never been so loud.

"They know there's plague within the palace," Nakhtmin said, "and they think that if Pharaoh's own children have been taken, then it must be because of something he's done."

For three days, the chanting never stopped. We could hear angry Egyptians calling for mercy in the name of Amun and cursing the Heretic Pharaoh who had brought them plague. I stood near the window and pressed my face against the wood, closing my eyes and listening to the rhythm of the cries. "He will never be known as Akhenaten the Builder. They will call him the Heretic Pharaoh until eternity." I thought of Nefertiti alone in her chamber, hearing the news that four of her children had died, and whenever I looked at my son at Heqet's breast my eyes stung with tears. He was so young. Much too small to fight off something so great, and I held him to me at night and tried to be thankful for the time I had with him.

In the day, we listened to the roll of the death carts outside the palace. We stopped our quiet games of Senet when the wagons went by, wondering whose body was to be stripped and buried anonymously for eternity, without any cartouche to tell Osiris who they had been when he returned to earth. I begged the servants who delivered our food to bring us more rue, but they all said there was none left in the palace.

"Have you checked the cellars? It could be stored amid the wine. Look at the barrels and read the names."

"I'm sorry, but I cannot read, my lady."

I took a reed pen and ink from my box and wrote the name of the herb on the back of one of my medical papyri. I hesitated before tearing it off, then took the strip to the woman in the hall, pressing it into her hand. "This is the herb. Look for this name amid the barrels. If you can find it, take some and put it under your door. Bring as much as you can carry to my sister and to my parents. Bring the rest to us. If there is a second barrel, pass it out among the survivors."

She nodded, but before she left I asked her, "What do they give you to walk among these halls of death?"

She turned back to me and her eyes were haunted. "Gold. Every day they pay me in gold, and I keep the rings in my chamber. If I survive, I will give it to my son to be trained as a scribe. If I catch the Black Death, he will do with it as he pleases."

I thought of Baraka and felt my throat begin to close. "And where is your son?"

The heavy lines around her eyes seemed to soften. "In Thebes. He is only seven years old. We sent him away when there was news of the death."

I hesitated. "Did many servants send their children to Thebes?"

"Yes, my lady. We all thought you would have, too, and the queen—" But she stopped at the look on my face, wondering if she had said too much.

"Thank you," I whispered. "If you find the rue, bring it at once."

She came the next day with a basket of herbs. "My lady?" She knocked eagerly and Nakhtmin opened the door just enough to see her face. "Will you tell my lady I found the herbs and did just as she said. I placed some under my door and brought a basketful to Vizier Ay."

Nakhtmin beckoned me with his hand and I took his place at the door, leaving it open only a crack. "And the queen?"

The woman hesitated. "Pharaoh Neferneferuaten-Nefertiti?"

"Yes. Did she take it?"

The woman lowered her head and I guessed at once. "Pharaoh Akhenaten answered. I want you to go back and place it above their door."

The woman gasped. "What if someone sees me?"

"If anyone asks, tell them you place it on my sister's orders. Pharaoh will be locked inside. He'll never know." The woman backed away and I touched her arm. "No one shall say otherwise," I promised. "And if he asks the queen, she will know it was me and she'll say she commanded it."

But the woman still hesitated, and I realized what she was waiting for.

I frowned sharply. "I have nothing to give you."

She looked down at the bracelet I was wearing. It wasn't gold, but it was made of turquoise stones, a gift from Nefertiti. I took it off and pressed it roughly into her hands. "You will hang it everywhere," I made her swear. "You will twine it into garlands."

She placed the bracelet into her basket. "Of course, my lady."

I didn't see the servant again for seven days. I had to trust she'd done what I'd paid her to do, while the cries in the palace halls grew more urgent. I could hear women in sandals running down the tiled halls. Some beat on locked doors in their delirium, and I could imagine their terror. But we kept our doors locked and didn't leave our chambers. On the eighth night after the servant appeared, a woman whose child had died beat on our door in delirium and cried desperately for us to open it to her.

"She doesn't want to die alone," I realized, and began holding Baraka closer to my chest, knowing that our time together was short.

"You can't press him so tightly. You will hurt him," Heqet remonstrated.

But my panic rose. "The food won't last. We will die of hunger if we don't die of plague. And our tomb is not finished! A sarcophagus hasn't even been carved for Baraka."

Heqet's eyes grew wide. "Or my son," she whispered. "If we die, we will all die nameless in here."

Nakhtmin shook his head furiously. "I won't let it happen. I won't let it happen to you. To either of you."

I looked down at our son. "We should pray to Amun."

Heqet gasped. "In Pharaoh's palace?"

I closed my eyes. "Yes. In Pharaoh's palace."

▣ ▣ ▣

When the sun rose the next morning, there were no new signs of plague, no fresh Eyes of Horus. We waited another day, then two, and slowly, when seven days had passed and all we had left to eat was stale bread, courtiers began to emerge from their chambers.

I saw the servant who had risked her life for gold.

She had survived the Black Death. She would send her son to school to become a scribe. But so many others were not so lucky. Broken mothers came stumbling out of their chambers, and fathers who'd lost their only sons. I saw Maya, bent and frailer than he'd ever looked. The light had gone out of his eyes. As we emerged, there were whispers that the Pharaoh of Egypt was ill.

"With plague?"

"No, my lady," the woman who'd placed rue over my sister's door said quietly. "With an illness of the mind."

Bells tolled in the palace, calling viziers and courtiers and all the servants that were left back into the Audience Chamber. Now, in the room where hundreds had once stood, only a handful remained. Immediately, I searched the chamber for my parents.

"*Mawat!*" I rushed into my mother's arms and she wept over Baraka, pressing him to her chest until he let out a cry. Nefertiti looked down from her throne at us. I could not read the expression on her face, but she held Akhenaten's hand in hers. Below them sat Meritaten and Ankhesenpaaten. Their family of eight had been reduced to four, and even young Ankhesenpaaten sat still and silent, muted by what she must have seen in the nursery while her sisters lay dying.

"We should leave Amarna," my mother whispered. "We should leave this palace for the palace in Thebes. Terrible things have happened here." I thought she meant the curse of the plague, but when my father clenched his jaw, I realized that they were referring to something more.

I looked between them. "What do you mean?"

We moved away from the dais so we wouldn't be overheard. "On the seventh day of quarantine, Pharaoh insulted the king of Assyria."

"The king?" Nakhtmin repeated.

"Yes. The king of Assyria sent a messenger with a request for three ebony thrones. When the messenger came, he saw that there was plague and hesitated. But he had orders from his king and he came into the city, traveling all the way to the palace."

"Then guards called on Pharaoh instead of your father and Akhenaten sent him away," my mother blurted. "With a *gift.*"

Nakhtmin heard the ominous timbre of my mother's voice and glanced at my father. "What kind of gift?"

My father closed his eyes. "A child's arm riddled with plague. From the nursery."

I stepped back; Nakhtmin's face became grave. "The Assyrians have thousands of troops," he warned darkly.

My father nodded. His tone was certain. "They will move against Egypt."

"It's too dangerous to be here," Nakhtmin stated, and I knew that it was no longer my decision to stay. We had lived through Black Death. Amun would not be so generous when the Assyrians fell upon Egypt. He looked at me. "There's nothing more we can do."

▣ ▣ ▣

"Wait for the funeral. Please," Nefertiti begged.

"We are going tonight. The Assyrians will be on Egypt's doorstep and your army is not prepared to stop them."

"But there will be a funeral tonight," she said desperately. "Stay with me," she whispered. "They are my children. Your nieces."

I hesitated at the look in her eyes. I asked quietly, "What have they done with the bodies?"

Nefertiti trembled. "Prepared them for burning."

I covered my mouth. "No burial?"

"They were victims of plague," she said savagely, but her rage was not directed at me. I thought of Meketaten and little Neferuaten, the flames rising around them as they burned on a pyre. Princesses of Egypt.

"But we will leave for Thebes immediately after," I said sternly. "And if our parents are wise, they will take Tiye and come with us." Our aunt was still sick, but not with the plague. It was a sickening of the heart. She'd watched over the nursery where Anubis had struck. She'd seen her grandchildren sicken and die. Meketaten, Neferuaten, Nebnefer. And there'd been others: the sons and daughters of wealthy merchantmen and scribes. When I went to see her, my eyes burned with tears. "Stay with us," I'd begged her. "Don't you want to stay to plant in your garden?" She'd shaken her head and grasped my hand. "Soon, I will plant in the gardens of eternity."

Nefertiti was shaking her head at me now. "Father's not going anywhere," she said. "He wouldn't leave me."

"The people are angry," I warned. "They are dying of plague, and they blame it on their Pharaohs. They believe Aten has turned his back on them."

"I can't hear this. I can't hear it now," she swore.

"Then you will hear it when it is too late!"

"I can fix it!"

"*How?* When the king of Assyria unwraps his gift, what will you do? Do you think the kingdoms of the East haven't heard of Akhenaten's rashness? Why do you think they write to Father and not to him?"

"He has visions . . . Visions of greatness, Mutnodjmet. He wants to be loved . . . so much."

"The way you do."

"It's not the same."

"No, because he will do anything for it. And you are rational. You are our father's daughter, which is why he likes you best." She started to speak, but I carried on. "Which is why he will stay here with you, even if the city falls down around him. Even if all of us were to die. But is it worth it?" I demanded. "Is immortality worth this price?"

She didn't answer. I shook my head sadly and walked away. I found Nakhtmin with Baraka in the hall leading to our chamber.

"Heqet will come with us," he said. "There are no barges going in or out of Amarna. We can go by horse, then find a barge outside the city. We will go nowhere near the workers' houses. We'll ride straight for the gates and the men will let us through," he said confidently.

"But we can't go until night," I told him. "There will be a funeral. I know what you are about to say, but she can't face it alone. She can't."

"It will be a funeral pyre, then?" he asked.

I nodded. "Little Neferuaten . . ." My lips trembled, looking at Baraka in his father's strong arms. "I don't know how she stands it."

"She stands it because she is strong and there is nothing else to do. Your sister is no fool, for all that she supports Akhenaten. And she is no weakling."

"I could not bear it," I said, and he put his hand under my chin, raising my eyes to his.

"You will never have to. I am taking you away from here, whether you want it or not."

"*After* the funeral."

Bells tolled when the sky had grown dark, and the priests of Aten who had lived through the plague gathered in the courtyard in the palace of Amarna. We all wore garlands of rue. A pyre had been built by nervous servants—plague could be lurking in any stone—but we gathered together, veils covering our faces, and the women cried. My mother leaned against my shoulder for support, while my father stood beside Nefertiti, the two of them defiant towers of strength.

The sound of weeping from Kiya was unbearable to hear. She was heavily pregnant, and I was surprised that in her weakened state she had survived the plague.

But then, little Baraka had survived it, too.

I watched her deep, heart-wrenching sobs, and I thought of how cruel it was that no one was with her but the few women she had left. Panahesi stood near the pyre in his robes of office, while Nefertiti held on to Akhenaten's hand, afraid to let it go.

"Do you think they are with Aten?" Ankhesenpaaten asked. She was a different child now, sullen and withdrawn.

"I think they are with Aten." I pressed my lips together at the lie. "Yes."

She turned her face back to the flames, which had begun on the farthest side of the pyre. The bodies had been wrapped in sheets of linen, sprinkled with rue. The flames leaped toward the sky, engulfing the princesses in fire. Flesh cracked and sizzled and the smell was acrid. Then Prince Nebnefer's clothes caught flame and the shroud around his body disintegrated, revealing his face. A scream split the courtyard and Panahesi grabbed Kiya. Akhenaten looked between his grieving wives and something in him broke.

"This is the fault of Amun worshippers," he shouted. "We have been betrayed. This is Aten's punishment," he cried, his sanity breaking. "Find me a chariot!" His Nubian guards stood back. "A chariot!" he shouted. "I will go to every home and break down their doors in search of their false gods. They are worshipping Amun in my city. In Aten's city!"

He was mad. The rage showed in his face.

Nefertiti gripped his arm. "Stop!" she cried.

"I will tear apart the families whose houses have false gods," he swore. He wrenched his arm away from her, throwing back his cloak and jumping into the chariot that had been brought. The two horses whinnied nervously and he raised the whips. "Guards!" he commanded, but they stood back, afraid. There was plague in the city, and no one wanted to risk their life. When Akhenaten saw that no one would join him, he commanded the gates to be opened regardless.

"You will keep them shut!" Nefertiti's voice boomed.

The guards looked between the Pharaohs, wondering whom to obey. Then Akhenaten galloped toward the heavy wooden gates and Nefertiti shrieked, "Open them! Open the gates!" before he crashed.

Akhenaten never stopped. The gates swung open in time to let the rider and his wild chariot through. Then the Pharaoh of Egypt disappeared into the night as the flames rose higher in the courtyard, engulfing the bodies of his children.

Nefertiti stepped forward into the light. The crook and flail of power were in her right hand. She clenched the left. "Bring him back to me!"

The guards hesitated.

"I am the Pharaoh of Egypt. Bring him back"—her voice rose—"before Amarna is destroyed!"

A servant rushed out from the palace weeping, and the courtyard seemed to turn as one.

The girl fell before Nefertiti. "Your Highness, the Dowager Queen has passed."

The keening in the courtyard now grew to hysteria, and my father moved to Nefertiti's side, speaking quickly. "If he returns, it could be with plague. We must release the inhabitants of the palace. Find barges and get them outside the city. The servants will remain. Your children—"

"Must go," Nefertiti said selflessly. "Mutnodjmet can take them."

I was shocked.

"No!" Meritaten cried. "I won't leave you, *mawat.* I won't leave Amarna without you."

My father assessed Meritaten's will.

"I won't leave the palace," Meritaten swore.

He nodded. "Send Ankhesenpaaten with Mutnodjmet, then. They can stay in Thebes until Akhenaten regains control." My father looked toward the palace. He closed his eyes briefly, the only respite he was allowed. "Now I must see my sister," he said.

I could see the physical toll that power had taken on my family. My father's eyes appeared sunken in his face, and Nefertiti seemed to shrink beneath the weight of so much loss. And now the woman who had brought us to power was gone. I would never see her sharp eyes again, or listen to her breathy laugh in my garden. She would never look at me with the power to see my thoughts, as if she was reading them as plainly as a scroll. The woman who had reigned at the side of the Elder, Amunhotep the Magnificent, and taken his role when he was too tired to want to rule, had passed into the Afterlife.

"May Osiris bless your passage, Tiye," I whispered.

Women were shrieking and children ran scampering down the halls to the Audience Chamber. "Pharaoh has fled! Pharaoh has fled!" a servant cried, and the call was echoed inside the servants' quarters and throughout the halls. I saw women running past open windows, shouting to one another, carrying armfuls of clothing and jewelry. "The gods have abandoned Amarna!" someone shouted. "Even Pharaoh has left!" Women pushed children through the acrid smoke of the courtyard so they could reach the docks. They took chests filled with their clothes while the men carried the remainders of family possessions. Servants were fleeing with courtiers and emissaries. It was madness.

My family rushed into the palace, but Nakhtmin stopped me before we reached the Audience Chamber. "We can't leave your family in this state," he said. "Pharaoh is gone. When the people outside the palace discover that he's disappeared, your family will be in danger."

"We will be in danger if he returns," I said desperately. "He could return with plague."

"Then we will quarantine him."

"The Pharaoh of Egypt?"

"Without your father's approval, I would not have you," he explained. "We owe him this. Stay with Baraka and Heqet and be ready to leave at a word's notice. Take Ankhesenpaaten, too. I'm going to find your sister. She must be ready to quarantine him if he returns."

When the guards stumbled in with the half-conscious king, bloodied and singed from fires he had set to his own people's homes, what remained of the court sprang into action.

"Place him in the remotest chamber and lock the door! Give him food for seven days and let no one in. On the threat of death, no one shall let him out." My father supervised the quarantine while next to him Vizier Panahesi was silent. "Do not go to him," my father warned.

"Of course not," Panahesi snapped.

When Akhenaten realized what was happening to him, the doors had already been locked and sealed. His screams could be heard throughout the palace, demanding his release, calling for Nefertiti, then finally begging for Kiya.

"Is somebody watching Kiya?" my sister demanded.

Guards were set upon Kiya, who wept when she learned that Akhenaten had been confined to his chambers like a prisoner. On the second day, she was the one who let the palace know with her shrieks of terror that Akhenaten was coughing blood, and that the scents the guards smelled from beneath the king's door were sweet, like honey and sugar. By the third day, the coughing had stilled. By the fourth, there was silence.

Six days passed before anyone would confirm what we already knew.

The Heretic Pharaoh had been brought before Anubis.

When Nefertiti was brought the news, she went to weep in our mother's arms. Then she came to me. He had been a selfish king, a flawed ruler, but he had been her husband and her partner in all things. And he was the father of her children.

"We must abandon this city," my father said, entering the chamber with Nakhtmin on his heels.

Nefertiti glanced up at him and her grief was untouchable. "It is the end of Amarna," she whispered to me. "When we're dead, it's all we'll have to speak for us, Mutny, and it's crumbling." Her dream, her vision of immortality and greatness, was to be covered in sand and left to the desert. She closed her eyes, and I wondered what she saw there. Her city in ruins? Her husband, ravaged by plague? She had heard the reports of men in the streets, burning their own houses in protest of Akhenaten. His image was being shattered across the city and defaced on temple walls. At first sign of the plague, Nefertiti had commanded Thutmose to close his workshop and flee. It was the one selfless thing she had done. But there was nothing left to build in Amarna. It had been built, and now it was being destroyed.

My father warned sharply, "They are burning their houses, and the palace will be next if the army flees. We must bury Akhenaten."

Nefertiti sobbed.

"But Panahesi took Akhenaten's body to the temple," I said. "He is giving him a burial now."

Nakhtmin froze. "He did *what*?"

I glanced between my husband and my father. "He took the body to the temple," I repeated.

Nakhtmin looked at my father.

"Find Panahesi!" my father shouted to the cluster of soldiers in the hall. "Don't let him leave the palace."

"What's happening?" I asked.

"The treasury is next to the temple. Panahesi hasn't gone to bury

Akhenaten," Nakhtmin said. "He's gone to take the gold and challenge your sister's reign." My husband turned to my sister. "You must release Horemheb from prison. Release the general and the men will follow him, or you can risk Panahesi getting to the army first with Aten's gold. And if Kiya has a son in her womb, all of Egypt will be lost."

Nefertiti stared, and it was as if she wasn't seeing us anymore. Tears marked her cheeks and she closed her eyes. "I don't care what happens," she said. "I don't care."

But Nakhtmin walked briskly to her, taking her by the shoulders. "Your Highness, Pharaoh Neferneferuaten-Nefertiti, your country is under siege and your crown is being threatened. If you remain here, you will die."

Her eyes were open, but they were lifeless.

"They will kill Meritaten or marry her to Panahesi, and Ankhesenpaaten's life will be forfeit," Nakhtmin said.

Nefertiti's face lifted, almost imperceptibly. Then her eyes grew hard. "Release him from prison."

Nakhtmin nodded, then disappeared down the hall and out into the darkness.

My father turned to me. "Do you trust your husband?"

I stared at him. Nakhtmin could release Horemheb from prison and together they could take the crown. "He would never do that," I promised.

Rebellion swept through the streets. Egyptians were taking up pitchforks and scythes, gathering whatever weapons they could. Every hour a servant ran into the Audience Chamber with news: They had attacked the Temple of Aten in the hills. They were marching on the palace, demanding the return of their gods, a return to Thebes, and the burning of Amarna.

Kiya sat in a chair below the dais, her face a mask of agony. I tried to imagine what she felt. She was the Second Wife to a dead king. Her child would have no father. And when the child came, if it was a son, he would be a threat to Nefertiti's crown.

Only Panahesi could salvage her destiny.

The doors of the Audience Chamber opened and Nakhtmin entered with Horemheb behind him. Prison had not been kind to the general. His hair had grown past his shoulders and a dark beard shadowed his jaw. But there was fire in his eyes, a crazed determination that I had never seen in any man before. My father stood up. "What is the news?"

Horemheb advanced. "The people stormed the Temple of Aten. The body of Pharaoh was burned beyond salvation."

My father looked to Nakhtmin, who added, "The people have stormed the treasury as well. The gold is secure, but seven guards were killed. As well as Vizier Panahesi."

There was a chilling scream. Kiya stood from her chair, her thighs red with blood. But Horemheb was advancing upon the throne. "I have been in prison on order of your husband, *Your Majesty*."

"And I am reinstating you, General," Nefertiti said swiftly, ignoring Kiya's screams. There was no time for anything but the throne. "You shall take control of the army with General Nakhtmin." She returned my husband's position. But Kiya's blood was coming thick and fast.

"My box!" I shouted. "Someone bring me my yarrow!"

"And how do I know you will not betray me?" Horemheb demanded of her.

"How do I know you will not betray *me*?" Nefertiti asked.

I called for servants to find water and linen.

"The reign of Aten is done," Nefertiti added. "I will compensate you for what you have lost. Bring me to my people so that I may tell them that a new reign has come upon us."

"And the Hittites?" Horemheb demanded.

"We will fight," she swore, gripping the crook and flail. "We will wipe them from the face of the East!"

I rushed to make a pillow out of a linen robe for Kiya. "Breathe," I told her. When I looked around the Audience Chamber, I saw that we had been abandoned. Only seven servants remained, the loyal few who had not fled to Thebes. "We must get her to another room!" I cried, and the servants helped me to carry her.

"Please don't let her kill my child," she whispered. Kiya gripped my hand with such fury that I was forced to look into her eyes. "*Please.*"

I realized of whom she was speaking. "She would never . . ." The words died on my lips.

The servants took her into a guest chamber and laid her on the bed, placing pillows behind her.

"We don't have a birthing chair," I said. "I won't—"

Kiya screamed, digging her nails into my flesh. "Raise my child," she begged.

"*No.* You will survive this," I promised. "You will get well." But even as I said this, I knew she would not. She was too pale, the child was coming too early. Beads of sweat lined her brow.

"Swear you will raise him," she pleaded. "Only you can protect him from her. *Please.*" And in a gush of water, the screaming child came. A prince. A Prince of Egypt. Kiya looked down at her son, his lusty wails piercing an empty guest chamber without any amulets or images of Tawaret, and her eyes filled with tears. A knife was brought and the cord was cut. Kiya fell back against the cushions. "Name him Tutankhaten," she said, grasping my fingers as if we'd never been enemies. Then she closed her eyes, and the peace on her face was gentle and soft. She exhaled, and her body grew rigid.

A servant washed the child and wrapped him in linen, pressing the tiny bundle into my arms, and I looked down at the boy who was to become my son, the child of my sister's most bitter rival. I lay him on his mother, so he could know the feel of her breast and that she'd loved him. Then tears welled in my eyes and I cried. I cried for Kiya, for Nefertiti and her children, for Tiye, and for the infant Tutankhaten, who would never know his mother's kiss. Then I cried for Egypt, because in my heart I knew we had abandoned our gods and brought this death upon us.

It looked as though a windstorm had swept through the palace.

Within days, the hangings were torn down, the cabinets emptied, the storage rooms picked clean. Whatever didn't fit in our caravan of ships would remain in Amarna, to be collected later by servants or by the sands of time. Beer remained in the depths of the cellars, as well as bottles of Akhenaten's favorite wine. I took some of the oldest reds for Ipu and stored them with my herbs. The rest would remain until someone broke into the palace and pillaged its stores, or the guards left behind grew desperate enough to raid Pharaoh's cellar. After all, no one would check, and who knew if we'd ever return.

There was no formal good-bye as we stood at the quay. All that mattered to my father was that we moved swiftly. Nefertiti's grip on the crook and flail of Egypt could be broken by a usurper in the army, or a High Priest of Aten, or an angry follower of Amun. Anything might happen, and everything depended on the people's support. The people no longer believed in Amarna. They wanted a return to the old gods, and my father and Nefertiti would give it to them. As we sailed for Thebes, no one thought of what we were leaving behind.

On the prow, Nefertiti looked toward Thebes as she had once done as a girl.

"There will have to be a ceremony," my father said, coming to stand by her. There was a chill in the air. The breeze on the water was crisp.

"A ceremony?" Nefertiti asked numbly.

"A renaming ceremony," my father explained. "The princesses must no longer use Aten in their name. We must show the people we have forgotten Aten and have returned to Amun."

"Forgotten?" Nefertiti's voice broke. "He was my husband. He was a visionary." I saw true affection for him as she closed her eyes. He'd made her Pharaoh of all of Egypt. He'd given her six children. "I will *never* forget."

"Nevertheless, it must be done."

Chapter Thirty

THEBES

1343 BCE

first of Pachons

WE STOOD BEFORE the columns of the temple, looking down to the avenue of ram-headed sphinxes that crouched in the sunset's glow, reminders of what Amunhotep the Magnificent had built and what his son had tried to destroy. The bald-headed priests of Amun and the nobility had gathered. The High Priest of Amun raised his vessel in the air, and I held my breath before the water fell, washing away the name of the Pharaoh who had nearly destroyed Egypt.

"Tutankh-aten, in the name of Amun, god of Thebes and father of us all, you are now Tutankh-amun in the eyes of Osiris."

Nakhtmin held Tut's little head steady as the water washed over him, a child yet too young to understand the significance of his name, while Nefertiti stood beside her daughters.

Ankhesenpaaten knelt upon the ground, baring her neck to the sacred water so that she could become Ankhesenamun. Then the High Priest called for the princess Meritaten, but Nefertiti stepped forward and said forcefully, "No."

There was a brief commotion as those who had gathered realized what she was doing.

"Not Meritaten. She will rule with me. She will be my consort and reminder of our past. Anoint her Meritaten, Queen of Egypt, so that the Aten priests will know they are not abandoned."

Either Nefertiti was clever, pacifying the abandoned Aten priests, or she was not willing to erase the husband who had crowned her Pharaoh of Egypt.

My father inhaled sharply and the High Priest forced an agreeing smile. He took a second vessel filled with oil, raising it above Meritaten. The little princess stepped forward with a grace beyond her seven years, then lowered her head and accepted her crown.

The High Priest hesitated. "And how shall I anoint the Pharaoh of Egypt?" he asked Nefertiti.

The crowd turned to my sister and she looked at me. "As Smenkhare," she announced.

Strong is the Soul of Ra.

Nefertiti had taken an official name without reference to Aten, making it clear to the people that this was a different reign, a return to the time when our empire had spanned from the Euphrates to the mountains of the south. Now there was Egypt and Nubia alone; Akhenaten had given it all away: Knossos, Rhodes, the Jordan Valley, Mycenae. I turned to see Horemheb salute Pharaoh and thought, *It shall not always be this way. Someday Egypt will be great again.*

I looked at Nakhtmin. "You won't return with Horemheb to fight the Hittites?" I asked him.

He smiled down at our sons in their nurses' arms. "No, *miw-sher.* There will be enough work to do here. Soldiers who have never been taught properly under Akhenaten will need to be trained. I can do that. Horemheb will have to make do with someone else."

"But who?" I worried.

"Ramesses, perhaps." My husband indicated a decorated soldier with hair as red as the flaming sun. "He's been commander of the fortress of Sile and will be a vizier someday. I fought with him in Nubia. He's smart as a scribe and a gifted soldier. No one else can outshoot him with the bow and arrow."

"Except you."

Nakhtmin smiled and said nothing to deny it.

That evening, Pharaoh Nefertiti promised the people great victories. In the dazzling vulture-headdress of Nekhbet, the great goddess of war, she vowed that Egypt would take back the land the Heretic had been foolish enough to let slip away.

"We shall take back Rhodes, Mycenae, and Knossos! We shall march into the deserts of Palestine and reclaim the territory that Amunhotep the Magnificent made a vassal to Egypt. And we will not stop until the Hittites are driven from Mitanni back into the hills from which they came!"

The army sent up a cheer to deafen the gods, and only I could see what becoming Pharaoh had cost her. There were lines around her eyes where there had not been before, and a hardness about her countenance that Tiye used to have. My sister raised her fist in the air. "With the protection of Amun, Egypt cannot fail. The reign of the Heretic Pharaoh is done!"

The men cheered as if she had already delivered them victory.

The shields in their hands were new, melted from vessels in the Temple of Aten, and the stone-tipped spears had come from the hundreds of sculptures that had once stood in the halls of Riverside Palace. And while Nefertiti raised her arms triumphantly, I was not fooled. I imagined her beautiful villas filled with sand, and the palace with its windswept curtains standing empty, and I could only guess how heavy her crook and flail must be. Still, she had not lost everything. They could destroy Amarna, her glittering city overlooking the Nile, and they could use her statues for tinder, but they could not erase her. She could still etch her name on the monuments of Thebes.

"There will be no more heresy!" she cried. "Amun, the great god of Egypt, has returned!"

Behind the pylons, my father nodded. He had written to the king of Assyria, sending a gift of seven gold thrones—payment for a single plague-ridden arm. Only time would tell if seven thrones were enough, or if there would be war in Assyria as well.

My mother stood beside me. "All that's left is Meritaten," she murmured. "There will never be a prince."

"There's Ankhesenamun," I told her.

We watched the four-year-old princess creep nearer the Window of Appearances. She had all of Nefertiti's wild beauty and none of Meritaten's seriousness. She would be full of mischief when she was older.

When the army marched out, ten thousand strong to the kingdom of Mitanni, Nakhtmin touched my elbow. Across the Audience Chamber, Nefertiti said, "You're not leaving, are you?"

I looked at my sister with the crook and flail of Egypt in her hand, still worried that she was going to be alone. "I have two sons across the river waiting for me."

"But you'll come back in the evenings, won't you? You'll come every day?"

"We'll come every evening," I promised. "I'll bring Baraka and Tut so they can grow up with their cousins." She frowned deeply, and I said, "He's my son, Nefertiti. He's no more a Prince of Egypt now than Baraka or Nakhtmin."

Nefertiti bit back what she wanted to say. "But you will come," she repeated.

"Yes," I replied, and added to myself, *As I have always done.*

◙ ◙ ◙

Heqet was singing softly to Baraka and little Tutankhamun, hovering in the open window that looked out over the sweeping gardens. She looked up when she heard our footfalls along the path, then rushed out to the loggia to greet us.

"A woman named Ipu was here to see you, my lady. She left this." Heqet indicated a small box on the table. "She's says it's something new she found. She thought you might want it for your garden."

I opened the wooden lid, and inside was a small, pink flower still attached to its root. It was in bloom, and I ran my finger over its delicate petals. They were long and smooth, the texture of linen that's been woven very fine. I studied its perfect color, the shade of a setting sun. To have my garden, my home, and my family, to be able to step into the sunshine and feel the warm soil beneath my hands and the life growing beneath my feet . . .

Heqet stopped what she was doing. "Are you well, my lady?"

"Yes. I am simply glad to be home."

Heqet straightened, surveying the painted walls and linen baskets. "And what will you do now without the court?" she asked me.

"I will fulfill my destiny," I said. "In my children's nursery and in my garden."

I knocked on the painted door with its carved image of a ship at sea.

"My lady!" Ipu's squeal of pleasure echoed in the streets.

Her cheeks were plumper and her hair had grown past her shoulders. The wail of a tiny voice broke out behind her, where Kamoses was waiting in his father's arms. I was astonished at how he had grown. "Look how big!"

"More than a year now. And he's such a pleasure that I'm ready to do it again." She rested her hand on her stomach and smiled. "In Mesore."

I gasped. "Oh, Ipu . . ."

"Look who's talking!" she cried. "You are the mother of two sons." She stepped back to look at me and beamed. "Oh, my lady. After so long." She embraced me, then ushered me inside.

"Welcome home," Djedi said. He looked healthy and contented. Plague had not come to any city but Amarna, and I tried not to think what that meant.

"So this is Kamoses," I said, trying to imagine that this was the same baby I had waved farewell to a year ago on the quay. "He is handsome. He has your nose," I told Ipu.

"And Djedi's eyes. The midwife says he'll be wealthy."

"How does she know?"

"Because his first cry was *nub*."

I laughed loudly. "*Gold?* I have missed you, Ipu."

"And Ipu has missed you." Djedi grinned. "You were all she would talk about."

"Amarna is all anyone would talk about," she confided. "No one knew what to believe. First a Durbar, then a coregent, then plague. Is it true"—her voice fell—"that Pharaoh sent an arm to the king of Assyria?" I nodded, and Ipu shook her head. "Tell me everything. I want to know *everything*."

So I told her of the Durbar and my sister's coronation, then of the Black Death and Akhenaten's offering. I described the deaths of Nefertiti's youngest, the death of Nebnefer, and finally Tiye. When I spoke of Akhenaten's ride through the city, Djedi placed Kamoses in his crib. He could not believe he had gone out unescorted to tear down forbidden images of Amun. "Pharaoh was full of rage," I told him, but it was impossible to explain the bitterness in Akhenaten's eyes when he watched his children burn in the city he had built for Aten.

"When they forbid the barges from leaving Amarna, we thought everyone inside would perish," Ipu admitted, and her eyes grew teary. "Including you and Nakhtmin."

I embraced her. "And we had no way of knowing whether the plague had spread. It was frightening for us, too." Something rubbed against my leg and a large, heavy body appeared in my lap. "Bastet," I exclaimed. I looked at Ipu.

"He followed me from the workshop one evening and never returned. You can take him back now," she added, but I saw the hesitation in her eyes.

"Of course not. You must keep him," I said earnestly. "He would have died with all the other palace cats had you not saved him."

"They slaughtered the *miws?"*

"Every animal in the palace was put to death."

"Where did they bury the bodies?" Djedi asked.

"Carts came and took them away."

"Without amulets?" Djedi whispered.

"And without tombs?" Ipu cried.

"Mass graves. Holes dug in the ground and covered with sand."

The pair of them were silent.

We walked to my house later in the warm evening, and Ipu wanted to hear the story for a second time of Kiya's deathbed request that I should take her child. I told it again, and even the fussy Kamoses was quiet, as if he too were spellbound by the tale.

"Nothing has happened as I imagined it," said Ipu. "Egypt is a land turned upside down. You are raising a Prince of Egypt," she marveled.

"No, not a Prince of Egypt," I said firmly. "Just a little boy."

We fell into a quiet routine in Thebes, and there was a peaceful rhythm to our life. Men came from around the city to visit Nakhtmin, telling him tales of what had been happening in Thebes while Amarna was being ravaged by plague. Then they tried to tempt him back to war, saying it was a waste of his time to teach soldiers when he could be leading men to victory in Rhodes. The soldiers stood outside our house and shook their heads and looked accusingly at me.

"He is the finest general in Pharaoh's army," Djedefhor said. "The men can't understand why he won't return. They begged me to come here and ask him. Horemheb is hard. He is mirthless, and the men don't love him the way they love Nakhtmin."

I thought again of my father's words, *Do you trust him?* and looked out to where Nakhtmin was instructing my sister's soldiers. The muscles were hard beneath his kilt, his brow was seeded with sweat. I smiled. "They will simply have to content themselves with the knowledge that he's turning their boys into men."

"But what will you do while you're not at court and he's not fighting?"

I laughed at the earnestness in Djedefhor's question. "Live a quiet life," I said. "And someday Nakhtmin will teach our sons to be soldiers or scribes."

Djedefhor looked at me strangely. "Sons?"

"There is Tut," I reminded him sharply.

We both stared across the garden to where two boys were crawling beneath the shade of an old acacia. Heqet was there, watching over them. "Kiya's son," he said, then added, "a possible Prince of Egypt."

"Never," I replied. "He'll be raised here, away from court. Meritaten will be Pharaoh next, then Ankhesenamun."

I knew what he wanted to say. That there had to be a prince for Egypt, that there had always been and there always would be. But instead he said simply, "I assume you've heard of the deal that's been struck with the Aten priests?"

"That they were given a fortnight to shed their robes for the vestments of Amun?"

"Yes. And some refused."

I glanced at him in shock. "But they can't refuse. They'll have nowhere to go."

"They will have the homes of Aten believers. There are many, my lady. Children who never knew Amun and followers who only left Amarna when their houses were burned. There could be trouble from them."

That evening, I entered the Hall of Books in the palace and a young scribe led me to my father. His back was turned to me. In his hand was a sheaf of papyrus bound by leather. "Father?"

"Mutnodjmet." He turned around. "I thought I heard you."

"What are you doing?"

He put down the sheaf of papers and sighed. "Studying maps of Assyria."

"Then seven thrones were not enough?"

"No. They have allied themselves with the Hittites," he replied.

I sighed. "Akhenaten did great damage. Why did Nefertiti allow it?"

"Your sister did more than you realize. She kept him occupied while your aunt and I dealt with Egypt's affairs. She took gold from the Temple of Aten so that we could keep the army fed and pay foreign kings to remain our allies. Loyalty does not come cheap."

"Akhenaten never paid the army?"

"No." My father passed me a significant glance. "Nefertiti did."

We stood in silence. "How did she hide the gold?" I asked him.

"She disguised it as projects for Aten. And it was not just a handful of copper deben. It was chests full of gold."

"And what of the Aten priests now? A soldier tells me they will be trouble for Nefertiti."

"If she continues to meet with them."

"On her own?" My voice was too loud. It echoed in the Per Medjat.

"And against my advice." But my father didn't ask me to try and change her mind. She was twenty-seven years old. A woman and a king.

"But why would she meet with them?"

"Why?" He heaved a heavy sigh of his own. "Why? I don't know. A sense that she owes them something, perhaps."

"But what could she owe them? They are killing Amun priests. Perhaps she is hoping to bring it to an end," I suggested.

"The fighting? That will never end. They believe that Aten is the god of Egypt, and the people believe in the power of Amun."

I settled back against the wall. "So there will always be war."

"Always. So be thankful you have the peace of your garden. Perhaps your mother and I will take refuge there when the cares of Thebes become too heavy."

"As they are now?"

He smiled grimly. "As they are now."

Chapter Thirty-One

1335 BCE

Akhet, Season of Overflow

BARAKA'S MUSCLES GREW taut as he drew back a feathered arrow, sending it swiftly to its target at the edge of the courtyard in a flash of red and gold.

"Well done," Nakhtmin praised.

Baraka gave a satisfied nod from the grass. He looked like his father, with the same wide shoulders and crop of dark hair brushing the nape of his neck. It was impossible to tell that he was only nine. He could have been a boy of eleven or twelve.

"It's your turn now," Baraka said, moving back so Ankhesenamun could step up to the target.

"I bet I can hit closer than Tut," she bragged. "While you've been studying, I've been out here practicing with Nakhtmin," she taunted Tutankhamun. She drew her small arm back and the bow tautened.

"Steady," Baraka advised.

The arrow flew, slicing very near the center of the target, and Ankhesenamun let out a squeal of delight. Baraka covered his ears.

"Very good," Nakhtmin said approvingly. "You're becoming a fine soldier, Ankhesenamun. Soon your mother is going to have to let you practice with my students."

"I'd like to be a soldier someday!"

Nakhtmin looked across the bower at me. No child could have been more different from her father.

"Come," she crowed. "Let's row back to the palace and show my mother what I can do."

"Do you think the queen will like that?" Baraka asked practically.

Ankhesenamun pushed back her forelock of youth. In two years, she would shave it and become a woman. "Who *cares* what Meritaten thinks? All she does is read scrolls and recite poetry. She's like Tutankhamun," she accused, and Tut took offense.

"I'm nothing like the queen!" he protested. "I hunt every day."

"You also recite poetry," she goaded.

"So what? Our father wrote poetry."

Baraka froze, and Ankhesenamun covered her mouth with her hands.

"It's fine," Nakhtmin cut in swiftly.

"But Tut said . . ." Ankhesenamun didn't finish.

"It doesn't matter what Tut said. Why don't we visit your mother now and show her what you can do? She'll be waiting for us anyway."

The sun had nearly set. We would be expected soon in the Great Hall of Malkata. While a pair of servants rowed across the river, Ankhesenamun leaned over in the bark.

"You shouldn't have said that about Father."

"Leave him alone," Baraka said, defending Tut. "He was your father, too."

She set her jaw. "I bet Mutnodjmet wouldn't approve of it."

"Approve of what?" I smiled innocently, and all three children looked up at me.

Ankhesenamun did her best to look morally superior. "Speaking about the Heretic King. I know you wouldn't approve of it," she said.

"My mother says he shouldn't be spoken about, especially in public, and that he's the reason there's rebellion in Lower Egypt. If he hadn't abandoned the gods and created the Aten priests, they wouldn't be fighting in the north, and our priests in Thebes would be safe at night because there'd be no one attacking them or leading revolts."

"Your mother said all that?" Nakhtmin asked curiously.

"Yes." But Ankhesenamun was still staring at me, waiting for my answer, and eventually everyone in the bark turned to see what I would say.

"Perhaps it is better not to speak of the Pharaoh Akhenaten in public," I admitted and Ankhesenamun gave Tutankhamun a wise look. "However, there is nothing wrong with remembering the good a person did."

Ankhesenamun stared at me. Nakhtmin raised his brows.

"He wrote poetry." I hesitated. "And he was skilled with the bow and arrow. That is where the two of you might have inherited it from."

"My *mother* was good with the bow," Ankhesenamun contradicted.

"That's true, but Akhenaten was especially swift." And at once, I thought of the woman in the Audience Chamber trying to save her child by fleeing from the plague. I drew my cloak closer to my chest, and Ankhesenamun leaned over in the bark as if there was an important question she needed answered.

"Was my father really a heretic?" she asked.

I shifted uncomfortably on my cushion, avoiding Nakhtmin's gaze. "He was a great believer in Aten," I said carefully.

"Is that why mother meets with the Aten priests, even though Vizier Ay says that it's dangerous? Is it because our father believed in Aten and she feels sorry?"

I met Nakhtmin's glance. "I don't know," I replied. "I don't know why she meets with them when everyone's told her it's a dangerous thing. Maybe she still feels sad."

"About what?"

"About being deceived by Aten when Amun is the great god of Egypt," Baraka declared.

▣ ▣ ▣

Nefertiti met with the Aten priests despite her viziers' protests, against all common sense and my father's warnings.

"I will fix this," she swore, walking the battlements of the new wall around Thebes. With age, her delicate beauty had hardened into something knifelike and more defining. She was thirty-one now.

"But what if there's no fixing it?" I asked. "They're criminals. They want power, and they're willing to kill to have it again."

She shook her head firmly. "I won't allow there to be discord in Egypt."

"But there will always be discord. There will always be disagreement."

"Not in my Egypt! I will talk with them." She gripped the crenellations and stared out beyond the Nile. The sun beat down on the freshly cut stones, baking them in the heat of Mesore. From here we could see the entire city: my villa across the River Nile, the towering images of Amunhotep the Elder, the Temple of Amun, and hundreds of royal statuary.

"What can talking do? These men have killed Amun priests," I said. "They should be sent to the quarries."

"I'm the People's Queen. There shall be peace in this land while I'm its ruler."

"And how will meeting with them achieve it?"

"Perhaps I can convince them to turn to Amun. To stop fighting." Nefertiti glanced sideways at me to see if I was listening. "I have so many visions, Mutnodjmet. Of an Egypt that stretches again from the Euphrates in the east to Kush in the south. Of a land where Amun and Aten can both reside. Tomorrow, I'm meeting with two Aten priests. They have petitioned to have a temple—"

"Nefertiti," I said firmly.

"I can't grant them the use of Amun's temples. But their own temple... Why not?"

"Because they will still want more!"

She grew quiet, looking out over Thebes. "I will make peace with them," she vowed.

* * *

The next evening I rushed into the Per Medjat and my father looked up, startled. "Have you seen Nefertiti?" I asked.

"She's in the Audience Chamber. With Meritaten."

"No. Thutmose saw her with two Aten priests. She swore she would meet us in the Great Hall, but she isn't there!"

His eyes met mine, and then we were running. The hour for petitioners was already done. We burst through the doors of the Great Hall and the palace guards tensed. "Find Pharaoh!" my father shouted, and the fear in his voice sent a dozen men springing into action, opening doors, shouting Nefertiti's name. From down the hall, we could hear the men calling, "Your Majesty!" as we opened doors, finding nobody.

A sick feeling bore into my stomach, a feeling I'd never had before.

Nakhtmin found us in the Great Hall. "What's happened?"

"Nefertiti! No one can find her. Thutmose says he saw her talking with two Aten priests." He saw the fear in my eyes, and at once he was moving down the hall and commanding his men to lock every door in the palace. "Let no one out!" he shouted.

Ankhesenamun came with Tutankhamun by her side. "What's happening? Who's missing?"

"Nefertiti and Meritaten. Go into the Audience Chamber and don't come out." I thought of the Window of Appearances, where Nefertiti sometimes took messengers to show them the city. The children hesitated. "Go!" I demanded.

I ran through the palace, sweat from beneath my wig trickling into my eyes. I threw off the hairpiece, not caring where it landed or who picked it up. "Nefertiti!" I shouted. "Meritaten!" How could they both be gone? Where could they be? I rounded the corner to the Window of Appearances, then opened the door.

The blood had already spread across the tiles.

"Nefertiti!" I screamed, and my voice echoed through the palace. "NEFERTITI! This can't be happening!" I rocked her against me. *"It can't be happening!"* I held my sister's body against my chest, but she was already cold. Then my father and Nakhtmin were standing beside me.

"Search the palace!" Nakhtmin shouted. "I want every chamber searched! Every cabinet, every chest, every door into the cellars!" He could see the knife on the floor, he could see how deep the cut to Meritaten's side was.

I collapsed in a heap over my niece. "Akhenaten!" I screamed so that Anubis could hear me. They had been *his* priests, *his* religion. My father tried to part me from Nefertiti, but I wouldn't be parted. He bent down next to me and we both held our queen, my sister, his daughter, the woman who had ruled our lives for thirty-one years.

My mother came running with Ankhesenamun and Tutankhamun behind her, despite my orders.

"In the name of Amun . . . ," my mother whispered. It was too late to tell the children to leave. They had seen what the Aten priests had done.

"Be careful!" I cried. But what was there to be careful of?

Ankhesenamun bent down and touched her sister. Fifteen years old and her life cut short. She looked over at me, and Tutankhamun closed Meritaten's eyes.

I held Nefertiti's body closer to mine, trying to press her spirit into me, to bring it back.

But the reign of Nefertiti was finished. She was gone from Egypt.

"Shh," I heard Nakhtmin whisper to my son. "Your mother's not well."

"Should I bring her chamomile?" Baraka asked.

"Yes." Nakhtmin nodded. My husband moved to my bedside, looking down at me, then he unstrapped his sword and sat by my side. "Mutnodjmet," he said gently. *"Miw-sher."* He caressed my cheek. "I'm sorry, but I have come with bad news. I wanted to give it to you before you heard it from someone else."

I swallowed my fear. *Gods, don't let it be my mother or father.*

"Your sister's body has been desecrated. Aten priests stormed the mortuary and tried to destroy her."

I threw off my linen covers. "I must see her!" I cried.

"Don't." He held my arm. "The damage is . . ." He hesitated. "Extensive."

I covered my mouth. "To her face?" I whispered.

He lowered his gaze. "And chest."

The places where the *ka* resided. They had tried to obliterate her soul. They had tried to kill her in death as well as in life! "But why?" I screamed, stumbling from my bed. "Why?"

"The embalmers will fix her," he swore.

But I was wild with rage. *"How* can they fix her? She was beautiful!" I crumpled in his arms. "So beautiful."

"The embalmers know how, and then they will entomb her secretly tonight. Already a new sarcophagus has been made. Tut can use hers someday. He will be Pharaoh next."

Our Tut? Only nine years old? "But how will Osiris know her face?" I sobbed.

"They have her statues from Amarna. They'll carve her name on every wall of the new tomb. Osiris will find her."

But my tears came harder. I couldn't stop them. I looked up at

Nakhtmin through my pain, realizing for the first time what he had said. "And the funeral?"

"Tonight. No one will go but your father and the High Priest of Amun. It's too dangerous. They could find her and destroy her a second time." He gathered me in his arms. "I'm so sorry, Mutnodjmet."

They wept for her in the streets. She was their queen, their Pharaoh of Egypt. She had restored Thebes to them and had rebuilt the shining temples of Amun. I stood at the window of the Audience Chamber, watching the masses that crushed against the gates, covering them with amulets and flowers. Some were hysterical, others came silently, and I felt as if my heart had turned to stone, it was so heavy inside of me.

Nefertiti was gone.

She had sent our army to victories in Rhodes and Lakisa, but never again would she wear the headdress of Nekhbet and raise her arms to greet the people. I would never hear her laughter or see her sharp eyes narrow with displeasure. I heard my father's footsteps in the hall. *He's come to look for me.* The door to the empty Audience Chamber creaked open and the sharp slap of his sandals disturbed the silence.

"Mutnodjmet."

I didn't turn.

"Mutnodjmet, we are meeting in the Per Medjat. You should come now. It is about Tutankhamun."

I didn't reply, and he came to stand at my shoulder.

"She was buried with care," he informed me. "With all the statues of Amarna and the riches of Thebes." His voice gave away his deep sadness and I turned. The love he'd had for her was wrought in the lines on his face. He looked so much older, but there was still Egypt to rule. There would always be Egypt, with or without Nefertiti.

"It's not fair." I choked back a sob. "Why would the Aten priests kill her? *Why?*"

"Because she created passionate believers," he said. "Believers willing to do anything to silence someone who was attacking them."

"But she was Pharaoh!" I cried. "What does killing her achieve? What does it get them?"

"Fear. They are hoping the next Pharaoh will fear them so much that he will let their temples stand. They don't see that unless the next Pharaoh returns Aten's temples to Amun, he is dead anyway."

"Because the people will rise," I realized.

My father nodded.

"So it's either the people or Aten's priests as enemies."

"And no Pharaoh would stand against his own people."

I blinked away my tears. "Time should stand still," I whispered. "It shouldn't go on."

My father watched me silently.

"All of Egypt should have crumbled before she died! And Meritaten . . . only fifteen years old." The terror and loneliness of living in a world without Nefertiti overwhelmed me. "What will we all do?" I panicked. "What will our family do?"

"We will prepare for a new reign in Egypt," my father said. "And we will meet in the Per Medjat when you are ready."

Chapter Thirty-Two

Peret, Season of Growing

KING TUTANKHAMUN ASCENDED the dais to the Horus thrones with the Princess Ankhesenamun by his side, and I watched my father whisper into his ear the way he had done with Nefertiti.

"Your father is the power behind the throne once more," Nakhtmin observed.

"Only this time it is for our son." A faint breeze stirred the summer heat, laden with the scents of lotus blossom and myrrh. I grasped my husband's hand. "I will never escape it, will I?"

"The Horus thrones?" Nakhtmin shook his head. "No, it doesn't seem that you will. But this time will be different," he promised. "This time Egypt will prosper, and there will be no rebellion under Pharaoh Tutankhamun."

"How do you know?"

"Because I am here, and because Horemheb will destroy the Hittites and return victorious for the glory of Amun. In fifteen years, Aten will be forgotten."

A shiver passed through me as I thought of Nefertiti's city lying in the sand, swept away by the winds of time. Everything she had worked so hard for had failed. But there was Ankhesenamun. I looked up at the dais and the little girl who looked so much like my sister, and I found it strange that I should be sitting in the same chair I had occupied when Nefertiti had ruled. How much would this child remember of her mother? She turned her gaze in my direction, the same dark eyes and willowy neck, and I wondered what she and my son would write together on the pillars of eternity.

Afterword

NEFERTITI'S STORY IS one that can be pieced together from the hundreds of images excavated at Amarna. Devoted to art, she and Akhenaten covered the city with carvings of themselves and Aten, a minor deity that Akhenaten elevated to supreme status. And so that no one could confuse him with any other Pharaoh, the portraits of Akhenaten and his royal family were created to be distinct. Their long necks, elongated heads, and feminine hips are unique to the Amarna period. In many ways, Nefertiti and Akhenaten revolutionized Egyptian art. But it was their heretical abandonment of Amun for which they were remembered, and for which Horemheb would destroy Amarna block by block upon becoming Pharaoh, with Mutnodjmet as his queen, as is recorded in history.

Historically, the Pharaoh Horemheb married Mutnodjmet after the rest of her family had died, for she represented the last royal link to the throne. There is circumstantial evidence that Horemheb took Mutny by force as his wife. In *The Heretic Queen,* the sequel to *Nefertiti,* these last tumultuous years of Mutny's life are described, as is the fascinating reign of her daughter, Queen Nefertari. However, in *Nefertiti* I chose to depict Mutny's earlier years, when she married for love.

It would also be prudent to note that many names in this book have been changed for the convenience of the reader. For example, the city of Akhet-aten is called by its present name of Amarna, while Waset has been changed to its modern-day equivalent of Thebes. Much of this novel is faithful to history: from such household details as the interest the ancient Egyptians had in aging their wine to the paintings on the dais in Malkata. However, some liberties have been taken with personalities, names, and minor events. For instance, no one can be certain how Mutnodjmet felt about her sister's vision of an Egypt without the Amun priests. But in an image of her found in Amarna, she is seen standing alone, her arms at her sides, while everyone else enthusiastically embraces Aten. In a period where art attempted to portray reality for the first time, I found this significant. And while Nefertiti did have six daughters with Akhenaten, so far as we know she never produced twins.

Other historical uncertainties remain: Did Amunhotep the Younger ever have a coregency with his father? Did Nefertiti ever rule on her own? How old was Nefertiti when she died? What killed Tiye? These are mysteries that thus far can only be answered by conjecture, and in the end I chose the interpretations that seemed most probable.

In the years to come, some of these questions might be answered by the discovery of the Amarna mummies. Although much of Kiya's funerary equipment was found in Tutankhamun's tomb, little to nothing remains of what belonged to Akhenaten or Nefertiti. Some archaeologists contend that a cache of mummies found in tomb KV35 are the bodies of Nefertiti and the Dowager Queen. If so, they were stunning beauties even in death. If not, the search for two of the most powerful women in Egypt's history continues.

Glossary

Alabaster: A hard, marble-like mineral mined in Alabastron, a village in Egypt.

Ammit: The god of karmic retribution, who was often depicted with the body of a lion and the head of a crocodile. During one's passage through the Afterlife, if a person's heart weighed more than Ma'at's feather of truth, Ammit would eat their souls and condemn them to oblivion.

Amun: The most important god in Egypt and the creator of all things. His wife was Mut.

Ankh: A symbol of life, resembling a looped cross.

Anubis: The guardian of the dead, who weighed the deceased's heart on the scales of justice to determine whether they should continue their journey into the Blessed Lands. He was often depicted as having the head of a jackal, since jackals were seen to lurk near the Valley of the Kings, where the dead resided.

Aten: A sun disk worshipped during the reign of Akhenaten.

Bastet (or Bast): The goddess of the sun and moon. She was also a war goddess, depicted as a lion or a cat.

Bes: The dwarf-god of fertility and childbirth.

Calendar:

SEASON	MONTH	FESTIVAL	DATES
Akhet Autumn	Thoth	Wag Festival	July 19–August 17
	Phaophi	Opet Festival	August 18–September 16
	Aythyr	Festival of Hathor	September 17–October 16
	Choiak		October 17–November 15
Peret Winter	Tybi		November 16–December 15
	Mechyr	Festival of Isis	December 16–January 14
	Phamenoth		January 15–February 13
	Pharmuthi		February 14–March 15
Shemu Summer	Pachons		March 16–April 14
	Payni	Feast of the Valley	April 15–May 14
	Epiphi		May 15–June 13
	Mesore		June 14–July 13
The Epagomenal Days			July 14–18

Canopic Jars: Four burial jars in which a person's most important organs (liver, lungs, stomach, intestines) were preserved for the Afterlife. Each jar was carved with one of the heads of Horus's four sons.

Cartouche: A circle with a horizontal bar at the bottom on which the king's name was written.

Crook and flail: The Pharaoh held these implements as a symbol of royalty and to remind the people of his role as shepherd (crook) and provider (flail, used for threshing grain).

Cuneiform: A pictographic language inscribed on clay tablets and first used by the Sumerians. It was later used by the Hittites.

Deben: Rings of gold, silver, or copper that had fixed weights and were used as units of currency.

Faience: Glazed ceramic used for small beads or amulets.

Hathor: The goddess of joy, motherhood, and love. She was often depicted as a cow.

Horus: The falcon-headed god of the sun and sky.

Ibis: A wading bird with a long, curved bill.

Isis: The goddess of beauty and magic. She was also revered as a wife and mother.

Ka: A person's spirit or soul, which was created at birth.

Khepresh crown: A blue ceremonial crown of war.

Kohl: A mascara and eye shadow made from mixing soot with oil.

Ma'at: The goddess of justice and truth. Ma'at was often depicted as a woman with wings (or a woman wearing a crown with one feather). During the Afterlife, a person's heart would be weighed against one of her feathers to determine whether they were worthy of passing into the Blessed Land. The word *Ma'at* came to stand for the principles of justice, order, and propriety, which every Egyptian was responsible for upholding.

Mawat: Mother.

Miw: Cat.

Montu: The hawk-headed god of war.

Mortuary temple: A temple (often distinct from the tomb of the deceased) built to commemorate a person's life.

Mut: The goddess of motherhood and the female partner of Amun. She was often depicted with the head of a cat.

Nemes crown: A royal crown made of a head cloth that was striped blue and gold. It is the crown depicted on Tutankhamun's sarcophagus.

Osiris: The husband of the goddess Isis and the judge of the dead. He was murdered by his brother, Set, who scattered pieces of his body across Egypt. When Isis gathered his body parts together, she resurrected him, and he became the symbol of eternal life. Osiris was often depicted as a bearded man dressed in mummy wrappings.

Papyrus: A type of reed plentiful on the Nile Delta, which could be dried and smoothed, then used for writing.

Per Medjat: Library.

Pschent crown: The red and white double crown symbolizing both Upper and Lower Egypt.

Ptah: The god of builders and artists.

Pylon: A gate or stone entryway, often accompanied by statues on either side.

Ra: The god of the sun, who was often depicted as a hawk.

Renpet: An entire year, according to the Egyptian calendar, which comprised 365 days (twelve months of thirty days each, with an extra five days added to the end).

Sarcophagus: A stone tomb or coffin, often covered in gold.

Sekhmet: The lion-headed goddess of war and destruction.

Senet: Considered to be the world's first board game, Senet later became a religious symbol and was often depicted in tombs.

Senit: Little girl.

Set: The god of storms, chaos, and evil, who killed his brother Osiris. When he was not depicted with the head of an unknown animal, he was shown as having red hair.

Shedeh: A favorite Egyptian drink made from either pomegranates or grapes.

Sistrum: A small bronze (or brass) instrument made from a handle and a u-shaped frame on which small discs were placed. When shaken, the instrument made a loud, tinny noise.

Tawaret: The goddess of childbirth, who was often depicted as a hippopotamus.

Thoth: The god of scribes and the author of the famous *Book of the Dead*. He was credited with inventing both writing and speech, and he was often depicted as an ibis-headed god.

Uraeus: The cobra crown that symbolized kingship. The cobra was depicted with its hood flared, and it was thought to be able to spit fire into the eyes of the wearer's enemies.

Vizier: An adviser to the royal family.

Acknowledgments

FIRST AND FOREMOST, I would like to thank my father, Robert Francis Moran, for instilling in me a passion for history. You were my greatest champion and my staunchest advocate, and I miss you more than words can ever express. It will always be my deepest regret that you never saw *Nefertiti* published, but I must trust that from where you are, you know it now. I would also like to thank my mother, Carol Moran, for being my closest friend, my greatest confidante, and my support in every meaning of the word. Without you, *Nefertiti* would not exist. Your kindness and love is an inspiration to me.

I cannot forget to thank my husband, Matthew Carter, whose generosity with his time also made writing possible. You are my first editor and my most beloved fan. Thank you for believing so deeply in me and for putting up with so many long writing hours.

Of course, writing is not a solitary endeavor once a work is produced and sent out into the world. I owe an immense debt of gratitude to my peerless agent, Anna Ghosh, who believed in me enough to wait while I wrote *Nefertiti*. Thank you, Anna, in more ways than you know. Danny Baror has been an amazing foreign agent, seeing to it that *Nefertiti* can be read in more than sixteen foreign languages and counting. And to Allison

McCabe, my incredible editor who contributed immensely to the novel that is here before you, I am deeply indebted. Your eye for detail is unsurpassable. Working with you has been such a pleasure, and I have especially enjoyed your photos of Audrey. Long may she reign as the finest Italian Greyhound in New York.

For all of the wonderful help I have received since writing *Nefertiti*, becoming an author does not happen in a vacuum, either. Most authors can look back on their past and see the events and experiences that have shaped who they are and what they eventually write about. For this reason, I am grateful to the Los Angeles Museum of Natural History for offering summer classes in the sciences for children. These classes sparked an interest in history that my father molded and my teachers refined. I am thankful as well to Pomona College and Claremont Graduate University for helping to send me to Israel on the archaeological dig that inspired me to write in the genre of historical fiction.

I have also been blessed in my academic career to come across teachers who have been great inspirations: Gayle Hauser, Ed LeVine, Kenneth Medina, Ernestine Potts, and Professor Martha E. Andresen, who made Shakespeare come back to life from the sixteenth century.

And, of course, I owe a debt of thanks as well to the team at Crown. My production editor Cindy Berman and proofreader extraordinaire, Shelley Bennett, spent hours upon hours making sure that among all the births and deaths in *Nefertiti*, there were no timeline inconsistencies. This was a Herculean task, and between their sharp eyes and my husband's, every month in Nefertiti's life has been accounted for. Sarah C. Breivogel and Dyana Messina have been amazing publicists, casting the publicity net far and wide for *Nefertiti*. Publishing is always a group effort, and to everyone who contributed to *Nefertiti*'s success at Crown, I am deeply appreciative.

Last, I would like to put on record how lucky I have been in having friends and family who've always believed in my writing career: Robert William Moran, Tracy Carpenter, the Armstrong-Carters, my Markstein family, my Moran family, Cathy Carpenter, Judy Indig, Bobbie Kenyon, and Barbara Ballinger . . . just to name a few. Fellow author M. J. Rose, your advice on all things publishing-related has been simply invaluable. And to my wonderful cast of teaching assistants without whom I would never have had the time to write: Monica Castañeda, Cynthia Castellanos, Jésica Castillo, Dilery Lovillo, and Catherine Perez. Thank you all so much.

A READER'S GROUP GUIDE

Nefertiti brings a fascinating chapter of Egyptian history to life. This guide is intended as a starting point for your discussion of this captivating story of two sisters, one of whom is destined to rule Egypt.

1. Thousands of years after the Pharaoh's ruled Egypt, this ancient civilization continues to fascinate the world. Why were you drawn to Nefertiti? What aspects of Egyptian life do you find interesting?

2. History remembers Nefertiti as a great beauty. What other parts of her personality are highlighted in *Nefertiti*? How does she use her good looks to her advantage? How do they hurt her? Have you ever known a woman like Nefertiti? Overall, is this a positive portrayal of her as a queen? As a sister?

3. Discuss Mutnodjmet and Nefertiti's relationship throughout the novel. In what ways are they jealous of each other? What makes two women who are raised together differ so greatly? What traits do they have in common? Can you think of a relationship you've had with a sister or friend that was similar?

4. Nefertiti knows she must convince Amunhotep that she is more than his mother's choice of bride. How does she do it? How does Kiya attempt to keep him? What do their powerful fathers do to create an intense rivalry between these women? What is the nature of the Pharaoh's relationship with each? Who do you think Amunhotep loved more? Why?

5. Do you feel Amunhotep is a tragic figure or a villain? What makes you think this? How would he be received today?

6. General Nakhtmin is impressed by Mutnodjmet from their first meeting, while she pretends to be uninterested in him. Why? What finally convinces her to admit her love for him? Why do Nefertiti and Amunhotep oppose the marriage?

7. Was Nefertiti's father, Vizier Ay, a wise man or was he a slave to his ambitions? Discuss the level of loyalty he asks from Mutnodjmet. In what ways does she disappoint him? In what ways does their relationship seem modern?

8. When the Elder dies Amunhotep becomes Pharaoh of both Upper and Lower Egypt—meaning he is free to do as he wishes. Nefertiti is

entitled to the dowager queen's crown but doesn't take it. What does she do instead? Why doesn't Nefertiti demand this symbol of all she has worked to attain? What does it mean for her family?

9. Desperate for a son, Nefertiti asks Mutnodjmet to take her to visit a shrine to Tawaret, the hippo goddess of birth. What does the fact that Neferetiti calls on the old gods in times of trouble say about her belief in Aten? Why does she ask her sister to pray for her? Discuss the importance of religion throughout the novel.

10. When the plague comes to Amarna, Mutnodjmet decides to stay instead of leaving for the safety of Thebes. Why? What would you have done in her position?

11. What happens to Amunhotep? How is his fate justified? Does Nefertiti deserve what happens to her? Why or why not?

A CONVERSATION WITH MICHELLE MORAN

Q: What inspired you to write about a queen who's been dead for more than three thousand years?

A: My love-affair with Egyptology began in the summer of 1998 on an archaeological dig in Israel. While our team was working to unearth an ancient trading post, we came across a scarab, proof that the Egyptians had traveled north, perhaps selling cloth, incense, or Nubian gold. Looking at the mysterious lapis stone in the dirt, untouched for who knew how many years, I was hooked. It wasn't long before I found myself wandering through Egyptian exhibits in Los Angeles, London, and Berlin, where the stunning bust of Nefertiti rests behind a case of polished glass. Even three thousand years later it fills the viewer with the same awe that citizens of Amarna must have felt when they saw her. I wondered who she was, and what her story must have been. As I began research into Nefertiti's life, I was surprised to discover that while many books and internet sites were devoted to her, there were no fictionalized accounts exclusively about her reign—one of the most enigmatic of any Egyptian Pharaoh-Queen. Spurred on by Nefertiti's untold story, I visited Egypt on an historical tour two years later, gathering books and writing down impressions of what had once been the most powerful kingdom in the ancient world.

Q: Did Mutnodjmet really exist?

A: Yes, Mutnodjmet really existed, as did Nefertiti, Queen Tiye, Akhenaten, Vizier Ay, Lady Kiya, General Horemheb, General Nakhtmin . . . Suffice it to say that almost every character in the book was based on an historical personage.

Q: So how much of the story is true?

A: While the main historical events are accurate, such as Ay's rise to power, Akhenaten's obsession with Aten, the dream of Amarna, and Nefertiti's unparalleled influence at court, liberties were taken with personalities, names, and minor historical events. For instance, no one can be certain how Mutnodjmet felt about her sister's vision of an Egypt without the Amun Priests, but in an image of her found in Amarna she is standing off to one side, her arms down while everyone else is enthusiastically embracing Aten. In a period where art attempted to portray reality for the first time, I found this significant. And while Nefertiti did have six daughters with Akhenaten, she never—so far as we know—produced twins the way she did in the novel. Historical uncertainties revolve as well around the questions of whether Amunhotep the Younger ever had a coregency with his father or whether Nefertiti ever did rule on her own. These are questions that can only be answered by conjecture, and I went with what seemed most plausible given the historical evidence.

Today, some of these questions could be answered by a firm identification of the Amarna mummies. Although much of Kiya's funerary equipment was found in her son Tutankhamun's tomb, little to nothing remains that was Akhenaten's or Nefertiti's. How old was Nefertiti when she died? What killed Tiye? Dr. Joann Fletcher contends that a cache of mummies found in tomb KV35 are the bodies of Nefertiti and the Dowager Queen. If so, they were stunning beauties even in death.

Q: Isn't there evidence that Nefertiti was banished to the Northern Palace toward the end of her husband's reign?

A: No. This belief was predicated upon an inscription on the Northern Palace which archaeologists believed read "Nefertiti." The name had been removed from the palace while Nefertiti was still alive and replaced with the name of Princess Meritaten. If Princess Meritaten had truly removed her mother's name from the palace, it would indeed seem to indicate a daughter taking the place of her mother. However, the inscription was later discovered to actually read "Kiya." After Kiya's death, Nefertiti and her daughter set out to erase the existence of Nefertiti's only real rival. Unfortunately, many internet sites haven't taken the time to update their information, so the erroneous theory of Nefertiti's banishment persists.

Q: Is it true that Akhenaten had Marfan Syndrome?

A:There is absolutely no anthropological or DNA evidence to suggest this was the case. Those who believe that Akhenaten had Marfan Syndrome—a genetic disorder characterized by unusually long limbs and curvature of the spine—do so simply because some of his statues show a man with long arms and an elongated head. It is essential to remember, however, that Akhenaten purposefully changed the artistic style which all of his predecessors had used, creating a new style known today as Amarna Art. For as many images as there are of Akhenaten with a long, leonine face and feminine hips, there are just as many images from when he was a child displaying none of these features. During the Amarna period, all of Akhenaten's family begins to appear with long arms, elongated heads and large hips, even Nefertiti. It is highly unlikely that the entire royal family had this connective tissue disorder, particularly in light of Nefertiti's bust which resides in Berlin and shows none of the characteristics that those with Marfan Syndrome typically display.

Q: What evidence is there to prove that Nefertiti ever ruled as Pharaoh on her own?

A: This depends on which Egyptologist you ask and what camp they fall into. Amunhotep IV changed his name to Akhenaten, and when Nefertiti became coregent with her husband she changed her name to Ankhkheperura-Neferneferuaten. It is not beyond the limits of plausibility, then, to imagine that Nefertiti later became Pharaoh Ankhkheperura-Smenkhkara, who ruled briefly after Akhenaten's death. A beautiful gold figurine in Tutankhamun's tomb depicts a female Pharaoh (not a queen) walking atop an ebony leopard. Egyptologists have dated the figure back to Akhenaten's reign, which means there is only one possibility of who this feminine ruler of Egypt could be: Nefertiti. There is also evidence of foreign correspondence during Pharaoh Ankhkheperura-Smenkhkara's time that points to Egypt's Pharaoh being Nefertiti. Readers who wish to find out more can consult the work of Dr. Joann Fletcher, who wrote *The Search for Nefertiti: The True Story of an Amazing Discovery* and was featured on the Discovery Channel. Dr. Fletcher stirred up quite the controversy with this book and her announcement that she had discovered the body of Nefertiti.

Q: In the novel you write about the ancient Egyptians using toilet seats and copper razors. Is this accurate?

A:Yes, these and other "modern conveniences" in the novel have been around for more than three thousand years! Dating as far back as 1500 BCE, palaces were more comfortable than you or I might imagine. The wealthy shaved with copper razors, and bathrooms were discovered in Amarna equipped with toilet seats that matched the limestone sink bowls. Royal women regularly applied face cream, eye shadow, and lipstick. Women had elaborate containers for their makeup, and very wealthy women carried handheld mirrors made of polished brass the way women carry purses today. In fact, it might surprise you to know that much like today's celebrities, one of Nefertiti's daughters even had her own perfume line.

Q: If Nefertiti ruled on her own, then who would have been her queen?

A: Just as Hatshepsut made herself Pharaoh and her daughter queen, Nefertiti would have named her own eldest daughter Meritaten as her consort. Surprising though this may seem, rulers of Egypt searched for balance—the feminine with the masculine—and in religious ceremonies it was necessary to have a female part which Pharaoh, as a "man," couldn't play.

Q: If there is evidence that Mutnodjmet married the general Horemheb, who later became Pharaoh, why does she fall in love with general Nakhtmin in the novel?

A: I chose to have Mutny fall in love with General Nakhtmin because there is circumstantial evidence that Horemheb took Mutnodjmet by force as his wife. If that was the case, then theirs was certainly not a love match. However, Mutny might have been married, or at least in love, before Horemheb made her his queen. Horemheb married Mutnodjmet after her family died, and she was the last royal link to the throne. Since the book focuses only on Nefertiti's reign, I wanted to depict Mutnodjmet's early life when she married for love and not because she had to.

Q: You mentioned that there is circumstantial evidence that Horemheb married Mutnodjmet by force. What evidence would that be?

A: The circumstantial evidence comes from the fact that Horemheb had no royal link to the crown. There are Egyptologists who contend that Horemheb used the marriage to legitimize his ascension to the throne. To further strengthen his reign, he quickly destroyed everything that Nefertiti and Akhenaten had built. I couldn't fathom Mutny marrying willingly and then standing quietly by while the monuments that were supposed to write her family's name in eternity were destroyed, block by block. Horemheb was methodical in his attempt to erase her family's name from history, and he very nearly succeeded.

However, there are just as many Egyptologists who would argue that this is all—as I pointed out—circumstantial, and that there is no hard evidence of the marriage being unwanted by Mutny. As I wrote in my Author's Note at the end of the novel, I went with what seemed most convincing to me.

Q: Are the poems written by Akhenaten in the novel real?

A: Yes, they are translations of his *Hymn to the Aten*, which is considered one of the finest examples of Egyptian poetry ever discovered. It also has similarities to Psalm 104 in the Bible.

Q: In the novel, many of the names are changed from what they were in Nefertiti's time. Why is that?

A: As I explain in the Author's Note, some of the names were changed for convenience. For example, I thought that the city of Akhetaten, which Akhenaten built, sounded too close to his own name. In order to avoid confusion, I used the modern day name of Amarna. In the case of Thebes, Egyptians would have known the city as Waset, but I chose to go with the name more people would be familiar with today.

Q: Was there really plague in ancient Egypt?

A: Yes. In fact, in 2004, *National Geographic* published an article about tracing the bubonic plague's fleaborne bacteria to ancient Egypt. As far back as 3500 BCE, the Nile rat was probably transferring these deadly bacteria to humans, who had disturbed its habitat and settled near the river. The *Ebers Papyrus*, written nearly three hundred years before Nefertiti's reign, describes a disease that produces a bubo, going on to say that "when the pus has petrified, the disease has hit." This medical text was almost certainly describing the disease we know now as the bubonic plague.

Q: Your experience as a debut author has been one that many writers might dream of. Within the first month of publication, Nefertiti landed on a national bestseller list, and has now been translated into more than twenty languages. Do you have any advice for aspiring novelists?

A: Learn as much as you can about the business of writing. Because we writers feel an emotional connection to our stories, we tend to feel that publishing is also emotional. If I'm nice, they'll publish me. If I send them chocolate with my query letter, they'll see what a good person I am. But for publishers it isn't personal, and most of the time it's not emotional either. It's about numbers and sales and—at the end of the day—revenue for the company. So learn everything there is to know about the business before you send off your material, especially once your material is accepted for publication. That's when business savvy matters most, and knowing important publishing terms like galleys, remainders, and co-op is extremely important when trying to figure out how you can best help your book along in the publication process. Learn everything you can, but above all, keep writing!

Q: You travel a great deal, particularly to historical sites. On your website it says that you and your husband were married in a sixteenth-century

chateau in France and that you take an historically themed trip together every year. How have your travels influenced your writing?

A: Traveling has been enormously important in my career. My adventures end up inspiring not only what I'm currently writing but what I'm going to write about in the future. For example, on a trip to Alexandria in Egypt, I was afforded the amazing opportunity of participating in a dive to see the submerged remains of Cleopatra's city. More than ten thousand artifacts remain completely preserved underwater: sphinxes, amphorae, even the stones of Marc Antony's summer palace. By the time we surfaced, I was Cleopatra obsessed. I wanted to know what had happened to her city once she and Marc Antony had committed suicide. Where did all of its people go? Were they allowed to remain or were they killed by the Romans? And what about her four children?

It was this last question that surprised me the most. I had always assumed that Cleopatra's children had all been murdered. But the Roman conqueror, Octavian, actually spared the three she bore to Marc Antony: her six-year-old son, Ptolemy, and her ten-year-old twins, Alexander and Selene. As soon as I learned that Octavian had taken the three of them to Rome for his military triumph, I knew at once I had my next book. And when I discovered what Cleopatra's daughter lived through while in exile—rebellion, loss, triumph, love—I absolutely couldn't wait to start writing.

Q: You have written three novels set in the ancient world, but your fourth novel, *Madame Tussaud,* will take place during the French Revolution. What made you decide to switch time periods?

A: I wanted to write on Tussaud because I found her life utterly compelling. She joined the gilded but troubled court of Marie Antoinette, then survived the French Revolution only by creating death masks of the beheaded aristocracy. During her lifetime, Marie (the first name of Madame Tussaud) met absolutely everyone, from Thomas Jefferson to Voltaire to Empress Josephine. When looking for a subject to write on, I search for someone whose story is simply unbelievable. Someone who has lived through events that will have the reader saying, "Now there's no way that could have happened!"

An Excerpt from

The Heretic Queen

a novel

MICHELLE MORAN

Prologue

I AM SURE that if I sat in a quiet place, away from the palace and the bustle of the court, I could remember scenes from my childhood much earlier than six years old. As it is, I have vague impressions of low tables with lion's-paw feet crouched on polished tiles. I can still smell the scents of cedar and acacia from the open chests where my nurse stored my favorite playthings. And I am sure that if I sat in the sycamore groves for a day with nothing but the wind to disturb me, I could put an image to the sound of sistrums being shaken in a courtyard where frankincense was being burned. But all of those are hazy impressions, as difficult to see through as heavy linen, and my first real memory is of Ramesses weeping in the dark Temple of Amun.

I must have begged to go with him that night, or perhaps my nurse had been too busy at Princess Pili's bedside to realize that I was gone. But I can recall our passage through the silent halls of Amun's temple, and how Ramesses's face looked like a painting I had seen of women begging the goddess Isis for favor. I was six years old and always talking, but I knew enough to be quiet that night. I peered up at the painted images of the gods as they passed through the glow of our flickering torchlight, and when we reached the inner sanctum, Ramesses spoke his first words to me.

"Stay here."

I obeyed his command and drew deeper into the shadows as he approached the towering statue of Amun. The god was illuminated by a circle of lamplight, and Ramesses knelt before the creator of life. My heart was beating so loudly in my ears that I couldn't hear what he was whispering, but his final words rang out. "Help her, Amun. She's only six. *Please* don't let Anubis take her away. Not yet!"

There was movement from the opposite door of the sanctum, and the whisper of sandaled feet warned Ramesses that he wasn't alone. He stood, wiping tears from his eyes, and I held my breath as a man emerged like a leopard from the darkness. The spotted pelt of a priest draped from his shoulders, and his left eye was as red as a pool of blood.

"Where is the king?" the High Priest demanded.

Ramesses, summoning all the courage of his nine years, stepped into the circle of lamplight and spoke. "In the palace, Your Holiness. My father won't leave my sister's side."

"Then where is your mother?"

"She . . . she's with her as well. The physicians say my sister is going to die!"

"So your father sent *children* to intervene with the gods?"

I understood for the first time why we had come. "But I've promised Amun whatever he wants," Ramesses cried. "Whatever shall be mine in my future."

"And your father never thought to call on me?"

"He has! He's asked that you come to the palace." His voice broke. "But do you think that Amun will heal her?"

The High Priest moved across the tiles. "Who can say?"

"But I came on my knees and offered him anything. I did as I was told."

"*You* may have," the High Priest snapped, "but Pharaoh himself has not visited my temple."

Ramesses took my hand, and we followed the hem of the High Priest's robes into the courtyard. A trumpet shattered the stillness of the night, and when priests appeared in long white cloaks, I thought of the mummified god Osiris. In the darkness, it was impossible to make out their features, but when enough had assembled, the High Priest shouted, "To the palace of Malkata!"

With torchlights before us we swept into the darkness. Our chariots raced through the chill Mechyr night to the River Nile. And when we'd crossed the waters to the steps of the palace, guards ushered our retinue into the hall.

"Where is the royal family?" the High Priest demanded.

"Inside the princess's bedchamber, Your Holiness."

The High Priest made for the stairs. "Is she alive?"

When no guard answered, Ramesses broke into a run, and I hurried after him, afraid of being left in the dark halls of the palace.

"Pili!" he cried. "Pili, *no! Wait!*" He took the stairs two at a time and at the entrance to Pili's chamber two armed guards parted for him. Ramesses swung open the heavy wooden doors and stopped. I peered into the dimness. The air was thick with incense, and the queen was bent in mourning. Pharaoh stood by himself in the shadows, away from the single oil lamp that lit the room.

"Pili," Ramesses whispered. *"Pili!"* he cried. He didn't care that it was unbecoming of a prince to weep. He ran to the bed and grasped his sister's hand. Her eyes were shut, and her small chest no longer shook with the cold. From beside her on the bed, the Queen of Egypt let out a violent sob.

"Ramesses, you must instruct them to ring the bells."

Ramesses looked to his father, as if the Pharaoh of Egypt might reverse death itself.

Pharaoh Seti nodded. "Go."

"But I tried!" Ramesses cried. "I begged Amun."

Seti moved across the room and placed his arm around Ramesses's shoulders. "I know. And now you must tell them to ring the bells. Anubis has taken her."

But I could see that Ramesses couldn't bear to leave Pili alone. She had been fearful of the dark, like I was, and she would be afraid of so much weeping. He hesitated, but his father's voice was firm.

"Go."

Ramesses looked down at me, and it was understood that I would accompany him.

In the courtyard, an old priestess sat beneath the twisted limbs of an acacia, holding a bronze bell in her withered hands. "Anubis will come for us all one day," she said, her breath fogging the cold night.

"Not at six years old!" Ramesses shouted. "Not when I begged for her life from Amun."

The old priestess laughed harshly. "The gods do not listen to children! What great things have you accomplished that Amun should hear you speak? What wars have you won? What monuments have you erected?"

I hid behind Ramesses's cloak, and neither of us moved.

"Where will Amun have heard your name," she demanded, "to recognize it among so many thousands begging for aid?"

"Nowhere," I heard Ramesses whisper, and the old priestess nodded firmly.

"If the gods cannot recognize your names," she warned, "they will never hear your prayers."

Also by Michelle Moran!

The Heretic Queen
$15.00 paper
(Canada: $18.95)
978-0-307-38176-7

A devastating palace fire has killed the Eighteenth Dynasty's royal family—all with the exception of Nefertari, the niece of the reviled former queen, Nefertiti. Soon Nefertari catches the eye of the Crown Prince, and despite her family's history, they fall in love and wish to marry. Yet all of Egypt opposes this union between the rising star of a new dynasty and the fading star of an old, heretical one. While political adversity sets the country on edge, Nefertari becomes the wife of Ramesses the Great. Destined to be the most powerful Pharaoh in Egypt, he is also the man who must confront the most famous exodus in history.

Cleopatra's Daughter
$25.00 hardcover
(Canada: $29.95)
978-0-307-40912-6

The marriage of Marc Antony and Cleopatra is one of the greatest love stories of all time. Feared and hunted by the powers in Rome, the lovers chose to die by their own hands as the triumphant armies of Antony's revengeful rival, Octavian, swept into Egypt. Their orphaned children—the ten-year-old twins named Selene and Alexander—are taken in chains to Rome. As they come of age, they are buffeted by the personal ambitions of Octavian's family and court, by the ever-present threat of slave rebellion, and by the longings and desires deep within their own hearts.

Available wherever books are sold